C8 000 000

THE SHEIKH'S
Untamed Bride

THE SHEIKH'S
COLLECTION

January 2016

February 2016

March 2016

April 2016

THE SHEIKH'S
Untamed Bride

SARAH MORGAN
JACKIE BRAUN
KRISTI GOLD

First Published in Great Britain 2016
by Mills & Boon, an imprint of HarperCollins*Publishers*
1 London Bridge Street, London, SE1 9GF

THE SHEIKH'S UNTAMED BRIDE © 2016 Harlequin Books S.A.

Lost to the Desert Warrior © 2013 Sarah Morgan
Sheikh in the City © 2010 Jackie Braun Fridline
Her Ardent Sheikh © 2002 Harlequin Books S.A.

Special thanks and acknowledgement are given to Kristi Gold for her contribution to the TEXAS CATTLEMAN'S CLUB: LONE STAR JEWELS series.

ISBN: 978-0-263-91823-6

009-0116

LOST TO THE DESERT WARRIOR

SARAH MORGAN

Bestselling author **Sarah Morgan** writes lively, sexy contemporary stories for Mills & Boon. *RT Book Reviews* has described her as "a magician with words" and has nominated her books for their Reviewers' Choice Awards and their "Top Pick" slot. In 2012 Sarah received the prestigious RITA® Award from the Romance Writers of America. She lives near London with her family. Find out more at www.sararahmorgan.com.

CHAPTER ONE

'The Persians teach their sons, between the ages of five and twenty, only three things: to ride a horse, use a bow and speak the truth.'
—from *The Histories by Herodotus*, Greek historian, about 484-425 BC

'SHH, DON'T MAKE a sound.' Layla slammed her hand over her sister's mouth. 'I can hear them coming. They mustn't find us.'

She wished she'd had time to find a better hiding place. Behind the long velvet curtains in her father's private rooms hardly seemed like an obvious place for concealment, and yet she knew in some ways this was the safest place. No one would think to look for the princesses here. They were never allowed in his bedroom. Not even today, on the day of his death.

But Layla had wanted to see for herself that the man who'd called himself her father lay cold and still in his bed and wasn't about to leap up and commit some other sin against her or her sister. She'd stood there, hidden by the curtain, and heard him seal her fate with his dying breath. His last words hadn't expressed regret for a life misspent. There had been no demand to see his daughters, nor even a request to pass on a loving message to make up for years of cold neglect. No apology for all the grievous wrongs. Just one last wrong—one that would seal her fate forever.

'Hassan must marry Layla. It is the only way the people will accept him as ruler of Tazkhan.'

Hearing footsteps, Layla kept her hand pressed over her younger sister's mouth. Her forehead brushed the curtains and she could smell the dust. The dark was disorientating and she held herself rigid, waiting for the curtains to be flung back, afraid that the slightest movement would give them away.

From behind the protection of rich, heavy velvet she heard several people enter the room.

'We have searched the palace. They are nowhere to be found.'

'They cannot just have vanished.' The voice was harsh and instantly recognisable. It was Hassan, her father's cousin, and if his last wishes were carried out, soon to be her bridegroom. Sixty years old and more power-hungry even than her father.

In a moment of horrifying clarity Layla saw her future and it was blacker than the inside of the curtain. She stared into darkness, feeling her sister's breath warm her hand, afraid to breathe herself in case she gave them both away.

'We will find them, Hassan.'

'In a few hours you'll be addressing me as Your Excellency,' Hassan snapped. 'And you'd better find them. Try the library. The older one is always there. As for the younger one—she has far too much to say for herself. We're flying her to America, where she will be out of sight and out of mind. The people will soon forget her. My marriage to the eldest will take place before dawn. Fortunately she is the quiet one. She has nothing to say for herself and is unlikely to object.'

He didn't even know her name, Layla thought numbly, let alone her view on the world. She was 'the eldest'. 'The quiet one'. She doubted he knew or cared what she looked like. He certainly didn't care what she wanted. But then neither had her father. The only person who cared about her was currently shivering in her grasp.

Her young sister. Her friend. Her *family*.

The news that they were planning to send Yasmin to America intensified the horror of the situation. Of everything that was happening, losing her sister would be the worst.

'Why rush into the marriage?'

Hassan's companion echoed Layla's thoughts.

'Because we both know that as soon as *he* finds out about the old Sheikh's death he will come.'

He will come.

Layla knew immediately who 'he' was. And she also knew Hassan was afraid. So afraid he couldn't bring himself to speak the name of his enemy. The formidable reputation of the desert warrior and rightful ruler of the wild desert country of Tazkhan frightened Hassan so badly it was now forbidden to speak his name within the walled city. The irony was that by banning all mention of the true heir to the sheikdom he had increased his status to that of hero in the minds of the people.

In a small moment of personal rebellion, Layla *thought* the name.

Raz Al Zahki.

A prince who lived like a Bedouin among the people who loved him. A man of the desert with steely determination, strength and patience, who played a waiting game. Right now he was out there somewhere, his exact whereabouts a secret known only to those closest to him. The secrecy surrounding him increased tensions in the Citadel of Tazkhan.

Footsteps echoed on the stone floor of the bedroom.

As the door closed behind them Yasmin pulled away, gasping for air. 'I thought you were going to suffocate me.'

'I thought you were going to scream.'

'I've never screamed in my life. I'm not that pathetic.' But her sister looked shaken and Layla took her hand and held it firmly as she peeped around the heavy velvet curtain.

'They've gone. We're safe.'

'Safe? Layla, that wrinkled, overweight monster is going to marry you before dawn and he's going to send me away to America, miles from home and miles from *you*.'

Layla heard the break in her sister's voice and tightened her grip on her hand. 'No, he won't. I'm not going to allow him to take you away.'

'How can you stop it? I don't care what happens, but I want us to stay together. It's been the two of us for so long I can't imagine any other life. I need you to stop me opening my mouth when I should close it and you need me to stop you living your life in a book.'

Her sister's voice was soaked with despair and Layla felt crushed by the weight of responsibility.

She felt small and powerless as she stood alone against the brutal force of Hassan's limitless ambition.

'I promise we won't be separated.'

'How can you promise that?'

'I don't know yet. But I'm thinking…'

'Well, think fast, because in a few hours I'll be on a plane to America and you'll be in Hassan's bed.'

'Yasmin!' Shocked, Layla gaped at her sister, who shrugged defiantly.

'It's true.'

'What do you know about being in a man's bed?'

'Nowhere near as much as I'd like. I suppose that might be one of the advantages of being banished to America.'

Despite their circumstances, a dimple flickered at the corner of Yasmin's mouth and Layla felt a lump in her throat. No matter how dire the circumstances, her sister always managed to find a reason to smile. She'd brought laughter to places without humour and light into the dark.

'I can't lose you.' She couldn't even bear to think of that option. 'I *won't* lose you.'

Yasmin peered cautiously across the room. 'Is our father really dead?'

'Yes.' Layla tried to find some emotion inside herself but all she felt was numb. 'Are you sad?'

'Why would I be sad? This is only the fifth time I've ever seen him in person and I don't think this one counts so that's only four times. He made our lives hell and he's still making it hell even though he's dead.' Yasmin's unusual blue eyes darkened with fury. 'Do you know what I wish? I wish Raz Al Zahki would ride into the city on that terrifying black stallion of his and finish off Hassan. I'd cheer. In fact I'd be so grateful I'd marry him myself and give him a hundred babies just to make sure his line is safe.'

Layla tried not to look at the figure on the bed. Even dead, she didn't want to see him. 'He wouldn't want to marry you. You are the daughter of the man responsible for the death of his father and his beautiful wife. He hates us, and I cannot blame him for that.' She hated herself too, for sharing the blood of a man with so little humanity. For sharing in his shame.

'He should marry *you*. Then no one would be able to challenge him and Hassan would be finished.'

The idea was so outrageous, so typical of Yasmin, Layla's instinct was to dismiss it instantly and preach caution as she always did. But how was caution going to help them when her marriage was only hours away?

Her mind picked at the idea gingerly. 'Yasmin—'

'It is said he loved his wife so deeply that when she died he made a vow never to love again.' Yasmin spoke in an awed whisper. 'Have you ever heard anything so romantic?'

Layla's courage evaporated along with the idea. *She*

couldn't do it. 'It's not romantic. It's tragic. It was a terrible thing.'

'But to be loved that much by a man as strong and honourable as him—I want that one day.'

Yasmin stared into the distance and Layla gave her a shake. 'Stop dreaming.' The whole thing was alien to her. The only love she knew was her love for her sister. She'd never felt anything remotely romantic when she'd looked at a man. And nothing she'd read on the subject had led her to believe that would change in the future. She was far too practical a person, and it was the practical side that drove her now. 'If they take you to America I'll never see you again. I'm not going to let that happen.'

'How can you stop it? Hassan is at his most dangerous when he's afraid and he's terrified of Raz Al Zahki. He won't even allow his name to be spoken in the city. But everyone *does* speak it, of course. Especially the women. I've been listening.'

'You've been to the *souk* again? Do you have no sense of danger?'

Yasmin ignored her and her voice was an awed whisper. 'They say his heart is frozen into ice and only the right woman can melt it. It's a bit like the legend of the Sword in the Stone you read me when I was little.'

'Oh, Yasmin, grow up! A man's heart cannot be frozen into ice unless he finds himself lost in Antarctica with insufficient equipment. A heart is responsible for pumping blood around the body. It cannot be "frozen" or "broken".' Exasperated, Layla wondered how two sisters could be so different. Their experience was the same, except that Layla had protected Yasmin from the worst of her father's actions. 'This isn't legend, this is *real*. Stop romanticising everything.'

'They think he will come.' This time there was an undertone of excitement in her sister's voice. 'He has been playing a waiting game while our father and Hassan plotted. With our father dead, he has to have a plan for taking up his rightful place as Sheikh. Hassan is terrified. The council is terrified. They have extra guards on the doors at night. They've sent patrols into the desert, although goodness knows why because everyone knows Raz Al Zahki knows the desert better than anyone. No one is sleeping because they're afraid he might enter the Citadel at night and murder them in their beds. Frankly, I wish he'd just get on with it. If I bumped into him in the dark I'd show him the way.'

Layla covered her sister's lips with her fingers. 'You need to be careful what you say.'

'Why? What else can they do to me? They're splitting us up! I'm going to America and you're going to marry Hassan. How much worse can it get?'

'I'm not marrying Hassan.' Layla made her decision. 'I'm not going to let that happen.'

'How can you stop it? Hassan can only be the next ruler if he marries you. That's a pretty powerful motivation.'

'Then he mustn't marry me.'

Yasmin looked at her with pity. 'He is going to make you.'

'If he can't find me, he can't make me.' Not daring to give too much thought to what she was about to do, Layla sprinted to her father's dressing room and removed a couple of robes. She thrust one at her sister. 'Put this on. Cover your hair and as much of your face as you can. Wait here for me behind the curtain until I come and fetch you. I need to get something from the library before we leave.'

'The library? How can you think of books right now?'

'Because a book can be many things—a friend, an escape, a teacher—' Layla broke off and hoped her sister didn't notice her high colour. 'Never mind. The important thing is that we're going away from here. It will be like the game of Hide we played as children.' She caught her sister's horrified glance and wished she hadn't used that reference. Both of them knew what that game had really meant. She changed the subject quickly. 'Those horses you love so much—can you actually ride one if you have to?'

'Of course!'

Her sister's hesitation was so brief Layla told herself she'd imagined it.

'And I've read extensively on the theory of riding and the history of the Arabian horse, so between us I'm sure we'll be fine.' She hoped she sounded more convincing than she felt. 'We'll take the back route to the stables and ride into the desert from there.'

'The desert? Why are we riding into the desert?'

Layla felt her mouth move even though her brain was telling her this was a terrible idea. 'We're going to find Raz Al Zahki.'

The wind blew across the desert, bringing with it whispers of the Sheikh's death.

Raz Al Zahki stood at the edge of the camp and stared into the darkness of the night. 'Is it truth or rumour?'

'Truth.' Salem stood next to him, shoulder to shoulder. 'It's been confirmed by more than one source.'

'Then it is time.' Raz had learned long before to keep his feelings buried, and he kept them buried now, but he felt the familiar ache of tension across his shoulders. 'We leave for the city tonight.'

Abdul, his advisor and long-time friend stepped forward. 'There is something else, Your Highness. As you predicted, Hassan plans to marry the eldest princess in a matter of hours. Preparations for the wedding are already underway.'

'Before her father's body is even cold?' Raz gave a cynical laugh. 'Her grief clearly overwhelms her.'

'Hassan must be at least forty years older than her,' Salem murmured. 'One wonders what she gains from the match.'

'There is no mystery there. She continues to live in a palace and enjoy benefits that should never have been hers to begin with.' Raz stared at the horizon. 'She is the daughter of the most ruthless man who ever ruled Tazkhan. Don't waste your sympathy.'

'If Hassan marries the girl it will be harder for you to challenge the succession legally.'

'Which is why I intend to make sure the wedding does not take place.'

Abdul shot him a startled look. 'So you intend to go ahead with your plan? Even though what you're suggesting is—'

'The only option available.' Raz cut him off, hearing the hardness in his own tone. It was the same hardness that ran right through him. Once, he'd been capable of warmth, but that part of him had died along with the woman he'd loved. 'We have considered every other option, and—' He broke off as he heard a commotion in the darkness and then lifted a hand as his bodyguards emerged silently to flank him.

They were men who had followed him for fifteen years, since the brutal slaying of his father. Men who would die for him.

Abdul thrust himself in front of Raz and that gesture touched him more than any other, because his trusted advisor was neither physically fit nor skilled with weapons.

Gently, but firmly, he moved him to one side, but Abdul protested.

'Go. *Go*! It could be the attempt on your life we have been expecting.'

Aware that Salem had his hand on his weapon, Raz fixed his gaze on the slim figure of a boy whose arms were gripped by two of his men. 'If my death were the objective then surely they would give the responsibility to someone I could not so easily crush.'

'We found him wandering in the desert along the border with Zubran. He appears to be alone. He says he has a message for Raz Al Zahki.'

Knowing that his men were protecting his identity, Raz signalled for them to bring their captive forward.

His hands were tied and as they released him the boy stumbled and fell to his knees. Raz stared down at him, noticing absently that his robes swamped his thin body.

It was Salem who spoke. Salem, his brother, who rarely left his side. 'What message do you have for Raz Al Zahki, boy?'

'I have to speak to him in person.' The words were mumbled and barely audible. 'And I have to be alone when I do it. What I have to say is just for him and no other.'

The guard closest to him gave a grunt of disgust. 'Someone like you wouldn't get close enough to Raz Al Zahki to wave from a distance, let alone be alone with him, and you should be grateful for that. He'd eat you alive.'

'I don't care what he does to me as long as he hears what I have to say. Take me to him. *Please.*'

The boy kept his head bowed and something in the set of those narrow shoulders drew Raz's attention.

Ignoring Salem's attempts to hold him back, he stepped forward. 'So you're not afraid?'

There was a brief pause. The wind blew across the desert, whipping up sand and catching the edges of the boy's robe. He clutched it desperately.

'Yes, I am afraid. But not of Raz Al Zahki.'

'Then you need to be educated.' The guard dragged his captive to his feet and the boy gasped in pain. 'We'll keep him here tonight and question him again in the morning.'

'No!' The boy struggled frantically in the man's grip. 'By

morning it will be too late. I have to speak to him now. Please. The future of Tazkhan depends on it.'

Raz stared at the boy, half shrouded by robes that were too big for him. 'Take him to my tent.'

Salem, Abdul and the guards looked at him in disbelief.

'Do it,' Raz said softly, but still the guards hesitated.

'We'll strip-search him first—'

'Take him to my tent and then leave us.'

Abdul touched his arm, his voice low. 'I have never before questioned your decisions, Your Highness, but this time I beg you, at least keep the guards with you.'

'You think I can't defend myself from someone half my height and weight?'

'I think Hassan will try anything at this late stage in the game. He is frightened and desperate and a desperate man should never be underestimated. I think it could be a trap.'

'I agree.' Salem's voice was hard. 'I'll come with you.'

Raz put his hand on his brother's shoulder. 'Your love and loyalty means more to me than you can possibly know, but you must trust me.'

'If anything happened to you—'

Raz felt the weight of it settle onto his shoulders. He, better than anyone, knew that there were some promises that shouldn't be made. 'Make sure I'm not disturbed.' He dismissed his bodyguards with a single movement of his hand and strode into his tent.

He closed the flap, muffling the sound of the wind and protecting them from prying eyes.

The boy was on his knees in the furthest corner of the tent, his hands still tied.

Raz studied him for a moment and then strolled over to him and cut the rope with a swift movement of his knife. 'Stand up.'

The boy hesitated and then stood in a graceful movement, only to fall again a moment later.

'I don't think I can stand—' The words were uttered through clenched teeth. 'My legs are stiff from riding and I injured my ankle when I fell.'

Raz looked down at the slender body bowed at his feet. 'Tell me why you're here.'

'I'll talk to Raz Al Zahki himself, and no one else.'

'Then speak,' Raz commanded softly, and the boy lifted his head in shock.

Under the concealing robes, dark eyes widened. 'You're him?'

'I'm the one asking the questions.' Raz sheathed his knife. 'And the first thing I want to know is what a woman is doing creeping around my camp in the middle of the night. What are you doing walking into the lion's den unprotected, Princess?'

Layla was in agony. Physical agony from her fall from the horse, and emotional agony from the knowledge that her sister was missing and alone in the vast emptiness of the baking desert and it was all her fault.

She was the one who had suggested this stupid, crazy plan. She, who never did anything stupid or crazy. She, who studied all available evidence before she made a decision, had acted on impulse. Which just proved that a cautious nature wasn't to be mocked.

It would have been better had Hassan sent Yasmin to America. At least then Layla would have known she was alive.

As it was, Yasmin was lost, and she was now a captive in the desert camp of Raz Al Zahki, a man who had more reason to hate her than any other.

A man who knew who she was.

Staring into those cold black eyes, she suddenly knew the meaning of the phrase 'between a rock and a hard place.' If her cousin was the hard place then this man was the rock. He stood legs spread, handsome face unsmiling as he stared at her. His body had the muscular structure of a warrior's, his shoulders broad and hard. She knew he had suffered terribly and yet there was no sign of suffering in face. This man wasn't broken, he was whole and strong—at least on the outside. There was nothing soft about him. Nothing vulnerable. Even before he'd revealed his identity she'd sensed his place at the head of the pack. He had the confidence and authority of a man born to lead others, and even though Layla had expected nothing less still he intimidated her.

'You knew who I was the whole time?'

'Within five seconds. You have a memorable face, Princess. And very distinctive eyes.'

It was the first personal comment anyone had ever made to her and it took her by surprise.

She'd studied him on paper and committed all the facts to memory, from his year and place of birth to his impressive military career and his degree in engineering. She knew he was a skilled rider and an authority on the Arabian horse. She knew all that, but was only just realising that facts could only tell you so much about a man.

They couldn't tell you that his eyes were darker than the desert at night or that the power he commanded on paper was surpassed a thousand times by the power he commanded in person. They couldn't tell you that those eyes were capable of seeing right through a person to the very centre of their being. They couldn't tell you that meeting those eyes would make your heart thunder like the hooves of a hundred wild horses pounding across the desert plain.

She was fast realising that a list of dates and qualifications didn't convey strength or charisma.

Unsettled that the facts had given her such an incomplete picture, Layla remembered what her sister had said about the rumours. That Raz Al Zahki was a man who knew women. Before he'd fallen in love he'd been wild, and afterwards he'd locked it all away. Every emotion. Every feeling.

'How do you know me?'

'I make a point of knowing my enemy.'

'I am not your enemy.' And yet she could hardly blame him for thinking that, could she? His family had suffered terribly at the hands of hers. They stood on opposite sides of an enormous rift that had divided their families for generations.

'Which brings me to my second question—where is Hassan? Or is he so lacking in courage he sends a woman with his messages?'

Layla shivered, but whether it was his tone or his words that affected her she didn't know.

'I'm not here because of Hassan. I was with my sister, Yasmin, but I fell from the horse.' She saw his beautiful mouth tighten. 'I'm sorry—I—you have to help me find her. *Please*. She's alone in the desert and she won't have a clue how to survive.' The thought filled her with despair but still he showed no emotion. No sympathy. Nothing.

'So where is Hassan?'

'He could be back at the palace, or he could be out there looking for us. I don't know.'

'You don't know? And yet this is the man you're supposed to be marrying in a matter of hours.'

And if Hassan found Yasmin first—

His words slowly seeped into her numb brain. 'You know about the wedding?'

'I know everything.'

'If you think I want to marry Hassan then clearly you *don't* know everything.' The tent was dimly lit, but there was enough light for her to see the flash of surprise in his eyes.

'How did you leave, if not with his consent?'

'We escaped. My sister loves horses. She took the fastest horse in the stables. Unfortunately she omitted to tell me she couldn't control him.' Layla rubbed her palm across her bruised back. 'He proved too much for both of us.'

'*Both* of you?' A dark eyebrow lifted. 'You rode one horse?'

'Yes. We're not that heavy and we didn't want to be separated.' Layla didn't tell him that she'd never ridden before. This man was renowned for his horsemanship. She had a feeling he wouldn't be impressed by the fact she knew everything about the breeding history of the Arabian horse, but nothing about the reality of riding one. 'Something scared him and he reared up. I fell and he bolted with Yasmin on his back. She won't be strong enough to stop him. She's probably fallen, too.' Panicking, she tried to stand up again, but her body protested so violently she sank back onto her knees just as two large dogs bounded into the tent.

Terror sucked the strength from her limbs. She was at eye level with the two beasts as they came to a standstill, teeth bared.

Raz said something to them and they whimpered and sank down to their bellies, huge eyes fixed on him in adoration.

'Saluki?' The fear was so sharp Layla could hardly breathe. 'You own Saluki?'

'You recognise the breed?'

'Of course.' Her mouth felt as if she'd swallowed all the sand in the desert. If dogs could smell fear, she was doomed. 'The Saluki is one of the oldest breeds in existence. They have been found in the Pyramids of Egypt, mummified alongside the bodies of pharaohs.' She didn't reveal that her familiarity with the breed came from a darker, more personal experience. An experience she'd tried to block from her mind.

'You said you were escaping. What was your destination?'

'You. You were my destination.' Reminding herself that the dogs were unlikely to attack without provocation or command, Layla kept utterly still, watching the animals. 'We were trying to find you.'

'On the night your father died? From the lack of tears it would seem you have inherited his lack of sentimentality.'

Was that what he thought?

Shocked, Layla almost corrected him, but she knew this wasn't the right time. Misunderstandings could be corrected later. Or maybe they didn't even matter. 'It was my father's dying wish that I marry Hassan.'

The darkening of his eyes was barely perceptible. 'So why come looking for me?'

She'd practised a hundred alternative ways to say what she wanted to say but every word vanished under that icy scrutiny. 'You are the rightful ruler, but if he marries me that weakens your claim and strengthens his.'

There was a sudden stillness about him that suggested she had his full attention. 'That still doesn't tell me why you're here.'

Only now did Layla realise just how much she'd been hoping he'd be the one to say it. He was praised for his intelligence, wasn't he? Couldn't he see for himself why she was here? Couldn't he see the one solution that would solve this once and for all?

But perhaps he could see and chose not to look.

'I don't blame you for hating us.' The words tumbling out of her mouth weren't the ones she'd rehearsed but when she looked at him all she could think of was the loss he'd suffered. 'If I could change who I am then I would, but I'm asking you to put that aside and do what needs to be done.'

'And what,' he prompted softly, 'do you believe needs to be done, Princess?'

No man had ever asked her opinion. Not once since the day she took her first step to the day she and her sister had slid out of the window of their father's bedroom. Not once had anyone treated her as anything but a weapon in the considerable armory of the house of Al Habib.

But this man had asked her.

This man was listening to her.

He was regal, she thought, proud and sure of himself. In that moment she caught a glimpse of why so many trusted him and protected him. He was as different from Hassan as the ocean from the desert.

'You *know* what needs to be done. You have to take your rightful place. You have to end this before Hassan finishes what my father started. Before he ruins our country in the selfish pursuit of power...' She paused, wondering whether to mention Yasmin again but deciding this man would be motivated more by his duty to his people than sympathy for her sister. 'And to do that you have to marry me. Now. Quickly. Before Hassan finds me and takes me back.'

CHAPTER TWO

HE'D BEEN PLANNING to do whatever was necessary to prevent her wedding to Hassan taking place. Yet he had not considered the option of marrying her himself, nor had any of those surrounding him dared to suggest it despite the fact it was the obvious solution.

The tactician in him could see the benefit. The man in him recoiled.

He'd thought there was no price he wouldn't pay to fulfil his duty.

He'd been wrong.

Tension rippled down his spine. He felt as if he were being strangled.

'No.' He'd trained himself to shut down emotion but that skill suddenly failed him and his refusal came from somewhere deep inside him. Some dark part of himself he no longer accessed. 'I had a wife. I don't need or want another.' His voice sounded strange. Thickened by a hundred layers of personal agony. One of the dogs growled, a threatening sound that came from low in the animal's throat. He saw her gaze flicker to the dog and sensed her fear although he didn't understand it.

'I know about your wife.' Her brief hesitation suggested she was about to say something else on that topic, but then she gave a little shake of her head. 'Obviously I'm not suggesting myself as a replacement. This would be purely a political arrangement, advantageous to both sides.'

Raz tried to detach his mind from the pain he carried around inside himself. 'Political?'

'Hassan's position is precarious. Marriage to me is his way of securing his place as my father's successor. He has no support in Tazkhan and has never taken the trouble to earn it. For him, ruling is about what he can gain rather than what he can give and that approach makes him neither popular nor secure.'

Raz hid his surprise. He'd listened to men talk for hours on the problems facing Tazkhan and yet this girl had summarised the situation in four blunt sentences, devoid of emotion, exaggeration or drama.

'Perhaps he didn't expect your father to die so soon.'

Again there was hesitation, and it was obvious she was being selective about what she told him. 'Hassan knows that the only way he will be accepted is to marry me, and he is willing to do anything to make that happen. Do not underestimate him.'

Her words were like the scrape of a knife over an open wound because he'd done exactly that. In his righteous arrogance he'd thought himself untouchable and as a result he'd lost someone he'd loved deeply.

'You seem very familiar with the workings of his mind.'

'I've studied him. I think there is a strong chance he is clinically disturbed. He demonstrates some of the elements of a sociopath, shows no remorse or guilt for any of his actions.'

Her words were serious, those beautiful, almond-shaped eyes steady on his.

'He has no care for the feelings or opinions of others and an overinflated idea of his own importance. He is a dangerous man. But you already know that.'

'Yes.' He did know. What surprised him was that *she* knew.

Raz realised he'd made assumptions about her based purely

on her bloodline. He also knew she was right that the marriage had to be prevented. He didn't reveal that he'd had his own plans for making sure it didn't happen.

There was no doubt her plan was better. Permanent.

And safer for all concerned.

Except for him.

For him, it meant breaking a vow.

His tension levels soaring into the stratosphere, Raz paced the length of the tent.

Whichever way he looked at it, it felt like a betrayal. It pulled him down and tore at him. 'I cannot do it.'

'Because I am the daughter of your enemy?' She spoke in the same calm voice. 'Aristotle said "a common danger unites the bitterest of enemies". We have a common danger. I am proposing we unite. It is the right thing to do and you know it.'

Raz turned with a snarl that drew the dogs to their feet. 'Never assume to guess what I am thinking, Princess.'

Her head was slightly bowed but he could see her eyes were fixed in terror on the two animals now crouched low on the floor of the tent.

'I beg your pardon.' She held herself absolutely still, her voice barely more than a whisper. 'It seems a logical solution to me. I assumed it would seem so to you.'

It did. The fact that his emotions defied logic frustrated him. 'Do you apply logic to everything?'

'I didn't apply logic when I chose to steal a horse and point him towards the desert, so the answer has to be no, not to everything. But to most things. I find generally the outcome is better if the action is given the appropriate consideration.'

He'd never met anyone as serious as her.

He wanted to ask if she'd ever laughed, danced or had fun, and then wondered why he was even interested.

'You are suggesting something I cannot contemplate.'

'And yet you know it is the right thing for Tazkhan. So

your reluctance must be because you once had a wife you loved so very much.'

Raz felt the blood drain from his face. The tips of his fingers were suddenly cold. Anger sharpened his brain and tongue. 'Logic, if not an instinct for self-preservation, should be warning you that you are now treading on ground that is likely to give way beneath your feet.'

'I did not bring up that topic to cause you pain, but to try and understand why you would say no to something that is so obviously right.' Her fingers shook as she smoothed the robe she was wearing. 'You loved her and exchanged promises, and now you never want to marry again. I understand that.'

'You understand nothing.' He heard the growl in his own voice. 'You have condensed a thousand indescribable emotions into one short sentence.' The force of his anger shook him, and it clearly shook her too because her eyes flickered to the entrance of the tent, gauging the distance. Raz felt a rush of shame because whatever his sins, and God knew there had been many, frightening women wasn't one of them.

She spoke before he did. 'I'm sorry.' Her tone was a soothing balm against the raw edges of his pain. 'And you're right, of course. I don't understand what you're feeling because I've never loved anyone that way. But I understand that what you lost is somehow linked with your decision never to marry again. And I just want to make clear that what I'm suggesting has nothing to do with what you had before. Ours would be a marriage of political necessity, not of love. Not a betrayal of her memory, but a business arrangement. If you marry me, you take your rightful place as ruler of Tazkhan. You would be unchallenged.'

Not a betrayal of her memory.

So maybe she did understand him better than he'd first thought.

'You think I'm afraid of a challenge?'

'No. But I know you love your people and want to give Tazkhan a peaceful and prosperous future.' Suddenly she sounded very tired, very alone and very young.

Raz frowned as he tried to remember her age. Twenty-three? Younger?

'And what do you gain from this arrangement, Princess? How do you benefit from entering into a marriage where feelings play no part?' In the flickering candlelight he could see a hint of smooth cheek beneath the voluminous robes, but very little else except those eyes. And her eyes were mesmerising—as dark as sloes and framed by long, thick lashes that shadowed that smooth skin like the setting sun. Suddenly he wanted to see more of her. He wanted to reach out and rip off the robes that concealed her and see what lay beneath the folds of fabric. He'd heard whispers about the beauty of the elder princess and ignored them all because her physical attributes had been of no interest to him.

Disturbed by the sudden flare of his own curiosity, he stepped back. 'How do you benefit from this "business arrangement"?'

'If I am married to you, then I cannot be married to Hassan.'

'So I am the lesser of two evils?' Could that truly be the reason? Raz struggled to decipher her intentions. She seemed innocent and yet she came from evil. She appeared to speak the truth but those who surrounded her spoke only lies. Feeling the weight of responsibility, he suppressed his instinct to trust her. 'You are expecting me to believe that you crept out of the Citadel tonight, stole a horse and rode aimlessly into the desert in the hope of tripping over me so that you could propose marriage?'

'I had more to lose by staying than leaving. And it is well known that there are plenty of people who know your whereabouts, Your Highness. I trusted that someone would bring me to you.'

She'd called him 'Your Highness'. It was an acknowledgement he wouldn't have expected from her, given that they were on opposite sides.

Raz narrowed his eyes. 'Your loyalties are easily shifted.'

'My loyalties are to Tazkhan, but I understand that you are afraid to trust me. I do have other reasons—more personal ones.'

'What other reasons?'

'If he finds her, Hassan intends to send my sister to America.' Desperation shook that steady voice. 'He wants her out of the way.'

'Why would he want her out of the way?'

'Because we are stronger together than we are apart and he wants to weaken us. Because my sister has an uncomfortable habit of speaking her mind and she becomes harder to control with each passing day. She is dreamy, passionate, and challenges everything. And Hassan hates to be challenged.'

'And you don't challenge him?'

'I see no point in poking an angry dragon with a stick.'

'And where is your sister now?'

'I don't know.' There was fear and anxiety under the veneer of calm. 'The horse galloped off. I'm scared she might have fallen and been injured. I'm scared Hassan's men will find her before you do.'

Raz lifted an eyebrow. 'That is almost inevitable since I'm not looking for her.'

'But *will* you look for her? Once I'm your bride, will you also offer your protection to my sister?'

So that was why she was here, he thought.

She'd risked everything for love. Not romantic love, perhaps, but love all the same.

'So to keep your sister with you, and protect Tazkhan, you

would marry a stranger. That is the least romantic proposition I have ever heard.'

'Possibly. But we've already established this is not about romance. You wouldn't want that and neither would I.'

'Why wouldn't you?'

'I am not a romantic person, Your Highness.'

That matter-of-fact statement might have been unremarkable had it come from someone several decades older than she was. Her eyes were dark, luminous pools of pain and he wondered how those eyes would look if she smiled.

'You don't believe there can be love between a man and a woman?'

'Yes, I do believe there can be. Just not for me. I'm not like that. I don't have those feelings. I'm a very practical person,' she said with disarming honesty. 'As you don't want love either, I assume that won't be an obstacle for you.' She brushed it aside as easily as the desert winds shifted sand.

She had no idea, he thought. No idea that love was the most powerful force known to man. No idea how much havoc could be wrought by that emotion.

But *he* knew.

He'd been caught in the wake of devastation and still ached from his injuries.

'You say that this is a political arrangement to secure the future of Tazkhan, but for a marriage to be legal and binding in our country it requires more than simply the exchange of vows and rings.'

Her spine was rigid and her eyes were fixed on the ground in front of him. 'I am aware of that. It's important that Hassan isn't able to challenge our union so I've already familiarised myself with Tazkhan marriage laws.'

Raz found himself intrigued and exasperated in equal measures. 'So you understand what marriage entails?'

'You're referring to the physical side and, yes, I understand that. I know it has to be a full and proper marriage. I accept that. It won't be a problem.' She'd dipped her head so that the folds of her robe almost obscured her features. 'From what I've read, it shouldn't be a problem for you, either. A man doesn't need love in order to be able to perform the sexual act.'

'Perform?' Raz was torn between amusement and disbelief as he stared down at her. Under the protective folds of the robe she was shy, fragile and clueless. 'What exactly have you been reading? Whatever it is, it sounds an unusual choice for a girl like you.'

'I'm not a girl. I'm a woman.'

Not yet. The thought flew into his head and he stared at her for a long moment.

'You are contemplating a lifetime with a man who cannot love you.'

'But you will respect me.' Lifting her head, she looked him directly in the eyes. 'You will respect me for making the decision to do the right thing for Tazkhan. And that is all I need.'

Raz stared at her for a long moment.

Respect.

Was that really all she needed?

It sounded like very little, and yet right now he wasn't sure he could deliver even that.

Feeling the weight of responsibility pressing down on him like a thousand tons of sand, he turned and strode to the doorway of the tent. 'I need air.'

I need air.

Layla sagged. She needed air, too. She couldn't breathe. She was suffocating under the heavy fabric of the robes and the stifling heat in the tent and she was terrified she'd blown everything by mentioning his wife. And as for the rest of it— she'd never thought talking about sex could feel so uncomfortable. It was a natural act, performed by animals—of which man was one—since the dawn of time. Why a discussion on the topic should leave her hot and shaky she had no idea.

It was *him*.

There was something about him—a raw physicality that made her understand for the first time why women talked about him in dreamy tones.

Confused, exhausted and desperately worried about Yasmin, all Layla wanted was to strip off the robes she'd taken from her father's rooms and lie down.

She looked longingly at the low bed covered in richly coloured silks that dominated the far side of the tent.

His bed?

Just for a moment she had an image of him lying there, strong limbs entwined with the beauty who had been his wife, sharing their love. The image shocked her. Apart from images of the sculptures of Michelangelo she'd never seen a man naked, so she had no reason to be imagining one now.

Her body ached from head to foot and she wanted to stretch her limbs and examine her bruises, but she was too afraid to move with the dogs guarding her.

She watched them as she carefully tried to ease herself into a different position.

The bag she'd tied under the robes pressed uncomfortably against her hip and she pulled out the two books she'd taken from the library. One was her favourite—a book she'd read so many times she almost knew it by heart. The other—

'What is that?' His voice came from the doorway of the tent and Layla jumped and dropped both books onto the thick rug that carpeted the floor of the tent.

'Books. Just books. I brought them from home.'

Before she could snatch them back he stooped and picked one up. And of course it was *that* one.

There was a tense silence while he scanned the title of

the volume. Dark eyebrows rose in incredulity. 'The *Kama Sutra*?'

'If I'm proposing marriage then it's important I have some knowledge of what is required. There is no skill that cannot be mastered with sufficient studying. I'm ignorant, and in my experience ignorance is never bliss.'

She could hear the blood throbbing in her ears. She felt her mouth dry as if she had swallowed all the sand in the desert and her heart pounded like the hooves of the Arabian stallion who had thrown her onto the sand with such disdain.

His prolonged silence was more humiliating than a refusal and she was grateful for the semi-darkness of the tent that gave her at least some protection from his scrutiny.

Her expectations of this encounter had been modest. She hadn't exactly expected him to embrace the idea of marriage with enthusiasm, but she'd thought he'd say *something*. She certainly hadn't expected him to walk out of the tent.

But perhaps the thought of marrying her sickened him. Perhaps people were wrong and Raz Al Zahki *wouldn't* do anything that needed to be done for his country. Perhaps even he wouldn't stoop so low as to marry the daughter of the man who had destroyed his family.

Perhaps he didn't want a woman whose knowledge of the world had been gained from the contents of her father's library.

'You're not going to need this.' He handed the book back to her and her face burned like the desert in the midday heat

Tears formed a hot burning ball in the back of her throat and she almost choked on it.

He was refusing to marry her.

'I understand. In that case I need to try and find my sister myself, before Hassan does. He is at his most dangerous when he is angry and he will be very angry.' She struggled to her feet, but her legs cramped from kneeling for so long in one position and she lost her balance.

He caught her and scooped her into his arms.

Afraid of being dropped to the ground for the second time in one day, Layla gripped his shoulders and her fingers dug into an unyielding layer of solid muscle.

In her day-to-day life at the palace she didn't encounter men like him. Her father had surrounded himself with men like Hassan: men whose flesh was softened from inactivity, sycophants whose purpose in life was to indulge to the fullest.

She doubted Raz Al Zahki had ever overindulged in his life. He was lean, athletic, super-fit—and dangerous in every way.

As she turned her head, her eyes met the fierce black of his. Curiosity turned to fascination. Her eyes dropped to his mouth, now terrifyingly close to hers. Hassan's mouth was full and fleshy, but this man's lips were firm and perfectly shaped. His face was beauty blended with hardness. Hardness in the savage slash of his cheekbones and the lean line of his darkened jaw. Hardness in the grim set of his mouth and the glint in his eyes. And that hardness gave him an edge of danger. Even she, with no expertise or interest in men, could see why women might describe him as spectacularly handsome.

Something tightened deep in her stomach. Heat washed across her skin and poured through her veins.

They stared at each other and then his mouth compressed. He strode across the tent and lowered her onto the silken cover draped over the large bed, standing over her, powerful and imposing in every way.

'Where does it hurt? Explain your injuries.'

That curt command jolted her out of her dreamy state of contemplation.

Layla told herself there was no reason to feel intimidated. He couldn't help his height. He couldn't help his powerful build. And she could hardly blame him for not smiling in the circumstances.

He'd asked about her injuries.

All the talk of romance and emotions had stressed her beyond belief, so the practical nature of his question soothed her. She preferred the definable to the indefinable and her injuries were definitely definable.

'I ache all over, but particularly my legs, my back and my arms. I suspect it's a mixture of stiffness from unaccustomed muscle use and bruising from the fall. Based on the symptoms, I don't believe anything is broken.'

His eyes gleamed with irony. 'Presumably you have studied medical texts along with Aristotle and the *Kama Sutra*? Your reading matter is diverse, Princess.'

She didn't tell him she hadn't even started the *Kama Sutra*. 'I read a lot.'

'You read. Your sister talks.' He studied her for several long and deeply unsettling minutes. 'Take the robe off.'

'What?' Feeling like a tiny mouse in the sights of a predatory eagle, Layla stared at him. 'Why?'

'Because I want to assess the state of your injuries for myself.'

'I don't have any injuries,' she said quickly. 'Truly, it's just muscular. Superficial. Nothing for you to worry about but I appreciate your concern.' She'd been desperate to be out of the robes, but now she was equally desperate to keep them on. The thought of removing them in front of this man unsettled her.

With a sigh he sat down on the bed, his thigh brushing briefly against hers. 'You say you want marriage and yet you're afraid even to remove your robe in my presence? Are you proposing that once we're married we go to bed fully clothed?'

'No, of course not. That's different.'

'*How* is it different?'

He was testing her. He thought she couldn't do it.

Desperation blew away modesty. If he refused to marry her she would never see Yasmin again.

'I will be fine. I will take the responsibilities that come with the role very seriously.'

'Responsibilities?'

'Physical intimacy is one of the responsibilities of a wife. I understand that. I understand exactly what is involved.'

'Are you sure?' Those dark eyes swept her face with disturbing intensity. 'How much of the *Kama Sutra* have you read, Princess?'

If she said she'd read the whole thing cover to cover would he marry her?

Layla opened her mouth and then closed it again, because she knew her skills at lying were on a par with her horse-riding abilities. 'Not much.' She hoped honesty wasn't going to kill her future. 'In fact just the title so far. But I'm a fast reader,' she added quickly, afraid that her lack of knowledge might put him off. 'And *you* have experience.'

For some reason just saying that made her body warm.

Because looking at his face made her feel hot and uncomfortable she stared instead at his hands, but for some reason that didn't make her feel any better. She felt as if she'd had a shot of adrenaline straight into the heart.

'You are reluctant to take off your robe,' he said softly, 'but once we're married you are going to be naked when you share my bed.'

Layla felt her stomach curl. Everything inside her twisted and heated. She felt dizzy and strange.

Nerves, she thought. 'Does this mean you're agreeing to my suggestion?'

Without warning he lifted a powerful hand and pushed back the swath of fabric covering her head. His handsome face was taut and unsmiling, as if he were weighing up a decision of enormous importance.

Layla tried not to flinch even though the gentle brush of those strong fingers against her cheeks made everything inside her clench. She told herself he had every right to look at the woman he might marry.

Was he looking to see if she were as beautiful as his wife? Or was he deciding if he could look upon her every day and not see the face of her father and Hassan and think of the destruction they'd caused in his life.

He continued to look, his gaze disturbingly intense as his fingers trailed slowly over her cheek.

She knew her face was flushed. She could feel the heat and knew he would be able to feel it, too, with those fingers that seemed in no hurry to cease their exploration of her skin.

Her heart started to pound.

The seconds passed and a minute became two minutes and longer.

His forefinger traced the line of her jaw.

His eyes dropped to her mouth.

Layla was rigid with discomfort. She had no idea of the correct etiquette in this situation. Was she supposed to do something? Say something? Was it some sort of test?

She remembered Yasmin telling her that his wife had been stunningly beautiful.

Was this all about comparison?

When he spoke, there was something in his tone she couldn't identify. 'You are brave.'

Torn between relief that there was at least one thing about her he liked and disappointment that such close examination hadn't uncovered anything else to commend her, Layla felt obliged to tell the truth. 'I'm not very brave. I ran away from the palace.'

'And you ran to me and offered me everything, even though deep down the thought of it frightens you.'

'I'm not frightened.'

'So far I believe you have been honest with me. I advise you not to change that.'

She hesitated. 'I don't think you'll hurt me.'

His eyes darkened. 'I will inevitably hurt you—as you would know if you'd read the book.'

Was he talking physically? Out of her depth in a conversation that felt like a swim in boiling oil, Layla had never felt more mortified in her life. 'If there is pain then I'll bear it.'

'You seem determined to pursue this course, but what you are proposing will tie us together for a lifetime, so I urge you to think carefully and be sure this is what you want.'

'That's why I came to you and suggested it.' Surely the facts spoke for themselves? Why did he keep asking her? 'The alternative is being tied to Hassan for a lifetime and you must see that lacks appeal for so many reasons.'

There was a glimmer of something in his eyes. It might have been admiration or it might have been pity or even humour.

'You have strength and honesty and I respect those traits. If respect is truly all you need from a relationship then I can promise you that. It will be done.' He rose to his feet, sure and confident and very much the one in control. 'I will send Salem to find your sister and instruct him to bring her here. I agree that there is no time to lose, so you and I will be married within the hour. I will send someone to help you prepare. Oh, and princess...' He paused by the entrance to the tent, his eyes a wicked shade of black. 'You have no need of that book. When the time comes I will teach you what you need to know.'

CHAPTER THREE

'I AM TO search for a princess who talks too much? What sort of a description is that? Every woman I know talks too much.' Salem sat relaxed on his horse, a look of incredulity on his handsome face as he looked at his brother. 'If the stallion she stole is the one we think it is, he was bred for speed and endurance. He could have carried her for miles. She could be anywhere. Or lying dead somewhere in the desert.'

'The fact that she talks too much should make her all the easier to find and we both know that with your abilities you can track anyone.' Raz rode alongside him, controlling a horse who snorted and pawed at the sand, yearning for speed. 'Be careful. Hassan will be looking for her and the horse. And also for you.'

'And for *you*. You should not be asking me to leave you at this time.'

'I'm not asking you. I'm giving you an order.'

'Is it true that you are going to marry the Princess tonight?'

Salem's voice was soft and Raz kept his hand steady as he soothed the horse.

'It is the right thing to do. The only thing.'

'It may be the right thing for Tazkhan, but is it right for *you*?'

Raz ignored the question. 'You will do everything in your power to find the younger sister.'

'You vowed never to marry again.'

No one but his brother would have dared make such a personal remark and the words were like the sharp flick of a whip.

'There is more than one type of marriage. This will be a marriage of the head, not of the heart.'

'And the Princess?' There was a creak of leather as Salem shifted his position in the saddle. 'She's young. Is that the life she wants?'

'She claims that it is.'

'Does she know about—?'

'No.' Raz interrupted him before he could finish the sentence. 'But she understands exactly what I am able to offer her.'

'And you trust her? You can live with her, knowing who she is?'

'I will learn to live with her.' He blocked thoughts of her heritage and instead thought of her sitting huddled on his bed, gripping the oversized robe in clenched hands. He thought of the book she'd chosen to bring from the library to equip her for her new role. *Thought of the courage it must have taken to come to him.* 'She has very little life experience.'

'Whereas you have decades too much. You're not an easy man to know, Raz—are you being fair to her?'

'I will endeavour to be as fair as possible.' Frowning, Raz released his hold on the reins and urged the stallion forward. 'You're wasting time. The key to my bride's happiness will be finding her sister safe and well. Make that happen.'

Salem rode away from him. 'Just watch your back, brother.'

'His Highness instructed us to bring you clothes.' The girl dropped a dress on the bed. Resentment and animosity throbbed from her and it was obvious she wished she had not been the one chosen for the task.

'Thank you.' Having washed away the dust from her fall in the water that had been hastily provided, Layla stared at the exquisite fall of silk, caught at the waist with a silver belt. 'I didn't expect a dress.' Especially not a dress like this one. *A romantic dress.* Where had he found it?

She remembered his comment about romance and felt a flash of panic that Raz Al Zahki would think she was secretly nurturing dreams about their relationship, and then remembered that he was the last person to encourage such a delusion.

He didn't want this any more than she did.

'You cannot marry His Highness in dusty robes that swamp you. You have to look your best on your wedding day.' There was censorship in her tone and something else. *Jealousy?*

Feeling desperately alone, Layla missed her sister more than ever. She suppressed the urge to point out there was no reason for anyone to feel jealous. That this marriage was driven by loyalty to his country and no other emotion.

Surely it was obvious?

'The Sheikh and I met for the first time a few hours ago.'

'But you have been chosen as the one to warm his bed and his heart.' The girl removed the bowl of water that she'd placed by Layla's feet. 'You carry a big responsibility.'

The words did nothing to ease the churning in her stomach. Layla knew she'd warm the bed simply by lying in it, but she also knew that wasn't what the girl meant. She did not feel it appropriate to point out the absurdity of being chosen to warm his heart when his heart was in his thoracic cavity and more than capable of maintaining its own temperature. No, what the girl was *really* pointing out was that she was filling the gap left by his wife. Suddenly Layla realised that it was all very well to speak blithely of a different sort of marriage but in the end this union was about a man and a woman spending their lives together, and she had no idea if he would even be able to treat her with civility, given everything that had happened.

But what difference did it make? Her alternative was marriage to Hassan and nothing could be worse.

Rationalising that, Layla only half listened as the girl braided her hair and continued to praise Raz in terms close to hero-worship. She was aware of the worsening throb in her head and the steady gnawing of anxiety about her sister. And beneath all that there was anxiety about herself. About what lay ahead. About *him*.

It was all very well to state bravely that this was what she wanted. Quite another thing to contemplate the reality.

I will inevitably hurt you—as you would know if you'd read the book.

'The book' was safely tucked away in her bag, along with the other book she'd smuggled out of the Citadel. Raz had told her she didn't need to read it but she couldn't think of anything worse than relying entirely on someone else for information.

She wished she could have time alone to study it before the wedding, but there seemed to be no chance of that and she couldn't argue with his decision to proceed as quickly as possible.

Hassan would be out looking for her. *And for Yasmin.*

She winced as the girl's fingers encountered a fresh bruise.

'His Highness told me you fell from your horse. It's a shame that you can't ride because he is a magnificent horseman.'

The implication being that he couldn't have picked a worse match in her.

Her confidence plummeting as each of Raz's qualities was revealed, Layla sank into gloom. She was starting to wonder if this might not have been the worst idea of her life.

And then she heard noise from outside the tent and sat up,

clutching the towel, terrified that Hassan might have found them. 'Who is that?'

'The wedding guests. A Bedouin wedding gives everyone a chance to dress up and celebrate. Word has spread that His Royal Highness Raz Al Zahki is to marry Her Royal Highness Princess Layla of Tazkhan.' There was a brittle note to her tone. 'Even though it is short notice, he wants as many of the local people here as possible. It's important that it is witnessed.'

He wanted rumour spread. He wanted Hassan to hear and be afraid.

'Even when I'm married to Raz Al Zahki, Hassan is unlikely to step aside.'

'His Highness will know what to do.'

Layla was surprised by how much faith people seemed to have in him. She was used to living in an atmosphere of negativity and resentment, not of trust.

Nothing about this new life seemed familiar, and certainly not the dress.

She had never worn anything so beautiful. Her hair, now shiny and clean, was concealed by a veil and her eyes had been accentuated by kohl. The shiny gloss the girl applied to her mouth felt sticky and strange and Layla felt utterly unlike herself.

Any hopes she'd had of being able to sneak a look at the *Kama Sutra* died as she was immediately led outside. It seemed that she and Raz Al Zahki agreed on at least one thing, and that was that the marriage should take place as fast as possible.

And clearly he had also decided that there should be as many witnesses as possible, because a surprising number of people had poured into the desert camp in the time it had taken her to wash and change.

The wedding itself was a blur, conducted with an urgency

driven not by feelings of sentimentality but by the knowledge that any delay could give Hassan an advantage.

Layla kept her gaze focused ahead of her, aware of what felt like a thousand pairs of eyes fixed on her—some curious, others with unconcealed hostility.

And all the time she was aware of Raz next to her, tall and powerful, doing his duty for the good of his people, his own personal wishes set aside.

The event held no emotional meaning for either of them, but they stood side by side, spoke the words required of them, and Layla felt a rush of relief that came from the knowledge that no matter what happened now Hassan couldn't make her his wife.

As Raz turned towards her relief was washed away by reality.

She was now living in the enemy camp with a man who had no reason to feel anything but animosity and contempt for her.

The fact that this was a marriage of expediency didn't seem to bother the guests, who danced and celebrated until Layla was almost dropping with exhaustion.

And he noticed, of course, because it seemed he noticed everything—from the slightest change in the wind's direction to a child who had wandered off unattended.

'Come.'

Just a single word, but delivered with such authority that it didn't occur to her to contradict him. Or maybe it was that she was too preoccupied with what lay ahead.

She hoped the physical side of their relationship didn't require too much input from her because she was fairly sure she was going to fall asleep the moment she lay flat.

They were halfway towards the tent when there was a sound in the distance. She heard horses and shouts and Raz tightened his hand over hers and hauled her close to his side.

Moments later two men she recognised from her arrival at the camp galloped up with the Sheikh's stallion—that same huge black beast that had become as much of a legend as its master.

Layla strained her ears to catch what they were saying and then gasped as firm hands grasped her and swung her onto the back of the animal. Less than thrilled at being back on a horse so soon after her last experience, she clutched at the stallion's mane feeling unbalanced and horribly unsafe.

Moments later Raz vaulted on behind her and locked his arm around her waist.

'I'm sorry to do this to you when you're still bruised after your last encounter with a horse, but Hassan has discovered your absence.' His mouth was right by her ear. 'Right now he is doing everything in his power to find you. It isn't safe to stay. We must move on.'

'But now that we're married—'

'That does not make it safe. No matter what circumstances led to our marriage, you are mine now and I will protect you. You have my word on that.'

Layla heard the steel in his voice and wondered if he were thinking of his wife.

Did he blame himself for not preventing the accident that had killed her?

Had she given him yet more responsibility to add to the load he already carried?

'Could we use a different mode of transport? I'll slow you down. I can't ride.'

'I am the one doing the riding. You are merely the passenger.'

'I'll fall off.' She glanced down and then wished she hadn't. It was a long way to the ground. The stallion was enormous and she felt the power of him beneath her, felt the quivering suppressed energy, and remembered how the horse Yasmin had taken from her father's stables had shot forward like an arrow from a bow, leaving her in an aching heap on the sand.

His arm tightened around her. 'I will *not* let you fall.'

'Can't we use a helicopter or a Jeep or something?'

'One of my men is flying the helicopter and another is taking a Jeep to provide a decoy. They will not expect us to be on horseback. It is the safest way.'

Thinking that he had a very different idea of the definition of 'safe', Layla gripped tightly with her legs and felt the warm flanks of the quivering horse pressing against her bare thighs. 'I'm not dressed for this.'

Even as she said the words a cloak was wrapped around her and he said something to someone close by.

'There is no time to change. You will be fine. Trust me.'

Layla was about to point out that she didn't trust him any more than he trusted her, but the horse sprang forward and she squeezed her eyes shut.

'Is it wise to ride at night?'

'No. Which is why Hassan will not look for us on horseback.'

'Is that supposed to be comforting?' She thought she heard him laugh but decided it must have been the wind, because who could find such a dangerous situation amusing?

'I know this area as well as you know the palace. We are following the stars and the riverbed. Now, relax and go with the rhythm of the horse. You are very tense and that will make the whole thing more uncomfortable,'

Go with the rhythm of the horse...

She told herself that last time she hadn't had a skilled rider in control or a strong male arm wrapped around her.

'Pull the scarf across your mouth.'

She released her rigid grip on the horse's mane to do as he instructed.

She wanted to ask where they were going, but knew the

question was not only superfluous but also potentially hazardous because the hooves of the horses sent sand flying into the air and she only had a thin layer of scarf protecting her. So she kept her mouth closed and tried to remember what she'd read about riding, and then realised it didn't matter because *he* knew and was driving the horse forward, controlling the animal with one hand on the reins while the other remained firmly locked around her waist.

She was aware of the dull thud of hooves on sand, of the feel of Raz's thighs pressed hard against hers and the brush of the cool night air on her face. A sensation tore through her that she didn't recognise and it took her a few moments to realise it was exhilaration. With the responsibility for controlling the horse in someone else's hands, the ride on the back of this powerful animal was the most exciting, breath taking experience of her life. In her restricted, regimented life this was the closest she'd ever come to freedom, and it felt so good she smiled behind the protective covering of the scarf. She couldn't remember when she'd last smiled, but she was smiling now as each pounding stride of the horse took her further away from Hassan. It felt like the end of something—and then she remembered that Hassan was unlikely to give up that easily.

And Yasmin was out in the desert alone and lost.

Her smile faded.

She hoped Salem's knowledge of the desert was as good as it was reputed to be and that he'd find her sister quickly.

They rode for several hours, until time blurred and sleep overcame her. Several times she was jarred awake as her head hit his shoulder, and eventually he shifted position to give her somewhere to rest her head.

'Sleep, Princess.'

And she did, because her body gave her no choice, exhausted by the exertions of the past twenty-four hours. Her

last coherent thought before her brain shut down was that
sleeping against his chest like this was the safest she'd felt
in her life.

CHAPTER FOUR

SHE WAS SNUGGLED against him, lulled to sleep by the movement of the horse.

The closeness of her disturbed him as much as the realisation that she was nothing like he'd imagined her to be when people had spoken her name. He'd visualised someone pampered and privileged. Someone spoiled and entitled. When he'd first seen her in his tent he'd assumed she was an opportunist, switching sides to protect herself before the inevitable shift in power.

At some point from her arrival in the camp to her falling asleep against him his view on her had become clouded, and now he was forced to admit he didn't know what he was dealing with.

Dawn rose over the desert, and in the distance he saw the familiar shape of trees and tents clustered around the small, lush oasis that marked one of his favourite places on earth.

His heart clenched as it always did when he arrived here.

Perhaps he shouldn't have brought her, but what choice did he have?

Alerted to their presence, people emerged from tents. The rising sun glinted off the dunes and Raz brought his horse to a halt.

'Princess?' He spoke the word softly and she stirred against him, her hand locked on the sleeve of his robe.

Raz looked down at that hand. Her fingers were slender and he realised this was the first time he'd seen any part of her other than her face. 'Layla!' He used her name for the first time and she came awake with a start, her eyes blurred with sleep as she tried to focus and orientate herself.

'I fell asleep?'

'For several hours.' He held the stallion steady and then dismounted in a smooth movement. 'Swing your leg over the saddle and I'll help you down.'

She did it without fuss, but the moment her feet touched the ground she winced and gripped the horse for balance. They'd ridden for hours and she was already aching and bruised from her ride from the Citadel. He knew virtually nothing about her but suspected only dire need would drive her to steady herself against his horse.

The stallion gave a snort of disapproval and threw up its head in disgust.

Raz put his hand on his horse's neck and spoke calmly. 'Your muscles will soon become accustomed to riding.'

'I'm fine, really.'

'You are hoping never to see another horse in your life,' he said dryly, 'but horses are an essential part of my life. I own several stud farms. Two in the US, one in England and one here in Tazkhan.'

'I know. Your aim is to promote the highest standards in breeding. You specialise in endurance and racing. People send mares from all over the world to be covered by your stallions. You rode in the endurance team on your favourite horse, Raja.'

He hid his surprise. 'You know a great deal about my horses.'

'I know nothing about your horses.' This time she was the one to speak in a dry tone. 'But I will try very hard to learn.'

'Is that what you want?'

She hesitated. 'Of course. Although I can't promise I'll show any aptitude. I'm not very coordinated and I'm not sure animals like me much.' Hesitant, she reached out and patted the stallion's neck. 'Is this Raja? I'm incredibly grateful to him for not throwing me off.'

'I bred him. He was sired by my father's stallion.'

'He's beautiful. But big.'

Presumably her legs had steadied because she stepped back and looked around her for the first time.

'Where are we? We can stay with these people? In their homes? Will we be welcome?'

There wasn't a place in the desert where he wasn't welcome, but he didn't say that to her.

'The Bedouin pride themselves on their hospitality. A visitor may stay three days and three nights, after which he is considered sufficiently refreshed to be able to continue his journey.'

'Is that what we're going to do?'

Raz didn't reply. He wasn't used to sharing his plans with anyone, least of all the daughter of the man who had ripped his life into shreds. 'The oasis here is famed for its beauty. You can relax here, knowing you are safe.'

'And my sister?'

'When I have news from Salem I will tell you. And now I have things I must do.'

She didn't ask what things. She simply stared at the red-gold of the dunes as they rose against the sunrise as if she were seeing the desert for the first time, while Raz found himself looking at her profile. She had to be exhausted and in pain after the long ride, but she hadn't once complained.

He wondered what she was thinking.

Was she still relieved not to have married Hassan?

Was she nervous? Regretting her decision to marry a man she didn't know?

On impulse he reached out to touch her shoulder, and then changed his mind and withdrew his hand. 'The waters of the oasis are good for muscle ache.'

'I'll remember that, thank you.'

A young woman emerged from one of the tents and Raz felt a sudden rush of tension. In an ideal world he would have prepared for this encounter with more care, but the world was rarely ideal.

'This is Nadia. If there is anything you need she will help you.'

Nadia looked from him to Layla, unable to hide her dismay. 'So it's true? You married her?'

Her voice shook and Raz shot her a warning look.

'Yes. And you will make her welcome.'

For a moment he thought she was going to refuse.

Their eyes met and suddenly he wondered whether her feelings about this development were more complicated than he'd imagined.

Nadia's breathing was shallow, but she gave a brief nod. 'Of course. Come this way, Your Highness.' The correct mode of address was spoken through clenched teeth, but Raz decided to overlook that for now.

His sudden marriage would have come as a massive shock to Nadia. It was fair that she be given time to adjust.

Raz saw Layla glance towards him and wondered if the other girl's open hostility had upset her.

Or perhaps she was suddenly realising that this marriage was real.

Out of the frying pan into the fire?

'Bathe, eat, rest,' he told her quietly, 'and I will see you later.'

Bathe, eat, rest.

All of it seemed to be leading to one thing. The night.

I will see you later.

Layla tried not to think about it. It was something to be done, that was all. She would endure it as she had endured the long gallop on the horse and a thousand other discomforts in her life. Really, how bad could it be?

'His Highness gave instructions that you are to swim. He says it will ease the pain in your muscles.' Nadia was barely civil as she led her towards the tents, but Layla was starting to get used to that attitude from everyone close to the Sheikh.

She felt as welcome as a scorpion in the heel of someone's boot.

All the same, she wondered what the other girl's relationship was with him. She'd seen the look they'd exchanged and it had been obvious to her that they knew each other well.

She wondered if the woman had been his lover, but told herself she had no reason to mind even if she had.

Baking hot under the desert sun, Layla removed her cloak. Nadia turned pale.

'Where did you get that dress?'

Layla glanced down at herself and noticed that the silk was discoloured by sand and dust from the ride. 'I was given it. Why?'

'No reason.' Nadia's lips were bloodless. 'I will leave towels on the rocks, Your Highness, and lay out clean clothes in the tent for you to change into when you have finished.'

'I can't swim,' Layla admitted. 'Is the oasis deep?'

Nadia led her along a narrow path. 'Not if you enter the pool by the rocks on the far side.'

The rocks on the far side.

Layla committed that to memory because she didn't want to get it wrong.

Nothing about her first glimpse of the camp had prepared her for the beauty of the oasis. Shaded by date palms, the still pool of water looked temptingly cool after the long, dusty ride.

This part of the pool was secluded, the view from the

other tents obscured by palms and citrus trees. Just one tent stood close by and Nadia gestured with her head. 'That is His Highness's tent. I will leave clothes there and put food in the tent. If you need anything, just call, but the pool is safe in the daytime. I'll go and fetch towels.'

Layla didn't ask what happened at night. She was too busy wondering who had given up their tent for the Sheikh.

It was obvious it had prime position, set apart from the others and opening onto what effectively became a private pool.

But not *that* private.

Layla glanced around her, aware that anyone could walk past at any time.

Having only ever undressed behind a locked door, she decided to keep her dress on. It was ruined anyway, so she might as well get one last use out of it.

Removing the belt, she walked to the rocks at the far side of the pool, as Nadia had instructed, and slid into the water.

Stretching out her legs, she felt for the bottom with her feet—but there was no bottom.

Too late, she realised how deep it was and clung tightly to the slippery rock with her fingers, trying to pull herself out again. Just as the thought flashed into her head that Nadia had deliberately sent her to deep water she sank under the surface, dragged down by the weight of the saturated dress.

Trying not to panic, Layla attempted to haul herself up, but her fingers slipped and she sank under the surface, choking.

Water flooded through her mouth and her ears and she kicked hard, but the dress wrapped itself around her ankles, pulling her down.

Just when she'd thought there was no way she was ever going to get out of this alive she felt a disturbance in the water next to her and strong hands hauled her upwards, towards the light. Layla broke the surface of the water, gasping and coughing.

'Are you trying to drown yourself?' His black hair plastered to his head, Raz lifted her onto the rocks and then launched himself out of the water next to her, water streaming from the gleaming, pumped muscles of his bare chest. 'What were you thinking, swimming in a dress?'

Layla couldn't answer. She was too busy coughing and trying not to be sick.

Cursing softly under his breath, he smoothed her soaked hair away from her face. 'You are all right now. You are safe. It was lucky I decided to come back and check on you.'

'I went under—'

'Because you chose to swim in your dress,' he breathed, and she shook her head.

'I never intended to swim. I can't swim. I was just going to dip myself in the water.'

'Fully clothed?'

It sounded ridiculous, spelled out like that, and her face turned fiery hot. 'I thought someone might walk along and see me. The dress was ruined anyway so I thought I'd just keep it on and paddle.'

'In the deepest end of the pool?'

'I thought it was the shallow end.' Layla glanced up at him, puzzled, and saw his eyes darken dangerously.

'Why would you think that? Who told you it was the shallow end?'

She wasn't going to tell him that when there was already friction. 'It was my fault,' Layla muttered 'I should have checked for myself.'

Without speaking, he unfastened the back of her dress. 'Take this off. Go to the other end of the pool where the water is only waist deep. You will be safe and undisturbed, I promise.'

'Where are you going?'

'There is a conversation I need to have and it would seem

that it can't wait.' His voice vibrating with anger, he vaulted to his feet and strode back towards the tent.

Moments later Layla heard his voice and winced, because it was obvious to her that however much Nadia had loathed her before this, she was going to loathe her a thousand times more by the time Raz had finished ripping strips from her in that icy voice of his. She thought she heard muffled sobs and closed her eyes, because the whole situation was turning into a complex mess and without the facts she had no idea how she was supposed to handle it.

Taking refuge in the practical, she peeled off the soaked dress and forced herself back into the water again—more because she didn't want to let fear beat her than because she wanted to wash. This time she was relieved to feel the bottom under her feet. As he had promised, the water only reached her waist and she washed herself quickly, still shocked by how close she'd come to drowning in this beautiful place.

The sun sent sparkles of light dancing over the still surface of the pool. Somewhere nearby she heard children playing, their laughter cutting through the stillness of the baking hot air, and the sound surprised her because she hadn't expected to hear children.

She couldn't think of the time she'd last heard children laugh like that. It reminded her of when Yasmin had been very young and Layla had been constantly putting her hand over her mouth to stifle her giggles in case the sound drew unwanted attention. But here no one was trying to muffle the sound and the children played happily, unrestricted.

Thinking of her sister brought a lump to her throat.

Where was she now?

If only she were at least alive, Layla would never complain about anything ever again.

Listening to the children, she was tempted to go and watch them, but then decided she'd encountered enough hostility for one day. Instead she wrapped herself in the towels that had been left for her and walked the short distance to the tent, hoping that Nadia wouldn't be there.

Stepping inside, she stopped in surprise.

She'd expected something basic, but this tent was not only fully furnished but luxurious, decorated in rich reds and deep purples. There was a seating area piled with soft cushions and a low bed covered in silk sheets, with a thick cover for cold desert nights.

It was idyllic.

It was—Layla swallowed hard—*it was romantic.*

Someone had laid food on a low table near to the door, but Layla wasn't hungry. She couldn't even think about food after everything that had happened. Did Nadia really hate her so much she would want her dead? And what had Raz said to her that had caused her such distress?

Feeling sick from nerves and oasis water, she pulled on the clothes and sank onto the cushions.

Despite worry about Nadia, and anxiety for her sister, her mind was dominated by thoughts of the night ahead.

She would have spent the day reading, but her books had been left behind at the first camp so she had nothing but her imagination to occupy her time, and by the time Raz finally appeared she was so worked up she jumped out of her skin.

'You startled me.'

His gaze rested on the untouched food and a faint frown touched his forehead. 'You haven't touched the food. Are you unwell after the incident earlier?'

'No. I just wasn't hungry.'

'If you do not eat you will make yourself ill.'

She didn't tell him that she already felt ill. That nerves had created an uncomfortable lump in her stomach, leaving no room for food. 'I won't be ill. I'm very fit.'

'But you can't swim?'

'There is nowhere to swim in the palace so I've never had opportunity.'

'Then that's something we must fix.' A ghost of a smile touched his mouth. 'Swimming in the oasis is one of life's pleasures.'

Her heart was pumping so fast she worried she was going to pass out, and when he took her hand and drew her towards him she stopped breathing.

'I am sorry for what happened to you.'

'Is Nadia—?'

'I don't want to talk about Nadia. She has no relevance to what is happening between us and I've dealt with her. Now you need to relax.' His voice soft, he smoothed her hair back from her face. 'You are very tense and there is no need to be.'

Behind him, through the crack in the tent, she could see the sun turning dark red as it set and it shocked her because she hadn't realised it was so late.

'I'm not tense.'

'Yes, you are, and that is hardly surprising.' His fingers lingered in her hair. 'This is not how you dreamed your wedding night would be, I'm sure.'

'I never dreamed about it. I'm not a dreamy person, Your Highness.'

'Raz.' He let a strand of her hair twist itself around his fingers, frowning as she flinched away from him. 'You don't have to be afraid of me.'

It wasn't fear that made her stomach cramp, but she wasn't sure what it was because it was a feeling she didn't recognise.

All she knew was that she'd never felt more uncomfortable in her life. He clearly thought she'd spent her formative years dreaming of weddings and happy endings whereas nothing could have been further from the truth.

'I am not a romantic person,' she reminded him. 'I thought

I'd made that clear. I hope that won't be a problem. I assumed you wouldn't want that.'

What if he did?

Perhaps he was expecting her to fall instantly in love with him and she knew that was never going to happen.

The heat in the tent was stifling and he was standing close to her. *So close she could feel the heat and power of him.* The breath was locked in her throat and Layla had no idea what she was supposed to do next. Was he expecting her to kiss him? Was he supposed to go first or was she? Both together?

Layla desperately wished she'd had time to study the various options.

She wished she'd read *that* book long before now, instead of grabbing it as an afterthought on the run from the palace and her old life.

The gaps in her knowledge were glaringly obvious. For a start, she was confused by how long he'd stood there just looking at her. She'd assumed it would all be over quickly. Instead he seemed to be taking his time. His hand had migrated from her hair to her cheek and the slow, exploratory stroke of his fingers unsettled her.

Her tummy tightened into a knot and her pulse leaped and pounded.

She wanted to look away but his gaze drew her to him, holding her eyes with his. And then his eyes flickered to her mouth and that made her feel strange, too. As did his next words.

'So what *did* you dream about when you were growing up in the palace?'

How was she supposed to answer that? Every day had been focused on survival. On protecting her sister. 'I didn't really dream. I prefer to focus on things that are real. Tangible.'

'You had no wish for the future?'

'If I did then it was a hope that the future would be bet-

ter than the present.' She saw him frown slightly and felt his
thumb slide slowly over the line of her jaw.

'The present was hard for you?'

What could she say? However hard it had been for her, she
knew it must have been so much harder for him. He'd lost his
father and the woman he'd loved. 'I had my sister.'

A faint smile touched the corner of his mouth. 'You're
being evasive, but I'll overlook it for now because the past
has no place in our bedroom.'

Our bedroom.

Her heart was pounding furiously and she found herself
trapped by his dark gaze as he slid his hands into her hair
and tilted her face to his.

'If I do anything you don't like you must tell me,' he
breathed.

She'd just had time to think that was a very strange thing
to say, because she had no expectation of liking any of it,
when he lowered his head.

Anticipation held her rigid.

That sensuously curved mouth hovered close to hers, pro-
longing the moment of contact. Just as Layla was beginning
to wonder whether there was a reason he was taking so long,
whether there was something she was supposed to be doing
that she wasn't, he slanted his mouth over hers and kissed her.

The gentleness threw her. Braced for something quite different, she found the slow, deliberate movement of his lips on
hers shocking. Equally unexpected was the sudden tightening of her stomach and the warmth that rushed through her
body and into her limbs. The feelings intensified but still his
mouth moved over hers while his hands, buried in her hair,
held her head trapped.

She felt his tongue trace the seam of her mouth, teasing,
coaxing, and she parted her lips, shocked to feel his tongue
delve into her mouth.

Something—*nerves*?—made her shaky? and she closed
her hands over his arms to steady herself, her fingers moving over the solid muscle of his biceps. His physical power
was undeniable, and she remembered the way he'd controlled
the stallion and lifted her out of the pool. But he used that
strength lightly now, his hands gentle as he smoothed her hair
away from her face and kissed her mouth, all the time watching her through slumbrous dark eyes that made her aware of
every part of herself.

Layla had never felt anything like this before, and she felt
a flash of panic because she was a person who liked to understand things and rationalise them. But there was no understanding the searing heat that shot through her body and
pooled low in her belly.

Releasing her head, he curved one arm around her back,
slid the other around her waist and pulled her into him. She
felt the strength and power of his thighs and the hardness
of him. Pressed against the evidence of his masculinity, she
discovered that the works of Michaelangelo didn't tell the
whole story.

Layla was confused by the torrent of sensation that flooded
her skin and seeped into her nerve-endings.

'Kiss me back.'

His husky command was spoken against her lips and she
stared up at him, unable to see him properly in the darkness
but knowing her mouth was just a shadow away from the
dangerous curve of his.

Kiss me back.

Wishing she had more knowledge of technique, Layla tentatively touched her lips to his. She wanted to ask, *Is this
right?* But then she felt his arm tighten around her waist,
drawing her closer. Pressed this close to him, she felt hot
and unbalanced in every way. She knew her cheeks were
flushed, knew he could taste her confusion on her lips, but

still he kissed her and the slowness of it, together with the long drawn-out ache of anticipation and something else she couldn't name, was agonising.

He kissed her until their surroundings faded and the only thing in her vision was him, and then he lifted her in his arms and carried her to the bed. The practical side of her prompted her to tell him she was capable of walking, but she thought it might be a lie so she kept silent and wondered how nerves could weaken limbs.

The light in the tent was dim, but not so dim she couldn't see his face, and she remembered Yasmin dreamily telling her how handsome he was—how he was 'hot'. At the time Layla hadn't understood how a word used to describe temperature could be used as a positive indicator of visual appeal, but now she realised that looking at him made her *feel* hot. Burning hot. Her skin, her lips and other more sensitive parts of her that she rarely had reason to think about. And while he was kissing her he extracted her from her clothing. The ease with which he accomplished that feat was almost as embarrassing as being naked in front of him.

Grateful for the semi-darkness, she somehow resisted the desperate urge to cover herself. Never in her life had she felt so out of her depth and inadequate, and she lay there, her breathing shallow, staring up at him as he wrenched off his shirt, all the time watching her with eyes almost black in the candlelight.

Layla held her breath because even she, with her limited experience and previously limited interest in the masculine form, could see that his was perfectly proportioned.

Unable to help herself, she let her gaze slide over bronzed, muscular shoulders, down over his chest with its haze of dark hair, and lower still to his board-flat abdomen. She didn't look lower and he slid his fingers under her chin and lifted her face, forcing her to look at him.

'You're scared.'

'No.' Her voice was a whisper. 'But I wish I'd read more.'

'Not all the answers can be found in books.' His thumb brushed the corner of her mouth and his fingers slid into her hair, cupping the back of her head. 'Perhaps you know more than you think you do. Follow your instincts.'

As he drew her head down to his she wanted to tell him that she didn't have any instincts when it came to men, but her tongue wouldn't form the words. Instead it tangled with his, and she heard herself moan into the heat of his clever mouth.

And she discovered she *did* have instincts, because it was instinct that had her sliding her hands into his hair, clutching his head, meeting his hot, seductive kisses with her own. And instinct had her pressing herself closer to him. Later, she'd wonder how a kiss involving her lips could have an effect on her whole body, but right then she wasn't capable of wondering about anything except what was going to happen next.

'Next' was his mouth on her neck—slow, lingering, as everything he did was slow and lingering—and she lay still, hardly breathing as the warmth of his tongue traced the line of her shoulder and moved lower, to her bare breasts.

Her nipples were standing erect and she watched in tense fascination as he paused with his mouth close to that sensitive part of her. She felt the warmth of his breath brush over her skin, followed by the slow, deliberate flick of his tongue as he skilfully teased and toyed with that part of her that had never been touched before. Sensation shot right through her, pooling in her pelvis, until she found it almost impossible to keep still, until the urge to cry out was so powerful she had to bite her lip to stay silent. And what he did to one nipple he did to the other, and when he finally lifted his head and looked at her she found it impossible to look away.

For a moment they stared at each other.

There was a hardness in his eyes, a coldness she wished

she hadn't seen, and then he leaned across the bed and blew out the candle, sending the tent into darkness.

She could no longer see, but she could feel, and the feelings became more acute because everything was focused on that one sense—touch.

The warmth of his palm rested low on her abdomen and she wondered if he knew how much she was aching, just how badly she needed—needed *something*. But of course he knew. She remembered Yasmin's breathless statement that he was supposed to be a skilled lover and knew now that it was true.

No wonder he hadn't bothered returning her book.

I will teach you everything you need to know.

The fact that he knew her body better than she did embarrassed her, but nowhere near as much as when he gently spread her thighs and shifted lower on the bed.

Shocked, and feeling intensely vulnerable, Layla gave a soft gasp as his hand moved with sure, leisurely ease over her abdomen and lower still. He took his time, but whether that was out of respect for her inexperience, patience or just a maddening ability to know how to ramp up the tension until she was at screaming pitch, she didn't know. All she knew was that she was moving her pelvis against his hand, and then his fingers were there, sliding skilfully over that part of her, exploring her with slow, knowing strokes of strong, clever fingers, until her breathing was shallow and her hands fisted in the sheets.

She hadn't known it was possible to feel this.

She couldn't see his face, couldn't see anything except darkness, and that darkness intensified feeling because she never knew what was coming next. She felt him shift above her, then move lower, and this time he put his mouth on her *there*. Shock rocketed through her and her hands moved to push him away, but he caught both her wrists in one hand and held her securely, so that all she could do was lie there and let him do exactly what he wanted to do. And what he did was sinfully good, and he did it again and again, until her body quivered and heated, until she was slippery wet and sensitive, embarrassment blown away by sensation. And with each erotic slide of his tongue the feelings intensified, until the heat of it was so maddening she thought she'd explode.

She knew there was something more, that her body was trying to reach something, somewhere, and she squirmed and shifted, trying to relieve the unfamiliar feelings, and then he shifted position in a lithe movement and came over her, his hand under her bottom.

'I will try not to hurt you...'

His voice was husky and he slid his hand down her thigh, encouraging her to wind her legs across his back. Like this, she was open to him and she was once again grateful for the darkness as she felt the silken power of him against her and the warmth of his breath against her mouth as he lowered his head to kiss her again.

He licked at her lips, kissing her gently as he stayed still, letting her grow used to the feel of him against her. It was shockingly intimate with her legs wrapped around him, and for endless moments he held himself still. Then he eased forward and entered her slowly, gently, holding himself in check with ruthless control, taking it so slowly that the discomfort seemed minimal in comparison to the building frustration. Pain and pleasure mingled. Layla felt herself clench around the hard thickness of him, felt the heat and power of him stretching her, and when his hand tightened on her bottom she lifted herself against him and heard a low sound rumble in his throat as he sheathed himself deep. Her breath caught. The intimacy of it shocked her and she curled her fingers over his biceps and then up to his shoulders, aware that he was holding himself still and knowing that he did it for her.

'Are you all right?'

His voice was low and very male, and she opened her eyes, even though she couldn't see him, and said yes, even though she wasn't sure it was true.

She wasn't all right. With him so deeply inside her she felt shaken and unbalanced, as out of her depth as she had in the pool. Only this time instead of drowning in water she was drowning in sensation.

She didn't know what was happening, but she knew she wanted this, *needed* this, and when he lowered his mouth to hers and kissed her she kissed him back, her tongue tangling with his.

He eased back slightly and then moved into her again. She felt her body yield against the male thickness of him, discovered that if she relaxed it was easier, that when he shifted his angle the pleasure intensified and poured through her in long, wicked waves of ecstasy. He was deep, deep inside her, his hand locked in her hair as he controlled the rhythm, all the time kissing her. And she recognised nothing that was happening to her body, *knew* nothing—but he did, and he used that skill and experience to drive her higher and higher, until something strange happened, something unfamiliar and intensely exciting, until screaming ecstasy exploded into an almost unbearable shower of sensation that made her cry out despite her attempts to stay silent.

He trapped the sound with his mouth, kissing her through it as she felt her body tighten around the smooth, hard length of him. She felt the sudden tension of his shoulders under her fingers and then heard him groan deep in his throat as her body drove his over the edge. It was the most thrilling, explosive, intense experience of her life and afterwards Layla lay still, crushed by the weight of him and the knowledge that she had lived with herself for twenty-three years and yet not known herself at all.

She'd had no idea she was even capable of feeling that way.

Her illusions about herself had disintegrated. She'd never thought of herself as romantic, nor particularly physical. Nothing in her past had prepared her for what she'd just experienced. And she realised that delving into a book for information wouldn't have made a difference, because there were no words that could adequately describe what she'd just experienced.

Nothing she'd read could have prepared her for pleasure.

Shattered by the experience, her expectations blown apart, Layla lay there, not knowing what words were appropriate. They'd shared the ultimate intimacy and yet outside the silken haven of his bed they were strangers.

She lay rigid, feeling as if she should say something, trying out various sentences in her head. But before she could utter any of them she felt him rise from the bed. Her burning skin chilled instantly and that chill spread through her bones as rapidly as the heat had done.

Shattered and confused, Layla lay still in the darkness, listening as he dressed. Was this normal?

Was it usual for a man to stand up and leave the bed afterwards?

Or did his response have something to do with his wife?

Was that why he'd blown out the candle? Had he been imagining that he was with someone else? Or was it that he couldn't bear to look at her?

It sounded as if he were going to stride out of the tent without looking back, but then he paused, his hand on the heavy fabric that protected them from the heat of the sun and the cold of the night. Moonlight shone through the slit in the tent and in that moment Layla saw him. Saw the hard, savage lines of his handsome face and the emptiness in those cold eyes that were as black as a starless night.

She stared at him in silence, trying to read him, trying to understand what was going on and failing.

She had no idea what that look meant. No idea what was going through his head.

And now she wished she'd kept her eyes closed. Pretended to be asleep. Anything, to avoid a situation in which she was clueless.

Should she speak?

Was he waiting for her to say something?

And then, before she could decide whether to speak or not, he turned and strode out of the tent, leaving her alone.

CHAPTER FIVE

HE RODE RAJA deep into the desert, trying to escape the weight of his feelings but failing, because wherever he went they followed. His mouth was dry with the bitter taste of betrayal, the past a deep ache inside him that wouldn't heal.

There were so many issues demanding his attention, but the only thing on his mind was Layla.

He'd felt nothing but contempt for her family for so long that when she'd arrived in his camp and offered herself to him he'd treated her proposal with suspicion. Even when it had become clear to him that her life had been very different from the one he'd imagined for her, his feelings towards her hadn't warmed.

But now?

The scent of her clung to his skin and her soft gasps echoed around his head, refusing to be silenced by his own vicious conflict.

As if sensing his tension, the horse under him stamped impatiently. Raz soothed him gently with his hands and his voice until Raja calmed and stood still.

He had a sudden vision of Layla smuggling the *Kama Sutra* from her father's library before leaving the only home she'd ever known. He thought of her climbing onto a horse, even though she didn't ride, and then going in search of him even though she knew exactly how he felt about her family.

And then he thought about her standing still and straight next to him, speaking her vows in the hope that the union would ensure the safety of her sister, and writhing under his hands as he'd shown her what her body could do.

The thought of it sent heat rushing through him and he cursed softly.

He told himself that respect and powerful sexual chemistry didn't change the fact he wasn't ready to feel anything for another woman. Nor did it change the fact that he didn't want her feeling anything for him.

Nothing changed the fact that this marriage politically motivated.

Was she all she seemed to be, or was she a clever opportunist who had the sense to change sides for her own protection?

His suspicions were deep-set, rooted in a lifetime of bitter feud.

So why did the knowledge that he'd hurt her rub at his nerves like sand wedged in his boot?

Staring at the sunrise, he told himself it was a good thing.

He told himself that anger was a thousand times safer than those softer emotions that could fell a man faster than a samurai sword.

'Your Highness.'

It was Abdul, never far from his side and as much a father to him as his own had been.

'You should not be out here alone.'

'I don't appear to *be* alone.'

Ignoring the irony in his voice, Abdul touched his arm. 'This is hard for you, but you did the right thing marrying her.'

'Did I?' He heard the harshness in his own voice and winced, because he wasn't in the habit of revealing his weaknesses to those around him. 'We need to keep an eye on Nadia.'

'Yes. I can imagine she is very upset. But no doubt Her Highness will deal with that sensitively. She seems like a very sensible young woman.'

Sensible? Raz could have agreed with him, but he knew it wasn't her logic or her ordered thought-processes that teased and tormented his brain.

It was something far more intimate and a thousand times more dangerous.

Layla awoke slowly, aware of the sounds of animals, the laughter of children, the hum of voices. None of them belonged to Raz.

The side of the bed where he would have slept was cold, the pillow smooth and untouched.

Her body ached from her night with him, making it impossible to blot it out or forget.

He'd come to her in darkness and then he'd walked away.

Had he known how his touch had made her feel?

Of course he had. His expertise had never been in question. From the first touch to the last, he'd known exactly what he was doing to her.

Layla rolled onto her back and stared up at the roof of the tent.

But as for the rest of it—as for how she felt inside and in her head...

How could he understand that when she didn't understand it herself?

She'd thought she knew herself very well but it turned out she didn't know herself at all, because she hadn't known she was capable of feeling like *that*.

Sheltered by the silk sheets, she slid her hand over her breasts, still tender from the touch of his mouth and the roughness of his jaw. He'd touched her *there* and then he'd—

'Your Highness?' Nadia stood in the entrance to the tent,

her expression frozen as she saw the clothes piled on the floor. 'I have instructions to help you dress and fetch you anything you need.'

What did she need?

Layla had no idea. She felt like a jigsaw someone had dropped. She had no idea how to fit the pieces back together because she no longer recognised the picture. And she had no idea how to make peace with Nadia. It didn't feel good to watch the other woman's pain and know she was somehow the cause.

It was the first time they'd seen each other since the incident in the pool, but Layla decided that Raz had already said whatever needed to be said so didn't raise the topic.

'There is nothing I need, thank you.' She watched as Nadia moved around the tent, placing food on the rug and laying out fresh clothes. She wanted to ask where Raz was, but didn't want to reveal how much she minded his absence—especially not to this girl, who clearly resented Layla's presence and wished she were anywhere but there.

Layla wondered again if she were in love with Raz herself. Was that the reason for the rigid expression and the fact she didn't meet her eyes? Or was it because of who Layla was?

In the end concern for him overruled pride.

'Have you seen His Highness?'

Nadia paused in the entrance of the tent. 'The rumour is that he has gone to find Hassan and talk to him. If he is killed it will be *your* fault.'

The girl blurted out the words and then left the tent, leaving Layla alone with nothing but her conscience to keep her company.

The news that he'd gone to find Hassan disturbed her—not because she underestimated Raz's strength, but because she knew just how duplicitous Hassan could be. He was neither honest nor honourable, and she knew better than most that he was at his most dangerous when he was cornered.

Should she have voiced her suspicions to Raz?

Weighed down by her worry, the hours dragged past. Without access to the library Layla had nothing to distract her from her thoughts, no hope of reaching a state of relaxation. She would have loved to talk to someone but no one came near her. Even Nadia stayed away, and Layla realised that when she'd suggested this marriage she'd given no consideration to how others would feel about it.

Did they all think she'd put Raz at risk?

What if Nadia was right and by coming to him she'd created trouble?

What if Hassan found them here?

It felt like the longest day of her life, and she spent most of it alone, sitting by the oasis, aware of the unfamiliar soreness and aching in her body.

Several times she heard children laughing and the sound reminded her so much of her sister that a lump wedged itself in her throat. Where was she? Had Salem found her? Was she in trouble? *Dead?*

If Hassan had found her before Salem then the chances were she was already in America.

As darkness fell the noise of chatter faded, leaving only the sounds of the desert at night.

Layla lay still on the bed, staring at the single candle that had been lit for her, so tense she could hear her own breathing in the silence of the tent.

Would he come?

Would it be like the night before?

The question swirled around in her head until eventually she fell asleep. When she woke it was light, his side of the bed was still cold, and she had her answer.

He hadn't come.

She was still alone in the bed and she had no idea if Raz had even returned.

Seriously concerned, she swallowed her pride and sought out Nadia once more.

'I do not know where he is, Your Highness.' Her voice was frosty and hovered on the edge of rude. 'He never reveals his plans. And now he's brought you here the risk to him personally will be even greater.'

With no hard evidence with which to refute that challenge, Layla bowed out of the conversation. Guilt gnawed at her, driven by anxiety that Nadia could be right. Had she increased his problems? Had she made things worse, not better?

Or did his unexplained absence have nothing to do with Hassan?

What if it were driven by something even more personal?

Something to do with the night they'd spent together.

Was he thinking of his wife?

Layla spent a second day alone, with only her imagination for company, and was beginning another night the same way when she heard the sound of horses and knew it was him.

The rush of relief was quickly followed by other, more complex feelings.

All day she'd wanted to see him, but now he was here he wished she were on her own again. She had no idea what to say or what to do. She was hardly in a position to play the role of concerned wife, but still she *was* concerned.

Embarrassed, uncomfortable, and burning hot at the thought of the night before them, Layla sat rigid, wishing that there was a rulebook she could follow, an instruction manual—*anything* that might give her clues about how she was supposed to behave.

She heard his voice, deep and instantly recognizable, as he responded to people around him, but still he didn't appear in the tent. It seemed he had time for everyone except her.

Or maybe he was once again waiting for darkness. Maybe he just couldn't face looking at her.

As that explanation occurred to her embarrassment turned to humiliation.

Everyone would know the Sheikh had stayed away from his new bride.

That indisputable fact was a stark reminder that physical intimacy didn't mean emotional intimacy.

Curled up in a ball under the covers, Layla felt more alone than she ever had in her life.

At least back in the Citadel she'd had Yasmin. Her life had been wretched, but familiar. She'd known the rules, known what was expected of her and been able to rationalise every one of her thoughts and feelings.

Here, she was totally isolated, living with a man who apparently loathed her so deeply he couldn't bear to set eyes on her, tormented by emotions and feelings that were totally unfamiliar.

She heard a splash from nearby and assumed he'd gone for a swim in the oasis.

The fact that he hadn't even greeted her first upset her more than she could rationalise. She shouldn't care, should she? She wasn't *allowed* to care.

Layla hesitated for a moment, but then slid quietly out of the bed and peeped through the slit in the tent. It was dark, but without the pollution of the city there was sufficient light for her to make out powerful shoulders as he swam.

She stared at those bare, powerful shoulders, fascinated and shocked in equal amounts. If anyone had told her days ago she'd be hiding in a tent in the hope of getting a glimpse of a naked man she would have laughed at them. But this wasn't any naked man, of course. This was Raz. And because he'd blown out the candles she had yet to see his body.

And she couldn't really see it now—just the occasional

tantalising hint of male muscle and power as he swam with smooth, steady movements.

He reached the far side of the pool and turned. Layla shot back into bed, terrified of being caught.

By the time he walked into the tent she was safely under the covers with her eyes closed.

She heard his soft tread, then silence, and she knew he was looking at her although surely the lack of light would restrict his vision.

Feeling as if someone had set fire to her, Layla kept her eyes closed and tried to breathe evenly. She stayed completely still. Even when the mattress moved under his weight she didn't move.

She lay rigid, churned up inside by his reappearance, shocked that he'd stayed away for two days and then not even greeted her on his return, and shocked that such an action on his part could hurt so badly.

'A tip for the future. No one is that tense when they sleep.'

His voice was deep and soft and she turned, giving up the pretence. *What was the point?*

She saw that he had lit a single candle. Not much, but enough to send a golden shadow of light across the bed. *Enough for her to see his face.*

'Where have you been?'

Shock flared in his eyes. 'I'm not in the habit of disclosing my plans to anyone—least of all to a woman I met for the first time only three days ago.'

She wanted to point out that it might only have been three days but that he knew her more intimately than anyone, had revealed a part of her she hadn't even known existed, but she realised there were dark depths to him she hadn't begun to uncover.

'Has there been any news of my sister?'

His gaze was shuttered. 'None.'

Just one word but it made her feel sick, and suddenly all the daydreams were blown out of her head and replaced by stark reality. 'That's bad, isn't it? We should have heard something.'

'If she is alive then Salem will find her.'

'If?'

'Do you want false hope? Because I won't give you that. Lies destroy trust and create nothing but confusion. But until we have evidence that something has happened to her I urge you to stay positive. We have to hope she will have found a way to survive.'

'How? Neither of us spent any time in the desert when we were growing up.'

'And yet Tazkhan is ninety-eight percent desert. How can you serve a country when you are ignorant of the life its people lead?'

Thrown off balance by that unexpected attack, Layla sat up, clutching the silk sheet to her neck as she rose to her own defence. 'That is an unfair accusation. You know nothing of the life my sister and I led.'

'You were in a position of power and lived a life of luxury. There must have been something you could have done.'

Luxury? 'There was, and I did it. I came to you.'

Cold black eyes met hers. 'I am supposed to believe that was an altruistic act on your part? How do I know you didn't just have the sense to move to the winning side?'

It was like being slapped.

'If you believe that, why did you marry me?'

'Because your motivation has no impact on my decision. I am doing what is best for Tazkhan. My personal wishes have no part in this.'

'So when we were in bed you had to force yourself to do those things to me?'

His jaw clenched and his eyes narrowed. Two streaks of colour highlighted the hard, savage lines of his cheekbones.

'For a virgin whose first glimpse of a naked man was from behind a curtain, you suddenly have a great deal to say for yourself.'

She had the distinct impression that he was trying to pick a fight, and suspected she knew why. It was logical, wasn't it?

'You're angry,' she said softly, banking down her own feelings to try and understand his. 'You feel guilty and it's making you angry.'

'You know nothing about my feelings, Princess.'

'And you know nothing about *my* feelings, either. I may be inexperienced, and I admit I'm shy, but don't *ever* assume you know what my life has been. The reason my sister and I have no knowledge of the desert is not because we weren't interested but because we were unable to leave the city walls.'

'Did you ever try?'

Her heart was pounding. 'Yes.'

'And what happened?'

Her mouth was dry. The sudden emergence of a memory she'd squashed down brought sweat to her palms. 'There are some aspects of our past neither one of us wishes to revisit. I think we should both accept that and move on.' Her desperate statement earned her a long, questioning look.

'If your sister is in the desert then Salem will find her.'

He blew out the candle, there was a rustle of clothing as he undressed, and then he joined her in the bed.

Rigid with discomfort, heart pounding, Layla shot to the furthest end of the bed and lay still, hardly daring to breathe in case breathing brought her into contact with him. 'You think I came here to guarantee the continuation of some glittering lifestyle you've imagined for me and yet, feeling that way, you still want to share the bed with me?'

'We're married.'

'But you don't trust me.'

'Sharing a bed doesn't require trust, Princess.' Reaching

for her in the darkness, he hauled her against him. 'It simply requires sexual chemistry, and fortunately we have plenty of that.'

Layla wondered if he could feel her shivering. Wondered if he could feel the heat of her skin and the rapid beat of her heart.

She wanted to ask why he had to blow out the candle before he shared a bed with her, but before she could form words his mouth slanted over hers and his hand slid into her hair. As a concession to the desert heat and the sand she'd tied it back, but he freed it instantly and it tumbled down over her shoulders.

She felt his hand, warm and strong against her bare back, as he pressed her down onto the soft mattress and shifted her underneath him. She felt the weight of him, the strength and the power. Felt his lips move over hers in a kiss that created an instant response. It started deep inside her and then exploded outwards.

Intense excitement shimmered over layers of despair.

Was this how their relationship was going to be?

Days where they saw nothing of each other and nights spent in the dark?

Intimate strangers?

She wondered how his kiss could make her melt when her emotions weren't involved and tried to control her response to him, but her nerve-endings were already on fire and the erotic skill of his mouth left her with no choice but to kiss him back.

His mouth closed over her nipple and Layla moaned. Just like before, he used all his skill and knowledge to drive her crazy, until she was hot and desperate. The only difference was that this time she *knew*. This time she knew what was to come. And when he surged into her with sure, deep strokes she climaxed instantly, and again and then again, while he possessed and controlled her totally.

Afterwards Layla lay there, numb. Maybe she should be grateful for the protection of the darkness, but she wasn't. The knowledge that he could only make love to her if it was in the dark hurt her more than she would have thought possible.

She turned her head, plucking up the courage to talk to him about it, but before she could speak she heard a high-pitched cry coming from close by.

Layla sat upright, heart pounding. 'What's that? It sounded like a child.'

And then the screams began.

Raz moved quickly, his hand on the knife he kept strapped to his belt whenever he was in the desert.

The screams sliced through him, ripping his composure into shreds, because he knew who screamed.

His strides fuelled by a primal need to protect, he tore open the entrance of the tent next to his and saw the child sitting upright, eyes staring in terror, forehead glistening with sweat, as she screamed while Nadia stood there helplessly, hopelessly out of her depth.

'I can't get her to stop.'

In seconds he had the child in his arms, folding her tightly. 'What is wrong with her?'

He heard the raw edge to his tone but the girl simply shrugged defensively.

'She's awake but she won't respond to me. It's as if she's having a fit or something.'

He smoothed the child's hair, gazed into those staring eyes and felt an anxiety so acute it slowed his thinking. He prided himself on the speed and accuracy of his decision-making and yet now, when it was so important to get it right, his brain was motionless.

'Her breathing is fast. Her pulse is fast. Get someone medical in here immediately.'

A calm voice came from the entrance to the tent.

'It isn't a fit and she isn't awake.'

He turned his head and saw Layla, dressed only in a thin nightdress, her hair tangled and tousled from his hands. Her gaze was fixed on the child. 'She's having a night terror. My sister had them all the time at the same age. You shouldn't wake her.'

"She's already awake. Her eyes are open.' Nadia's eyes were cold and unfriendly.

Raz ignored her. 'You have seen this before?' Fear made his voice harsh, but Layla seemed calm and unflustered.

'Many times. It's very unsettling to witness, but I can assure you she will remember nothing of it in the morning. Who is closest to her? Who does she know the best?'

Her gaze flickered expectantly to Nadia and Raz drew a deep breath.

'Me.' The confession was dragged from him, because he hadn't yet decided how to broach this topic and this wasn't the way he would have chosen. 'I have the closest relationship with her.'

Was she shocked?

If so, she didn't show it. Nor did she question what that relationship was.

'In that case you should be the one to tuck her back into bed. Snuggle the sheets around her to make her feel safe. Talk to her quietly. It's not what you say that matters, it's the way you say it. You need to hold her securely. Blow out all the candles except one. Darkness helps. When she goes back to sleep, stay with her for about ten minutes. Once she is deeply asleep it's unlikely to happen again.' Having delivered that set of instructions, she looked at Nadia. 'We should leave. The fewer people the better.'

The other girl's expression was stubborn. 'She knows me.'

'It's better that way.' Layla's voice was firm. 'She needs quiet and just one person she trusts.'

'Do as she says.' Raz lowered his voice and eased the child back under the covers. She was quivering and shivering and it broke his heart to see her. His urge to call a doctor was powerful, but for some reason he was inclined to give Layla's suggestion a try, all the while wondering why he was following the advice of a woman he had no reason to trust.

She'd said it was the tone that mattered, so he spoke nonsense, reciting poetry from his childhood, his hand stroking those fragile shoulders until gradually the little girl calmed and relaxed under his fingers.

Her breathing slowed. Her pulse slowed with it. And as hers did so did his.

Her eyes fluttered shut, those eyelashes dark shadows against cheeks swollen by crying.

Raz sat until the change in her breathing told him she was deeply asleep.

His shoulders ached with tension. His head throbbed with it. Responsibility pressed down on him until he felt not as if he had the world on his shoulders but the universe.

Satisfied that she really was asleep, and unlikely to stir, he rose carefully to his feet and left the tent in search of answers.

Nadia was hovering outside, her expression defensive and defiant. 'I could have settled her. You should not have asked *her* advice.'

'How long has this been going on?'

Her hesitation told him everything.

'A while.'

That reluctant admission did nothing to ease his stress levels.

'*Why* wasn't I told?'

'You were away.'

'But everyone knows I wish to be told of anything that affects my daughter.'

'I didn't think it was significant. She doesn't remember it in the morning.'

Holding onto his temper, knowing that he needed time to cool down before he spoke what was on his mind, Raz clenched his jaw and gestured to the tent he'd just left. 'Stay with her.' Ideally he would have stayed himself, but he needed information so he strode back into his own tent and found Layla standing still in the middle of the room, her hands clenched into fists by her sides, stress evident in every rigid line of her body.

She'd lit the candles and the tent was bathed in a soft, gentle light that revealed sheets still rumpled and twisted from the wild heat of their lovemaking.

She turned as he entered the tent and their gazes locked and held.

Awareness rushed between them and sexual tension crackled like static in the air.

Now you're a woman, he thought, and then blocked that out because he knew this was not the time to address the other issues that were piling up.

'Thank you for your help. You knew what was wrong? You called it a night terror?'

'Yes.' Her confidence reassured him, because he was far from convinced he shouldn't have called for medical assistance.

'You have seen it before?'

'Many times.' Her voice was tight, her eyes shadowed by ghosts and darkness. 'My sister Yasmin started having them when she was five and it carried on for over a year. It might have been longer. I don't really remember. Every night, about an hour after she'd fallen asleep, she'd wake screaming, eyes wide open. She seemed to be awake, but she was asleep. The first time it happened I was just like you—I thought she was awake.'

'But she wasn't?'

'No, and it's very unsettling. It took me a while and some research to realise she was actually asleep.'

Of course she would have researched it. He knew virtually nothing about her, but he knew that much. 'And did your research suggest a cause?'

'There is no single cause, but there are different triggers. A fever, extreme tiredness, and—' She licked her lips and turned her head away so that he could no longer see her eyes. 'And stress. Stress can cause it.'

Guilt twisted inside him, because he knew without a doubt that the trigger in this case was very likely to be stress. And he knew the cause of the stress. 'And in your sister's case?'

'It was definitely stress.'

Still she didn't look at him, and he remembered her reaction to their conversation earlier.

You know nothing of the life my sister and I led.

Raz looked at the tension in those slender shoulders and realised he was looking at far more than a reaction to what had just happened in the tent next door. 'What was she stressed about?'

'This isn't about my sister.' She evaded the question. 'This is about the little girl. Has she been through a bad experience?'

How was he supposed to answer that?

The truth lodged somewhere behind his ribs, Raz turned away and paced to the far side of the tent.

It occurred to him that their relationship was already turning into a minefield of things they didn't talk about, issues they didn't address. The complications were endless.

'How did you stop it happening?'

'I couldn't stop it. I could only deal with it. And I tried to make her feel more secure so that she didn't go to bed scared.'

'She was scared?'

They were exploring two parallel lines of conversation and he was aware that she was avoiding his questions as skilfully as he was avoiding hers.

'They say overstimulation of the central nervous system can cause it. The temptation is always to shake them awake, but it's better if they can just go back to sleep.'

'So there was nothing you could do?'

'I tried very hard not to let anything frighten her.'

There are some aspects of our past neither one of us wishes to revisit.

He caught the bleak look in her eyes and realised just as there were layers to him she hadn't even glimpsed, so there were layers to her. And they were dark layers.

How could it be otherwise, growing up with a man like her father?

Only now did it occur to him how little he knew about his new bride.

An uncomfortable feeling spread down his neck and across his shoulders. 'Did she have reason to be frightened?'

'I started sleeping in the room with her. Sometimes that helped.'

'Layla, why was your sister frightened?'

It was only the second time he'd used her name and he saw her still.

Then she turned her back on him and picked up a robe, slipping it on and covering herself, shielding herself from him in every way. 'If you want to deal with the night terrors, the best thing is to talk to her family and find out what is likely to be causing them.' She fastened the robe around her waist. Her hair poured down her back, thick, shiny and as dark as a starless night. 'That shouldn't be a problem as you seem to know her well.'

Was that the second or third time she'd ignored his question about her life in the palace? Every time he raised it she deflected it. And suddenly he knew this relationship was going to be impossible if they shared nothing.

One of them had to make the first move.

'I do know her well. I know her better than anyone.' He had to push the words past his own natural reluctance to confide. 'She's my daughter.'

CHAPTER SIX

'YOUR *DAUGHTER*?' UNPREPARED for that revelation, Layla simply stared at him. 'You have a daughter?'

'She is six years old.'

He had a daughter.

She sank down onto the bed, her legs shaking, racking her brain for the information she had on him and discovering it to be depressingly sparse. 'I—I didn't know. I had no idea.'

She muttered the words to herself, examining this further piece of evidence to support her suspicion that it was possible to be intimate with someone and yet still know nothing about them.

It didn't make any difference that she'd shared something with him she'd never shared with anyone else. He was still a stranger.

'There are few who know, and those who do know better than to speak of it.'

His voice was flat and she looked at him blankly, shocked into silence and shaken by the enormity of it.

'Why don't people speak of it? Why would you hide the fact that you have a child?'

'I lost my father. I lost my wife—' He didn't finish the sentence. He didn't need to.

Layla knew her face matched the colour of his.

'No.' She shook her head in instinctive denial of that hypothesis. 'That wouldn't have happened.'

'How can you be sure?' His tone was raw. 'You insist on having evidence for everything—show me the evidence that my daughter would have been safe. Did your father live by a code of honour? Did he have boundaries beyond which he wouldn't go? If so, then please enlighten me, because I have seen nothing like that in my dealings with him.'

The shame of it covered her like a filthy, dark sludge. She wanted to dive into the oasis and scrub her skin clean. 'I can't show you evidence. I understand why you kept your daughter's existence a secret. But when I suggested marriage I would have thought—'

'What would you have thought? That I would have confided in you? You arrived in the desert out of nowhere. I married you because I saw the sense in what you proposed but let's not pretend that this marriage is a union of trust.'

His words shook her because in her head she'd started to spin a different scenario. When she looked at him all she could see was the burning heat in his eyes and all she could think of was his body, hard and hot against hers. Out of bed they were strangers but *in* bed? In bed they were as close as it was possible for two people to be and what they did in bed had started to dominate her brain. The craving inside her had intensified to the point that she found herself wishing the daylight hours away because at night there was a chance they'd be together. She found herself hoping desperately for the dark because it was only in the dark that he came to her. Swept away by the darkness and the wildness of the passion she'd started to imagine that this was real but now she realised she'd been deluding herself.

'That is all true, but I am your wife now and that also makes me—'

'Do not say the words.' His voice was thickened with emotion. 'Do not even think of yourself as my daughter's mother.'

The words slid under her ribs like a blade.

She tried to ignore the sharp pain that made it difficult to breathe. Used logic to remind herself that his response was understandable in the circumstances.

The fact that he would kiss her, touch her, didn't mean he trusted her with his daughter.

And she really couldn't blame him for that, could she?

Right now he was the powerful protector, ready to shield his daughter from any threat, and it was clear he considered that threat to be her.

Feeling his struggle to suppress the emotion that threatened to overwhelm him, Layla groped for the best way to handle the situation. 'At least tell me her name.'

'Her name is Zahra.'

'That's a pretty name. Does she know you have married me?'

'No.' He was brutally frank. Everything about him was designed to repel her gentle attempts to ease closer. 'There is no easy way to tell a child I have married the daughter of the man responsible for the death of her mother.'

The knife in her ribs twisted. 'Had I known you had a daughter I never would have suggested this marriage. I had no idea there was a child involved. It changes everything.'

'It changes nothing. This marriage was never personal so what difference would it have made?'

'I would not have sacrificed your daughter's happiness for—'

'For the future of Tazkhan? And what about your sister's safety? What about your own marriage to Hassan? Because that's why you came to me, isn't it? You wanted my protection.'

'Yes, that's all true. I was honest about that right from the start. But I didn't want those things at the expense of a little girl's happiness. A little girl who has already suffered a major trauma in her life.' Layla was shaking so badly she wasn't sure her legs would hold her. 'There is no way I would have foisted myself on her as a stranger. At the very least I would have suggested I take time to get to know her. To gain her trust.'

'That would have created a delay we could not afford, and this was never about building a relationship. And you are assuming you would have gained her trust.'

'I would certainly have worked hard to do that. I have experience with children. Give me the opportunity and I will prove it to you.'

The shutters came down on those eyes. 'No. We will wait and see if the night terrors settle and then re-evaluate.'

'Perhaps they would settle if she had someone she could bond with. Someone she is close to.'

He turned slowly, his eyes like ice. 'My relationship with my daughter is very close.'

'Yes, I can see that.' She thought about the way he'd soothed the child. About the anxiety and love on his face and the patience he'd shown. It had warmed her because she'd never seen a man like that with a child. 'But you're away a great deal. You have your business interests—'

'That is an inevitable part of life. When I can, I take her with me, and when I can't I make sure I return here as quickly I can.'

'But when you are away who looks after her?'

He didn't answer immediately. 'She is with Nadia, who loves her very much.'

Nadia?

Layla felt as if she were walking on eggshells. This wasn't the time to point out that Nadia had seemed out of her depth at the moment of crisis. 'How have you kept Zahra's existence a secret?'

'I have the support of many people.'

'But I don't.'

He glanced at her with a frown. 'What does that mean?'

'No one speaks to me. This marriage has not been welcomed by the people who love you.' Suddenly she felt overwhelmed by it all. By the distance that couldn't be closed by physical intimacy alone. 'How can this possibly work even on the most basic level? If you don't trust me, why would they?'

'Because this union was never about trust.' He towered over her, powerful and imposing. 'Most of them understand why we did this. They know it is the right thing.'

But not all of them.

Layla thought about the hatred she sensed in Nadia and wondered again if the cause of it didn't go deeper than dismay at seeing the Sheikh marry the daughter of his enemy.

'So what happens now? You have a daughter. Are you saying you don't want me to meet her?'

'For the time being, no. She is already having night terrors. I don't want to risk making those worse by introducing you to her.'

His belief that she might make it worse hurt more than she would have thought possible, but how could she, of all people, blame a man for wanting to protect his child?

She'd never had that and she felt the loss of it keenly.

'Of course, if that is what you prefer.' Layla's jaw was stiff, her thoughts a mess of pain as she thought what she would have given to have a father who fought so fiercely to protect her from harm. 'But I don't think it's the right decision.'

'You think you know better than me what is right for my child?'

'No, what I think is that you don't know me at all. You married me with a set of preconceived ideas of who I am, and I don't blame you for that, but we're married now and for this to work you have to start seeing me. The real me. I may not be able to swim or ride a horse, but I am good with children. I think if we are to become a family we need to start somewhere.'

'We have started somewhere.'

His gaze shifted to the rumpled sheets and then back to her and she felt a tiny shiver run through her. Right now he was distant and intimidating but she knew it wasn't fear that made her knees weak. Looking into those brooding black eyes, gazing at the dangerous curve of his sensual mouth, all she could think of was how it felt to have those lips on her body, how it felt when he filled her, possessed her, drove her mindless. Her skin still burned from his touch. Her head was dizzy with the memory of how he made her feel and she slid her fingers into her hair and shook her head in frustration.

'A relationship cannot just be about sex.'

His eyes held hers, hard and unsympathetic. 'It has to be, because I can give you nothing else.'

In the morning he was gone again.

If she'd thought their shared confidences would have moved their relationship forward, she was disappointed.

And this time when she heard children laughing she knew one of the voices belonged to his daughter.

It felt unnatural not to approach her and build a relationship, but he'd made his wishes clear on that matter so Layla sat in the shade on a smooth rock by the oasis and forced herself not to initiate contact with the little girl. And she seemed happy enough, playing with her friends, laughing as a child should laugh. Laughing without fear that the sound might draw unwanted attention.

The child laughed until darkness fell over the desert.

And then the screams started again.

Instinct drove Layla from her bed. Heart pounding, she came to a screeching halt outside the entrance to the tent.

He didn't want her near his daughter, did he?

Unless she wanted to create a rift between them she had to respect that decision.

Torn, she stood there, waiting for the child's screams to settle, telling herself that Nadia was there and would comfort the girl.

The screams grew louder and more desperate.

Sweat beaded on Layla's forehead. Just listening to it stressed her so badly her heart raced. The sound reminded her so much of Yasmin in the early days, and to stand there and do nothing demanded a self-control and thick skin Layla didn't possess.

Pressing her palm to her forehead, she breathed deeply and tried to calm herself. She told herself it wasn't her concern, that if she suddenly appeared in the tent it would probably just frighten the child even more. But none of that reasoning did anything to ease her urge to do something.

Why didn't someone else go to her? *Where was Nadia?*

Her will-power stretched taut, she lasted another five seconds before giving in. If Raz never spoke to her again, so be it. He hardly spoke to her anyway so it wouldn't be that much of a loss.

As she pushed aside the flap she expected to see Nadia, but the tent was empty apart from the little girl who sat alone in the enormous bed, shuddering and screaming at some imaginary terror. At her feet lay the two Saluki, whimpering and looking at the child in alarm and confusion, as if they sensed a threat but couldn't identify it.

Mouth dry, Layla stared at the dogs. Nothing but a screaming child could have propelled her forward.

Her heart was kicking at her ribcage—not just because to get to the child meant stepping over fur and teeth, but because the sound of the screaming brought back so many memories of Yasmin, terrified and clinging to her.

She threw one last glance over her shoulder, in case there was someone else who could do this, but there was no sign of Nadia or the bodyguards who were supposed to be in attendance.

Trying to look confident, she stepped over the Saluki as gracefully as a ballerina, braced to feel those sharp teeth close around her ankle.

The dog closest to the bed growled, a menacing rumble low in its throat, but it didn't move from its position.

Taking that as a good sign, Layla crawled onto the bed and snuggled down with the child, stroking her back and talking to her, hoping desperately that the tone of her voice would do the trick and the child wouldn't wake and realize that the comfort came from a stranger.

'There, you're safe now—and you need to go back to sleep.' She talked nonsense, and then decided a story might help. 'Once upon a time…' She told the same stories she'd told her sister at the same age, remembered them word for word, and the familiarity of the ritual soothed her as well as the child. She talked quietly until the little girl's breathing suggested she was deeply asleep while all the time the two Saluki lay by the bed, heads on paws, watching her.

Afraid that if she moved she'd wake the child, Layla stayed still, her fingers tangled in the dark curls that belonged to Raz Al Zahki's daughter. Looking down at that sweet, vulnerable face, now smeared with tears, she felt her heart twist.

What had she been through?

What had she suffered?

She'd stay just a while. Until she was sure the girl was asleep.

Then she'd return to her bed and he wouldn't be any the wiser.

The red ball of the dawn sun was rising up behind the mountainous dunes when Raz rode back into the camp two days later. His eyes were gritty from lack of sleep, his head pounding following long days spent in meetings with senior tribal members.

He needed sleep, but nowhere near as much as he needed a swim.

It was still early and everything was quiet and still. No one was stirring.

Having handed over his stallion to one of the waiting grooms, he made straight towards the tent where his daughter slept, noticing with a frown that there was no sign of the guard.

Fear for his daughter fuelled his stride.

Entering quietly, he stood for a moment on the threshold, his eyes adjusting to the dim light, relieved to see the dogs sprawled protectively at the foot of the bed.

The familiar sight of the lump in the bed brought relief rushing down on him—and then he realised that the lump was bigger than usual.

Stepping closer, he saw that there in the bed, with her arms wrapped around his daughter, was Layla.

Shock and surprise were replaced by anger, and then another, darker emotion he didn't dare examine too closely.

The dogs sensed the change in his mood and growled, and those growls woke the child. Her expression brightened as she saw her father and she sat up sleepily, the movement waking Layla.

Her eyes opened and her gaze met his, blank at first and then alight with consternation.

Sitting up, she clutched at the sheet. 'We weren't expecting you so early.'

'Evidently.' His tone was silky soft and he saw the colour return to her cheeks as she met his hostile gaze.

'I'm *pleased* you're early.' Zahra slid out of the bed, paused to hug and kiss the dog closest to her, and ran across to him, arms outstretched. 'Has Shakira had her foal?'

'Not yet.' Raz scooped her into his arms. Her hair brushed against his jaw and he felt his insides knot with love. It was a love that overwhelmed every emotion he'd ever felt. A love that made a strong man vulnerable. And he felt that vulnerability now as he held her and felt those slender arms tighten around his neck.

'When can we go and see her?'

'Soon.' He hugged her protectively, his eyes still on the woman in the bed. 'Zahra, I want you to play with your toys for a minute while I speak to Layla.'

'Can't she stay?' Zahra was openly disappointed. 'She hasn't finished the end of the story. We both fell asleep.'

'I can finish it later.' Without meeting his eyes, Layla slid out of the bed.

He saw her hesitate before allowing her feet to touch the ground and saw her hold her breath as she stepped carefully over the dog blocking her path, as if doing so required nerves of steel.

Oblivious to the atmosphere, Zahra smiled at her. 'When you've finished talking, can we play in the sand like yesterday?'

The news that she'd been spending her days with his daughter was the final straw. 'No, you cannot, because we are going riding.'

'Together?'

'Together.' Touched by her expression of delight, he put her down gently. 'Play with Isis and Horus for a moment.'

She needed no encouragement to play with the dogs, and they in turn fussed around the child, proving themselves better guards than the people he'd paid to stand over her and keep watch in his absence.

Keeping his anger in check, he left the tent, noticing that

one of the guards assigned to watch over his daughter was now standing outside, having no doubt taken a badly timed bathroom break.

Deciding to deal with him later, Raz followed Layla to the edge of the oasis, noticing that she stopped a safe distance from the water's edge.

'You deliberately went against my orders.'

'Yes, I did.'

She turned to face him, her expression calm. She made no excuses. Nor did she apologise and that surprised him.

'I thought I'd made my wishes clear on this matter.'

'Would you rather I'd left your daughter to scream, Your Highness?'

The news that Zahra had been screaming again sent ice down the rigid length of his spine. 'If she was screaming then it would have been better for someone familiar to comfort her. That was your advice.'

'And I stand by it. But there was no one familiar. She was alone.'

'My daughter is never alone. She is under twenty-four-hour guard and Nadia is with her at all times.' Even as he said it he remembered that the guard had not been present when he'd arrived, and her next words confirmed that.

'She was alone last night. And the night before. And the night before that. There was no guard and there was no Nadia.' She seemed more annoyed than intimidated. 'You weren't here. I made the decision I thought was best, Your Highness.'

'My name is Raz,' he said tightly. 'I think we are now sufficiently well acquainted for you to use it.'

'Evidently not, since you don't see me as fit company for your daughter.'

Raz breathed deeply. 'Nadia is supposed to stay with her at night.'

'Then no doubt that is something you will wish to explore with her.'

Listening to that calm appraisal, Raz realised just how much he'd underestimated her. He'd mistaken silence for a lack of opinion, and shyness for a lack of forcefulness, but it seemed his new wife had a layer of steel, visible only if someone pressed hard enough. On this she wasn't budging.

'Nadia would not have left her alone.'

'Are you accusing me of lying?'

'Perhaps it was a simple misunderstanding. Perhaps she went to fetch Zahra a drink or something to eat.'

'There was no sign of her at any point during the night, nor of the guard. I understand that as her nanny you believe Nadia to be the best person to care for her, but I'm providing you with evidence that she left the child alone. Why would you doubt me?'

'Because Nadia isn't Zahra's nanny. She is her aunt.' That confession was met by a tense silence.

For a moment she said nothing and simply stared at him. Then her mouth moved and finally words emerged.

'Her *aunt*?'

Raz stayed perfectly still. 'Nadia is my late wife's sister.'

'S-sister?' She stammered the word, visibly shocked. Again she said nothing, and then she shook her head briefly. 'And you didn't think that was worth mentioning? You let me turn up here in my wedding dress and you didn't even *warn* her or tell me who she was?'

'When would I have had the opportunity to warn her? We were married only hours after you appeared unannounced at my desert camp. Then we arrived here and she came out of the tent before I had a chance to speak to her privately.'

'It is no wonder she can barely look at me.' Her words were barely audible. 'It explains so much.'

'It does *not* explain why she would leave Zahra unattended.'

'Maybe it does. Maybe...' She frowned slightly and then stared at the still surface of the oasis. 'You should have told me. There is *so much* you should have told me.'

'Why would I tell you?'

'You really have to ask me that?' Her head was turned towards him, pain and accusation in her eyes. 'Because keeping secrets is doing nothing but harm. I understand that this is hard for you, I understand that you have to make love to me in the dark because touching me makes you think of your wife and that makes you feel guilty, and I understand that you don't want to be here during the day because it's like a slap every time you look at me. I understand that, given the way you feel about my family, you are reluctant to trust me with your child. I don't blame you for that. But it wasn't Nadia who comforted Zahra in the night, Your Highness. It wasn't Nadia who read to her and played with her. For the past two days it hasn't been Nadia who has cared for your daughter. It has been me.'

Raz was stunned into silence by her interpretation of the facts, but before he could respond she took a step closer to him.

'Do you think I'm not a caring person? Is that what you think?' Her voice vibrated with tension. 'Do you think I would have crossed a desert I didn't know, on a horse I had no idea how to ride, to find a man who hates me, if I weren't a caring person? Just in case the facts don't speak for themselves, let me tell you I'm a *very* caring person—and if you looked at the facts you'd be able to see that. And, yes, I was thinking of my sister and my future, but I also care about the people of Tazkhan. And before you dismiss that, based only on my bloodline, let me remind you that we can choose many things in life, but whom we are related to isn't one of them. I chose to go to your daughter in the night because I couldn't sit there and listen to her distress. And I chose to step over those horrible, scary dogs in order to comfort her. So *never* imply I'm not trustworthy enough to care for you daughter.'

The stillness of the baking desert heat intensified the silence.

Raz stood still, her words stinging as they sank into his flesh. 'Why do you find the dogs scary?'

'After everything I just said to you, *that* is the question you choose to ask?' She gave a choked laugh—a sound loaded with disbelief—and he frowned.

'Layla—'

'No. Enough.' Her voice was shaky as she backed away from him. 'This conversation is going nowhere. You don't want to come anywhere near me and you can't bear it when I come anywhere near you, so just leave me alone.'

CHAPTER SEVEN

LAYLA PACED THE width of the tent and back again, so upset she didn't know how to calm herself. Once again she was ripped apart by emotions new to her and she tried desperately to rationalise them.

Why *would* he trust her? He didn't know her. Of *course* he'd be reluctant to allow her near his child—a child whose existence he'd taken great care to keep secret from her family. It was a sign of his love for his child, and she was the last person ever to criticise a father for loving his child.

So why did his attitude towards her hurt so badly?

And why couldn't she share the same space with him and not think about sex?

Hyped up and unsettled, she picked up a ripe peach from the bowl on the table and then put it down again, knowing that she was already in possession of the answer. And the answer was that it hurt so badly because it *felt* as if he cared. When his mouth was on hers, when his hands were holding her face and his body was buried deep in hers, it felt as if he cared. And it felt incredible. So incredible she wanted more. And in wanting more she also wanted it to mean something.

The whole thing was turning her brain into a churning mess. She was used to using logic, but the feelings inside her defied logic.

With a murmur of frustration Layla turned and paced back

again, trying to filter out the facts, but even the facts were confusing. To be so intimate in bed and so distant out of bed was muddling her brain. In bed, the signals were that he cared. Out of bed, it was clear he considered her on a level with the life forms occupying the bottom of the oasis.

Having admitted that to herself, it horrified her when he strode into the tent and closed the flap between them and the rest of the world.

'Go away—' Her voice cracked and she stepped back from him, still reeling from their conversation and feelings that were new to her. She wanted to turn them off and had no idea how. 'Don't say anything else. I can't take any more right now. I got the message. If you really don't want me near your daughter I won't go near her, but please make sure that *someone* does because I can't lie here listening to her screaming.'

'And that is very much to your credit.' His voice was low, his expression guarded as he watched her pace from one end of the tent to the other. 'I came to tell you that you're wrong.'

She couldn't focus.

She couldn't concentrate on the conversation because she wanted to look at him all the time. Not just because he was a man who naturally commanded attention, or even because he was sensationally good-looking—although that had to play a part—no, it was something so much more personal. It was because he knew her in a way no one had ever known her before. Whenever he was near she felt as if they were being pulled together. She had to fight the impulse to walk up to him and touch him. And because she had no experience of feeling that way she had no idea how to cure herself.

She'd never felt like this before and it was driving her mad. They had huge issues, but all she could think about was the feel of his hands on her and the way it felt to be kissed by him.

Layla pressed her fingers to her forehead, trying to clear her brain, trying to harness her old way of thinking. *Trying to push out thoughts she didn't want in her head.* Her stress levels were running into the red, her grip on control so loose she was afraid the whole thing was going to slip from her grasp. She knew the only way to pull herself back together was not to be near him. She needed to be on her own so that she could rebalance herself.

'I probably am wrong. You know Nadia much better than I do. I don't have all the facts. If you think she's the right person to care for your daughter, it's not my place to disagree with you.'

'I don't mean that you're wrong about Nadia. I mean that you're wrong about the other things you said.'

She was so aware of him standing there that the whole conversation blurred in her head. 'What things?' Was this the ultimate in humiliation? To know a man could do those things to her and feel nothing and yet still her head could be full of nothing but him? Why couldn't she detach the physical from the emotional as he evidently could?

The intimate atmosphere suffocated her, and the way he was looking at her made her feel as if he'd touched her skin with the flame of a candle.

'I make love to you in the dark *not* because I am thinking of my wife, but because you are very shy and I am trying to be sensitive to your feelings. On that first night you would not even remove your robe to show me your bruises, so I assumed you would want to take that side of our relationship very slowly.'

Slowly?

Layla felt as if she were burning up inside. She thought about what they'd shared. *Was that slowly?* Trembling, she hid her damp palms behind her back. 'Oh.'

'You came to me clutching a copy of the *Kama Sutra*, but you hadn't even glanced between the pages and clearly had no idea of what lay ahead of you. I decided you might be less self-conscious if you were in darkness.' He paused to draw breath. 'I don't spend time with you during the day, that is true, but it's because I have a million and one demands on my time—not least the upheaval in Tazkhan. I have spent the past two days meeting with certain members of the council in secret. Hassan has disappeared. That is another reason I am particularly concerned about my daughter's safety right now.'

Still dealing with the news that he'd been thinking of her feelings, Layla felt her stomach lurch. 'Hassan has disappeared?'

'Yes, and until we know his whereabouts I don't want my daughter left alone.' He hesitated. 'Or you. He is a desperate man. Who knows what he could decide to do, given that he now has so little to lose? He has lost any chance of taking your father's place and he has few, if any, supporters among the people. Speaking of which, I have been learning a great deal of interesting information about you in the past few days.'

'You have?'

'I spent some time with the people. I visited hospitals and local schools—including a school where you apparently help out.'

'I love books and I like to help the children who struggle with reading. The school doesn't have enough staff to offer that sort of help.' Layla stammered over the words, horrified that he'd found out with such ease. So much of her life had been conducted with discretion, if not secrecy. 'Who told you?'

'Apparently the staff don't feel the need to keep it a secret any longer as your father is dead and Hassan missing. There is no shortage of people willing to tell me how good you are with the children and what an excellent decision I made in marrying you.'

She stood rigid, thrown by that news. 'But *you* don't think that. I know you don't. On that first night you left the tent because you felt guilty about what we'd done.'

'No. I felt guilty because the sex was incredible. I agreed to this marriage because of what it meant for Tazkhan, but what we shared that night went well beyond duty and I couldn't pretend otherwise.'

Shocked into silence by his honesty, Layla tilted her head and stared up at him, feeling a shift in their relationship. 'I didn't know—'

'That I felt that way? I would have thought it was obvious.'

His dry tone made her blush and the look in his ebony eyes made her stomach flip.

'Your Highness—'

'Raz.'

He was standing so close to her she could hardly breathe. She lifted her hand and placed it on his chest, feeling the steady thud of his heart under her fingers. 'Raz.' It felt strange to say his name. Strange to be this close to someone.

He cupped her face in his hands. 'Do you realise that, despite the intimacies we have shared, that is the first time you have spoken my name?'

'It felt wrong to use your name. You were a stranger.'

There was a prolonged silence. His eyes dropped to her mouth. 'But I'm not a stranger now.'

His self-assurance was in direct contrast to her own mixed-up, tangled emotions.

'You hate me.'

'No. But I admit it's a complicated situation.' A wry smile tugged at his sensual mouth. 'You are a person who likes facts, so I will tell you that the facts in this case are that nothing is going the way I thought it would go when you turned up at my camp that night.'

She wanted to reach up and sink her hands into that glossy dark hair. She wanted to pull his head down to hers and see if his kiss felt as good in daylight as it did in darkness. She wanted to give herself up to the emotion and the confusion and stop trying to rationalise the mess in her head.

'It's not going the way I thought it would go, either.'

'I owe you an apology for ordering you to stay away from my daughter. You should know that I am very overprotective where she is concerned and the past week has been a particularly unsettling time.'

Standing this close to him, it was a struggle for her to concentrate. 'I would never criticise any father for being overprotective.'

'Please understand that my reluctance to allow you near her was less about you as an individual and more about my determination to keep life as stable as possible for her. I thought Nadia was the perfect person to care for her. It seems I may have been wrong.'

'Maybe you weren't. As you said, there is probably some perfectly reasonable explanation for her absence.' What right did she have to comment on the behaviour of another person when she didn't even understand her own?

'Possibly, but at the current time we are unlikely to find that out.' There was an edge to his tone. 'She has gone missing, along with one of my guards. I suspect that when they both should have been with Zahra they were together. We are trying to find them. In the meantime I must thank you for being so incredibly kind to my daughter when she was upset.'

His apology was as unexpected and unsettling as it was touching.

She'd craved distance, but instead she had closeness and a new sense of understanding that simply intensified the feelings inside her.

'She is very sweet and good-natured. And I love her sense of mischief. She reminds me so much of Yasmin.'

'The people here have noticed your kindness to her and it

has done much to make them warm towards you. What are these stories you've been telling Zahra that make her so desperate to go to bed at night?'

'*One Thousand and One Nights*. I read them to my sister.'

His eyes glittered. 'So now you think you are Scheherazade?'

'Hardly. But I thought if I could relax Zahra before she sleeps she might be less likely to wake.'

'It was a good plan. Did it work?'

'It's too soon to know. I just wish I'd brought the book with me instead of leaving it at the first camp.'

'That was the other book you brought with you?'

'Yes. It's one of my favourites. I decided I could only carry two, because of the weight, so I picked that one.'

His hands were still on her face, his gaze intent on hers. 'And the *Kama Sutra*.'

'It was a matter of priorities.' She knew her face was hot against his palm. 'And ignorance.'

'You have no need to explain yourself to me and no need to feel embarrassed.' His eyes darkened. 'These last few days have been a terrible strain for you. The threat of marriage to Hassan, whom you clearly fear and loathe, escaping from the palace, losing your sister in the desert and then being picked up by my men. Marriage to a stranger, a near drowning, and then living with a husband with whom you've barely shared a conversation but are expected to undress for.'

Layla tried to smile. 'When you put it like that, it's no wonder I'm a little wound up.'

'A little?'

'A lot. I'd be a lot better if there was news of Yasmin.'

His hand dropped from her face. 'So far there is none, but that does not mean you should worry. Salem is renowned for not communicating.'

Remembering the dark, forbidding profile of the man she'd

seen only briefly on that first night, Layla found that of little comfort. 'What if he can't find her?' She blurted the words out, seeking reassurance.

'If anyone can find her it will be Salem.' Raz hesitated, as if he were deciding how much to tell her. 'He has a special set of skills.'

'But what if Hassan has already tracked her down? What if he has her right now?'

'Then Salem will find *both* of them and you can safely feel sorry for Hassan.'

Layla hesitated, because to make an accusation unsupported by solid evidence felt wrong. 'I have nothing but instinct on which to base this suspicion, but I think Hassan may have played a part in the death of my father.'

His expression didn't change. 'I'm sure you're right.'

The relief that came from having someone to discuss it with was overwhelming. 'You suspect it too?'

'Of course. The moment I heard about the Sheikh's sudden illness it was the first thing that came to mind. We have no proof, but we believe it was Hassan who ordered someone to tamper with the brakes of my car two years ago. I don't believe it was his intention to kill or injure my wife, because that would have brought him no political benefit. There is little doubt I was the intended victim, but sadly she chose that day to borrow my car.'

His voice was thickened with a mix of regret, guilt and anger, his pain so powerful she felt it as if it were her own.

'I'm sorry.'

'I do not hold you in any way responsible. But it is true that Hassan would do anything for power. He and your father were cut from the same cloth.'

She knew that, but it was the first time she'd heard anyone else say it. 'If he finds my sister—'

'I would trust my brother with my life and we must now

trust him with your sister's life.' He turned to look at her, the lines of his handsome face set and serious. 'When did you last eat?'

'I'm not hungry.'

'You've barely eaten in the whole time we've been together.'

'I've eaten.'

'We may be in the dark for much of the time, but that does not make me blind.' His tone was dry. He hesitated. 'Zahra is keen for me to take her riding today. I know your experience with horses to date has been less than encouraging, but if you would like to learn to ride it would give me pleasure to teach you.'

The thought of spending yet more time on a horse horrified her, but she could tell he was reaching out to her and didn't want to do anything that could be considered a rebuff. 'Teaching a beginner would drive you mad.'

'I have been teaching Zahra since she was able to sit unsupported. Believe me when I say that nothing you throw at me can be more of a challenge than putting an overexcited toddler on a horse.'

'You taught her to ride that young?'

'It is the best age. She has grown up around horses, as I did. It wouldn't surprise me if she chooses to make that her career in some way in the future.'

Career?

'You see her having a career?'

'Of course. And I can't see it being diplomacy, because my daughter is as outspoken as your sister.'

That fact clearly amused him, and Layla thought about the times she'd had to haul Yasmin away from a situation before her comments created havoc.

'You're proud of your daughter.'

'Very.'

The contrast between his love for his daughter and her own barren childhood was so vividly accentuated that the breath caught in her throat. Wondering what was wrong with her that she could envy a child, Layla stepped away from him.

'Thank you for the offer of riding lessons, but I don't want to intrude on your time with Zahra.'

He curved an arm round her waist, trapping her. 'You're still upset?'

'No.' All she had around this man were uncomfortable feelings. Feelings about him. Feelings about herself. She'd arrived here thinking she knew herself well and had discovered she didn't know herself at all. It was like being inside the body of a stranger. 'I just don't want to intrude on your relationship with your daughter.'

'You were the one who pointed out that you should be part of my relationship with my daughter.'

Did it make her a bad person that it was almost too painful to watch? 'You have a very special bond.'

'A bond that will not be threatened or broken by the presence of another person.' His eyes narrowed. 'But that isn't the issue, is it? Tell me what's wrong.'

'There is no issue. Nothing is wrong.' She tried to walk away but he locked his arm tightly around her waist.

'Your father wanted you to marry Hassan, so I assume from that your relationship with him was difficult. You don't have to hide it from me. I want to know. All of it.'

'Why? What difference does it make?'

'As you just pointed out to me, keeping secrets isn't going to do anything for the progression of our relationship.'

Did he see a progression? This was a man who had loved his wife totally and completely. A man who had vowed never to love again. What progression could there be? She could have asked, but she wasn't sure she could cope with the answer. They were together now, and nothing could change that.

'My relationship with my father wasn't just difficult, it was non-existent. You're so proud of Zahra and you want the best for her.' She stared at a point in the middle of his chest, trying to contain her emotions and relate only the facts. 'My father was never proud of me. His interest in us extended no further than how useful we could be to him. He met Yasmin just four times in his life.'

Shock flared in his eyes. 'Four times? That is all?'

'Five, if you count the day he died, when we were both hiding behind the curtain in his rooms.' Layla was surprised by her sudden need to confide when she'd lived her life relying on no one.

There was a long, tense silence. 'I had no idea. I assumed—' He broke off and rubbed his fingers over his forehead, apparently struggling for words.

'I cared for Yasmin. We've never been apart. She's the only person in the world I've ever been close to until—' She stopped, feeling her face burn. *Feeling his eyes on her.*

'Until me.'

'I know we're not close in *that* sense,' she said quickly. 'I know what our relationship is.'

'Do you?' His voice was soft and his eyes didn't shift from her face. Slowly his hand dropped. 'Then you're making more progress than I, because I truly have no clue what our relationship is.'

The air was thickened with a tension she'd never felt before.

Something changed when she was with this man. Something she couldn't put a name too, and didn't understand.

She wanted desperately to reach out to him, to touch him as he'd touched her, but she wasn't sure he'd want that and didn't have the confidence to risk being rejected.

'You should go to Zahra.'

'You will come too. It would please her if you were to join us.'

'I really don't—'

'And it would please me, too. Get dressed and meet us outside. Zahra's favourite treat is to have breakfast by the oasis, so we will do that and then fly the helicopter to Bohara—my home.'

'You have a home?' It was something else she hadn't known about him. 'All the rumours are that you live in the desert and move around for your own safety.'

'I do live in the desert, and I do move around—because how else is a man expected to know his people if not by living among them? But I also have a place that is mine. A stud farm just inside the border with Zubran. On paper it is owned by the Sultan of that country, who just happens to be a friend of mine.' When Layla stared at him he flashed her a smile. 'I don't spend all my nights in a tent. After the last few days I think you deserve a taste of luxury.'

'Just practise everything I taught you. I will keep you on a leading rein so there is no way she can run away with you.'

'That's comforting to know.' Layla sat rigid on the calm, placid mare and Raz hid a smile, oddly touched by her determination to ride even though she clearly found the whole experience uncomfortable and unnatural. So far she had fallen three times, but each time she'd insisted on getting back on the horse.

'If you want to give up, just tell me.'

'I don't want to give up. I won't give up.' Her jaw was set, her wrists inflexible as she gripped the reins.

'Relax,' Raz said mildly. 'If you relax you will not fall.'

'We both know I am going to fall whatever I do.'

But still she got back up again. He wondered if that was a skill she'd developed during her loveless childhood. But it hadn't been completely loveless, had it? She'd had her sister. The sister who was now missing.

He made a mental note to try again to contact Salem, even though he knew such persistence would irritate his brother. 'Relax your wrists and lower your hands slightly.'

She did as he instructed. 'At least it isn't as far to fall as it is from your stallion.'

'I promise I will not let you fall again. Don't grip the reins so tightly—you're pulling on her mouth.'

'I am?' Dismayed, she immediately loosened the reins and rubbed the mare's neck by way of apology.

He watched, intrigued by her and wondering how such gentleness could come from so much evil.

In all the rumours that had oozed from the corrupt walls of the Citadel there had been little about the princesses and most hadn't thought to question the detail of their existence.

'You're doing well.'

'We both know I'm not doing well, but I will learn. Just as long as I don't hurt an innocent horse in the process.' She balanced herself carefully and then risked a glance at him. It was the first time she'd taken her eyes off the horse's ears. 'Thank you for being so patient.'

'You are very easy to teach because you listen. Sit up straight. Sit down in the saddle. That's good.'

Her jaw was rigid and he could see her concentrating, going through his instructions one by one. The mare walked forward without fuss, as accommodating as he'd known she would be.

'She's very pretty. Is she pure Arabian?'

'Yes. She is brave, spirited and intelligent, like all of her breed. And very strong. She could carry you for days in the desert and not tire. It's the reason we choose this breed for endurance racing.' It occurred to him that she shared many of those qualities. 'The Arab horse is surefooted and agile in difficult terrain and bred for stamina. It can withstand the daytime heat of the desert and the cold at night.'

'You bred her?'

'My father bred her. He gave her to me as a foal but I am too heavy for her now. She taught Zahra to ride.'

'You mean *you* taught her.'

'The horse did most of the teaching.'

'Did your wife ride?'

She asked the question quietly and he realised how sensitive the situation must be for her.

'She didn't ride, but she was an artist and she loved to paint the horses. She spent hours studying equine anatomy and her attention to detail was astonishing. Her mother was an artist, too, and she always hoped that Zahra would be equally artistic. But Zahra only ever wanted to ride the horse, not immortalise its image on paper.'

'The greatest gift a parent can give is to allow a child to be who they want to be.'

Her wistful tone caught his attention.

'You have told me about your father, but nothing about your mother.'

'My mother died just after I was born.'

'So your sister—?'

'Yasmin is my half sister. Her mother was a model who caught my father's attention for a short time. She left when Yasmin was five and we haven't seen her since.'

It was a brief delivery of the facts, devoid of emotion, but he could imagine how much emotion was simmering below the composure that seemed to be part of her. *She'd learned to hold it all in*, he thought. *Learned to feel without expressing the feeling.*

'But you said *you* cared for your sister. How is that possible?'

She sat without moving, her gaze focused on the horse's ears. 'It's possible.'

'You were seven and she was five.'

'We learned what we had to learn.'

The mare, perhaps sensing the sudden tension of her rider, threw up her head and he saw Layla's fingers whiten on the reins.

'She is the most reliable horse in my stables, but if you feel unsafe you can always grab a piece of her mane.'

'It doesn't seem fair to make her suffer just because I'm nervous.' But her fingers closed gently and carefully around a hunk of the mare's mane.

Watching her, Raz felt himself harden. His gaze focused on those slim fingers. Heat shot through him as he remembered how those fingers felt against his skin.

He lifted his gaze from her fingers to her face, studying the curve of her cheek and the sweep of her inky lashes, and she must have felt his scrutiny because she turned her head and her eyes met his.

Raz felt that look all the way through him.

'Can she gallop yet?' Zahra cantered up, disturbing the moment, glued to the back of her horse as if she'd been born in the saddle, Isis and Horus running by her side. 'I want you to learn fast, Layla, so we can ride together. Isis and Horus can come with us too. They love it when we gallop.'

Layla had switched her attention from the horse to the dogs and Raz frowned.

'The dogs make you nervous?'

'I'm worried they might upset the horse.'

Her response made perfect sense, but he sensed something more and wondered if she'd been bitten as a child. That would certainly explain the fear he saw in her eyes whenever his dogs were nearby.

'Did you keep Saluki as pets when you were young?'

'No.' Her lips were bloodless, her slim fingers clenched in the horse's mane. 'Not as pets.'

'Layla…' He rode closer to her, his knee brushing against hers. 'If the dogs are a problem you must tell me.'

'The dogs aren't a problem. Zahra adores them and they adore her. They also guard her, which can only be a good thing.'

Her response was neutral and composed but he glimpsed something in her eyes—a shadow of something so dark and bleak he wasn't sure he even wanted to explore it further. He wondered again what her life must have been like. What it would have taken to drive someone like her to cross the desert to seek out a stranger.

The more he knew her, the more he realised that such impulsive behaviour was completely out of character. She was a woman who thought everything through, who relied on evidence to make decisions, and yet she'd chosen to risk everything to find him. She'd known nothing about him, and yet she'd preferred to commit herself to the unknown than spend another day in her old life. *So what did that say about her life?*

'When can we gallop?' It was Zahra who asked the question, circling her pony like a polo player as she waited impatiently for her father.

'Later,' Raz told her. 'I don't want to leave Layla.'

'Don't worry about me. I think I might have had enough for one day and so has this poor horse.'

Apparently relieved to have an excuse to finish, she rode the mare to a halt the way he'd taught her.

'You two gallop and I'll go back. See you at the stables. But I think I'll walk and lead her, if that's all right.'

Before she could dismount, Raz reached out and covered her hand with his.

'You are doing well.'

Her mouth twitched at the corners. 'We both know I'm doing terribly,' she said dryly, 'but thank you for saying that.'

'It's always harder to learn as an adult than as a child because your awareness of danger is more sharply focused.' And he suspected her awareness of danger was even more sharply focused than most. He watched her face, searching for clues, but her expression didn't change and he released her hand. 'Go and relax. Abdul will show you my library.'

'You have a library?' Her face brightened but Zahra shuddered.

'Who wants books when they can have horses?'

CHAPTER EIGHT

LAYLA SAT CURLED up on a low ottoman covered in rich red silk, a stack of books awaiting her attention and a chilled fruit juice on the table in front of her. Of all the rooms in Raz's beautiful home—*the home she hadn't known existed*—the library was predictably her favourite. Not just because of the walls lined with books, but because of the views. The doors opened over a courtyard with a central fountain that sent cooling water flowing over a majestic statue of a horse. And now, with the sun setting over the distant dunes, the courtyard was floodlit with a warm golden light.

It was the most beautiful place she'd ever seen.

On their arrival Raz had been called away, so it had been Zahra who had shown her round, predictably lingering in the stables and introducing Layla to every horse in the yard. The stables were beautiful, arranged around shady courtyards, and everywhere the sound of running water from fountains that offered a cool contrast to the parched desert.

After all the rumours about his Bedouin lifestyle she'd been surprised to discover that Raz owned a place like this, but what had really surprised her was the almost military efficiency with which it was run.

Here, horses were bred and trained in what was clearly a highly successful business. Smiling staff ran the place with smooth efficiency, allowing their elusive boss to come and go as security and his responsibilities demanded.

Used to the oppressive atmosphere of her rooms at the Citadel of Tazkhan, Layla felt a sense of peace and freedom she'd never experienced before. It wasn't just the ability to wander freely, but the absence of her father, Hassan, and all the others who had made her life so stressful.

She'd stood up, intending to explore the books on the higher shelves, when one of the dogs came bounding into the room, ears pricked.

Layla stood without moving and seconds later a woman rushed into the room and ushered the dog out, closing the door firmly behind the retreating animal.

'I apologise, Your Highness. I was feeding them and Horus went exploring. Please forgive me.'

Relieved that the overenthusiastic Horus was now on the other side of a closed door, Layla relaxed slightly. 'It's fine.'

'No, it isn't. His Highness left orders that the dogs weren't to be allowed near you. He was very strict about it. All the staff were informed.'

Layla stared at her. 'They were?' *He'd done that for her?*

'Yes, and I'm so sorry for what just happened.'

'Don't be.' She sank back down onto the sofa. She'd never given him an explanation for her fear of dogs, but he'd seen it and responded. She hadn't asked him to act, but he'd cared enough to instruct his staff to keep the dogs away from her. Realising that the girl was looking at her anxiously, Layla managed a smile. 'Don't worry. It's me, not the dogs. I'm sure the dogs are trustworthy.'

'Horus and Isis have had the run of this place since they were puppies, so it isn't always easy to keep them contained.'

'Keep who contained?'

Raz strode into the room at that moment wearing an exquisitely cut dark suit that suggested he'd come straight from meetings. His sudden appearance shattered her calm and sent her spinning straight back into that state of nervous tension that never seemed to leave her when he was around.

It was the first time she'd seen him since they'd arrived at his home but that didn't surprise her. She was fast coming to realise how hard he pushed himself and how seriously he took his responsibilities. Wherever he was, he rose before dawn, worked way past sunset, and still somehow managed to spend time with his daughter. Admittedly that time was usually spent galloping like two crazy people across the desert on horses that seemed half wild to her inexperienced eyes. His energy levels seemed limitless, his physical power, strength and stamina as much a part of him as those fierce black eyes that appeared to see under the surface she presented to the world.

And those eyes were on her now, stripping away her armour, seeing right through her. He saw her fear, knew how deeply that fear went, and the fact that he held that knowledge seemed as intimate as anything they'd shared in the darkness of the desert night. Somehow he'd accessed that most private part of her—her thoughts—and apart from her sister she wasn't used to sharing her thoughts with anyone. She wasn't used to revealing weakness. To do so made her feel as vulnerable as if she were standing naked in a crowd.

But he hadn't taken advantage, had he? He'd used the information, but he'd used it to her benefit not his. He hadn't mocked or ridiculed her response to the dogs. Instead he'd responded with gentleness and kindness. He hadn't just understood the depth of her fear, he'd tried to help.

The girl responsible for keeping the dogs under control was profuse in her apologies. 'I'm so sorry, Your Highness. Horus ran in here when my back was turned. I followed immediately,' she said quickly, 'and he didn't get farther than the door.'

Raz spoke in a low voice. Layla couldn't hear exactly what was said, but she saw the girl whiten and give a rapid shake of her head before backing away and leaving them alone.

'What did you say to her?'

He closed the door firmly. 'When I give an order I expect it to be obeyed, and I gave express instructions that the dogs were *not* to be allowed in the library or into whichever space you choose to occupy.'

'It's fine, really.'

His eyes held hers. 'But it isn't fine, is it? We both know it isn't fine even though you don't talk about it.'

Layla tried to steady her breathing but she knew it was a hopeless quest.

The moment it was just the two of them the atmosphere shifted.

She knew what sexual attraction was now. She knew it and she felt it right through her, from the tips of her fingers to the depths of her soul. It was the quickening of her heart when he walked into a room, the power of a shared look full of intimate promise. But most of all it was the constant longing to touch—the need to put her hands on his hard body and feel his hands on her. The craving was so intense it was almost visceral, and it surprised her because she wouldn't have thought the physical could have so much power over her. The feelings thrilled her and scared her because they were unfamiliar and uncontrollable.

Ignoring his reference to the dogs, Layla struggled to respond as her old self. 'Did you have a productive afternoon?'

'Yes, but the downside was that I neglected you on your first day here.'

'Zahra showed me round. We had fun together. And you don't have to worry about me—I'm used to occupying myself.'

'In the past, yes, but I don't want your future to be like your past.'

She put down the book she was holding. 'I love books. I'm always happy to read.'

'Because it's an escape? Do you feel the need to escape when you're with me?'

'No.' Her mouth was dry. She had no way of telling him how much her feelings unsettled her because she could barely articulate it to herself. 'I don't only read to escape. I read because I love the rhythm and flow of words. A good writer can create images with prose in the way an artist does with a brush.' And it was a good job she was a reader, not a writer, because she couldn't have found the words to describe how being with him made her feel.

'Then hopefully you can pass on some of your love of books to Zahra,' he said dryly, removing his tie and undoing his top button. 'To her, reading is an activity that takes her away from horses, which makes it something to be loathed and detested.'

'So we need to start by finding her some horse fiction.'

'Horse fiction?' His brows rose. 'Does such a thing exist?'

'Of course.' It was a relief to have something to focus on. She dragged her eyes from the addictive curve of his mouth and tried not to think how it felt when he kissed her. 'There are talking horses in *The Horse and His Boy* by C.S. Lewis, and I always loved *Black Beauty* because the story is told from the horse's point of view. I'm sure I can think of more.'

His eyes gleamed dark, his gaze disturbingly compelling. 'In that case you are now officially responsible for Zahra's reading—or lack of it.'

'It will be my pleasure. It's just a question of finding something to engage her interest. She is enjoying the stories I'm telling her at bedtime.'

'And on that topic…' He strolled across the room to her

and handed her a package. She unwrapped it cautiously, wondering how she hadn't noticed that he was holding something in his hand.

'Oh!' As the packaging fell away she felt her breath catch. 'It's my copy of *A Thousand and One Nights*. I thought it was lost forever.'

'It came with us when we travelled on that first night. I should have given it to you before now but I didn't think of it.' He was standing close to her. So close it would have taken nothing to reach out and touch him. 'I'm sorry I've neglected you today.'

'You didn't neglect me. I understand the pressures on your time.' What would happen if she touched him? She had no idea of the etiquette and no idea how to subdue the feelings that threatened to overwhelm her. 'I hope your meetings went well.'

'Very well. What did you do this afternoon?'

'I read. Explored a bit. Enjoyed the surroundings. I've never been this close to the border with Zubran before. It's beautiful. You've known the Sultan and his wife for a long time?'

'Mal and I have been friends since childhood. I often stayed in his house. His father and mine were close—' He broke off but she read his mind easily.

'United against a common enemy,' she said quietly. '*My* father.'

'We are not going to talk about that now.'

He cupped her face in his hands and the touch of those strong fingers on her skin made her go hot inside.

Was that really all it took? One touch. One touch and she was hopelessly lost. Suddenly all she wanted was more. Just how badly she wanted more was embarrassing to contemplate.

'I moved Zahra into the room next to ours so that if she wakes we will hear,' she said.

His finger traced her jaw. 'That was thoughtful of you.'

'And I met your cousin,' Layla said desperately. 'The one who manages this place. She is very impressive. And she was welcoming. I didn't know you had business interests. Hassan has no idea you own this. No one does. No one knows you have a home here.'

'Have you finished?'

'Finished?'

Those dangerous dark eyes burned into hers. 'You are chattering and I've never known you chatter before. You're nervous.'

'I'm not nervous.'

'You can be honest with me. I *want* you to be honest.'

How honest? Was he waiting for her to admit she thought about him every moment of every day? Did he want her to say she just wanted to tear off his suit, his tie, his perfect white shirt and everything else he was wearing until the only thing between them was bare skin? What would he say if she confessed that night had become her favourite time? That she wished away every hour of daylight in the hope he might come to her?

'I'm not nervous.'

He stared down at her—held her eyes with his as if he were drawing all her thoughts inside him so that he could read them and know every detail.

Terrified of what he'd find inside her head, Layla tried to pull away. But his free hand slid behind her back and he locked her against him with a strong arm.

She felt the hardness of his powerful body against hers and goosebumps raced down her spine.

'Raz—'

'My daughter is asleep,' he said softly. 'We should probably move this conversation to the bedroom so that we can hear her if she wakes.'

The bedroom.

'Yes.'

Except that it felt so good being this close to him she didn't want to move. Didn't want him to let her go.

Fortunately when he did it was only briefly, and then he took her hand and drew her close to him as he led her from library to bedroom. She was aware of every movement he made. Aware that he shortened his stride to match hers, aware of the brush of his arm against hers as he stepped back to allow her through the door first, aware that he drew her closer as they passed the door of Zahra's bedroom and the sleeping forms of the ever devoted Isis and Horus.

'They are very protective of her.' She followed him into his luxurious bedroom and he closed the door behind them.

'It has been that way since she was a baby. I believe they would give their lives for her, but I am conscious that you are uncomfortable around them so I have given orders that they should not be allowed to roam freely.'

'Zahra's safety is more important than the fact I'm a little nervous with dogs. They must be allowed to do as they have always done.'

'A *little* nervous?'

His eyes were gently mocking and she gave a half smile.

'Terrified—there, I admit to being that pathetic.'

'*Not* pathetic. Nothing about you is pathetic.' His expression serious, he pulled her towards him. Tension shimmered between them. 'You accused me of turning out the lights so that I didn't know I was with you, but the lights are still on and if you want them turned off you're going to have to say so.' His eyes were dark on hers and the hunger she saw in him shocked and thrilled her.

'I don't want you to turn them off.' She wanted to see him. *All of him.*

'You're sure?'

'Yes.' Just as she was sure if he didn't kiss her soon she'd be the one to do the kissing. In fact she was close to doing just that when he cupped her face and lowered his head to hers.

His mouth was hot on hers, his kiss sure and clever, and just like every other time the explosion of sensation was instantaneous and all-consuming. Just like every other time her mind blanked. She felt dizzy with it, and the fact that this time there was no doubt he knew who he was kissing somehow intensified all those feelings.

As his mouth seduced hers she felt his palms on her shoulders, easing off the simple, modest dress she'd selected earlier that day, felt the skilled glide of his fingers down her spine. And this time, whatever happened to her, *whatever she felt*, she was determined not to close her eyes.

Perhaps he sensed it because he took her hand and placed it on his chest. 'Undress me.'

His soft command made her pulse sprint.

She felt the steady thud of his heart under her palm and then her shaking, useless fingers fumbled with first one button and then another. But the speed of her fingers wouldn't match the desperation building in her and she gave a murmur of frustration and tugged at his shirt, sending buttons flying.

Layla froze. 'I'm sorry.'

'For what?' His eyes glittered down at her. 'For wanting me as badly as I want you? That isn't something to apologise for.'

Releasing her briefly, he wrenched off his torn shirt, leaving her face to face with his muscular male chest. She stared at the dark hair that shadowed the centre of his chest and then narrowed down and disappeared below the waistband of his trousers.

She wondered if he was going to make the next move. Felt his eyes on her as he waited.

Face hot, Layla reached for the fastening of his trousers.

She heard the sharp intake of his breath, felt his board-flat abdomen tense against her fingers, and paused.

'Do it.' His tone was raw. 'Do what you want to do.'

She was too self-conscious to do *exactly* what she wanted to do, but she undid the button and slid down the zip, freeing him. The only sound in the room was the harsh rasp of his breathing and she heard the sound change as she took him in her hand and stroked him.

He felt hot and hard, and the thickness of him in her palm made her own body heat. It was the first time she'd touched him like this and for a moment she stood still, unsure of herself, and then he covered her hand with his and showed her, guiding her movements, teaching her what no man had taught her before. And she learned fast what pleased him, discovered the instant high that came from hearing the sudden intake of his breath or feeling the bite of his fingers in her flesh as he struggled for control.

Her palm cradling the most intimate part of him, she lifted her face to his. 'I'm sorry you have to teach me.'

'That proves how little you know about men, because I'm *not* sorry.' His tone was rough and his features were as tense as his shoulders. 'I am traditional enough to be pleased that everything my wife has learned in bed she learned from me.'

Layla hid a smile. 'That's not very progressive, Your Highness.'

'In some areas progress is overrated.'

'It's your own fault. If you'd let me keep the book—'

'You will not need a book.'

His tone thickened, he pulled her into him, taking her mouth in a hard, burning kiss before he tumbled her back onto the bed. Dispensing with the rest of his clothes, he came down on top of her, his weight pressing her into the soft mattress.

'Tell me if I'm too heavy for you.'

'You're not. I like it. I like the feel of you. All of you.'

His gaze darkened and he shifted slightly so that she felt the roughness of his thigh against the smoothness of hers. 'I promised myself I'd be patient.'

'You don't have to be patient.' Layla gazed into his handsome face, so hungry for him she ached in every part of her body. She slid her palm over the smooth skin of his powerful shoulder and felt the tension there, felt his own struggle to hold back. 'I don't need you to be patient.'

'If anything I do makes you uncomfortable—'

'It won't.'

She was about to say that nothing he did could make her uncomfortable but he was kissing her again, the slide of his tongue against hers driving all rational thought from her head. He kissed her with slow, deliberate expertise, and although he'd kissed her like this before she discovered that the light changed everything because now she could see. She kept her eyes open and so did he, and she could see the fire in his eyes, the flare of heat as he looked at her, the raw hunger that she knew was mirrored in her own gaze.

She needed to see him.

Needed him to see her.

And if she'd been worried he couldn't look at her she wasn't any more, because it was soon obvious he couldn't *not* look at her as he slid down her body, exploring every shivering, trembling inch while the lamps threw golden shadows over her skin.

Layla watched as his fingertips grazed her nipples and then felt the skilled flick of his tongue. And then he took her in his mouth and the delicious heat of it intensified the ache in her pelvis until she was only able to stay still because the weight of his body was holding her down.

Her only outlet was to moan, and moan she did as she felt the brush of his erection against the soft flesh of her inner thigh. He eased away from her and slid his hand down one bare leg, parting her.

It was possibly the most intimate action of their relationship so far.

It was the first time he'd seen her. The first time any man had seen her. And she realised that the light offered no opportunity for modesty or concealment. Spread and exposed, there was no hiding, and when his gaze lifted to hers she knew her cheeks were burning.

'It makes me feel—'

'I know how it makes you feel,' he said softly, 'but you can trust me. I want you to trust me.'

Light shone from the two lamps positioned right by the bed. His eyes shifted from her flushed face to her breasts and lower still. To that part of her that lay between the shadows of her thighs—that part of her that now lay open to him. And if she were embarrassed it soon became clear that he wasn't. Nor did he intend to allow her to hide. Trembling with anticipation, she felt the warmth of his palm on the inside of her thigh, the gentle slide of skilled male fingers against her wet, sensitive flesh, and then he moved again and the next thing she felt was the scorching heat of his clever, knowing mouth.

Layla closed her eyes. He'd done this before but she was discovering that in the dark it was different. She knew how wet she was already, and then she felt his tongue on her and in her, parting her, exploring her in the most intimate way possible, until she was writhing against the silk sheets, only his firm grip on her hips keeping her still.

He drove her to orgasm again and again, and when he finally hauled her under him and thrust deep Layla was so dazed and disorientated, so weakened by pleasure, she could do nothing but move with him, lost in this new version of reality.

* * *

'Tell me about the dogs.'

He'd picked his moment carefully. Picked a time when she was at her most vulnerable. A time when she was more likely to trust him with those secrets she'd buried inside herself. Because she was wrapped in the curve of his arm he felt the tension ripple through her slender body as she tried to roll away from him.

'I can't.' The fear in her voice was so sharp it was almost visible.

'Try.'

'You don't understand—'

'I want to.' He wondered how far he could push before she shut herself down and refused him access. 'Were you bitten?'

Without warning, she pulled away from him and sat up. She stared blankly ahead of her and then drew up her knees and hugged them with her arms, as if giving herself comfort. 'When we were young Hassan used to make us play a game called Hide.'

'Hide and Seek?'

'*His* version of Hide and Seek. We were given an hour to hide and then—' The words seemed to jam in her mouth so he prompted her.

'Then they tried to find you?'

'Then they sent the dogs to find us.' Her voice was flat, the words factual, as if it were only by stripping out the emotion that she could bear to speak them. 'Saluki. Four of them. Although people keep them as pets, the Saluki is a hunting dog. But I'm sure you already know that. The Bedouin use them for hunting hares, gazelle, and foxes and other prey. In this case we were the prey.'

Shock stunned him into silence. When he finally managed to speak, he found himself devoid of words, because there simply were none. What could anyone say in response to a revelation of that magnitude? 'Layla—*habibti*—' The endearment flowed off his tongue so naturally he didn't notice. All his attention was focused on her.

'A Saluki is the fastest dog there is—did you know that?' She swept her hair away from her face with a shaking hand, her face ghostly pale in the dim light of the room. 'Some claim it's the Greyhound, but over long distances the Saluki is faster. Its paws are padded so they absorb the impact. Believe me when I say that no child, however terrified, could ever outrun a Saluki. I know because we tried.'

She was speaking quickly now, her breathing shallow, as if she were remembering what it was like to run with fear in her heart and menace at her heels.

The image she painted was so vivid Raz felt nausea settle in the pit of his stomach. He sat up slowly, staring at her frozen profile. 'You are saying he sent the dogs to hunt you?'

'It was Hassan's idea of entertainment. Yasmin was terrified—just terrified.' Her teeth were chattering as she remembered. 'Her little body used to shake so badly she couldn't run, but it didn't really matter because running was pointless. And they didn't want us to run. They wanted us to hide. Do you know how terrifying it is, waiting for the moment when they find you? Because they *will* find you. And you hear them before you see them—you hear them panting, and the muffled thud of their paws as they pick up the scent and follow your trail. And you brace yourself for that moment, never knowing if this time they'll rip you apart before the humans call them off. All you can do is close your eyes and hope.'

For the first time he noticed a mark on her upper arm—an old scar, a silvery twist of damaged flesh that ran from shoulder to elbow. Lifting his hand, he touched it with his fingertips and felt her flinch. 'They did this?'

'I used to lie on top of her...' Her voice whispered over the pain. 'And the dogs used to try and pull me off. And she was screaming and screaming and it drove the animals crazy and I kept telling her not to move, to try and keep still, because it made it worse. But it was impossible to lie still when you could feel the heat of their breath on your neck and hear that horrible, rumbling growl—'

It explained her behaviour whenever Isis and Horus were around. She was always still. She never moved. It explained her behaviour on that first night in the tent when she'd been frozen to the spot and he hadn't understood why.

Now he understood, and his anger was black and lethal as he pulled her into the circle of his arms, holding her as she shivered and shook. 'I will find him,' he vowed in a thickened voice. 'I swear to you I will find him and he will pay for what he did to you both.'

'He is already paying. What he wanted was power and he's lost that. Between us we've taken that from him and it feels good.'

'I will not allow Isis and Horus near you again.'

'I don't want that. I want to get used to them.' Her voice was fiercely determined. 'I *need* to get used to them. They're good dogs. I know they are. Nothing like the others.'

Her lips were bloodless, her eyes dark and bruised in the soft light. She was so pale he felt guilt rip through him

'I shouldn't have made you talk about it, *habibti*.'

'You were right to make me talk about it. Why should I expect you to share things with me if I share nothing with you? On that first night you asked why a woman would cross a desert on a horse she couldn't ride to find a man she didn't know. Now you know the answer.'

'Your father knew what Hassan did?'

'My father had no interest in us beyond our use to him in his political games.'

'I am starting to understand the reason for your sister's night terrors.'

'That was just part of it.' She eased away from him, her eyes wide with anxiety. 'You don't think Salem would use dogs to track her?'

'No. You can rest assured that Salem utilises far more sophisticated methods than dogs. By now he will have tapped his many contacts in various shadowy government organisations and be using the most up-to-date technology that exists.'

'I let her down. I was the one who made the decision to leave the palace, and because of me she is lost and alone.'

'You made the right decision. By leaving you took control away from Hassan.' He smoothed her hair with his fingers and lay down in the bed again, taking her with him. Keeping his arm round her, he pulled the covers over them. 'You're safe. I'll never let him touch you again. This is your life now. This is your home.'

'But when everything settles in Tazkhan you will have to move there. The people will expect it.'

Her voice was muffled against his chest and Raz stared up at the ceiling, the scent of her hair winding itself around his senses.

'It's what we do that matters, not where we live. We will sort something out that works for everyone. And in the meantime I'm going to make you forget that life. This is your life now and, yes, there is responsibility—but there should also be fun.'

'Fun?'

She sounded unsure, doubtful, as if she had no idea what he meant, and he realised how little thought he'd given to her life and just how wrong he'd been in the few thoughts he'd had.

'Dancing? Talking to new people? Wearing nice clothes?'

'I've never danced. I'm not sure I'd be very good at it if my experiences on a horse are anything to go by.'

'You've never danced?' His arms tightened around her. 'Then that's something else I need to teach you. Now, go to sleep. You're safe now, I promise.'

CHAPTER NINE

SHE WOKE ALONE and the level of disappointment that followed that discovery was shocking. And then she heard the sound of the shower and realised he was using the bathroom.

He hadn't left.

For once he hadn't walked away once the sun had risen.

Layla rolled onto her back and stared up at the ceiling, her head full of the night before. And not just because of the discovery that she had an unsettling capacity to enjoy sex.

He'd called her *habibti*.

It was the first time he'd called her that. She subdued the sudden lift of her mood with cold, calm logic. She'd been upset. Whatever lay between them, Raz Al Zahki was a decent human being. The endearment had been spoken out of comfort, not affection, and she'd be deluded if she pretended otherwise.

But it had been the first time in her life anyone had held her like that. The first time anyone had offered comfort.

And it had felt good.

And strange. She'd never shared her thoughts with another person. Not even Yasmin. Because her role had been to protect her sister, so she hadn't wanted to frighten her by revealing her own fears. Part of her felt vulnerable that she'd shown him so much of herself, that he knew so much about her.

'Layla?' Zahra hovered in the doorway, clutching a book, unsure of her welcome.

When Layla sat up and stretched out her arms the little girl bounded into the room, closely followed by the ever-protective Isis and Horus.

Despite her best efforts Layla felt her throat close and the fear spark inside her.

'*Bas!* Stop!' Raz thundered the command from the door-way of the bathroom and the dogs skidded to a halt, crashing into each other like clowns in a circus. There was something almost comical about the dopey way they looked at him but he didn't smile. 'Sit and stay, or tonight you'll be sleeping in the desert.'

The dogs gave a whine and obediently sank down, heads on paws.

Layla felt her heart-rate slowly normalise.

Raz transferred his gaze to her and she knew he was thinking about her confession of the night before, so she smiled and tried to keep it light. 'They know who's boss.'

'My dad is the boss. Everyone does as he says except me.' Zahra climbed onto the bed, still holding her book. 'Can we finish the story you started last night? You stopped at the exciting bit.'

Layla shifted across in the bed, relieved she'd thought to put her nightdress on in case Zahra woke in the night.

She was desperately conscious of Raz watching her, his bare chest still damp from the shower, a towel knotted around his waist.

'You can read for a while but then you need to pack.'

'Pack?' Zahra lost interest in the book. 'We're going on a trip? Can we ride?'

'Not this time. We're flying to Zubran for a party tonight.' Zahra's face fell. 'A party? That means I can't come.'

Raz strolled across the room and scooped his daughter into

his arms. 'You can't come to the party but you can come to Zubran. I need you there. I want your opinion on a mare I'm thinking of buying.'

Watching the two of them together, Layla felt something soften inside her. The fact that a father could care so much about his daughter's feelings and opinion was a revelation. It was something she hadn't witnessed before because she'd had no relationship with her own father.

Aware that Raz was looking at her with question in his eyes, she smiled. 'You are buying another horse? How many animals can one person ride?'

'She won't be for riding. She'll be for breeding,' Zahra told her seriously. 'I'm going to have a foal of my own to take care of. I'm going to pack right now.' Squirming out of her father's arms, she sped from the room.

Overwhelmed by emotions so intense and uncomfortable she could hardly handle them, Layla rescued the book from where it lay as the little girl had left it, in danger of snapping its spine.

'Layla?' His voice was soft. 'Talk to me.'

What was there to say? 'You're a good father.' The words were thickened by the lump in her throat. 'And she adores you.'

'You think that's a bad thing?'

'Oh, no! How could I? A little girl *should* adore her daddy.'

There was a tense silence. 'But it doesn't always happen that way, does it?'

'No. But life is full of things that shouldn't happen—as we both know.' She closed the book carefully. 'If you want me to encourage her to read, it's probably best not to mention the word *horse* while we have a book open.'

'I know, but in this case it was intentional.' The corners of his mouth flickered. 'I wanted her out of the room. I need to talk to you, *habibti.*'

Habibti.

Her stomach flipped. What reason did he have to call her that this morning? Or did he think she still needed the comfort? 'What about?'

'I want to make sure you are comfortable about tonight.'

'The party? What exactly does it involve?'

'It is a fundraiser for a children's charity supported by the Sultan of Zubran and his wife, Avery. I think you'll like her. She used to run a highly successful party planning business and her events are always spectacular. This one promises to be no exception.'

'A fundraiser?' Layla felt no excitement. Just pressure. 'What exactly is my role at an event like that?'

'Your role is to enjoy yourself. Something I suspect you haven't done anywhere near enough in your life.' Droplets of water clung to his powerful shoulders and his hair was still sleek and damp from the shower. 'Did you never attend formal functions at the Citadel?'

'Never. My father never raised funds for anyone except himself and neither did Hassan.' Thinking of Hassan made her feel sick, and this time her concern wasn't just for herself and her sister. 'If you appear in public at a high-profile event like this one, won't you be a target?'

'The only people who know in advance that we will be there are the Sultan himself and his wife. I would trust them with my life. *Have* trusted them with my life on more occasions than I care to count. And although I take sensible precautions I don't live my life in hiding. I am easy enough to find if someone knows where to look.'

As they both knew.

Their eyes met briefly and she felt a new intimacy—and something she hadn't felt before. A warmth. *A new level of understanding.*

And something else. A chemistry so intense it thickened

the air and created a tension that unsettled her. They were talking about serious issues and yet part of her just wanted to place her hand on the hard swell of his biceps and her lips on the dark haze of hair at the centre of his chest.

'What about Zahra?' Somehow she managed to speak. 'What will she do while we're at the party.'

'She will be safe in Zubran. She has been there many times and it is sufficiently familiar that hopefully her night terrors will not return.' His gaze lingered on her face. 'Since you started reading to her at night and settling her down there have been no more bad dreams.'

'I know. And I'm pleased.'

'I can't thank you enough.'

'No thanks are needed.'

'And now it is your turn,' he said softly. 'We need to re-place those bad dreams of yours, and those memories, with something much happier. Starting with this party.'

'But if Hassan guesses where you are going—'

'I don't anticipate that Hassan will pay us a visit, but if he does then it will save us the bother of finding him.' His gaze held hers for a moment. 'So, how do you feel about the party? I don't want to overwhelm you, and I know how anxious you are for news of your sister, but I would very much like you to have fun and enjoy yourself.'

Layla couldn't imagine enjoying herself in the company of a large number of strangers but she didn't want to say so. 'I'm already looking forward to it.'

'I've promised to take Zahra riding this morning. Will you join us?'

Was it her imagination or had those dark shadows she saw in his eyes lessened? Was it wishful thinking on her part to think he seemed happier and more relaxed?

'I think the two of you should ride together.'

'Join us.' He brushed her cheek with the backs of his fingers. 'Abdul will stay with you and we will all ride slowly.'

But of course he didn't know the meaning of *slow*, pushing his animal to the limit as he sped into the distance in pursuit of his young daughter, who seemed to embrace their extreme ride with the same enthusiasm as her father. The horse's tail was lifted high and trailed like a banner in the wind, his curved neck betraying his enviable lineage. Even Layla, whose knowledge of horses came entirely from books, could see the animal was beautiful.

It made her sick with nerves just watching, but she had to admit it was good that Zahra didn't seem afraid either of horses or the Saluki who ran next to them.

If her childhood had been different would she have been the same?

Would she be the one galloping across the sand and whooping with excitement?

'You are doing so well, Your Highness.' It was Abdul, as kind and solicitous as ever as he rode by her side as Raz had instructed.

'We both know I'm not, but thank you for the encouragement.' She stared enviously at Raz and Zahra, now just specks in the distance.

'We are all born with different gifts,' Abdul said quietly. 'His Highness has a particular gift with horses, but he has also had the benefit of many years of experience. He was virtually raised on horseback. The moment he could sit unsupported he was put on a horse—I think he was about six months old. He rode with his father every day until he could control the animal himself. Then he rode alone. And he has a tendency to take what many would see as appalling risks, so I would beg you do *not* aspire to emulate him.'

'Not much chance of that.' She felt a pang that she wasn't confident enough to share that interest with him, but she knew that even if she rode each day and every day for the rest of her life she'd never be as good as Raz.

'You have your own gifts.' Abdul reached across and showed her how to shorten the reins. 'And those are to be valued every bit as much as His Highness's skills with a horse. You have courage and patience, as you have shown on numerous occasions over the past week. His Highness is growing more relaxed by the day and we have you to thank for that.'

'You think so?' Perhaps it hadn't been her imagination. 'Will you be coming with us to Zubran?'

'Yes, because His Highness will have talks with the Sultan.'

'And will you be at the party, Abdul?'

'Sadly, no, Your Highness. But I feel sure you will enjoy it.'

'Will I?' Layla wasn't convinced. 'I have no idea what I'm supposed to wear.'

'On that topic I have taken the liberty of contacting Her Royal Highness the Sultana of Zubran. She has generously agreed to assist with your wardrobe needs as there has been no opportunity to provide what you will require for such an event.'

'I don't want to put her to any trouble.'

Abdul cleared his throat. 'Perhaps it is indiscreet of me to say this, but I can assure you that there is nothing Her Highness enjoys more than dressing people in clothes of her choosing. Zahra loves going to see her for that very reason. And you will find Her Highness to be a very warm and caring person once she has finished organising your life and telling you what you should be doing.'

Layla was amused and intrigued. 'So she isn't dominated by the Sultan?'

'It is very much a marriage of equals,' Abdul said dryly, and Layla felt her heart squeeze as she watched Raz ride into the distance.

Theirs wasn't a marriage of equals, was it?

She couldn't ride. She couldn't swim. She was terrified of his dogs. She had no idea what was expected of her at this party.

What exactly *did* she have to offer him?

The realisation that she was hopeless at all the things that were important to him disturbed her, as did the thought that tonight they would be making their first public appearance together.

Never having been allowed to mingle with her father's guests, Layla felt as if she were back in the oasis with the waters closing over her head.

'I'd be delighted if Her Highness would help me with my wardrobe.'

If it came to a choice between inconveniencing the Sultan's wife and embarrassing Raz she'd pick inconvenience every time. But as it turned out Abdul was correct in his summation that their hostess would be only too delighted to take responsibility for her wardrobe.

'You've been hiding out in the desert together? I have never heard anything more romantic in my life! But romance can only take a girl so far and then she needs a decent spa day.'

Avery was the most elegant, capable, efficient person Layla had ever met, and within minutes they were curled up on a low sofa in an opulent room hung with beautiful tapestries and sipping tea.

'Mmm. Whenever we're in the desert Mal makes me drink the Bedouin variety, which is delicious, but you can't beat Earl Grey. Now, tell me all the details and leave nothing out.'

'Details?' Layla sat stiff and formal on the edge of the sofa, but Avery slipped off her shoes and curled her legs under her.

'I'm going to give you a tip, because once you and Raz are back in your rightful place in the palace at Tazkhan you're going to be throwing open those gilded doors and entertaining the whole world and your legs will feel as if they've been trapped between clamps: whenever you can before a big event take the weight off your feet. And now tell me if it's true that you escaped from the palace and rode into the desert on your father's wild stallion? It's too romantic for words.'

'It wasn't romantic. It was horrible in every way. And I don't think the horse was wild, precisely—at least not until we climbed on its back. Then it was certainly less than impressed—'

After a moment's hesitation Layla told Avery the whole story, and by the end of it she felt so relaxed she'd even removed her shoes.

'So you married for the good of Tazkhan, but now you're in love? That is the happiest ending I've heard in a long time.'

'Oh, no, that isn't true!' Startled, Layla stiffened. 'I'm not in love.'

Avery's brows rose. 'No? So when you say "Raz this" and "Raz that" in every sentence it's just because you're—' she waved a hand in the air '—sorry, but I only know one reason to mention a guy in every single breath and that's l-o-v-e. Either that or obsession, and you don't strike me as the obsessive type.'

Love? Layla stared at her blankly. 'I can't be in love. I'm not that sort of person.'

'Trust me, love is indiscriminate. It strikes all types without mercy. I didn't think I was "that sort of person" either and now look at me. I'm someone who has to control everything around them, but take it from me that love can't be controlled. Believe me, I've tried.'

'That's different. You and His Highness knew each other for a long time before you were together. Whereas Raz and I—' Her skin heated as she thought about the intimacies they'd shared. 'We are strangers. We have known each other only a few weeks.'

'I actually find that quite erotic.' Avery leaned back against the arm of the sofa. 'Strangers forced together. I presume you've actually…?' When Layla coloured Avery smiled. 'Mmm, and I'll bet it was good. Raz is super-hot. But don't tell Mal I said that.'

'He was so in love with his wife.' The words fell from Layla's lips before she could stop them and she saw Avery's eyes narrow.

'Yes, and that was tragic. But it happened. Stuff happens.' The laughter had gone and her husky voice hinted at layers of depth beneath the sophisticated social skills. 'It's called life. Sometimes life delivers a steaming pile of crap right in your lap, and when that happens all you can do is keep moving forward. You keep walking. You get out of bed, you move, and eventually you start living again. And that's what he's doing.'

'But this marriage wasn't his choice. It was mine.'

'Raz Al Zahki has never done anything that wasn't his choice. He is tough, single-minded and as stubborn as his brother and my husband.' Avery reached across and squeezed her hand. 'And he made a *good* choice. I'm thrilled we're going to be neighbours.'

'I'm nothing like his wife. I can't take her place.'

'Would you want to? Personally, I'd hate to be a clone of another person. You probably don't want my advice, but I'll give it anyway because I can't help myself: don't try and replace her.' Avery unfolded her long legs and slipped on her shoes. 'Be yourself. Be *you*. If you want to learn to ride, then learn. But only if it's what you want to do. You should probably learn to swim, but only so that his psycho sister-in-law can't have the pleasure of drowning you. The point I'm making is that if you are *you* then any relationship you form together will be real.'

Layla felt her mood lift for the first time in days. Maybe even longer. 'That makes sense.'

'Of course it does. I only ever talk sense—as I'm forever telling my husband. Now, drink some tea and tell me about your sister.'

At the mention of her sister Layla felt her happy mood evaporate. 'She's still missing.'

'Yes.' Avery's expression was sympathetic. 'Everyone is looking for her. And Salem is exactly the right person to be in charge of that.'

'Everyone says that, but he didn't look particularly friendly when I saw him.'

'I didn't say he was friendly.' Avery swept a sheet of blonde hair away from her face. 'No, he definitely isn't friendly. Dark. Moody. A bit scary, I suppose. But in a totally hot way. Exactly the right person to find your sister.'

'Why? Why does everyone keep saying that?'

Avery put her cup down carefully. 'You don't know?'

'All I know is that Raz seems to trust his brother with his life.'

'As well he would. Salem isn't just his brother—he's ex-Special Forces. After everything that happened in their family he left to set up his own private security firm. He handles *our* security—although I'm convinced that's just Mal trying to monitor my movements when I'm buying shoes.'

Layla laughed, but her mind was picking over what she now knew of Salem. On that first night he'd stepped in front of his brother to protect him, even though Raz was obviously well able to defend himself. 'He hasn't been in contact.'

'He's a man.' Avery selected a date from the bowl on the table. 'Men never call when they're supposed to, and Salem keeps everything close to his chest. Which isn't a bad place to be, I have to say, because he's all muscle and very sexy.' Catching Layla's expression, she grinned. 'Sorry, I'm trying to cheer you up. I honestly do believe that Salem will find her. He's the best.'

'But if she were alive surely he would have found her by now?'

'Maybe he has. Maybe he's lying low for some reason—such as the fact Hassan is a crackpot and no one knows exactly where he is.' Avery nibbled the date. 'Is she a resilient girl?'

Layla thought about her sister and everything she'd endured. 'Yes.'

'Shy? What would she do if she were picked up by a Bedouin tribe, for example?'

'Talk them to death?'

Avery's brows rose. 'It sounds as if Salem will have his hands full when he finds her. You don't know him, so you'll have to take it from me that he's very serious. And everything he does is top secret so he's not much of a talker.'

'Then how do you know so much about what he does?'

'Just one of the perks of being married to the boss, sweetie.'

Layla sifted through the information at her disposal. 'But if Salem is really as serious as you say he is going to strangle my sister.'

'Yes, it does sound like an interesting match. I predict that she will be a pleasant interruption from his usual life. Now, have some more tea. And eat something. Because it's ages until dinner and I'm always too busy mingling to eat much at these things.'

Avery topped up the cups and Layla breathed deeply.

'I have no idea what is expected of me tonight.'

'You're our guest. All we expect of our guests is that they enjoy themselves. In fact I insist on it or I'll assume my party is a dismal failure.' Seeing the expression on Layla's face, she gave a warm smile. 'Just enjoy the time with Raz. Sounds as if the two of you haven't had much time to get to know each other outside of a crisis situation, so this is a perfect opportunity to explore a whole different side to your relationship.'

'But I knew what was expected of me in the crisis. I knew I had to stop the wedding, find Raz, find my sister—it was stressful, but there was a purpose to it. I don't understand the purpose of a party. That isn't what our relationship is about.'

'Maybe it should be. Maybe you just don't know how to relax because you've never been allowed to. The purpose of tonight,' Avery said, 'is for you to spend time together. Be a couple.'

'I've never been part of a couple. I don't know what I'm doing.' Layla's desperation to talk to someone overrode her natural shyness about the topic. 'Raz is—experienced. I'm worried I'm not the woman he needs.'

Avery stared at her for a long moment and then gave a slow smile that transformed her face from beautiful to pure seductress. Suddenly Layla saw exactly why the Sultan had fallen so hard for her. She was strong and independent, but never at the expense of her femininity.

'Trust me, you are *all* the woman he needs,' Avery said.

Layla gave a helpless shrug. 'I don't know myself anymore. I thought I had such a clear idea of who I was and what I wanted, and then suddenly it turns out I'm wrong.'

'Not wrong, but people change and adapt according to their circumstances.' Avery sipped her tea. 'People grow and learn. Or at least the people worth knowing do. For the record, I'm glad Raz found you. He deserves someone like you. And you deserve him.'

'He was forced to marry me.'

'Stop saying that! Did he marry you kicking and screaming? I didn't think so. Now, finish your tea—we're going to make sure that by the time you and Raz make it back to the bedroom tonight he is going to be a desperate man.'

'I won't be comfortable wearing anything too revealing.'

'Don't worry. The true secret of allure is not to show all but to hint at what you are hiding.'

Layla gave a choked laugh. 'You want him to unwrap me?'

'Well, that's one alternative.' Avery stood up. 'Personally, I have a preference for a scenario where you unwrap yourself and make him watch but not touch. The theme of tonight's ball is Desert Nights. It has so much potential, don't you think?'

CHAPTER TEN

RAZ PACED THE length of the royal rooms that had been allocated to them for their stay and glanced at his watch for the sixth time in as many minutes.

Of Layla there was no sign, and he wondered how she'd coped with being plunged into the centre of a big working palace with people she didn't know. From the little he'd learned about her past he knew she'd had little exposure to glittering social gatherings such as the ones run by the Sultan and his wife. And he'd known Avery long enough to be sure she would have extracted every last scrap of detail from Layla, and suddenly wondered if it had been unfair of him to leave them together for so long.

The Desert Nights Ball—an annual event organised by Avery as a fundraiser for disadvantaged children—was about to begin and their presence was expected.

He pulled out his phone and was about to call Avery when Mal appeared in the doorway of his suite, flanked by his security team.

'I have been sent by my wife to tell you that they will meet us downstairs.'

Raz slid his phone back into his pocket. 'I expected Layla to be here.'

'She's spent the day shopping and lunching with Avery, so expect to find her exhausted.' Mal dismissed his guards with a discreet gesture and walked into the guest suite, closing the door behind him. 'Apparently they want to surprise you. And by that I mean that my wife has taken over, as always. I hope that isn't a problem?'

'I appreciate Avery's help. Layla isn't used to large social gatherings and she's quite shy. I'm worried she'll find it overwhelming.'

Mal gave him a speculative look. 'You care about her?'

'Does that surprise you?'

'Does it surprise *you*?'

'Yes.' Seeing no reason not to be honest with his friend, Raz paced over to the window. 'Yes, it surprises me. She is nothing like I expected her to be. I admit it. I made an assumption about who she was based on what we know about the rest of her family.'

'Most people would have done the same.'

'Perhaps, but it isn't something I'm proud of.' He knew now how desperate things must have been for Layla to choose to ride a strange horse into the desert with no fixed destination. She was careful, cautious—and with reason. Those were the qualities that had kept her alive. 'I suspect her life was hell.'

'Now, that comes as *no* surprise to me.' Mal's voice was hard. 'If you want my honest opinion, she is lucky to now be married to you and is probably feeling nothing but relieved.'

Was she? He realised he knew very little about what she was feeling because she kept her thoughts to herself. Except for that single occasion when she'd lost control and spoken out about the secrets he'd kept from her, she'd made no comment on her new life. He knew that much of what she did was driven by her desire to please him, to compensate in some small way for the sins her father had committed.

'She is very brave. She rides even though she hates it, and although she is scared of the dogs she insists they are allowed to roam free. She refuses to be beaten by fear.'

'Then hopefully it will not be long before she realises that with you there is nothing to fear.'

'I think tonight might be stressful for her.' And he realised he didn't want it to be. He didn't want it to be another task she had to endure, another challenge. He wanted her to relax. He wanted her to have fun and enjoy herself without constantly looking over her shoulder.

Mal was watching him. 'And what about you? This is the first time you have made a public appearance with another woman.'

It was something else that hadn't occurred to him. 'I don't care what people think, but *she* will care.' And people would be speculating about their relationship, his feelings about being married to the daughter of his enemy.

'We will all ensure that she is protected as much as possible. She will receive a warm welcome from all of us and that will help.'

But would that be enough?

'She isn't used to crowds.'

'If you sense she is bothered by it then of course you must leave early,' Mal said immediately. 'No one will be offended. Come up here and spend some time alone. My staff will serve you dinner—anything you need, just ask. You are like a brother to me. I hope you know that.'

Quiet words, but spoken with such sincerity that they unlocked something inside him.

'I do know that. For the past decade you've—'

'You would have done the same for me.' Mal cut him off before he could express his thanks. 'I am glad you've found Layla.'

'She's never danced before. Can you imagine that?' His tone raw, Raz lifted a hand and pressed his fingers to his forehead. 'Her life was *nothing* like I imagined it to be.'

He thought of two small girls, huddled together while they

listened to the dogs approaching. Had an image of the scar on her arm where those dogs had come too close. Knowing how hard it had been for her to share that with him, he had no intention of sharing it with anyone else.

'Having met both her father and Hassan on a few occasions I prefer to forget, I have no trouble believing you.'

'She has no idea how to enjoy herself. I don't think she knows who she really is.'

Mal hesitated and then reached out and squeezed his shoulder. 'Give her time. Her life has changed overnight. She has lived with people she couldn't trust, so it will inevitably take a while for her to realise she can trust *you*. It must be a relief to her to be living with you after the life she has led.'

Was it? He realised that since this whole thing began he'd barely thought further than his own needs. 'I have no idea how she feels about living with me,' Raz said honestly.

Mal raised an eyebrow. 'Don't take this the wrong way, but I think you underestimate your qualities. Not that I claim to be an expert on the minds of women, as my wife is always swift to point out.'

His wry tone made Raz smile. 'Your wife is an amazing woman.'

'She is pregnant.' Mal spoke the words in a rough tone tinged with male pride and then gave a half smile. 'I wasn't supposed to tell anyone that.'

'Congratulations.' It was Raz's turn to reach out. 'I'm pleased for you both.'

'I'd rather you didn't—'

'I won't mention it.'

'Good, because I would be in serious trouble. There will be a public announcement in due course.'

'I shall look suitably surprised.'

Mal glanced towards the door. 'I am the host. I should go downstairs and greet the early arrivals. Join me?'

They walked into the opulent ballroom together and Avery immediately walked up to Raz and kissed him on both cheeks.

'It's good to see you, my friend.'

Dressed in ivory silk, she looked stunning and Raz smiled. 'And it is good to see you. Thank you for looking after Layla.'

'I love her,' Avery said simply. 'She's the kindest, most sweet-natured person. And very, *very* beautiful—but of course you've already noticed that because you're a man. She's nervous, so please say the right thing when you see her. And if you need help working out what that is, don't be afraid to ask.'

Raz didn't respond. He was looking over Avery's shoulder to Layla, who was dressed like something from the *Arabian Nights*. Her dress was midnight-blue shot with silver, high at the neck, cut narrow at the waist. Her hair fell in a smooth sheet, dark as ink over the shimmering fabric. Her beautiful eyes were accentuated by subtle make-up.

'And just in case you're that guy who never asks for help, the word you're looking for is *stunning*,' Avery murmured, and then took Mal's arm and guided him towards the arriving guests, leaving Raz alone with a shimmering, dazzling version of Layla.

She looked at him through the dark sweep of those thick eyelashes that had caught his attention from the first moment he'd seen her.

'Did your meetings go well?'

She sounded composed but he saw the uncertainty in her face and knew that Avery was right about her being nervous.

His mouth on those lips, Raz struggled to focus. 'Very well. And I see you and Avery had a busy afternoon.'

'We had fun. We talked and then we shopped.'

Her eyes sparkled and there was an excitement in her expression he'd ever seen them. It was as if someone had switched on a lightbulb inside her. She had a new confidence.

She carried herself differently. He wondered what had brought about the change.

Was it just the dress?

'You look stunning.'

'She told you to say that. I heard her. But thank you, anyway.'

'I said it because it's true. And I would have done so without prompting.' He looked into her eyes and then reached out and drew her against him, his hand resting on the dip of her narrow waist.

'Can I ask you something?'

'Anything.'

'You mentioned dancing—' Her gaze slid to the dance floor, which shimmered and sparkled under clever lighting. 'I'd really like to try it.'

Hiding his surprise, Raz took her hand. 'Then let's try it.'

Intrigued by the change in her, he led her towards the dance floor, exchanging only the briefest of greetings with people as they moved through the crowd, all his attention focused on her.

He noticed Avery in the centre of the dance floor with a man Raz recognised as the French ambassador while Mal was deep in conversation with the man's wife.

When she spotted them Avery immediately escorted the dazzled ambassador back to his wife before grabbing Layla by the hands.

'Don't you *love* this song?' She swirled and shimmied, arms above her head, and Layla watched her curiously for a moment and then joined her, following Avery's lead as she danced, her movements more subtle, more discreet as she learned to match the flow of her body with the beat of the music.

It was a skill that seemed to come naturally too her. Raz felt tension throb through him as he watched her move with sensual grace, her long hair flowing like liquid silk around her shoulders as she discovered a love of dancing. Her happiness at that discovery was evident from the smile on her lips and the unselfconscious way she twirled with Avery, her enjoyment as infectious as the rhythmic beat of the music.

Raz watched her, hypnotised by the change in her, knowing he was witnessing the transformation from unsure girl to sexually aware woman.

Avery caught his eye and gave him a knowing look before twirling Layla into his arms.

She landed against his chest with a gentle thud, off-balance from the dancing and laughing in a way he hadn't heard her laugh before. And he found himself smiling too, because it was impossible not to smile with her eyes sparkling into his and her arms wrapped around his neck as she tried to balance herself.

'I'm dizzy.' Her fingers closed over his biceps. 'Did I embarrass you?'

Was this the first time in her life she'd done something for herself without thought to others? 'No.' His mouth was close to hers, his gaze locked on hers. 'You could never embarrass me.'

By chance, or more likely because the ever-observant Avery had organised it, the rhythm of the music changed from loud and throbbing to soft and smooth and Raz drew her against him, his hand pressed low on her back.

He felt her body relax against his, knew people were watching curiously and tightened his grip on her protectively, hoping she didn't notice the interest and lose that sudden burst of unselfconscious enjoyment that he was finding as addictive as a drug.

Her enchantment with dancing reminded him of that magical moment when a newborn foal staggered to its feet for the first time, balancing on shaky legs as it realised there was a whole new world to explore.

His grip on her must have tightened, because those exotic, beautiful eyes lifted to his in silent question.

Raz felt as if someone had kicked his legs out from under him.

Sexual energy crackled between them, scorching hot and intense. His hand was on her back and he felt the change in her, felt her response to the chemistry as her eyes dropped to his mouth and lingered there.

This time there was no shyness in her gaze, just curiosity, and something far, far more dangerous that came from the knowledge she'd acquired over the past week. Her eyes darkened like the sky before a storm, those eyelashes a silky veil of temptation. And then her lips curved into a happy smile and she leaned her head against his chest, the softness of her hair brushing against his jaw, the scent of it yet another drugging assault on his senses.

Fighting the impulse to drag her from the dance floor, Raz closed his eyes and gathered her close, blocking out everyone around them.

Time passed unobserved until the pace of the music increased and she tilted her head back and looked up at him.

He slid his fingers into her hair, pleased that Avery hadn't suggested she wear it up. 'Do you want to carry on dancing or would you like something to eat? Maybe a drink?'

'The beat has changed.'

'It's a different dance. I can teach you.'

'You must be tired of having to teach me everything.'

Her eyes were soft on his and he tightened his grip on her, pressing her closer until their bodies touched from waist to thigh.

'No, I am not tired of teaching you.' His arm was curved around her and the contours of her body fit perfectly against his. Sexual arousal slammed into him and he felt the answering tremor of her body and knew she felt the same. Her fingers dug into his shoulder. 'You're enjoying yourself?'

'Yes. Very much.'

'Did you have fun with Avery?'

'Yes. I've never talked to another woman before. Not like that.'

'What did you talk about?'

Colour streaked along her cheeks. 'Life.'

'Your life, *habibti*?'

'Not specifically. She talked a bit about you and Salem. She is obviously very fond of you both.'

'Those feelings are returned. Mal has been a friend for as long as I can remember. He and I were at the same party the night he first met Avery. It was like watching two asteroids collide. Everyone in the vicinity was hit by the explosion and the subsequent fallout.' They both glanced towards the edge of the dance floor, where Avery was deep in conversation with Mal, their connection so close it felt like intruding to watch it.

'They're perfect together.'

There was a wistful note in her voice and Raz tilted his head so that he could see her face.

'I thought you weren't romantic?'

Her eyes were fixed across the room on Avery and Mal who were indulging in a last brief exchange before greeting their guests. Remembering what Mal had told him earlier, Raz could guess what the exchange was about.

'I'm not. Not for myself. That doesn't mean I can't be pleased when other people find love.'

He looked down at the glossy curve of Layla's mouth and suddenly wanted to be alone with her, away from the curious glances and the speculation.

'Let's get out of here. The Old Palace is famed for its water gardens. They were a gift from Mal's father to his mother on their marriage.' Keeping his arm around her, he guided her outside.

'Should we be doing this? There are people waiting to speak to you.'

'Then they can wait. I have been doing nothing but speaking to people. Tonight is for us.' He wondered how often before in her life she'd been able to please herself and decided he probably didn't want to hear the answer.

'It's peaceful here.' Tilting her head back, she stared up at the stars. 'I love the sound of the water. It reminds me of your home.'

'*Our* home.'

She hesitated, then pulled away from him and sat down on the low wall that surrounded the bubbling fountain. 'Did your wife love it there? Was it her favourite place?'

He stiffened in instinctive rejection of the personal nature of her question and then saw the anxiety in her eyes and realised how much courage it had taken on her part to ask it. 'Nisa preferred the city. She grew tired of moving around. She was made impatient by the restrictions placed on our movements. She wasn't always careful.'

'I shouldn't have asked.'

But she *had* asked, and emotion settled in his stomach like a solid lump. 'The day she was killed—she wasn't even supposed to be in the desert. She had been staying in the city but had come out to surprise me. I had ridden one of the horses and she climbed into my four-wheel drive. They had tampered with the brakes and she was inexperienced at driving in the desert. Had I been the one at the wheel then perhaps—' He broke off, knowing that 'perhaps' was a useless word. 'She couldn't control the vehicle. It rolled and she was crushed.'

He felt her arms slide round his waist.

'I'm sorry. I'm sorry you lost her. I'm sorry for any part my family played in that. For all of it.'

'An individual is responsible for his own actions. I have never blamed you.' But he understood how hard it must be for her and knew he was the one making it hard.

'It hurts you to talk about it.' Her voice was soft in the semi darkness. 'I apologise. I shouldn't have asked. I've spoiled the moment.'

'You have a right to ask, and you've spoiled nothing.'

'I have no rights, Your Highness. We both know that.'

Sadness shadowed the dark depths of her eyes and Raz pulled her to her feet and took her face in his hands, forcing her to look at him.

'You are still calling me Your Highness after everything we have shared? Have we not moved further on than that?'

'You married me because it was the right thing to do for your people, and in doing so you ignored your personal wishes.'

'Maybe that was true at the time of the wedding, but it isn't true now. Do you think I was ignoring my personal wishes last night? Do you think what we do together has anything to do with my responsibilities?'

'Raz—'

Her hand was on his chest, her eyes on his, and he lowered his head, his mouth hovering above hers.

'Do you think this isn't personal? Does this not feel personal, *habibti*?'

Layla felt everything inside her tighten and spin out of control. Staring into his dangerous black eyes, she felt the world around them fade to nothing. The distant sound of chatter was replaced by the pounding of blood in her ears and her vision was filled with nothing but him.

She felt the roughness of his cheek against the softness of hers, the warmth of his breath and the bite of his strong fingers in her hair as he held her head for his kiss. But he didn't kiss her. Not quite. And the anticipation was electrifying. She felt his tension as powerfully as he evidently felt hers.

'Do we have to stay?' She almost whispered the words. 'Would it be possible to leave?'

His dark brows met in a concerned frown. 'You're not happy? Then we will leave.' Without pressing for further explanation he took her hand and led her towards some steps that led past a cascade of fountains to the rear entrance of the Old Palace. 'We can reach our rooms from here.'

She walked with him through an arched entrance, up spiral stairs, along opulent corridors with gilded mirrors and ornate tapestries, past uniformed staff and the odd exotically clad guest until they reached their private suite.

'I should not have taken you this evening,' he breathed. 'Forgive me.'

'Why do you say that? I had fun. Such fun.'

'You wanted to leave.'

'But not because I wasn't enjoying myself.'

'Then why?'

Layla hesitated, and then stepped forward and placed her hands on his chest. 'Because of this. Because of what I want to do.' She felt him tense. Saw the shock in his eyes as he realised her reasons for abandoning the party were not the ones he'd assumed they were.

'Layla—'

'Don't speak.' She wanted the illusion. No matter what lay between them, tonight it was all about the chemistry and she didn't want to shatter that with words. Whatever emotional hurdles they faced, physically there were none.

This time her fingers were swift and sure as she undressed him. Within seconds he was naked from the waist up, his trousers riding low on his waist, revealing a gloriously masculine chest, every line of muscle clearly delineated as he stood in front of her. Her fingers slid up his chest to his shoulders and then lingered on the hard swell of his biceps. His physical strength fascinated her, and she traced the shape of his muscles with the tips of her fingers, hearing his breathing change, feeling the tension in him as he held himself still and let her explore. She took her time because she wanted to discover and memorise every inch of him. After her fingers she used her lips, her tongue retracing the line her fingers had taken. And still he stood still, although she sensed the effort it took him to do so.

Candles flickered in all corners of the room, sending shafts of shimmering light across them, turning his chest from bronze to gold.

Without hesitation she undid his trousers and dropped to her knees in front of him, her hair falling in a sweep of dark silk over her shoulders.

She glanced up at him and his gaze clashed with hers and held.

Then slowly, gently, she took him in her mouth and saw his eyes close, his jaw clench. She felt the thickness of him in her mouth, tasted the silky, salty heat of him, until he groaned deep in his throat and closed his hands in her hair, easing her away from him.

'Give me a minute—'

His voice was thickened, his eyes dark with something she hadn't seen before, and then he pulled her to her feet and their mouths came together at the same time. This time there was nothing gentle about the kiss, no tentative exploration or patient instruction, just raw, undiluted passion. His hands were locked in her hair and then ripping at her dress as they kissed, so hungry for each other they staggered slightly and sent a lamp flying from its place on a table.

Raz caught it in his hand and she laughed against his mouth. 'Good catch, Your Highness.'

'If it had fallen we would have had Security swarming all over this place.'

Without lifting his mouth from hers he replaced the lamp and urged her back towards the bed, but Layla twisted at the last moment so that this time he was the one on his back on the bed and she was the one on top.

Her hair fell forward onto his chest and he slid his fingers into it.

'I love your hair.'

Smiling, she licked her way down his chest, heard him groan deep in his throat as she moved lower again, exploring him intimately, until his hands closed on her hips and he shifted her over him, his impatience evident in the hard bite of his fingers.

His hair-roughened thigh brushed against the softness of hers and she lowered herself onto him, watching his eyes turn deep, dark black as he drove deep into her. Layla moaned with the sheer pleasure of it, moving instinctively, until he locked his fingers over her hips to control her movements.

'Give me a minute—'

His tone was raw, right on the edge of control, and she leaned forward to kiss his mouth, licking at his lips until he muttered something unintelligible and caught her head in his hands. They kissed like wild things, the heat a pulsing, pounding force, his body hard in hers as they drove each other to the same peak and over the edge. She felt him pulse inside her, watched his face as he lost control, as pleasure gripped them both and spun them into ecstasy.

Afterwards, she curled against his chest and felt his hand come up to touch her hair.

He didn't speak and neither did she, because she'd learned how easily words could destroy and she wanted to preserve the moment. Preferably forever, but if not forever then at least for now.

And in the aftermath of their loving, while they both lay bathed in intimacy, she knew that Avery had been right.

She loved him.

The realisation was overwhelming, terrifying and puzzling all at the same time.

But most of all it was shocking. Shocking to learn yet another thing about herself. When she'd made the decision that marriage to Raz was the best solution, she'd braced herself for living with a stranger, but she was fast discovering that the stranger she was living with was herself.

She realised that her life before him had been as dry and empty as the vast desert. Because she'd never known anything else she'd assumed that was all there was, but now she knew differently. She'd thought she knew herself well, but had discovered she'd only known one small part of herself. And as for knowing *him*

They say his heart is frozen into ice.

She knew that wasn't true.

She lifted her head and looked at him, staring down into the fierce black of his eyes. To describe him as handsome was to do him a disservice, because his appeal went so much deeper than that. Etched in those striking features was a strength that was more than surface deep.

Something flickered in those ebony depths and she saw all her own questions reflected back at her.

Without speaking he lifted his hand and pushed her hair away from her face. It was impossible not to react to his touch because it seemed everything she felt about this man was exaggerated and out of her control.

She felt a stab of envy for his wife, whom he had loved so deeply, swiftly followed by guilt that she could feel that way about someone no longer alive.

A few weeks ago she hadn't known anything about love. She'd felt disconnected from the poets' description of the agony and heartache that came with love and loss. She'd never seen any evidence to support the theory that hearts could break, shatter or be frozen into ice.

She'd been willing to believe in love, but had never expected to experience the reality.

But now she had both experience and evidence. She felt the pain of it heavy in her chest, the ache behind her ribcage growing by the hour.

Raz frowned slightly and just for a moment she thought he was going to say something. Then he gathered her close and pulled the covers over them both.

'That was amazing. *You* are amazing.'

Layla said nothing because she had no idea what to say.

When she'd made the decision to suggest marriage to him she'd been prepared to live in a loveless partnership. Any alternative hadn't occurred to her, because although she'd been willing to believe love existed for other people she'd had no evidence to suggest she was capable of it. All she'd wanted was respect and kindness. She'd been ignorant of the impact of sexual attraction and ignorant of the power of love.

But now she knew about both.

And she knew love hurt.

'Do you have to go away, Daddy?'

Raz turned at the sound of his daughter's voice and saw her standing watching him, her expression forlorn. Layla hurried towards her, trying to distract the little girl with the promise of a swim.

Raz noticed she didn't look at him.

It had been two weeks since the party in Zubran, and since their return Layla had been withdrawn and quiet. So quiet he was becoming increasingly concerned.

He made a mental note to talk to her about it immediately on his return.

'I have to go, but it's only for one night.' He scooped Zahra into his arms. 'When I come back we will ride together, I promise.'

As if realising that she should say something, Layla roused herself. 'Where are you going?'

'I have another meeting with the Tazkhan Council—this time to discuss arrangements for formalising my position.'

'So will we be moving to the city?'

It was Zahra who asked the question, but he wondered if that was what was bothering Layla.

'We will live there for some of the time, but not all.' He watched Layla's face but her expression didn't change.

As his security guards made the final preparations around him he drew Layla to one side. 'You are very quiet. Is something worrying you?'

'Nothing. I hope your meeting goes well.'

She was detached and formal and he knew this wasn't the right time to push her. Not with his daughter watching and his security team hovering in the background.

'I will be back tomorrow.' He lifted his hand to her face, intending to kiss her, and then let his hand drop, shocked by the impulse. They were in public, their exchange witnessed by a dozen other people.

Before he could say anything she stepped back. 'Safe trip.'

CHAPTER ELEVEN

LAYLA LAY AWAKE in the bed, sleep chased away by the ache in her chest.

Maybe a heart *could* break.

She'd read about people who lost partners only to die themselves.

Maybe such a thing was possible. Just one more thing she'd been wrong about.

It was almost a relief that Raz was away for a night because she didn't know how to be with him any more. She didn't know how *not* to show him that she loved him, and she didn't know how to stop herself falling harder and deeper.

Unable to sleep, she decided to read for a while and pressed the switch for the light by the bed. Nothing happened. Assuming the bulb had blown, she leaned across and tried the other one. When that didn't work either she pulled on a robe, slid on her shoes and walked out of her bedroom and onto the terrace. Stars twinkled in the sky and everything was quiet.

Too quiet.

Lights should have been burning in the house and outside on the terrace, but everything was in darkness and the fountain was silent. There was no sound of running water, no sounds at all.

It was eerily quiet.

Layla wondered if there had been a power cut and was

about to go back to her room and find a torch when she realised that there were no security guards outside Zahra's room.

Her heart stopped and she ceased to breathe for a few seconds.

No lights. No guards.

Grateful that there was enough moonlight for her to see the way, she walked quickly to Zahra's bedroom, adjacent to hers. There was sufficient light for her to see Isis and Horus curled up on the bed next to the little girl, and for once she was relieved to see them.

Her heart was pounding hard and her hands were clammy, and she stood for a moment, trying to rationalize the situation. The most likely explanation was a blown fuse or some other electrical fault.

Was she overreacting?

Possibly, but all she could hear in her head were Raz's words.

Show me the evidence that my daughter would have been safe.

She didn't have evidence, and she knew better than to underestimate Hassan at any time—least of all now, when he was likely to be at his most desperate.

What if he had somehow discovered that Raz had a daughter?

What if he decided to use that fact?

No matter that she might be overreacting. She couldn't risk letting Raz lose someone else he loved.

'Zahra…' Keeping her voice soft, she reached out a hand towards the sleeping child.

Isis opened one eye and looked at her.

Keeping as far away from the dogs as possible, Layla gave Zahra a gentle shake. 'Wake up. We're going on an adventure.'

Zahra snuggled under the covers. 'It's dark.'

'I know. The dark is going to make it extra exciting. We're going to have fun.'

The child yawned sleepily. 'Where are we going?'

Where? It was a good question.

For a moment Layla's mind blanked, and then she knew exactly what she had to do. Something she'd done many times before. 'We're going to play a game called Hide.' Her mouth dried at the memory, because those games, too, had been played in the dark. Pulling back the covers, she tugged the little girl into her arms, trying desperately not to frighten her. 'We'll just put on your coat in case it gets cold.'

'It's night-time. Why are we playing a game at night-time?'

'That's the best time to play it. I used to play it with my sister when she was your age. There are rules.' She manoeuvred Zahra into the coat. 'First, you mustn't make a sound. Second, you have to do exactly as I say. If I tell you to keep still you have to keep still. If I tell you to run you have to run.'

'This game sounds like fun, but why can't we play it tomorrow?'

Layla caught a flash of light out of the corner of her eye and saw lights approaching in the distance. Torches? Headlights?

Sure now that the threat was real, she cuddled the little girl close. 'Because it's going to be more fun to play it now. We have to go.'

Still sleepy, Zahra glanced back at the bed. 'Can Isis and Horus come too?'

Already halfway to the door, Layla eyed the dogs, watching her from the bed. 'Yes. Good idea. But we have to move quickly.'

Zahra called the dogs and they bounded across the bedroom. 'But who are we hiding from, Layla? What's the point of playing Hide if no one is going to try and find us?'

'We will find a safe place and see how still and silent we

can be. We're going to practise and then, when we're really, really good at it, Daddy can play it with us when he comes home.' Layla knew she was making no sense, and she was so afraid she could hardly make her legs move. Half walking, half running, she kept chatting and pretending it was all a game, trying not to frighten Zahra.

Because she knew now that they were being hunted.

She *felt* it, and the terror rushed over her as familiar and terrifying as it had been when she was a child.

'Zahra, listen to me.' It was a struggle to keep her voice light. 'If you didn't want anyone to find you where would you go? Where is the *best* hiding place around here?'

'Dahl Al Zahki. The Desert Caves.'

Layla had a dim memory of Raz pointing them out to her on a ride earlier in the week. 'Are they close?'

'We can ride there in five minutes.'

Ride.

Layla closed her eyes and faced the inevitable. 'Let's do it.'

'If you really want to be fast we should take Raja.'

'Your father's stallion?'

'I can ride him. You can just hold onto me. I *like* this game.' Zahra was wide awake now and bouncing in her arms. 'I'm glad you woke me up.'

They reached the stables and Layla turned and again saw the flash of lights in the distance. *How long did they have?* 'We'll take Raja. It's a great idea. But how will we find the way?'

'I know the way and so does he. He was born here. My daddy had him from a foal. But you'll have to help me up because he's too big.'

Somehow Layla managed to get both of them on the enormous horse and Zahra giggled.

'His coat feels all warm on my legs. I've never ridden in my nightie before.'

Layla pulled the coat round the child and resisted the temptation to look down. It felt as if her life had come full circle. She'd begun this new chapter by stealing her father's stallion and riding it into the desert, and now she was ending it in a similar way. Only this time she was determined not to fall.

'Go, Zahra. Get us out of here.'

'You've never galloped before.'

'Then it's time I learned and I know you'll be the perfect teacher. Isis—Horus—' she hissed their names '—come.'

The stallion sprang forward, needing no encouragement to unleash all that restrained power. Layla's breath caught and then she was hanging on, trying to remember everything Raz and Abdul had taught her about relaxing into the rhythm.

It was the most terrifying, uncomfortable few minutes of her life, but with each long, pounding stride she knew they were drawing away from whoever was at the other end of the light, so she concentrated on not falling off and let Zahra do the rest.

'We're here.'

They arrived at the caves and Layla slid off the horse, landing with an uncomfortable thud on the uneven ground. Zahra slid into her arms and the dogs stayed close. 'We need to get inside.'

'No. We have to tie Raja up or he could wander off and Daddy will be angry.'

'We'll take him with us deeper into the caves. We need to be out of sight.'

She shone her torch once and saw several tunnels leading off the main cavern. 'Over there—that's a good place to hide.'

'Why are you so good at finding hiding places?'

'Because I used to play this game with my little sister when she was your age.'

But she'd made a cardinal mistake. The horse had provided a quick escape vehicle, but by bringing the animal there was no way they could disguise their presence. 'We have to let Raja loose, Zahra. We *have* to.'

With luck the people tracking them would follow the horse, thinking they were still together.

'No! We can't do that. Daddy will be angry.'

'I'll take the blame. I'll tell him it's all my fault. But we have to let him go.'

'No! I won't let you—'

But Layla had already removed the reins and given the enormous stallion a slap on the rump. Delighted to be free of his reins, Raja launched himself into the darkness while Zahra gave a sob.

'He will hurt himself. He'll—'

'He's going to be fine.' Layla grabbed the child in her arms and sprinted across the cave. Zahra was squirming so badly she almost dropped her.

'But, Layla, he doesn't—'

'Hush.' Layla slammed her hand over the child's mouth and pulled her behind the rocks. 'I can hear someone coming. Don't be frightened, but do not make a sound. Not a sound. Isis—Horus—*down*.' The dogs slunk behind the rock obediently and lay down with them just seconds before lights shone into the cave.

'Don't be scared,' Layla whispered, holding Zahra tightly in her arms. 'I've got you.'

'They cannot both have vanished.'

It was Hassan's voice, speaking the same words he'd spoken the night she'd last seen him. Layla closed her eyes, back in her father's bedroom on the night of his death, only this time the person she was protecting was Raz al Zahki's child.

She hugged Zahra against her, keeping her hand over her mouth as she had done so many times with her sister, and all the time she was wondering how Hassan could possibly have known they were here. How had he even found out about Zahra's existence?

'They have to be here. There is nowhere else they could have hidden.'

Recognising Nadia's voice, Layla felt shock punch through her.

So now she had her answer.

She felt Zahra wriggle and held her tighter, but the sudden movement had dislodged something and sent stones tumbling, the sound magnified by the cavernous walls of their hiding place.

Layla realised she had nothing with which to defend them both. No knife. No weapon of any sort with which to protect Raz's child.

'Stay there, and whatever happens don't move.' Whispering the words, she stood up and moved out from behind the rock just as torchlight swept across the cave and dazzled her eyes.

'It's *her.*' Nadia's voice was thickened with contempt. 'If she's here then the child will be with her.'

'Zahra is asleep in her bed. I left her there when I ran. I assumed it was me you wanted. Well, here I am.' Layla walked forward and saw the glint of Nadia's eyes.

'She's lying. She's never far from the girl because she thinks that's the way to get Raz to love her.'

Before Layla could respond Hassan stepped into the beam of light. She felt a shiver run down her body from neck to toes as she remembered all the occasions he'd stood over her trembling body when she'd run from him as a child.

Determined that Zahra wasn't going to know that same fear, she stood as tall as she could. But he simply smiled.

'The best way to look for something is to hunt it and I know just how to do that.'

He snapped his fingers and before Layla could work out

what he was doing she heard the sound of panting and four Saluki shot into the cave towards her.

Her knees liquid, she stumbled back towards Zahra, determined to protect her, the terror so acute she could hardly walk.

She should have anticipated that he'd use Saluki.

She could hear the dull thud of their paws as they raced across the cave towards her, heard the sharp patter of stones dislodged, the low whine and the panting of the dogs as they drew closer. And then she was on her knees beside Zahra, shielding her, covering her, determined to protect her even if it meant the flesh was torn from her bones.

She braced herself for the feel of hot breath on her neck and then pain, but the growling intensified and Isis and Horus sprang in front of them. And then there was nothing but the most terrifying snarling as the dogs clashed, swirling together in the darkness in some macabre dance that sent dust and fur flying.

'Isis!'

Horrified, Zahra tried to go to them, but Layla held her tightly, wondering helplessly how two dogs could possibly be a match against four. And even if she'd wanted to help she couldn't, because the dogs were wild as they fought each other and she couldn't make out Isis and Horus from Hassan's beasts. The best she could do was take advantage of the distraction.

'Is there another way out of these caves?' She spoke the words urgently but the little girl shook her head.

'Not without ropes.'

It wasn't the news Layla wanted, but just as she was about to carry Zahra deeper into the caves there was the sound of vehicles approaching at speed. The next moment the whole cavern was filled with light and there were shouts and something that sounded like gunfire.

Layla flattened Zahra down on the ground.

The snarling became a whimper.

And then she heard the harsh tones of Raz's voice and knew that the guns and the lights belonged to his security team. Almost melting with relief that she was no longer alone, she snuggled Zahra close, afraid to move until she was sure it was safe.

All around them was pandemonium. Layla kept low, knowing that the best thing she could do was not make the situation more dangerous by moving around.

'Layla? *Layla!*' His voice was raw and desperate, the emotion painful to hear, and she knew she had to reassure him.

'It's fine,' she called out. 'She's safe. She's here with me. They haven't touched her.'

Before she could stop her Zahra wriggled out from under her and started to run towards her father, but then she stopped dead.

'Isis? *Isis!*'

Layla saw that the dog was lying still, her blonde fur coated in blood, while Horus stood guard over her body, a sombre sentinel.

'Oh, no—' Layla ran towards Zahra but the little girl was already on her knees beside the dog, sobs tearing through her chest as she tried to cuddle her.

'Don't die, Isis. Daddy, don't let Isis die. Please *do something.*' She scooped the dog's head onto her lap, stroking, rocking, making a terrible keening sound.

Her distress was so painful to witness Layla felt tears on her own cheeks. She reached the child at the same time as Raz.

'Let me look at her.'

His voice was calm and steady, but Layla noticed that his fingers shook slightly as he gently examined the dog. He snapped a command over his shoulder and someone appeared with a flashlight so that he could take a closer look.

'She's been bitten. We need to stop this bleeding.'

'Here—' Layla ripped off the cord that was holding her robe together and dropped to her knees beside him. 'Make a tourniquet. That should do until we can get her back home.'

Her hands were over his and together they tied it firmly and then tightened it. It was the first time she'd touched a dog voluntarily, but she didn't even think about it until she felt something cold and damp nudge her palm and saw Horus standing next to her, looking at her with anxious eyes.

'Good boy.' Layla hesitated and then reached out and stroked his head. 'She's going to be all right.'

'No, she isn't. They saved us from that bad man,' Zahra sobbed, 'and now Isis is going to die.'

'She is *not* going to die.' Delivering a series of orders, Raz rose to his feet in a fluid movement and peeled his daughter away from her beloved pet. 'But we have to get her help, *habibti*. We have to get her home right now. And you need to come home, too. You need to be brave and put your trust in others.'

Zahra clung to him, her little body shuddering with sobs, and Layla rubbed the tears from her own cheeks so that she could help as Raz's men gently lifted Isis and took her limp body to the nearest vehicle, accompanied by a worried Horus who refused to leave her side.

Layla turned to Raz. 'Where is Hassan?'

'He has been arrested, along with Nadia, who apparently masterminded tonight's episode. They are both being taken to Tazkhan for questioning.'

Layla stared at him, still stunned by the discovery that Nadia had been involved. 'I assumed Hassan had forced her in some way. Why would she do that?'

'Jealousy.' Raz's mouth was grim. 'She was jealous of her sister. Apparently she had some deluded idea that I'd marry *her*. It is something I only discovered in the past few hours.

It explains so much about her behaviour and I am angry with myself for not seeing it sooner.'

'Why would you?' Layla shivered and rubbed Zahra's back gently. 'We need to get her home.'

His gaze lingered on hers. 'How can I ever thank you?'

'You don't need to thank me.'

Raz inhaled deeply. 'There is much I need to say to you.'

Layla was too exhausted to contemplate a conversation. 'It can all wait.'

'The vet says Isis will make a good recovery and Zahra is finally asleep.' His handsome face drawn and tired, Raz walked across the bedroom. 'I have put a mattress next to the dog and both Abdul and Horus are sleeping with her for now, along with four of my security team. It's like a menagerie down there. All I need is for Raja to join them and the circus that is our life will be complete.'

The fact that he'd said 'our' warmed her, as did the wry humour in his voice, but Layla wasn't fooled. She knew how raw he was feeling because she felt the same way. She was still so shocked by everything that had happened she felt disconnected.

The warm sunshine and the soothing sound of the fountain in the courtyard beyond the doors to their bedroom were a contrast to the long, terrifying hours of the night before.

Knowing that she wouldn't be able to rest, she'd taken a hot shower, scrubbed away the physical evidence of their flight through the desert and changed into a practical outfit of trousers and a loose shirt, intending to go and sit with Isis and Zahra.

'I'm so relieved Raja is all right. Zahra was beside herself when I turned him loose, but at that point I was still hoping they wouldn't find us. I'm sorry. I didn't know what else to do.'

'You did the right thing. I still can't believe you rode my

stallion.' Raz shook his head and looked at her in naked disbelief. 'How did you do that?'

'I didn't. I just sat on him. It was Zahra who rode him. It's a good thing she takes after you.'

There was a glint of anger in his eyes. 'They arranged for me to be away last night. They arranged for you to be alone. If you hadn't woken—' He raked his hand through his hair, visibly tense. 'Why did you? Did you hear something? Did they disturb you?'

'No. I wasn't asleep.' She didn't tell him she'd been lying there thinking about him. 'I turned the light on to read and nothing happened. At first I thought it was the bulb and then I realised the whole place was dark and there were no guards. Just like that night—' Realisation dawned and she felt the colour drain from her face. 'Just like that night in the desert a few weeks ago.'

'Yes. That was to have been their first attempt to take my daughter and use her as leverage against me, but you foiled that one, too, by climbing into bed with her. They didn't anticipate that. They weren't prepared for the two of you. But this time they were.'

'How did you find out?'

'I arrived in Tazkhan and had an illuminating conversation with the senior council members, all of whom were surprised by my arrival. As soon as I realised what had happened I returned as quickly as I could, but I was terrified I was going to be too late.' He pulled her into his arms. 'You were so brave. You took my daughter into the desert and you took the dogs with you, and I know how much you fear them.'

'Not any more. I took them because I thought they might protect Zahra and they did. They were unbelievably brave.' She shivered as she relived those awful moments. 'I didn't know how two could possibly win a fight against four, but now I do. Isis and Horus love her so much they would have died for her, and that love gave them ten times the strength of Hassan's dogs. I've never seen anything like it.' Remembering moved her so much that tears sprang into her eyes and spilled onto her cheeks. 'Sorry—I think I'm just very tired.' Embarrassed by her loss of control, she lifted her hand to brush them away, but he was there before her, his fingers gentle as he stroked away her tears.

'You must be exhausted, and *so* stressed after everything that has happened.'

'I'm just relieved. And worried about poor Isis.'

'I am assured by the vet that she is going to be fine. And, on the subject of being fine, I have good news about your sister. Salem contacted me half an hour ago, when we were with Isis. He has Yasmin safe.'

'Really?' The tears still flowed and Layla wondered what on earth the matter was with her that she couldn't get through five minutes without crying. 'You're sure? It's really her?'

'Salem says he has never met a woman who talks as much as she does.'

'Then it's *definitely* her.' Layla was laughing with relief and happiness as she hugged Raz. 'Thank you. You were right to have faith in your brother.'

'So now we have your sister safe, Hassan and Nadia off the scene and Isis recovering, perhaps we can finally focus on our own relationship, *habibti*. There are things I must say to you.'

Not now.

She kept her face pressed to his chest so that he couldn't see the change in her expression. She couldn't cope with any more trauma in one night. *Couldn't cope with hearing him tell her again that he couldn't ever love another woman.*

'There is nothing to say. And we ought to check on Zahra—'

'Zahra is fine for the moment.' He eased her away from him so that she was forced to look at him. 'I have never felt fear as I felt it tonight.'

Hearing the change in his voice, Layla pushed down her own feelings. It was selfish of her to think of herself when he was also in shock. 'It must have been terrible for you, being so afraid for your daughter.'

'I wasn't only afraid for my daughter.' He took her face in his hands and the expression in his eyes made her catch her breath.

'Raz—'

'*Don't* speak.' He covered her mouth with his fingers. 'There are things I have to say and I need to say them without interruption. I owe you an apology.' His words thickened. 'You came to me that night in the desert and I was cold, distant and uncaring. I was *so* hard on you and it shames me to remember it.'

'It shouldn't. I thought your behaviour was very restrained in the circumstances.'

'I should have asked more questions that night. I should have suspected that you had suffered great trauma. But I looked no deeper than the surface and I cannot forgive myself for that.'

'I probably wouldn't have told you even had you asked,' Layla mumbled. 'And you behaved very decently towards me, given everything my family has done to yours.'

'I pride myself on being fair and treating everyone as an individual. You are not responsible for the sins of your family.'

'But you didn't know that. Given everything that had happened, you would have been less than human had you not had reservations about me. You were protecting your family and you would not be the man you are had you not done that. It's one of the things I love about you.' The words slipped out without thought and she saw his eyes darken. 'Respect and admire you,' she said quickly. 'I meant that it is one of the things I respect and admire about you.'

'*Is* that what you meant?'

'Yes.' Trapped, she averted her head, but he caught her chin in his fingers and gently forced her to look at him. 'Raz—'

'You were the one who insisted on honesty in this relationship. You've never been afraid to tell me the truth before. You weren't afraid to tell me I was wrong to trust Nadia and that I shouldn't have kept my daughter's existence a secret from you. You weren't afraid to ask about Nisa, even though most people dare not broach that subject with me. Why would you be afraid to tell me the truth about your feelings?'

Why? Because she wasn't sure she could handle his response.

'Feelings were never part of the deal when we married.'

'That is true. But life does not stand still—as we have both discovered. People change. Feelings change. Pain we believe we cannot endure we somehow learn to live alongside. Although I am pleased to have your respect and your admiration, I would so much rather have the first thing you were offering, *habibti.*' His voice husky, he looked down into her eyes. 'Tell me why you were awake last night. The truth.'

'I couldn't sleep.'

'*Why* couldn't you sleep?'

It was clear he wasn't going to let it drop so Layla gave up, too wrung out to keep fighting him.

'Because I missed you. Because I *love* you—' It was a surprising relief to say it. A relief to finally acknowledge the emotions she'd been holding back. 'I love you. I didn't expect to, I didn't think I could, but I do. And I wouldn't have told you except that you forced the subject, and I hope it doesn't make things awkward because it really shouldn't.'

'Why would it make things awkward?'

Wasn't it obvious?

'Because I know you're not capable of loving another woman. Our marriage was driven by political necessity. We both know that.'

'It is true that it began that way, but sometimes it is less important how something begins, *habibti*, than how it ends.'

Ends?

It was shocking how quickly happiness could turn to misery. 'You want to end it?'

'No! I do *not* want to end it. Not ever. I'm trying to tell you that things have changed. Everything has changed. Including my feelings.' His tone raw, he hauled her against him. 'This is the most important conversation of my life and I'm making a mess of it. I'm *trying* to tell you I love you, too.'

Layla was pressed against him and she could feel the strong thud of his heart against her cheek.

His heart not frozen into ice but warm, healthy and capable of love.

Heat spread through her, driving away the chill that had been part of her since her flight through the desert.

Raz eased her away from him so that he could see her face. 'I loved Nisa. That is a fact and it will never change. We met as children—grew up together.' He frowned slightly, as if he'd never thought much about it before. 'She was always part of my life. I don't even remember either one of us making the decision to marry—it felt inevitable. And then when I lost her—'

Layla slid her arms round him, feeling his pain as her own. 'You honestly don't have to talk about this.'

'I want to. Since I met you it's been easier to talk about it. I was trapped in my old life, clinging to memories because moving on without her felt too hard. And then I met you.'

'That first night—'

'I felt guilty.' His voice was soft. 'It felt like a betrayal. Not just because I was with you, but because that night was so special. I didn't anticipate that what we shared would be so powerful. I rejected it precisely because the chemistry between us was so intense, *habibti*. I'd expected to feel nothing. Instead I felt deeply, and I didn't know how to handle those feelings.'

'I didn't expect you to love me. I didn't expect to love *you*,' Layla confessed honestly. 'I've never loved anyone except my sister. I've never looked at a man and felt anything until that night I met you for the first time. I'd never met a man like you. I'd never met a man who used his strength and power for good rather than personal gain.'

'You were so brave, arriving with nothing but two books.'

His eyes gleamed and she felt the colour darken her cheeks.

'You've taught me everything. It would have been nice to bring something to this marriage and teach you something in return.'

'You have.' Lifting his hand, he touched her cheek. 'You've taught me that life does not stand still. That love can come from unexpected places. That there is always hope. And you've taught me to love again, *habibti*. When you came to me I was so closed off. I couldn't even think about allowing another woman into my life. But instead of putting on pressure you just accepted me as I was and didn't try and change that.'

'I wouldn't want to change it. I know you loved Nisa.'

'Yes, but I've learned that loving you doesn't diminish what I felt for her. It took me a while to accept my feelings for you without guilt. She was part of my past, but you are my future. I consider myself fortunate to have fallen in love twice in a lifetime when many do not ever find themselves in possession of that gift.'

Layla swallowed. 'I didn't think I would. I didn't grow up with expectations of love and happy endings. It just wasn't what I thought about. When I came to you in the desert that night I wasn't thinking about love. All I wanted from this marriage was your respect. I used you as an escape from the life I had and because I knew that without me Hassan could not rule, and he is not a man who should be in a position of power. I didn't expect anything else. I didn't expect you to notice so much about me and be so caring. You think you were hard on me, but there were so many times when you tried to make life easier for me. You noticed I was scared of the dogs and tried to keep them away from me—' She choked slightly. 'No one has ever done anything like that for me before. No one has *ever* wanted to protect me.'

'I never cease to be impressed by your determination to confront everything you fear. Particularly riding my stallion!'

'He was remarkably tolerant. I wonder if he somehow knew he was part of our escape.' Layla gave a half smile. 'And Isis and Horus came too.'

'All your nightmares in one evening,' Raz said dryly, but his hand was gentle as he stroked her cheek. 'You are an example to all of us, *habibti*.

'My biggest nightmare was that something might happen to Zahra. I love her, too. She is so confident and trusting, and I hated the thought of that confidence and trust being crushed.'

'She told me you turned the whole thing into a game so that she wouldn't be scared.' He hesitated. 'When I saw her a moment ago she asked me if she is allowed to call you Mummy.'

'Oh—' Emotion wedged itself in her throat. 'But you—'

'One of the biggest sources of my guilt—and believe me there are many—is the fact that I told you not to think of yourself as my daughter's mother.' His handsome face was paler than usual. 'It was a terrible thing to say. I hope you will forgive me.'

'There's nothing to forgive. You were in the most awful situation, being forced to marry me and—' Layla broke off, her vision blurred by tears. 'Do you know what I think? I think I like what you said just now, about separating the past and the future. Can we do that? And if Zahra is thinking of me as her mother then the future is looking better all the time.'

He hauled her close. 'I didn't think I would ever feel this happy. I didn't think it was possible.'

'Me neither.' She hugged him tightly, feeling happier than she ever had in her life before. 'I love you. I love you so much.'

Raz slid his hand into her hair, his mouth close to hers. 'I will never tire of hearing you say that.'

'It was Avery who noticed the way I felt about you.'

The corners of his mouth flickered into a smile. 'Avery is a master at interfering in the lives of others.'

'But in a good way. She was the one who encouraged me to just be myself. I was very confused. I knew I loved you and I didn't know how to live with those feelings without sharing them with you. I didn't know how to be with you. She was the one who pointed out that I should be myself. Just me. That you deserved to know the real me.'

'And I fell in love with the real you.'

Raz lowered his forehead to hers and she slid her arms around his neck, dizzy with the feelings inside her.

'Could you say that again? Just one more time? I need to keep hearing it.'

'I will be saying it many times. I love you. I will love you forever and always,' he breathed, gathering her against him. '*Enti hayati*. You are my life, *habibti*.'

* * * * *

SHEIKH IN THE CITY
JACKIE BRAUN

Jackie Braun is a three-time RITA® Award finalist, a four-time National Readers' Choice Award finalist, and a past winner of the Rising Star Award. She worked for nearly two decades as an award-winning journalist, before leaving her full-time job to write fiction. She lives in mid-Michigan with her husband and their two sons. She loves to hear from readers and can be reached through her website at www.jackiebraun.com.

'Emily Merit gets her man in the end, but I still feel bad for saddling her with such a horrid younger sibling. If I'd treated my three older sisters a tenth as rotten, I wouldn't have survived childhood.'
—**Jackie Braun**

CHAPTER ONE

"I THINK I've finally figured out who the guest of honor is," Arlene Williams said from the kitchen door, where she was peeking into the Hendersons' well-appointed dining room.

Babs and Denby Henderson regularly entertained powerful lawmakers, renowned academics, award-winning playwrights and European nobility at their Park Avenue soirées. Emily Merit, who'd been their caterer of choice for the past five years, didn't doubt tonight's guest of honor was any less impressive.

"Well, don't keep me in suspense," she replied, tongue-in-cheek, as she plated the evening's desserts.

Her sous chef shot her a black look before saying, "I think he might be the hunky model in those underwear ads."

Emily glanced up at that. "The ones that are plastered all over the city's bus stops and subway stations?"

"And you claim to have sworn off men." Arlene grinned.

"I have, but those ads are impossible to miss."

Arlene peeked out again and her tone turned thoughtful. "Or he could be the actor who plays the CIA operative on *Restless Nights*. They both have that same sensual mouth."

Emily rolled her eyes. Where she'd sworn off men, she couldn't keep track of the number of guys Arlene had drooled over in the past month alone. "Get away from the door already and give me a hand with dessert."

"Uh-oh. He's…he's coming this way."

Emily frowned. Great. Just what she needed, an audience. She didn't like people in her kitchen when she worked, especially if they were only coming in to flirt with her assistant. Technically this wasn't Emily's kitchen, but the same principle applied.

"He's with Mrs. Henderson," Arlene added and let the door swing fully closed.

Emily relaxed a little upon hearing that. She figured she knew why they were coming to the kitchen. She'd met Babs five years earlier through her then-boyfriend, Reed, who had a business relationship with Bab's husband, Denby. One day when a catering company left the Hendersons in the lurch just hours before a dinner party, Reed had volunteered Emily's services. At the time, she was just out of culinary school and her only catering jobs had been casual gatherings for family and friends. She'd been scared to death, to put it mildly. But her cooking that evening was a huge hit, and the Hendersons proved to be the launching pad for her career.

As a client, Babs could be flighty and trying, but she knew lots of people whose pockets were every bit as deep as her own and—bless her—she'd made it her mission to introduce them to Emily. Thanks in part to the Henderson's patronage Emily had been able to renovate the kitchen in her otherwise modest East Village apartment without dipping into her savings for the restaurant she dreamed of opening one day.

The older woman was probably bringing her guest in for an introduction. In Emily's book the title of potential client was more important than what he did for a living, even if he really was the hunky model with the ripped abs and buff biceps in those underwear ads.

Arlene hoisted the tray of desserts, leaving the kitchen just before Babs swept in with the mystery man. The older woman wore vintage Dior and was doused in her usual Chanel. Her high-piled hair prevented Emily from getting a good look at Mr. Hunky.

"Emily, my dear, you outdid yourself this evening," Babs proclaimed in her usual dramatic fashion. Her smile sparkled as brightly as the large diamond pendant hanging low in her décolletage. "All of my guests are raving about the herb-crusted salmon." She turned and tucked her hand into the crook of the man's arm then, drawing him to her side. "And that includes my very special guest, Sh—"

"Please, call me Dan," he inserted.

He wasn't the underwear model, but Emily's mouth dropped open anyway. She couldn't fault her assistant for standing at the door half the evening gawking. God, he was gorgeous. Drop-dead so. The monosyllabic name, however, didn't suit him. It was too simple, too... Western.

Which was why she frowned and said, "Dan?"

"It is what you would call a nickname." His words were adorned with an accent she couldn't quite place, but its effect was potent. It had her hormones threatening to snap and sizzle like vegetables sautéing in hot oil. It bothered her that she wasn't completely immune. She wanted to be. God knew, after what had happened with Reed, she should be.

The man was saying, "I find that when I travel in your country it is easier for some people to pronounce than my given name."

That made sense, she supposed. Still, he didn't look like a Dan. Nor did he resemble the underwear model Arlene mistook him for, though he certainly had the body for it. He was tall with a lean, athletic build that accentuated the clean lines of the expertly tailored suit he wore. His face, however, was more angular and masculine than the male model in question, and slashes of dark brow set off a pair of enigmatic brown eyes. His hair was the color of onyx and cut short enough to be respectable, but still long enough to make a woman's fingers itch to weave through it.

She stretched out her hand, but only to shake his. "I'm Emily Merit."

His palm was warm against hers, his grasp light but

not as condescendingly loose as some men's could be. She found it easier to concentrate on his grip than the bizarre reaction her body was having to the benign contact. It now felt as if her sizzling hormones had been placed under the broiler.

When the handshake ended, Emily smoothed down the front of her mannish chef coat. Normally she wasn't vain, but his physical perfection made her painfully aware that her hair was pulled back in a severe, net-covered chignon and what little makeup she'd applied that morning most likely had worn off.

Babs spoke up then. "As I told you earlier, *Dan,* Mr. Henderson and I wouldn't dream of letting anyone else cater our gatherings. As far as we're concerned, she's the best in Manhattan."

Dan nodded and offered a smile that was every bit as warm as his hand had been. Forget broiler, her temperature was reaching kiln status. "Then I must have her."

Was he aware of the double entendre? His bland expression made it difficult to be sure. Emily certainly was. Before she could stop herself, she sputtered ridiculously, "But I...I don't even know your last name."

"Allow me to remedy that. It's Tarim." His expression was no longer bland. The corners of his mouth turned up and laughter lit his dark eyes. He was amused. Definitely.

Emily wasn't since it came at her expense. God, what was wrong with her? This was completely out of character, not to mention unprofessional. Though it shouldn't have been necessary, she reminded herself that she was a respected and sought-after chef who had graduated from one of the country's best culinary schools. She wasn't some silly schoolgirl conversing with the football team's star quarterback.

Babs cleared her throat. "Well, if the two of you will excuse me, I should get back to the party. Promise me you won't keep him occupied for too long, Emily. My other guests are eager to spend more time with him."

"I'll shoo him out as soon as possible," she said with a tight smile. She meant it, too. She planned to get down to business and then usher him out. As soon as they were alone, she said, "So, what can I do for you, Mr. Tarim?"

"Dan, please. And may I call you Emily?"

"By all means." Her name, which she'd always considered plain and old-fashioned, sounded almost exotic when he said it.

"I'm planning a small dinner party before I leave Manhattan. I would like to repay the generosity of those who have hosted me during my stay."

"Is this your first time in the city?" she inquired politely, even as she sneaked a glance at her watch.

"No. I am here several times a year for business purposes mainly. In the past, I've used the services of someone else to cater my parties, but the meal you prepared tonight has caused me to change my mind."

"Thank you. I'm flattered."

And she was. His clothes screamed expensive, which meant he could afford to hire any catering company he wanted. She wondered which one he'd used, though she didn't ask him. She'd discreetly inquire later. It was good to know who her competition was. Good for business and, depending on the caterer, good for her ego. For the past several years, she had slaved and sacrificed to build a client base and solidify her reputation for high quality. Knowing that those efforts had paid off also made it easier to accept their high cost to her personal life.

She thought of Reed then. They'd dated six years. Everyone, including Emily, had assumed they would wed eventually. Looking back now, though, she could see the cracks that had only gotten deeper and wider as she'd pursued her dreams. When catering had been a hobby or merely a part-time job, he'd seemed proud of her. When it turned into a real career, pulling in serious money and creating enough buzz to land Emily a mention in The *New York Times*, his enthusiasm had cooled considerably. When she began to dream about opening a restaurant, he'd done his best to talk her out of it, quoting statistics on the number of establishments that failed each year. Finally he'd found someone else: Emily's sister.

"The guest list will be small, no more than six guests and myself," Dan was saying, pulling Emily back to the present.

"When were you thinking?" she asked, mentally flipping through her appointment calendar.

"The Saturday after next. The notice is short, I know."

His expression held an apology. "As I said, I usually hire someone else to handle my dinner parties. But I'm hoping you will find room in your schedule for me. As my gracious hostess said, you *are* the best."

His lips twitched charmingly, but this time, immersed in the details of business, she was able to ignore the pyre of heat.

Dan, also known as Sheikh Madani Abdul Tarim, wasn't one to settle for anything but the best. Thanks to his position and wealth, he'd never had to. Still, he didn't consider himself demanding so much as discerning. Tonight's meal was first-rate. He had to admit, though, he hadn't expected the chef who'd created it to be quite so young.

Or so attractive.

Even wearing mannish attire and with her hair scraped back in that hideous fashion there was no denying the tug of male interest he felt. Of course, he wouldn't act on it. With the official announcement of his engagement fast approaching, he wasn't in the market for a relationship, casual or otherwise. Still, Emily Merit almost made him wish his future hadn't been decided when he was still a toddler.

He blamed it on her eyes. They were a rich combination of blues and greens, and reminded him of the Mediterranean Sea near his family's summer home. Her gaze was direct and assessing, making it clear that she considered herself his equal.

He liked that. As it was, his title and position intimidated too many people—male and female. Perhaps that was why he hadn't allowed the hostess to formally introduce him. And why he had decided to tell Emily Merit his name was merely Dan. He preferred anonymity every now and then, if only to keep himself grounded. As his father often told him, when he became ruler of Kashaqra, Madani would need to look out for the interests of all of the country's people.

That didn't mean he didn't prefer to get his way. So, he prodded, "Well?"

"Unfortunately I'm booked to make the meal and cake for a child's fifth birthday celebration that day."

It didn't seem like a huge obligation to him. "Will it take all day?"

"In most instances, it wouldn't." Her tone turned wry. "But this particular party is an hour outside the city in Connecticut and the parents are insisting on an epicurean feast."

"You don't agree with their menu choices," he gathered.

She sobered and said diplomatically, "It's not my place to agree or disagree with a client's menu choices."

"But?" Raising his eyebrows he invited her confidence.

After a moment she admitted, "I just don't think the average kindergartner will enjoy what they have selected. After all, certain foods are considered an *acquired* taste for good reason."

Madani found himself chuckling, charmed by her honesty. "What have they ordered? Caviar blintzes?"

"Close." She smiled and he spied a dimple lurking low on her right cheek. It lent an air of impishness to her otherwise classical features. "At least I managed to talk the mother out of an appetizer of duck liver pâté in favor of ham rolls. Even so, I'm pretty sure there are going to be plenty of leftovers. She wouldn't budge on the veal marsala or the side of roasted root vegetables."

"I guess this means you won't be available."

She nibbled her lower lip. The gesture was uncomfortably and unaccountably sexy. "I may be able to accommodate you," she said at last. "I have an assistant I could leave in charge of the birthday party. Of course, a lot depends on the time of your gathering and what you would like to serve."

Madani wasn't sure if his relief came from knowing Emily would be preparing the meal for his guests or from knowing he would have the opportunity to see her again. "I can be very amenable when the situation calls for it. When shall we meet to discuss the details?"

"I'm free tomorrow morning if you are."

He had three meetings lined up back-to-back before noon, but he nodded anyway. As he'd said, he could be amenable when the situation called for it. This one did, though he refused to explore why he felt that way.

Emily went to retrieve a business card. Handing it to him, she said, "I'm an early riser. Feel free to call any time after nine o'clock."

The card was still in Madani's hand and a smile on his face when he met his driver downstairs.

"I trust you had a good evening," Azeem Harrah said.

Azeem was not only Madani's driver, but a trusted confidant and sometimes bodyguard who traveled with him whenever he went abroad. The two men had been friends since boyhood. Azeem's father was a long-serving member of Kashaqra's parliament. His uncle sat on the country's high court. He was educated and at times outspoken, but above all he was loyal—to Madani and to Kashaqra.

"Very good. The Hendersons are generous hosts and the food was…exquisite." His smile broadened.

"I know that smile." Azeem laughed as he shifted the Mercedes into Drive and eased the vehicle into traffic. "A woman is behind it."

Madani grew serious. "You are mistaken, my friend."

"Am I?"

"Those days are over."

"Why?" Azeem challenged.

"You know why, even if you do not agree with my decision," he said.

"That is because it was *not* your decision," Azeem shot back. "I cannot believe you are going through with an arranged marriage. You!"

In Kashaqra, Madani was known for holding much more progressive views than his father, even though during the past three decades Sheikh Adil Hammad Tarim had ushered in much change.

"You know my reasons."

"Your father's health is fine, *sadiqi*," Azeem said,

using the Arabic word for friend. "The heart attack he suffered last fall was mild."

It hadn't seemed mild at the time. Madani closed his eyes, recalling anew the way his father's face had turned ashen just before he'd crumpled to the floor. They'd been arguing over this very matter. Arranged marriages were not set in stone. They could be nullified under a limited set of circumstances, none of which applied to Madani. Still, given Adil's position, he could have voided it, but his father wouldn't hear of it. His own union had been contracted and all had turned out well. He believed the same would hold true for his son.

"My engagement to Nawar is his wish, his will."

Azeem shook his head. He didn't understand. Madani didn't expect him to.

"Well, you are not engaged yet. There would be nothing wrong with a final...*fling,* I believe is the word the Americans use."

Madani gazed out the car's tinted window and let the conversation lapse. He wasn't officially engaged. That much was true. His betrothal to Nawar would be announced later in the summer. But he was not free. Indeed, in this regard, he never had been.

Emily arrived home just before midnight. She felt exhausted and invigorated at the same time. In addition to the enigmatic Dan, two other guests of the Hendersons' party had requested her business cards tonight. As it was, the Hendersons had paid her generously, per usual.

Of course, she'd had to hire a couple of extra hands to pull off the meal and serving, but deducting for expenses, wages and other incidentals, she still had a decent sum to deposit into her savings account come Monday morning.

It took her three trips to cart everything from the catering van to her fourth-floor apartment from which she also ran her business. Then she had to move the van to her spot at a paid lot half a block away. Once in her apartment she wanted to collapse on the couch, but she spent another twenty minutes putting away chafing dishes, serving utensils and other items before she finally propped her aching feet atop the coffee table in what passed for a living room.

The stack of mail cushioning her heels drew her attention. She hadn't had time for more than a cursory glance at the envelopes before leaving for the Hendersons that afternoon. Most contained bills. A few were junk mail. Only one was personal and would require a response. She pulled her feet to the floor and sifted through the pile until she found it. Even without opening the thick envelope she knew what was inside: an invitation to her younger sister's wedding.

On an oath, she ripped back the flap and pulled out a square of ivory vellum. The quality of the paper and the engraved lettering had cost their parents a fortune, but then nothing was ever too good for Elle.

Emily's younger sister could do no wrong. Even the fact that she was engaged to marry Emily's ex-boyfriend, who had not yet been an ex when Elle first began seeing him, elicited no censure from their parents. Rather, Emily had been called on to be more "understanding" and, later, to be "happy" that her flighty baby sibling was finally settling down.

Elle Lauren Merit and Reed David Benedict, together with their parents, request the honor of your presence at their wedding...

Emily got no further than that before crumpling the invitation in her hand. Out of respect for the tree that had been chopped down to produce the paper, she decided to toss it in the recycling bin rather than the garbage. But she had no intention of *honoring* Elle and Reed with her presence as they exchanged I Dos, any more than she planned to give in to her mother's urging that she don a bridesmaid gown and join the wedding party.

It wasn't that Emily couldn't forgive them. She wanted to believe she was bigger than that despite their monumental betrayal. No, it was the fact that neither of them had ever so much as acknowledged the pain they'd caused her or offered an apology of any sort. Quite the opposite. Elle had manipulated her illicit affair with her older sister's longtime beau into proof positive that true love could not be denied.

"It's destiny, Em. The answer to my prayers. Reed and I were made for one another," she'd had the gall to claim. As if Emily was supposed to feel so much better knowing her sister had been hot for her boyfriend from the very beginning.

Reed had been neither romantic nor idyllic. Rather, he shifted the blame for his infidelity squarely to Emily.

"If you weren't always so busy catering parties you might have noticed how unhappy I was," he'd told her when she'd learned of the affair.

His remark had landed like a sucker punch. "I have a business, Reed." A business he'd been only too happy to help her create and grow when it had been convenient for him.

"Don't remind me." He'd snorted in disgust. "You're very much in demand these days."

"Am I supposed to apologize for being successful?"

"No, but you shouldn't act so surprised that with so much free time on my hands I found someone else."

"That someone else is my sister!" she'd shouted.

He'd merely shrugged. "Elle understands me. She's not interested in having a demanding career and working long hours. She wants to be supportive of me so that I can advance in mine."

Gaping at him, Emily wondered if Reed had always been so chauvinistic or if her growing success had brought it out. Regardless, his attitude had her blood boiling.

"So, women can't have a demanding job or pursue their dreams without expecting the men they're involved with to stray. Is that what you're saying?"

"I'm saying no man wants to place second to a woman's ambitions."

While Reed clearly felt a woman should be thrilled to place second to a man's, his parting shot contained enough truth that Emily had decided if she was only entitled to one true love, it was safer for her heart to choose cooking.

Sighing now, Emily rose and, peeling off her stained chef's coat, headed in the direction of the bedroom that, a year ago—a lifetime ago—she'd shared with the man who would soon make her sister his wife.

CHAPTER TWO

EVEN though she had retired late, Emily rose just before eight o'clock, as was her practice. She was a morning person, even though these days her career often demanded late nights. Caffeine—and lots of it—helped her stay on her feet.

Her East Village apartment measured barely seven hundred square feet and offered an uninspiring view of the alley from its two hazy, south-facing windows. In addition to the one small bedroom where she'd passed the night, it contained a hopelessly outdated bathroom and a cramped living room that doubled as her business office. Its kitchen, however, was a work of art.

When she and Reed had moved in a few years earlier, splitting the down payment and monthly expenses, the kitchen had been horrendous while the other rooms hadn't been quite as space-challenged. The major renovation she'd treated herself to after he'd packed up his belongings and gone was responsible for that. As far as trades went, Emily figured she'd come out way ahead.

Gone was the galley that had barely allowed room for an under-counter refrigerator and persnickety electric stove. A wall had been knocked out, new wiring and plumbing installed. The new kitchen, which took up the space of the other three rooms combined, had a multi-burner gas cooktop, double ovens and a commercial grade refrigerator. It also offered plenty of counter space for food preparation and ample storage for her extensive collection of pots, pans, gadgets and appliances.

At this point in Emily's life, her surroundings reflected her priorities perfectly, and she would make no apologies for that.

One of the perks of working from home was that her morning commute could be accomplished in a dozen steps while wearing her pajamas. Emily was seated at her computer, tweaking the ingredients in a recipe for roast duck, when she heard a knock at the door. A glance through the peephole had her cursing.

It was Dan.

He appeared freshly shaved and was wearing a tie. Despite the limited view, she was sure he looked every bit as polished and sophisticated as he had when she'd met him at the Hendersons' the evening before. Meanwhile, she was clad in wrinkled drawstring pants and a snug white T-shirt that couldn't camouflage the fact that she wasn't wearing a bra. God only knew what her hair was doing.

To think she'd been concerned about her appearance last night! When she'd told him to call, she should have been more clear that she meant on the phone. And why, she wondered now, had she ever thought it a good idea to put her address on her business card?

Emily debated not answering his knock. She could get his number from Babs and contact him later in the day. But what if she couldn't? What if she failed to reach him and he decided not to hire her despite the interest he'd expressed the prior evening?

Okay, she had an overactive imagination, but this much she knew: It never paid to be rude to a client.

So, after running her fingers through her hair in the hope of taming it, she flipped the dead bolt and un latched the security chain. As she opened the door, she maneuvered her body behind it, using it as a shield so that only her head and one shoulder were visible. Pasting a bright smile on her face, she offered a greeting.

"Dan. Hello. This is a surprise."

"Good morning." His voice was as rich as the freshly ground roasted Kona beans in her coffeemaker, but his engaging expression faltered almost immediately. "You weren't expecting me."

"No." She let out a self-conscious laugh. "Or is that yes?" When his frown deepened she clarified, "You're right. I wasn't expecting you. Sorry."

"But I thought we had agreed to this morning? I believe you said I could call on you any time after nine."

"Yes." She coughed delicately. *"Call."*

He closed his eyes, grimaced. "You expected me to

telephone. My profuse apologies for the intrusion. I will *telephone* you later."

He dipped his head and stepped backward. She doubted he often found himself lost in translation, even if English wasn't his first language. His show of embarrassment helped to chase away some of Emily's. As he turned to leave, she put a hand on his arm to stop him.

"Don't go. You're here now and I'm free. Just give me a few minutes to dress."

Despite the invitation, he hesitated at the threshold. "Are you certain? We can reschedule our meeting. I have no wish to inconvenience you."

A man who didn't wish to inconvenience her. *Are you married?* The ridiculous question wanted to slip from her lips. Instead Emily waved her free hand and said, "Nonsense. Please, come in."

Modesty, however, had her turning away without waiting to see if Dan actually did so. Even before she heard the apartment door close, she was in her bedroom, a battered oak six-panel between them as she rooted through the contents of her jammed closet for something presentable to wear.

As the eldest child and only son of his country's ruler, as well as the president of what was becoming a thriving export business, Madani often traveled to the United States from his native Kashaqra. Thanks in part to his schooling, first at Harvard and later Oxford, he was fluent in seven languages, one of them English. When he'd told Emily Merit he would call in the morning, he should have been clearer. But he hadn't figured it would matter one way or another. How was he to know that the address listed on her business card was her home? Or that she would answer the door in her nightclothes looking sexy and sleep tousled?

As it was, when he'd awoken that morning she'd been on his mind. Now, after watching thin cotton cling to her curves while she'd hustled away, he had the uncomfortable feeling she was going to be a blight on his concentration for the entire day.

He should go. Blaming curiosity, he stepped inside the apartment instead.

The small living room opened into a surprisingly large kitchen. It was a chef's dream, he supposed, noting the double ovens on the far wall and the multiburnered, stainless steel stove. As for the array of gadgets on the countertop, other than the coffeemaker he was clueless to their use. While he enjoyed eating a good meal, he'd never prepared one.

Overall, the entire space wasn't as big as the smallest bedroom in the tower suite he maintained at The Mark for his frequent visits to the city, but she'd made good use of every inch. Sleek cabinetry ran the full height of the walls in the kitchen, and in the living area her computer and printer were tucked inside an armoire. The doors were open now, revealing a chocolate soufflé screen saver and a plethora of notes pinned to the corkboard that lined the interior of the doors.

She'd cleverly used stacks of cookbooks to form the base of a coffee table, over which was placed an oval of glass. The slip-covered sofa behind it was the room's only nod to comfort, but it was the brightly hued throw on the back of it that caught his attention. He recognized the craftsmanship and the centuries' old pattern. It came from his homeland.

"Would you care for some coffee?"

He turned at the sound of her voice. "Yes, thank you."

He followed her into the kitchen, where she poured him a cup and topped off her own.

"Cream or sugar?" she asked.

"Black is fine." He'd acquired a taste for Western coffee, though he preferred the sweetened variety of his country.

She'd pulled her chestnut hair into a softer-looking version of the style she'd worn the night before, minus the net, of course. For a moment he wished she'd left it loose as it had been when he'd arrived. He liked the way it had waved in defiance around her face before falling just past her shoulders. The pink blouse she wore wrapped at the waist, accentuating its smallness. Her trousers were tan and mannish in style, but the flair of her hips and the tips of a lethal-looking pair of pumps that peeked out from the cuffed hem kept the cut from appearing too masculine.

When he realized he was staring, he glanced away. "You have an impressive kitchen."

"Thanks. I like it."

"Was it recently renovated?"

"Less than a year ago." Something in her expression changed and her chin rose fractionally, as if in challenge. "My business is growing, so I decided to go all out. Besides, I spend most of my time in here whether I'm working for a client or just puttering for fun."

She sat on one of the stools lined up next to the island. He took the one next to hers and swiveled so he could face her.

"You cook for fun?"

"I'm afraid I can't help myself. I absolutely adore food."

His gaze skimmed over her, lingering on her slender waist. "And yet you are…small."

She laughed outright at what he realized too late was a rude observation for a man to make. Wincing, he said, "I shouldn't have said that. Sorry."

"Oh, no. Don't apologize." She laid a hand on his arm. "I can't think of a woman alive who doesn't like to be told she's not fat."

He felt his face grow warm. This made twice since arriving on Emily's doorstep that he'd embarrassed himself. He didn't care for the sensation. Indeed, he wasn't used to putting his foot in his mouth, especially where women were concerned. But the amusement shimmering in her blue eyes took away some of his chagrin.

"I only make that observation because a lot of the chefs I know are…more substantially proportioned," he said, trying for diplomacy.

She sighed. "Unfortunately that's a hazard of the profession. All those little tastes can add up over time."

"How have you managed to avoid it?"

"Exercise and nervous energy." At his frown she clarified, "I have a gym membership. I try to work out at least three times a week. The rest of the time I fret and pace, or so my assistant tells me."

Fret and pace? She seemed too confident for either. "Have you been in business for long?"

"Why do you ask? Are you having second thoughts about hiring me?" Amusement shimmered in her eyes again.

"No. Once I make a commitment I keep it."

"But you haven't committed. No contract has been signed," she reminded him lightly.

Madani thought of Nawar, his bride-to-be in Kashaqra, and of the long-held agreement between their families. No contract had been signed for that, either. But it was understood. It had always been understood. "Sometimes one's word is enough."

"I prefer a signature," she replied. "No offense. I just find it easier to do business that way since not everyone's word tends to be equal."

"True." He nodded, thinking of the deals he would finalize later that day. "Legally speaking, it's always best to have documentation. I run an export business… among other things."

"May I ask you a question?" At his nod, Emily went on. "Your accent, I can't quite place it."

"I am from Kashaqra." He thought of his homeland now, missing it since he'd been gone a month already.

It was bounded by mountains on one side and a swath of desert on the other. Due to his father's foresight and diligence, it had avoided the unrest that had plagued some of the other countries in the region. It was Madani's goal to continue that tradition. It was also his goal to see the export business he'd started continue to grow so his people could prosper.

Her brows wrinkled. "Geography wasn't one of my better subjects, but that's in the Middle East, I believe."

"Yes. Near Saudi Arabia. Even though we lack our good neighbor's oil riches, we are wealthy in other ways."

"How so?"

"Our artisans are unrivaled."

"In your humble opinion." She grinned and he caught the wink of that solitaire dimple.

Madani smiled in return, but meant it when he said, "I do not believe in being humble when it comes to praising the work of my countrymen. Indeed, it is my hope that eventually, in addition to finding markets for it abroad, it will entice tourists to come and visit our country."

"You make me eager to see their work for myself."

"You already have and obviously are a fan." At her surprised expression, he pointed to the sofa. "That throw was hand woven in a little village called Sakala. The pattern dates back seven hundred years and has been passed down from generation to generation. Mothers make it for their daughters when they are to wed. It is said to bring good luck to the union."

Her expression turned surprisingly cool. "Maybe I should give it to my sister."

"Your sister is to be married?"

"Yes." She sipped her coffee and changed the subject. "I had no idea that throw enjoyed such a rich history when I saw it hanging in the window of an eclectic little shop not far from here."

"Salim's Treasures," he guessed. The owner's wife had family in Kashaqra.

"Yeah, that's the one. I paid a small fortune for it," she admitted. "But I had to have it. The colors are so rich and vibrant."

"Vibrant." He nodded, but his gaze was on her.

The moment stretched before she glanced away. Was she embarrassed? Flattered? Should he apologize?

"We should get down to business," she said, ending the silence. "About your dinner party, did you have a type of cuisine in mind?"

Emily couldn't help being in good spirits after Dan Tarim left her apartment later that morning. It had nothing to do with the man, she assured herself, though she found him extremely sexy with his dark good looks and fathomless eyes. Rather, it was because she'd landed another catering job that, after deducting expenses and incidentals, would allow her to deposit a sizable chunk of money into her savings account. The man obviously didn't believe in doing anything halfway.

She felt the same when it came to her restaurant,

which she planned to call The Merit. It was inching closer to reality by the day. Another year or so and she would be able to approach the bank with her business plan. Given the number of restaurants that failed each year, even in a good economy, Emily knew she would have to show the bank why she was a good risk.

She could picture the place so clearly. The menus would be leather bound and tasseled. The tables would sport crisp white linens and be topped with candles to add an air of intimacy and romance when the lights were turned low. But the bow to convention would end there. The food would be eclectic and bold, a smattering of tastes from around the globe all given her signature twist. As such she felt the best location for it was somewhere in the Village.

Her thoughts returned to Dan. At the end of their meeting, she'd promised to work up menu selections for his approval by the end of the week. He'd been open to suggestions, which made him the kind of client she preferred, since that allowed her to be creative. He'd made only one request, one she would have no problem honoring since he was footing the bill. He had a fondness for white truffles and insisted at least one dish include them.

The Italian delicacy went for up to ten thousand dollars a pound, which was why Emily rarely cooked with it. Even the Hendersons, who were exceedingly generous when it came to trying to please their guests' discerning palates, had never requested a recipe that included the pricey tuber.

"I'm in heaven." Emily sighed as she lugged a stack of books holding her favorite recipes to the kitchen's island.

It only took the phone to ring for her to return to earth. Then, as soon as Emily heard her mother's voice, she descended a bit further south.

"My goodness but you've been hard to get in touch with lately," Miranda complained by way of a greeting.

Since her mother had forgone social niceties, Emily decided to as well. "Have I?"

"You know you have. You can try to avoid me, but you can't avoid the fact that your sister is getting married in August."

The M word landed like a bomb, obliterating what remained of Emily's good mood.

"I'm not avoiding it, Mom." The reply came out clipped, despite Emily's best efforts to sound blasé.

"I know this is hard for you, but it's really for the best in the long-term. He and Elle are so much better suited than the two of you were. When are you going to forgive them?"

When they ask me to, she thought.

"On their silver wedding anniversary?" her mother went on dramatically.

"That's optimistic," Emily muttered.

"You need to be a bigger person. Your sister is so happy and content. Your father and I have never seen Elle like this. It's what we've been hoping for for years. Can't you be happy for her?"

Guilt niggled. Her mother was good at planting the seed and then helping it grow. Miranda had been nurturing this particular one since Elle first flashed an engagement ring.

"I really do have to go, Mom."

"Elle's bridal shower is next Sunday."

"You know I can't come. As I've told you half a dozen times already, I'm booked that day." It was a lie. She had that particular Sunday free.

"Please try. For the sake of family harmony."

Emily hung up wondering why she was the only one expected to carry that load.

Dan flipped his cell phone closed on an oath as Azeem maneuvered the Mercedes through Manhattan traffic. This message, like the one before it, was from his mother. Given the time difference between New York and Kashaqra, Fadilah must consider the matter to be vitally important. That meant he couldn't avoid calling her back much longer.

"Is everything all right?" Azeem asked. "Your father?"

"Is well." Fadilah would not have been so vague if that were the case. "My mother says she *needs* to speak with me," he said wryly, knowing that would explain it all.

Azeem nodded. "She is the only woman I know who can make you squirm. But not for long, *sadiqi*. If you insist on going through with the wedding, Nawar will enjoy that right as well."

Though the words were offered in jest, the challenge was unmistakable.

"Drop me off at the next light," he said.

"But Mayhew's is at Fifth Avenue and Forty-Third," Azeem reminded him.

"I know. I want to walk the rest of the way." When his friend frowned, he added, "This is the first warm, sunny day we've had in nearly a week. I want to take advantage of it."

"As you wish." But Azeem's expression said he wasn't buying the explanation.

Madani glanced at his watch after the Mercedes drove away. It wasn't quite noon, which meant he still had forty minutes before his rescheduled appointment with a potential distributor. He started walking, his pace slow and leisurely. Even with heat rising from the street, the temperature was pleasant and the humidity low after a week of thunderstorms, making him glad to be outdoors and moving under his own steam. In Kashaqra, even with all of the amenities his wealth and position afforded, Madani enjoyed walking. In addition to being good exercise, it gave a man time to think, plan and put things into perspective. He needed to do that now, he decided, his thoughts returning to the phone message.

His mother probably wanted to discuss the engagement announcement or, he swallowed thickly, his wedding. Just thinking about marriage had Madani tugging his necktie loose as he strode down the sidewalk. As his parents kept reminding him, it was the next logical step in his life. He was thirty-two, educated, well-traveled and established. The time had come for him to take a wife and start a family. As the next in line to rule the country, it also was Madani's duty.

Turning matrimony into an obligation hardly made it any more palatable.

Still, he shouldn't complain. Nawar, the bride his parents had chosen for him, was beautiful in both face and form. She also was bright, only recently finishing up her PhD in economics at Kashaqra's leading university. Per her request, all talk of marriage had been postponed until she had completed her education, causing Madani to wonder if her pursuit of a doctoral degree was an indication of her own mixed emotions.

Here in the West, arranged marriages were considered archaic and unromantic. Even in his country many of the younger generation considered such alliances old-fashioned and unnecessary. After all, shouldn't picking a life partner be left to the two people involved?

Azeem, who to Madani's knowledge wasn't even seriously involved with anyone, was surprisingly outspoken on the matter, which in turn made him annoyingly outspoken in his dismay over Madani's decision to honor his arranged betrothal.

"You have an opportunity to lead even before taking your father's place," Azeem had hollered during one of their many arguments on the subject. "If you refuse to marry under these conditions, others would be willing to follow your example."

He'd considered that at one time, but he'd shaken his head. "It is done."

Madani hadn't just been referring to the fact that his betrothal to the daughter of one of his father's closest political allies had been arranged when he was still a toddler. As he'd told Azeem, it was his father's wish. What reason did he have to risk his father's health? Nawar would make a suitable wife. Besides, the notion of marrying for love seemed far-fetched. He'd spent time with plenty of women over the years, but he'd never felt the intense emotion the poets claimed existed.

For no reason he could fathom, his thoughts turned to Emily Merit.

"I was unaware you knew someone in this part of Manhattan," Azeem had said when they'd arrived outside her apartment building that morning. "She must be very pretty to have roused you so early after a late night. Am I to conclude you have changed your mind about a final fling with which to remember your bachelorhood?"

"This is a business meeting," he'd answered irritably. "Nothing more."

It *was* a business matter, but the pretty young woman he'd hired to cater his dinner party also had captured his interest.

CHAPTER THREE

THE FOLLOWING week, Emily was still on Madani's mind, which he supposed made sense since his personal assistant had given him the list of the RSVPs for his dinner party. He decided to call her.

She answered on the fourth ring, sounding cheerful if breathless.

"Hello, Emily. This is Dan Tarim."

"Dan, hi. You must be psychic. I've been thinking about you and was just about to call."

Her laughter, light and musical, floated over the line. He pictured her face with its errant dimple, blue eyes and soft mouth. Interest, an uncomfortable portion of it sexual, gave a swift tug.

"You've been thinking about me?"

"Yes. I've put together the most amazing menu for your guests."

"Menu," he repeated.

"As I promised, I want to run it by you before I purchase all of the ingredients, especially those pricey white truffles. And, of course, I will need a head count."

"Of course." He cleared his throat. "That's actually the reason for my call. One of my guests and his wife will be out of town, leaving just two other couples and myself."

"That's too bad. I'll adjust the portions accordingly." Then, "You don't have a date?"

"A date?"

"I only ask because Babs Henderson insists on an even number at her gatherings. I've known her to ask her social secretary to sit in to avoid going odd."

"No. I don't have a date."

"Really?" She sounded surprised. "Okay."

"You think I should have one?"

"Well, no. It's not a requirement or anything. I just thought that someone who looks like you would have one if not several women…" She coughed, clearly embarrassed. "Um, never mind."

Manhattan was far from his homeland, but Madani had spent enough time in the city that he knew plenty of women he could invite. Women who would drop everything to spend an evening in his company, even though he always made it clear, without going into too much detail, that a long-term relationship would never materialize.

He didn't feel he was being unfaithful to Nawar. After all, they were not officially engaged. In truth, they had met on only a handful occasions during which he'd been allowed no more than to brush both of her cheeks with his lips in his culture's customary greeting.

He pushed thoughts of Nawar and all other women away. All other women save Emily.

"When are you free to discuss the menu?"

"You want to meet?" She sounded surprised. "We can…or, if your schedule is full, I can e-mail you the proposed menu and we can go over it on the telephone."

"Is that how you normally conduct business?"

"Sometimes." She laughed, the sound again pleasing. "I've found that there's really no such thing as normal. Some clients want to try samples of the dishes I suggest. Others leave everything to me. And then there are the high-maintenance types who demand they accompany me to the grocery store."

"And you let them?"

"I don't encourage it, but for what I charge…" She cleared her throat. "You're a businessman. The client is always right, remember?"

"Indeed."

"So?" she prodded.

"When can we meet? And, of course, I'll want samples." He chuckled before adding, "I may even request to come shopping with you. Those who know me well will tell you I can be very demanding."

"Are you serious?"

"On all counts." Though he hadn't been till she'd called him on it. "Are you free Saturday night?"

"I'm a caterer." Her tone was dry.

"Day then." Which was for the best, he reminded himself. Even in his country, Saturday night was the territory of couples and dates.

"I have a dinner party for twelve at seven o'clock. It's going to take up a lot of my time since my assistant has asked for the night off. I plan to start some of my prep work the night before."

"So the morning should find you free."

Her laughter was exasperated now. "You don't take no for an answer, do you?"

"No. The customer is always right, remember?"

"Absolutely. Come by anytime between ten and noon. I can't promise samples of the meal I'd like to make for your guests, but we can go over the menu and I'll be happy to answer any questions you have."

"Very good. Until then."

For no reason he could nail down, Madani was smiling when he hung up.

Dan arrived at Emily's door promptly at ten the following morning. This time, she was ready for him. She answered his knock fully dressed and coiffed, her teeth brushed and her makeup applied.

She'd taken a little more time on her appearance than she normally did on a day that would find her toiling in her kitchen, but she wanted to present a crisp and professional image since she had a client coming over. Of course, that didn't explain why she'd opted to forego a white, standard-issue chef's coat in favor of a short-sleeved teal blouse that brought out flecks of blue in her eyes. Thankfully, enough sanity prevailed that she'd layered an apron over the dry-clean-only fabric before starting to chop the ingredients for one of the three appetizers she was to prepare.

"Good morning." His voice was as deep and rich as she remembered.

"Good morning."

He was dressed casually in tan slacks, a pair of broken-in loafers and a white oxford shirt. He wore no tie, which made sense since it was Saturday. Even so he radiated the same authority and sophistication he did wearing expensive, tailored suits.

Realizing she'd been staring at him while he remained in the hallway, she backed up and invited him inside.

After Emily closed the door, she turned to find that he was staring, too. At her apron.

"You are already working?"

"For hours now. I've been up since six, although I didn't get anything accomplished until after I'd had a cup of espresso. I was up a little late last night. Today's client called just before five yesterday afternoon with a last-minute menu change. It seems one of her guests has a shellfish allergy, so the shrimp appetizer I'd planned was a no-go." She lifted her shoulders in a shrug.

"A caterer's work is never done."

"Exactly." She flashed a smile as they walked into the kitchen.

"Are you like this every weekend?" he asked.

"When I'm lucky."

Dan frowned at her reply. "Perhaps you should consider hiring more assistants. It sounds as if you could use the additional help."

She could. That was true enough. But adding more employees to the payroll was out of the question. Their wages and the additional taxes would eat too far into her profits. Emily figured she could work herself to near exhaustion on weekends for however long it took to open her restaurant. What else did she have going on Saturday nights anyway? When The Merit became a reality, she would gladly hire a full kitchen and waitstaff, and take off nights here and there when the mood struck. Until then, caffeine would be her best friend.

Which prompted her to ask, "Can I get you something to drink? Espresso? Coffee? Tea, maybe?"

"Coffee, since I see that you already have a pot prepared." He nodded in the direction of the state-of-the-art brewing station she'd splurged on the previous Christmas.

"Yeah. I switched to French roast after the espresso." She grinned. "I figured I'd better pace my caffeine intake. I can't afford to get jittery when I'm working with knives."

He smiled in return as he settled onto one of the tall stools at the granite-topped island. At the moment, the island was littered with a cornucopia of fresh produce that had already been washed. Some of it would be used in a salad. Others would be chopped and added to the various dishes.

As she poured them both a cup, he reminded her she hadn't answered his question about hiring more help. Emily didn't feel it would be professional to discuss finances with a paying client, so she edited her response before speaking.

"I've always loved cooking and creating new dishes, which is why I do what I do for a living. So, I don't mind the extra work." She handed him his coffee and sipped her own.

"But what do you do for pleasure?" he asked.

The exotic lilt in his voice caused the last word to feather over Emily's flesh like a caress, and it had her stammering like a schoolgirl.

"I…I…I…read." If he hadn't been watching her she would have smacked her forehead at the lame response. She didn't have to know Dan well to figure out he was sophisticated, educated and cultured. He probably could lead Met patrons on a guided tour of the museum's Egyptian antiquities exhibit. And she was certain he spent his free time engaged in far more *pleasurable* pursuits. Meanwhile, she sounded provincial and antisocial.

But he said, "I enjoy reading as well. Who are your favorite authors?"

Somehow she doubted rattling off a bunch of chef's names was going to improve her image. He already must think she was a workaholic.

"I don't really have any favorites," she hedged. "If a book looks like it might appeal to me, I pick it up."

"Very open-minded." He nodded.

"What about you? Do you have a favorite author?" He probably leaned toward the classics. He probably read Socrates' *Charmides* for fun.

"Stephen King."

"Stephen King?" She set her coffee cup down on the counter with a clunk.

"You seem surprised."

And he seemed amused. Emily wrinkled her nose and averred, "It's just that I wouldn't be able to sleep at night if I read his stuff."

"I sleep like a baby."

Dan's lips quirked up, drawing her attention to his mouth. He had a sexy mouth, very sensual, as her assistant had noted that evening at the Hendersons'. At that moment, Emily could picture him sleeping, but not like a baby. He was all male and fully grown, lying between silk sheets and wearing… Emily cleared her throat. What was wrong with her?

"How on earth did we get on this subject?"

"We were talking about the long hours you work and what you do for pl—"

"Right!" She rudely cut him off, but she couldn't bear to hear that word slip from his gorgeous lips a second time, especially given the vastly inappropriate direction her thoughts had just strayed. "As I said, I really do love my job."

Work. Talk about work. Keep it about work, she coached herself, and decided it was time to get back to her cutting board.

"But with more employees you could take on more clients and still enjoy time for yourself. I am not familiar with your business. Do you cater large events?"

She shook her head. "No. I did a few large corporate parties when I was starting up. The money was welcome, but it felt a little too much like assembly-line work. I prefer small parties. I feel I have more control over the finished product that way."

"Ah." He dipped his head in understanding. "A perfectionist."

Emily chuckled. "My assistant would say I'm a control freak, but I like your word better."

"So this is your dream," he said, sounding almost wistful.

"For now."

"I am intrigued. What more do you want, Emily?"

The question was benign, but when a man looked like Dan Tarim, a woman kept imagining—or perhaps hoping—for subtext.

Motioning with her arms to encompass the kitchen, she said, "I have it all. What more could I want?"

"You tell me."

She almost wanted to, and not just about the restaurant, but the other hopes for her life, hopes she'd shoved to the back burner and rarely thought about these days: a husband. A family. A home.

Startled by the direction of her thoughts, she shook her head. "Another time, perhaps."

"Very well."

A bell chimed then and Emily crossed to the commercial-grade double oven. After donning protective mitts, she pulled out the dish inside and set it on a rack on the counter to cool.

The scent of cinnamon and apples wafting through the air was enough to make one's mouth water.

"That smells like heaven," Dan said. "What it is?"

"My favorite part of a meal: dessert."

"Is it apple pie?"

"Not quite. That seemed a little too American to serve with the French-inspired menu my client requested, so I opted for an apple-almond tart."

Dan walked over to inspect it, inhaling deeply as he went. "It looks too perfect to eat," he said. The apples were thinly sliced and perfectly arranged in a swirling pattern inside the thick crust.

"Wait till you see what I'm planning for you." When he turned she said, "A pear and caramel trifle heaped with whipped cream."

"That sounds like pure decadence." Dan's dark gaze turned intense and sensual enough to have her swallowing.

"P-perhaps *self-indulgence* would be a better word," she said.

Pleasure. Decadence. The man had an excellent grasp of the English vocabulary even though it was his second language.

"I prefer decadence." He smiled then and heat began to curl through her.

Though her hands were clean, Emily wiped them on the front of her apron. Her palms were damp. Overall, she felt uncomfortably warm. She blamed the oven and the rising temperature outside. Maybe she should turn up her air-conditioning. She glanced at Dan. He appeared perfectly comfortable and unperturbed.

It was time to get down to business, she decided.

"I think you'll approve of the rest of the meal I've planned."

With that, she went to her desk to retrieve the folder containing the menu for his dinner party.

Madani returned to his seat at the counter feeling a little off center. Thankfully he had long ago mastered the art of camouflaging his emotions. He wasn't sure how it had happened, but a simple conversation about dessert had turned into foreplay.

For him, at least.

In fact, ever since setting foot in her apartment-slash-place-of-business, he'd been acutely aware of Emily not as a chef but as a woman. He blamed his long hours this trip as well as the long absence of intimate female companionship for his libidinous thoughts.

Emily's appearance didn't help matters. She looked especially lovely today. Her hair was pulled back, no doubt out of deference for her work, but instead of a chignon, it was twisted in some fashion at the back that left it fuller in the front. The teal blouse was a good choice for her. It enhanced the color of her eyes and paired well with her creamy complexion. Without proper protection, her skin would burn in the hot sun of his homeland. He wondered if it was as soft as it appeared.

Dan sipped his coffee, which had grown cold. He, on the other hand, was becoming hot. Indeed, if they had spent another moment discussing decadent desserts, he might have wound up embarrassing himself.

As it was, he was pretty sure he'd embarrassed Emily. When she returned to the kitchen, he noticed that her cheeks were pink and she was careful to maintain her distance, even when she sat on the stool next to his, opened a folder and pushed it toward him on the counter. Should he apologize? He decided against it, partly because putting any of his veiled thoughts into words would surely only make matters more awkward.

Her expression was guarded, her voice crisply professional when she said, "We'll start with appetizers. You asked for two. Based on what you've told me about your guests and the kind of evening you have planned, I'm suggesting penne pasta with asparagus and basil. The portions will be larger than normal since you will be foregoing a salad course. In addition, and in a nod to your region of the world, I propose a hummus dish. It's made with chickpeas and lemon and uses yogurt instead of sesame paste. It will be accompanied by the customary wedges of toasted pita bread."

She glanced up, clearly expecting him to say something. So, he offered, "It sounds perfect."

"For the main course you wanted fish. I know you

were a fan of the salmon I made for the Hendersons, so I'm hoping you'll be similarly pleased with the sea bass I plan to simmer in a light white wine sauce."

She leaned closer and pointed to the photograph she'd included in the folder. He thought he caught a hint of floral fragrance beneath the aromatic scents of the kitchen.

Emily was saying, "As you can see, I propose pairing it with risotto, which will be seasoned and formed into cakes that will be skillet fried. The textures mix well."

"Textures?"

"The fish is fork tender. The crispness of the risotto cakes offsets that."

"That makes sense," he said, surprised at how much thought she put into planning a meal.

"Finally, I will steam green beans over which I will shave the truffles you requested. I chose green beans, because I wanted to let the truffles shine without too many other competing flavors."

"The star of the show," he said.

"Exactly. What's the point otherwise?" She glanced up and smiled. Talking about food had eased her earlier discomfort.

"Generally speaking, the meal is light, which is good considering what I've told you I will be making for dessert. Your guests will feel they are entitled to splurge."

"Very impressive. It appears you've thought of everything," he said.

"Well, that is what you're paying me for. Which

reminds me." She flipped the page. "Since you're visiting the city, I took the liberty of quoting you prices for china place settings and silverware. I have service for thirty, including all of the matching serving pieces."

"Thank you, but that won't be necessary. The accommodations I keep in Manhattan have everything I need."

She nodded. "I've also listed a selection of wines, both white and red, that would pair well with the courses. I can pick them up for you and include them in my final price, or you can purchase them on your own if you prefer. If you do want to purchase them separately, I can suggest a location. The owner is a friend and he will give you a discount if you mention you're a client of mine."

Madani skimmed the list she'd provided. Again, he found himself impressed with the breadth of her knowledge. "You have a good eye for wine," he told her. Some of the vintages she'd included were quite pricey, but all of them were well-regarded.

"Wine is often an integral part of the meal. As such it can either enhance the flavors of what I've prepared or detract from them." She shrugged then and her expression turned rueful. "Control freak, remember?"

He shook his head. "Not a control freak. A perfectionist." Even though Madani knew it was foolhardy, he reached over and touched her face. He planned the contact to be brief, just a light brush of his fingertips over the slope of her skin. But his fingers lingered and his hand opened until his palm cupped the side of her face. "And a lovely perfectionist at that. *Gamila.*"

Before he even knew what he intended, he'd leaned in and kissed her opposite cheek. Even though he was stunned at what he had just done, he drew back slowly. What madness was this, he wondered, that had him wanting to kiss her again and on the lips this time?

Emily sat very still. Her eyes were wide, her gaze intent. "What does that mean?" she asked in a voice that was barely above a whisper.

"I do not know," he replied haltingly, truthfully. He wasn't sure what emotion he'd intended to express with his forward behavior.

"You don't know?" She appeared puzzled. "But you just said it."

"Said it? Ah." It dawned on him then that she was talking about the word he'd used, rather than seeking an explanation for his actions. "*Gamila* means beautiful in Arabic."

Her cheeks turned pink again. "Oh." She cleared her throat then, shifted back on her seat.

"You are beautiful, Emily."

She didn't look at him. "I'm a caterer."

"And you cannot be both?"

He saw her swallow. "About the wine, what do you want me to do?"

Irritation snapped within him. "I'll see to the wine."

"Okay."

He modified his tone. "I have a couple of the ones you've suggested on hand, as well as a favorite of mine that I plan to serve. I think it will meet with your approval."

She nodded and stood. "Well, that's that, then. Unless you want to change or add something to the menu."

"One cannot improve upon perfection," he replied, following her lead and rising to his feet.

Emily collected the folder and handed it to him. "The cost is broken down on the front. I require an advance payment of half the total amount, which is nonrefundable once I've purchased the ingredients. The remainder is due the night of the party."

"Will a personal check do?"

"Certainly."

He drew his checkbook from his pocket, wrote one out and handed it to her, wondering at the sudden awkwardness he felt. It seemed he should say something more, if only so he could linger awhile in her company and determine why he found her so fascinating. But a glance at his watch revealed that he'd taken up too much of her time already. How had an hour managed to pass so quickly?

"I should let you return to work," he said.

"Unfortunately I need to. I have a lot left to do." They walked to the door. As she opened it, she added, "I'll be in touch."

"Gee, Em, isn't that usually the guy's line on the morning after?" a man drawled insultingly from the hallway, where he stood on the welcome mat with his hand raised as if to knock. He was fair-haired and nearly the same height as Madani. "And here poor Elle is worried that the reason you won't stand up in the wedding is you haven't gotten over me."

The man's gaze was as insolent as it was measuring when it shifted to Madani.

"Take care with your words," Madani said. He kept his voice soft, but the threat was unmistakable.

"Who is this guy, Em?"

"What are you doing here, Reed? What do you want?"

The man ignored her questions. Instead, he persisted, "Aren't you going to introduce me to your boyfriend? Maybe I can offer him some insights into your…likes and dislikes."

Madani took a step forward at the same time Emily laid a hand on his arm. "I'm sorry, Dan. This rude and obnoxious man is Reed Benedict, my sister's fiancé."

Sister's fiancé? Yet Reed's previous words implied he and Emily had been a couple.

"I see you're trying to connect the dots." The man named Reed winked as he stretched out a hand. "I wanted to keep it in the family."

Emily had called him rude and obnoxious. Madani silently added a few more adjectives to the list, and while he wasn't the sort of man prone to violence, he found himself wanting to take a swing at Reed's arrogant face. To keep from acting on the impulse, he curled his hand into a fist, which he kept at his side.

"I don't believe Emily wants you here. Maybe you should leave."

Reed lowered the hand Madani had refused to shake. "Word to the wise. Em doesn't like guys to speak for her. She's too *independent* for that."

The man's tone turned the trait into a character flaw. Incensed on her behalf, Madani asked Emily, "Shall I make him leave?"

She blinked in surprise. "As tempting as I find your offer, no. I'll give him five minutes of my time. You can go now. I'll call you later in the week."

Left with no choice, Madani bid her goodbye.

CHAPTER FOUR

ONCE THEY WERE ALONE, Emily let the full range of her wrath sharpen her tone. "What are you doing here, Reed?"

"Elle asked me to come." He sloughed off his sports coat as if she'd asked him to make himself more comfortable and flung it over one thick arm of the love seat. His voice held a sneer when he said, "I see that you've done a lot to the place since I've been gone."

The jerk smiled then, flashing several thousand dollars worth of veneers. She'd paid the bills for a couple of months so that he could afford them.

"I made it more suited to my needs," she agreed.

"Your needs. That's funny." His smile turned nasty. "I didn't think you had any."

The blow hit below the belt, just as he'd intended. Reed had always been good at stripping away her femininity, turning her into some sort of asexual automaton simply because she had dreams that went beyond being a showpiece on his arm.

It struck Emily then that she didn't feel that way around Dan. Okay, she didn't know the man well—hardly at all, come to that—but she had never been more aware of her femininity, her sexuality than when he was around.

She folded her arms, her confidence returning. "I'm busy today, so you'll have to get to the point of your visit."

"Busy. Always busy." He sighed. "Too busy, apparently, to make time for your family."

"Don't try to send me on a guilt trip, Reed. I have absolutely no guilt where you and Elle are concerned." She raised her chin a notch, a gesture she knew he found irritating. Sure enough, he scowled.

"She wants you at the shower tomorrow afternoon, Em. God only knows why since you're so bitter and jealous. You'll probably ruin the day for her."

Emily's brow rose. "Is this your idea of appealing to my better nature?" she asked, almost as amused as she was irritated.

"No. You don't have one of those," he shot back. "I never realized you could be so vindictive."

"Bitter, jealous *and* vindictive. Wow. That's some trifecta."

"I'm serious. Elle and I feel sorry for you. You spend every waking hour wrapped up in your work." He motioned toward the kitchen and shook his head. He'd never understood her, she realized now, wondering how she'd put up with his belittling comments. That much hadn't changed. "The kitchen in this place is now three times the size of the bedroom. Not that you probably care."

"I don't."

He shook his head. You're going to wind up sad and alone."

Even as she raised her chin, Emily swallowed, hating that he'd found yet another chink in her armor. "Don't waste your time pitying me, Reed. I'm really quite happy."

Happy and alone, a little voice whispered. *Happy with a thriving career*, she silently shot back. God, she was not only arguing with her ex, but she was arguing with her subconscious.

"Right." He shook his head. "You keep telling yourself that, Em."

She dropped her arms to her sides in exasperation and started for the door. "I'd say that your job here is done. You've delivered Elle's message."

"And?"

"Tell her I don't think I can make it, but if I manage to wrap things up early tomorrow, I'll stop in."

"That's big of you." His tone suggested he felt otherwise.

"Goodbye, Reed." Emily opened the apartment door and allowed a little of her own pettiness to seep through. "I'd say it was good seeing you, but it wasn't."

One step from leaving, he stopped. For an uncomfortable moment he stared at her. "It's hard to believe that we were ever a couple, let alone for so long. I don't know who you are anymore, Emily."

She could have said the same. Instead, she told him, "I

haven't changed. I always had these dreams, these goals. They're why I went to culinary school in the first place."

"Yeah, but I didn't think they'd pan out for you, at least not to the extent that they have."

"You thought I'd fail?" He wasn't the only one left wondering how they'd ever become a couple.

"Not fail exactly. I just figured that you would make a nice little hobby of it, you know?"

No. She didn't know. "A nice little hobby?" His lack of faith shouldn't have come as a surprise, let alone as a blow. Oddly, it hurt almost as much as his romantic defection had. "Well, Elle's goals shouldn't be a problem for you."

Reed's brow furrowed. "She doesn't have any goals."

"Exactly."

Emily closed the door behind him. She slammed it, actually. And even though she tried to banish their conversation from her mind, his prediction that she would wind up sad and alone pecked at her peace for the rest of the day.

Madani's eyes were closed as he reclined on the chaise on his terrace. The afternoon sun felt good on his face, as did the breeze that accompanied it. Music floated from the stereo, a languid melody with lyrics to match. He should have been relaxed. Indeed, he gave the appearance of being so. But he was far from it.

He'd returned from Emily's apartment several hours ago far too keyed up to work. He'd paced, put himself through a punishing workout with the free weights he kept in one of the spare rooms. Neither had helped.

Even sitting on the terrace doing nothing was proving difficult. He wanted to break something.

He had a feeling he would have felt this way even if he hadn't also had the misfortune of meeting her ex-boyfriend just before taking his leave.

Madani wasn't prone to snap judgments, but he'd made an exception in Reed Benedict's case. He didn't like him. The man had hurt Emily. That much was clear. He was marrying her sister. But it was the rude way in which the man had spoken to her that bothered Madani the most. His verbal jabs were proof that he disrespected her.

"I should have punched him," he muttered aloud.

"I hope you are not talking about me, *sadiqi*. Though only for your sake."

Madani opened his eyes as a chuckling Azeem stepped out onto the terrace.

"Not this time." Swinging his legs to the flagstone floor he rose. "Care to join me for a drink?"

"What kind of drink?"

"The only kind that counts when a man is in a foul mood."

Azeem's bushy eyebrows shot up at that. "An alcoholic beverage this early in the day? Something serious must be troubling you. Or could it be someone?"

The question hit a little too close for comfort. "Do you want a drink or not?" Madani snapped impatiently.

"Of course. I would never pass up an opportunity to

sample your cognac. I cannot afford such superior quality on the salary you pay me."

"Maybe I should sack you and be done with it."

His friend merely smiled. "If you'd like we can discuss the terms of my termination over the cognac."

When Madani returned with their drinks, Azeem had pulled a padded wrought-iron chair over from the table. "So, whom do you wish to strike?"

Picturing Benedict's overconfident sneer, Madani's blood boiled anew. "This…this fool of a man who… Forget it. He is not worth another moment of my time."

He would leave it at that, Madani decided. He handed Azeem one of the snifters and settled back on his chaise.

Azeem sipped his cognac. Nodding sagely, he said, "A woman is involved."

"Why must there be a woman involved?" Madani asked in exasperation.

"Because all too often men are fools where women are concerned." Despite Azeem's smile, his expression lacked its usual joviality.

"The voice of experience, my friend?"

Azeem merely shrugged. "Aren't we all fools at one time or another when it comes to women? Well, except for you, of course. Even as you prepare to marry one of Kashaqra's loveliest specimens, you will never be a fool for a woman. You do not believe in love."

Madani's eyes narrowed. "I have the feeling you have just insulted me."

"Never. I am but your humble servant." Azeem's lips twitched below his dark mustache.

"Now I know I have been insulted."

"So who is this woman?"

Madani swirled the cognac in his snifter. The color of the liquid reminded him of Emily's hair. "No one you know. I have just met her myself."

"Yet she weighs on your mind and inspires you to violence." Azeem's lips turned down in consideration. "That's quite an accomplishment."

Madani didn't care for his friend's summation since it was too close to the truth. He planned to change the subject, but the words that slipped out were, "She is so much more than what some people see."

"Including the fool?"

"Especially the fool." He snorted, drained his glass. "He had her and he didn't appreciate her."

Azeem hoisted his snifter, emptied it. "I know exactly what you mean."

The following morning, Emily knew to expect at least one phone call from her mother, if not half a dozen. Elle's shower was at two o'clock, which meant Miranda would be in overdrive.

Sure enough, the telephone in Emily's apartment rang just after she returned from a brutal workout at the gym. After a peek at the Caller ID, Emily was tempted not to answer, but Miranda would try her cell and then alternate between the two for the next couple of hours until

Emily finally picked up. Better to get this over with now so that she could attempt to enjoy the rest of her day.

Grabbing the cordless receiver, she flopped down on the couch. "Hi, Mom."

"Oh, I'm so relieved to hear your voice. Are you all right, honey?"

Hmm. This was a new tactic. "Why wouldn't I be?" she asked.

"Well, Reed and Elle are here, and Reed mentioned that a strange man was at your apartment yesterday."

Ah. Mystery solved. "The only strange man at my apartment yesterday was Reed. The other one was a client of mine."

"A client. Oh." Miranda sounded disappointed.

"Are you sorry it wasn't a serial murderer?"

"Don't be silly," her mother chided. "It's just, I guess I was hoping...well, you know."

"Hoping what?" Emily asked, perfectly aware she would regret doing so.

"That maybe you'd found someone."

She expelled an exasperated sigh. "Mom, you need to make up your mind. A moment ago you claimed to be worried that the man Reed met yesterday might have harmed me and now you're disappointed that I'm not involved with the guy."

"Oh, please," Miranda huffed. "Forgive me for being a little excited that you might have found someone. Reed mentioned that the man was there early in the morning."

"It was nearly eleven o'clock, Mother." Emily snorted.

"That's only early for Reed. I'd been up working for hours. And this was business. As I said, Dan is a client."

"Dan, hmm?"

"Yes. Dan. Generally speaking, I'm on a first-name basis with all of my clients."

"Client or not, Reed said the man was possessive of you. He said he was a little surprised that you allowed it."

Emily thought back on the exchange. Possessive? No, she wouldn't have allowed that. Protective was more like it. And that she didn't mind. Indeed, she smiled now, recalling the way Dan had told Reed to watch his words and later had offered to toss him out. Despite all of his refinement and sophistication, she had little doubt he would have done so—and quite handily—had she agreed. It almost made her wish she'd let him.

Forcing herself back to the present, Emily said, "Is this the only reason you're calling, Mom?"

"No," Miranda replied.

"I didn't think so," Emily mumbled. Heaven knew she couldn't get that lucky.

"Reed told me why he stopped to see you yesterday. He also told me the cool reception his request received." Miranda's voice lowered. "I'm really disappointed in you, Emily Josephine."

Emily massaged her forehead. She was pushing thirty and her mother was still trotting out her middle name in the hope of forcing her to toe the line. "For what, Mom? Not dropping everything to be at Elle's side today?"

She said it sarcastically, but her mother took her words at face value. "Yes."

"I've got work to do." Which wasn't a complete fabrication. She could always find something business-related to occupy her time.

But her mother called her on it. "That's a convenient excuse and we both know it. Just stop in for five minutes today, not just for Elle's sake but to put the rumors to rest."

That got her attention. "Rumors?"

"You know your aunt Dora. Your cousin Sara says she's claiming you're too broken up over losing Reed to put in an appearance."

"Hardly."

"I know," Miranda agreed with an airy sigh. "I told Sara to tell her as much, but Aunt Dora's already been on the phone to Aunt Betty and Aunt Sally. She told them that you're all but incapacitated with heartache and that's why it's unlikely you will be at the shower today."

Emily's molars ground together. She knew she was being manipulated. She knew it! Yet on the off chance her mother was telling the truth and the aunts were burning up the grapevine with tales of her woe, pride demanded that she put in an appearance.

Brokenhearted, indeed.

It struck Emily then that she wasn't. At least not as much as she should have been given the fact that she'd thought she and Reed would wed eventually. God, they'd dated for so long. She was ticked off, sure. As she saw it, she had every right to be. But the fact was, given the same set of opportunities, Emily would make the same choices all over again.

"What time will you finish playing Bridal Bingo and all of the other silly games?" she asked.

Miranda's tone was triumphant, confirming Emily's worst fears. "Oh, we'll be done with those no later than three."

"I can only stay an hour."

"Terrific." She pictured her mother rubbing her hands together in glee. Miranda—and Elle—had gotten their way. Again. "See you this afternoon, dear. Oh, and since your sister's bridesmaid dresses will be peach, we thought it would be nice for members of the wedding party to wear something in that color."

CHAPTER FIVE

EMILY CHOSE RED.

The dress' low cut was inappropriate for a Sunday afternoon not to mention a bridal shower. She didn't care. She paired it with lethal pumps and a kiss-off attitude. If she was riddled with remorse over her breakup with Reed and his subsequent engagement to her baby sister, it looked damned good on her, she decided, adding a bit more kohl liner to her eyes.

She finished off the dramatic look with lipstick in the same flaming shade as her dress. Yes, she was being defiant, but she wouldn't give in entirely to her mother's manipulations.

Miranda's mouth pinched tight when Emily walked through the door of her family's two-story Brooklyn home. The guests, which included all of the aunts and female cousins, as well as a gaggle of Elle's girl-friends, were gathered in the living room. Her mother jumped up from her place next to Elle and crossed to Emily.

"That's not peach," she hissed as she pretended to kiss her daughter's cheek.

"Nope. It's not even close."

Elle came up next, looking like a confection in her white eyelet sundress with its wide peach sash. Blond hair tumbled around a face whose pouty, glossed lips would have been right at home on the cover of a men's magazine.

Emily had once overheard their father say where Elle would stop traffic, Emily would be the one to give out the tickets. Darin Merit hadn't meant it as a compliment. She'd decided to take it as one anyway.

"Oh, Em!" Elle exclaimed, enveloping Emily in a hug that was tight enough to transfer the overpowering scent of her perfume to Emily's skin. "You've made my day! Your being here is truly the best gift of all."

This was said loudly enough for those at the far end of the room to hear without straining. The murmuring began almost immediately. Emily couldn't make out what the guests were saying, but their gazes were full of pity and speculation, making the words unnecessary.

"I brought you something anyway." She pulled out of the death grip long enough to fetch the gift she'd set on the console table in the foyer.

"Here."

"I'm sure I'll love it," Elle said, clasping the wrapped box to her bosom.

Emily doubted it. She hadn't had time to shop off Elle's gift registry and the sisters had never shared the same taste, Reed being the exception. "I've included the receipt just in case."

"Why don't you help yourself to some refreshment, Emily, and then join us," her mother suggested.

Emily glanced at the clock. It was five minutes past three. The games were done. She only had to endure this charade for another fifty-five minutes. Less than the amount of time it took for her to whip up a soufflé. Some punch would help, she decided. Especially if her aunt Sally had already managed to spike it with rum.

In the kitchen, she ladled up a glass of punch as red as her dress. A sip had her closing her eyes. "Bless you, Aunt Sally," she murmured and returned to the living room.

Unfortunately a glance around confirmed her worst fears. The only seat available was next to Aunt Dora.

"You look ready for a night on the town," Aunt Dora remarked.

"I'm going out later." The lie slipped easily from Emily's lips. "I won't have enough time to get back to my apartment afterward, so…" She sipped more punch.

"Oh?" Her aunt's face lit up. "Do you have a new man in your life?"

Her thoughts turned to Dan. "It's not serious or anything. We've just met."

"Is he handsome?" Her aunt's elbow dug into her ribs.

"God, yes. Drop-dead gorgeous is more like it." That wasn't a lie.

Dora reached over and squeezed her hand. "I'm so happy that you're moving on."

A mouthful of punch went down smoothly. "Oh, yeah. The ship has sailed," Emily confirmed.

She hoped that would be the end of it, but of course it wasn't. Dora found a new reason to pity her.

"It must be hard, though, to watch your baby sister get married first. Goodness, she's nearly six years younger than you are! But at least you're seeing someone now."

Emily made a noncommittal sound. Not that it mattered. Dora went on.

"And you still have time. You don't turn thirty for—what?—another year yet." Eight and a half months. Emily hadn't been counting. Until now.

Dora went on. "My Christine says a lot of women feel the need to have a career before settling down, just so they know what they're *not* missing once they do."

Ah, yes, Christine. The voice of experience. She was the same age as Elle and had tied the knot in a hastily ordered civil ceremony a month out of high school. Aunt Dora still claimed little Jimmy had been born premature, though no one in the family believed that at eight pounds, seven ounces he'd arrived two months early.

"It's a rat race out there," Emily agreed, managing to sound sincere. Another gulp of punch helped.

"All those long hours you put in and for what? So you can go home all alone?" Aunt Dora shook her head in dismay and reached over for Emily's free hand. "Thank

God you've met someone. Maybe now Elle won't get too much of a head start on you."

"That would be tragic." Her glass was empty, which was just as well. She was already feeling a bit tipsy.

A moment later, though, when her mother announced they would be playing a game to determine which guest knew Elle and Reed the best, Emily decided on a refill.

Madani had no reason to call Emily. The menu for the following Saturday was set, the down payment had been made. But as he prowled restlessly around his rooms at The Mark on Sunday afternoon, he tried to come up with one. As happened whenever he set his mind to something, he succeeded. Flipping open his cell phone, he punched in the business number from Emily's card. When her recorded voice greeted him, he cursed and hung up without leaving a message. Not one to give up, though, he eyed the card again. Her cell number was on it, too.

When she answered he could barely make out her voice over the din of conversation in the background. He assumed she was working, probably whipping up her magic in some wealthy socialite's kitchen.

"Dan. This is a surprise."

"It sounds as if I'm interrupting something," he said apologetically. "I'll hang up and let you get back to whatever it is you're doing."

"No!" Even with the background noise, her shout came across as desperate.

"Emily, is everything all right?"

"Not even close." Her tone was wry. "I'm glad you called, actually."

The pleasure he experienced upon hearing her say that was way out of proportion. Even so, he couldn't stop it.

"I…I need a favor," she said.

"Anything." He meant it.

"Have you ever been to Brooklyn?"

Azeem didn't say a word during the drive. He didn't have to. His smirk said it all, which was why Madani felt the need to explain, to put things into proper perspective. For his friend. For himself.

As they crossed from lower Manhattan to Brooklyn, Madani said, "It's not what you are thinking."

"What am I thinking?"

"That I have taken your advice. That I am having this, this *fling* you suggested."

"Aren't you?"

"No!" The protest only made him sound guilty.

"I make no judgments, Madani. I, better than anyone, know that the arrangement you have with Nawar doesn't make it a love match."

"No, but I am not having a fling."

Azeem shrugged with maddening indifference.

"Emily asked me to collect her." Indeed, her voice had verged on pleading. She'd promised to explain the situation to him in full later. "I am doing a favor for a friend. Nothing more."

"So, now she is a friend rather than a caterer." The smirk was back.

"She can be both, can she not? You are my driver as well as my friend," he pointed out.

"True." Azeem didn't sound convinced, though. "And perhaps you are a fool."

Azeem muttered it half under his breath, leaving Madani to wonder if he had heard correctly.

"What?"

"Nothing."

Madani stared out his window. A yellow taxi blasted past. Couldn't Azeem go any faster? A moment later, he ran a hand over his face. He should have shaved. Though a little scruff on a man's cheeks was in fashion these days, he preferred a smooth face when he went out with a woman. But this wasn't a date, he reminded himself. Nor was it business. It was…a rescue of sorts.

Twenty minutes later, Azeem pulled the car to a stop in front a comfortable-looking two-story house on an oak-lined street in Brooklyn.

"Are you sure this is the right address?" Azeem's tone was dubious.

"It's what she said."

He opened the car door and stepped out, feeling oddly apprehensive as he navigated the flower-lined stoop, and that was before he spied the pair of white paper wedding bells hanging over the door. Under the bells were the names "Reed and Elle."

What was he getting himself into? No doubt a

family drama every bit as melodramatic as his own tended to be.

He knocked anyway. A moment later an ample-chested matron opened the door. She eyed him frankly before breaking into laughter, and called over her shoulder, "Miranda, you didn't mention there would be male entertainment at this shower."

"Good Lord, Sally! Get away from the door."

Another woman appeared then. This one wasn't smiling. "Can I help you?"

"I've come for Emily."

"Emily?" She frowned.

"Emily Merit. Is she here?" he inquired politely.

"Yes." The woman pushed open the screen door and invited him inside, albeit reluctantly.

Stepping into the living room, Madani knew a moment of panic. It was filled with women, a good three dozen of them, and they were sizing him up like a prized camel.

He fell back on manners. "Good afternoon, ladies."

His gaze landed on Emily then. She was tucked between two large matrons. Where all of the other women were adorned in pastels, she wore red. Vivid, vibrant, sexy red. She uncrossed a pair of surprisingly long legs and rose to her feet. The dress flaunted her curves.

"Ah, my knight in shining armor has arrived." Her lips quirked with a smile that would have been right at home on a siren. The blood in his head started heading south. And this was before she said, "I'm sorry to have to leave the party early, but I have other plans for the rest of the afternoon and maybe the evening."

She sent a wink in the direction of the woman who had first opened the door.

"Em, aren't you going to introduce us to your…your friend?" a young woman asked.

Based on the corsage, he assumed her to be the guest of honor, making her Emily's sister. The two women didn't look much alike.

"Oh, yes. How rude of me. This is Dan. I'm catering a party for him, which makes him a client. Our relationship is *strictly* business." The way she said it implied otherwise.

"So, you're just going to leave?" the blonde asked petulantly. She was curvy and attractive, but not his type at all.

"Yep. Sorry. I am. But you know me, Elle. All work and no play. Dull, dull, dull." Emily's laughter was throaty and shot straight to his loins.

Swallowing, Madani watched her weave toward him through the crowded living room, stepping around guests, wrapped boxes and gift bags. Her gaze was smoldering and direct, if a little unfocused. When she reached him, she framed his face with her hands, rose up on tiptoe and kissed him full on the mouth.

That was all it took. Though he had no right, not to mention an audience, he kissed her back. How could he not?

Mmm.

The sound was like a gunshot in the quiet room. Had

he moaned or had she? Either way, the satisfied vo-
calization was fitting. This was good. Better than he'd
fantasized, he thought, admitting to himself that he had
indeed fantasized.

"Oh, for heaven's sake!" someone shouted. Her
mother, most likely.

Madani ended the kiss, but only because Emily had
begun to pull away. She appeared undaunted despite the
whispers going on around them. In fact, she grinned,
that impish dimple serving only to stoke his appetite.

"What do you say we get out of here?"

CHAPTER SIX

HIS REACTION NOTWITHSTANDING, Madani knew all was not as it seemed. Something more was going on. Emily confirmed as much the moment they were outside.

As he escorted her down the steps to his car, she drew to a halt. "I'm sorry about that."

"The kiss?" Even though he'd expected it, her apology served as a bucket of ice water. "I didn't mind."

She glanced sideways at him and her cheeks turned pink. "I meant it when I said you were my knight in shining armor. I planned to leave my sister's bridal shower early, but there seemed to be no way to exit gracefully without having to endure their pity, especially since I left my vehicle in the city and would have to call a car."

"Why would they pity you?"

Her tone turned wry. "Well, let's see, it probably has something to do with the fact that my baby sister is not only getting married first, she's marrying the man I dated for six years."

"Their betrayal must have hurt you deeply." He said it softly, reaching up to tuck a stray curl behind her ear.

She stilled, studied him. "You know, you're one of the few people who get that. My parents seem to think I should be delighted beyond measure that Elle is finally settling down, even if she's doing it with my ex, who *wasn't* my ex when she began seeing him."

Madani had wanted to take a swing at Benedict when they'd met the day before and that was without knowing what a duplicitous cretin he was.

"Elle, of course, blathers on about how she *always* had a crush on Reed and that *nothing* can stand in the way of true love."

"And Reed?"

Emily huffed out a breath. "He claims to be justified in cheating with my sister since my career can be so demanding."

"It sounds as if he felt threatened by you."

"Would you be?"

"Excuse me?"

She shook her head. "Never mind. Just a hypothetical question that I had no business asking." She sucked in a deep breath and let it out slowly. Though he thought she might say something more, she remained silent.

"I'll take you home."

At his signal, Azeem got out of the car parked at the curb and opened the rear door.

Emily grimaced. "Oh God. I didn't realize you had

a driver. I've put both of you out, and on a Sunday afternoon no less."

"Not at all. Azeem had nothing better to do." In a stage whisper, he added, "He really needs a social life. It's sad really. I worry about him."

She laughed, as he'd intended, and Azeem joined in.

"I'd have a social life if not for Madani. I'm always at his beck and call."

"Madani?" Emily glanced back at him.

"It's my given name."

She smiled, nodded. "It suits you. I like it much better than Dan. Would you mind if I called you Madani from now on?"

She could call him whatever she wanted. He merely nodded, though, and helped her into the backseat. Ignoring Azeem's raised eyebrows, Madani followed suit. As the Mercedes started back to Manhattan, Emily leaned her head back against the rest, closed her eyes and sighed.

"Bad day?" he asked softly.

"Yes. Thanks again for doing this. It's only a slight exaggeration to say I thought I was going to die in there." She turned her head toward him and opened her eyes. "Or go insane. My mother has that effect. Add in a couple dozen aunts and female cousins and…."

Since his mother and some of the other women of his family could produce the same reaction in him, he commiserated. "I think I know what you mean."

"The punch didn't help."

"The punch?" Had someone harmed her?

"One of my aunts spiked it with rum and, given the way my head feels right now, I'm guessing she didn't hold back." Her gaze lost its focus as she admitted, "I had three glasses."

"Ah. Punch." Not sure what else to say, he nodded.

"I wouldn't have had so much if not for the game. You wouldn't know this, being a man and from a foreign country and all, but women here play the most ridiculous games at bridal showers."

Out of the corner of his eye, Madani caught a glimpse of Azeem in the rearview mirror. His friend's eyes were watering from suppressed laughter. No doubt, Madani would be hearing about this later.

"I'll take your word for it. So what was this game?"

"Twenty questions to determine which shower guest knew the bride-to-be and her intended groom the best."

Madani winced on Emily's behalf.

"Yeah, exactly. What quality does Reed admire most about Elle?" she intoned breezily. "Who said I love you first? Where did they go on their first date?"

"The first date they had behind your back."

"Yep." She closed her eyes, nodded. "That would be the one."

No wonder she'd drank so much of the punch. No wonder she'd kissed him.

"I'm sorry, Emily."

"Thanks." She snorted then. "A couple of my aunts actually seemed surprised that I didn't win."

Hoping to lighten the mood, he asked, "What was the prize if you had?"

Her nose wrinkled. "A set of hand towels embroidered with Elle's and Reed's names and their wedding date."

"Perhaps it's for the best that you lost. That doesn't sound like much of a prize."

Her tone was wry. "You don't think so? Elle did, but then she believes the whole world revolves around her."

"From what little I know of her intended, he believes the world revolves around him. It would seem, then, that they deserve one another."

She grinned sideways at him. "You, Madani Tarim, are definitely a bright spot in what has otherwise been a dark day."

"I'm glad I could be of service." He tried to ignore the fact Azeem's shoulders were now shaking with mirth.

They drove in silence for the next few minutes. Madani's conscience, however, was not quiet. Take Emily directly home, it commanded. He ignored it, and instead asked, "Are you hungry?"

"I am. Starving, in fact. My mother made the food," she explained. "Everything was overcooked and overspiced."

"Obviously you didn't get your talent in the kitchen from her."

"No. My mother's family came from the South originally. Three generations removed, deep-frying everything from meat to vegetables remains sacrosanct. When I started cooking as a teenager, it was a matter of self-preservation." She smiled. His breath caught. "Then it clicked and I knew I'd found my calling."

At that moment, Madani felt a calling as well, an irresistible urge to be with her in the only way he could. "Have dinner with me, Emily."

"I'd love to."

Emily meant it, which was why she suddenly felt so nervous. Foggy as her brain still felt, she knew this wasn't a good idea. But sitting beside Madani, steeped in his warmth and the subtle scent of his cologne as the Mercedes sped through traffic, the exact reasons escaped her.

"Where shall we go?" he asked. "Do you have any preferences?"

Preferences? Indeed, yes, as a chef she had them. She was always eager to try new places or revisit those whose fare inspired her to make new creations. But at the moment her mind was dangerously blank. She couldn't think of the name of a single eatery either within the limits of Manhattan or the surrounding boroughs.

"Surprise me," she said. As if she really needed any more of those today.

Madani nodded and leaned forward to say something to the driver in their native tongue. Though Emily had no idea the content of his words, she liked their lyrical cadence.

"Will Azeem be joining us?" she asked politely as Madani settled back in his seat. She hoped the driver would. Surely having a chaperone along would ensure that things remained platonic, innocent.

Azeem grinned at her around his headrest. "Thank you for the invitation, but I believe there's a saying in your language about three being a crowd."

Emily managed a weak laugh. The kiss she'd planted on Madani in her parents' living room mocked her now. Nothing about it had been platonic or innocent. That had been her intent at the time, of course. She'd wanted to eradicate every last bit of pity oozing out of her aunts and cousins.

Poor Emily.

How many times had she heard that whispered during that hideous game? In some cases, a sympathetic glance in her direction had accompanied the words making it all but impossible to pretend she hadn't heard them.

And, okay, Em could admit that she'd used that kiss to prove to her mother and sister that she wasn't some spinster workaholic whose life lacked any trace of excitement or passion.

What she hadn't expected when she'd crossed the room and reached her intended target was for Madani to rest his hands on her waist, to draw her into his arms until they were pressed together from chest to thigh and then kiss her back.

And, oh, how the man could kiss. That much was obvious straight away, the brevity of the encounter notwithstanding.

The mere memory of it now sent heat curling through her. Even so, she shivered.

"Are you cold?" he asked.

Before she could respond, he'd ordered Azeem to turn down the air-conditioning and had peeled off his coat, which he then put around her shoulders.

Cold? No. Quite the opposite and now that she was all but cocooned in his scent her temperature threatened to shoot up by several more degrees. But she smiled, accepted his kindness and tried not to inhale too deeply lest she make a bigger fool of herself.

Emily was so preoccupied making nervous small talk for the next twenty minutes that she paid no attention to where they were heading until the car stopped. They were in Chinatown, she realized. They stepped out onto one of the narrow, winding streets just off Mott and not far from the heart of the ethnic neighborhood.

She gave no thought to masking either her surprise or her disappointment.

"Chinese food? But I thought…" Manners finally caught up with her and she let the comment go unfinished.

Madani read her mind. "You were under the impression I would take you to a place that serves the types of food found in my country."

"Well, yes," she admitted.

In truth, she had looked forward to it. Perhaps because of her profession, Emily had an adventurous palate. She enjoyed trying new kinds of cuisine, loved identifying the spices and reveling in the textures. She couldn't say she'd ever eaten Kashaqra's fare, but in general she loved Middle Eastern food. Over the years, she'd added her own twists to standards such as tabouli and fattoush, and incorporated them into clients' menus, always to rave reviews.

The scents that greeted her as she stood outside Fuwang's were not cumin and turmeric, but sesame and ginger. Madani took her arm as they strolled toward the main entrance. Paper lanterns and banners written in Chinese characters dangled overhead.

"I would, but I have found only one or two places that I believe reflect the true taste of Kashaqra's cuisine."

"Are they close to here?" she asked hopefully.

"Not far. But neither has what you would call ambiance."

"What, no tablecloths or candles?" she teased. "I'm really not that high maintenance. I'd rather a quality meal than a fancy dining room."

"These lack that as well. Takeout only."

"Oh."

"I decided you would think it presumptuous of me to bring you back to my suite to dine." His dark gaze dipped, lingered on her mouth. Food was forgotten, pushed back behind thoughts of that kiss.

"Actually it would be quicker to go to my apartment than trek all the way to The Mark on the Upper East Side." She was staring at his mouth now, too. Nice lips, soft and firm at the same time. Just as his hold had been. "If you wait too long things might get cold."

Emily coughed. God, had she really just said that? Talk about sounding presumptuous. In the hope of resurrecting her self-respect, she added, "The food, I mean."

His lips twitched with a smile, telling her that the extra words had only made it more obvious that her thoughts had strayed far from takeout meals.

Once again, Emily attempted to dig herself out of her self-dug hole. "But that's neither here nor there. We're in Chinatown."

Madani frowned now. "You do like Chinese food, don't you?"

She laughed, finally at ease now that the topic was something truly safe. "I just plain like food, Madani."

"Good, because I have a weakness for fried rice."

"Shrimp or chicken?"

He grinned, flashing straight white teeth. "Either, especially at Fuwang's."

Emily knew what he meant when their meals arrived half an hour later as they sat in the restaurant's sparsely populated dining room. Outside, the late June afternoon was winding down over a crowd on the sidewalk, but it would be a couple of hours yet before the dinner rush arrived.

Madani had ordered an appetizer of shrimp toasts, which they'd already polished off. Now, their waitress, a petite young woman dwarfed by the huge platter of food she carried, arrived with the rest of their meal.

There was so much of it.

Emily had gone for a traditional sweet and sour pork dish served with white rice. It wasn't exactly low-calorie with its sugary sauce and batter-dipped meat, but Emily figured she had endured the kind of day that begged for comfort food, and this fit the bill.

But she barely spared her plate a second glance after the waitress left. Madani had ordered hot sesame beef, but it was the side of shrimp-fried rice that held her attention. Peeking from the browned rice were a good dozen shrimp. Not salad-size either, but big enough to be classified as jumbo.

"I'm beginning to think I ordered the wrong thing," she commented.

"Would you like some?"

Though her mouth actually watered, she shook her head and said lightly, "We don't know one another well enough for me to eat off of your plate."

"That would be the second date?"

Uh-oh. The D word. Is that what he thought this was? What she had led him to believe? She nearly groaned. If he did, she had no one to blame but herself after that wholly inappropriate lip-lock. Sure, she'd explained it away afterward, but there was a reason for the saying: actions speak louder than words.

Over the quiet conversations of the other diners, Emily could hear music, airy flutes accompanied by the almost mournful sound of string instruments. It fit her current mood perfectly.

"Madani," she began.

He held up a hand, stopping her. "You are going to tell me we are not on a date. Am I right?" His gaze was as direct as his words.

"I think I may have given you the wrong impression earlier." She straightened in her seat, coughed. "Back at my parents' house."

"When you kissed me, you mean?"

Emily figured she had turned the same shade as the prancing dragon that adorned the festive wall mural. "Yes. Then."

"Will it offend you if I say I enjoyed it?" One dark brow shot up.

"I...I..." She might have continued stammering if he had not spared her by going on.

"You did not give me the wrong impression, Emily. Afterward, you made your reasons for kissing me very, very clear."

"Oh. Well...good." She shifted back in her seat, wishing those reasons were as clear to her right now as she studied his handsome face and considered leaning across the table to kiss him again. "I just wanted..." Uh-oh, don't go there. Starting over, she said, "It's just that we have a business relationship."

He smiled warmly. A little too warmly. "Yes."

"I think it would be best for it to stay that way." She said it and told herself that she meant it even as something she refused to admit might be disappointment did a little shimmy-shake through her stomach.

Emily thought she saw something dim in his dark

eyes, but his expression and demeanor remained unchanged. Indeed, his voice sounded matter-of-fact when he replied, "We are in perfect agreement."

They ate in silence for a moment. Then Madani plucked one of the plump shrimp from the browned rice with his chopsticks and dropped it onto the side of her plate.

A peace offering? Apparently so.

"Maybe, in addition to having a business relationship, we also can be friends?"

"Friends?" The word sounded foreign to her ears.

"Yes."

She blinked, smiled. "I'd like that. Truly I would. Friends."

As they finished their meal, Emily knew she should have felt relieved. It was for the best. After all, what else beyond friendship could come from this…this relationship? Madani would be leaving the country soon, returning to his homeland in the Middle East. She had dreams of her own to pursue after his departure, plans that would require every last bit of her energy and attention to be realized in full.

Yes, nipping any sort of romantic notion between them in the bud was for the best.

Between bites, she glanced over and caught him watching her. The pair of chopsticks she held in her right hand stilled and she stopped chewing. She nearly stopped breathing, as, during one long, poignant moment, a pair of dark eyes took her measure.

What do you see?

She desperately wanted to ask him. She wanted to demand an answer if necessary. A host of other questions bubbled to the surface then, too.

When his lips tipped up in a smile that set off her pulse, the only one Emily didn't want answered was why she suddenly felt like crying.

CHAPTER SEVEN

IT WAS a nice evening for a walk, breezy and warm without a hint of humidity in the air. The meal they'd eaten, while far from being heavy, gave Madani another good excuse to ask Emily if she'd care to take a stroll after they left the restaurant.

Friends could do that, he told himself, even as the way he was admiring her legs had meandered into an arena well beyond the platonic.

"But what about Azeem?" She turned and glanced around. Neither the driver nor the Mercedes was anywhere to be found.

"He will come when I call for him."

And Madani hadn't called yet. He'd planned to just before they finished their main courses. That was usually what he did to give his driver enough time to arrive at the curb. But he'd procrastinated, not ready for his time with Emily to end. And once they were in his automobile, under Azeem's knowing eye, it would.

"He doesn't mind just waiting around for his phone to ring?" she asked.

"Not very much." Madani smiled, though, knowing that his good friend would indeed grumble mightily to him about it later. He always did.

Emily switched the small clutch she held to her other hand and turned slightly as they walked, giving him, rather than the antiques and curio shops, her undivided attention. "I get the feeling the two of you are more than just employee and employer."

"We are," he said simply.

"Is it difficult, being both his friend and his boss?" she asked.

"It can be difficult at times," he began. As the son of Kashaqra's ruler, Madani was used to people doing as he requested without hesitation let alone question. Azeem was the exception. Thinking of Azeem's opinion of Madani's betrothal contract, he continued, "Azeem and I do not always agree, but he is one of the few people in my acquaintance who is not afraid to offer his true opinion even when he knows it will not be what I wish to hear. I respect him for that."

"You don't strike me as all that fearsome," Emily teased. "There must be another side to you I haven't seen."

If only she knew. Madani almost told her about his title then, just to discover if it would change the way she treated him. He hoped she would be like Azeem, able to see him first as a man and second as a ruler in waiting. But revealing his status chanced pulling his other secret out into the open. Though he had nothing to feel guilty about—Emily had initiated the kiss they'd shared earlier—he was enjoying her company too much. There was an ease, an intimacy to their conversation that surely would not exist were Emily privy to the upcoming announcement of his engagement.

She was saying, "Well, the fact Azeem speaks his mind around you makes him not only a friend, but a good one. I hope you appreciate his candor, even when what he says makes you uncomfortable or angry."

"Why do you say that?" Madani asked. Her tone, both wry and wistful, made him curious.

"Because I have a good friend—had, I guess, is the more accurate description at this point—who tried to tell me that Reed wasn't right for me. She tried to tell me that when push came to shove, he wouldn't be there for me. He wouldn't support my career. But I didn't listen to her." Emily lifted her shoulders. "I *wouldn't* listen."

"You did not want her to be right," he said, thinking of his arguments with Azeem on the betrothal agreement.

"Exactly. We argued about Reed on several occasions. I made excuses for his behavior. Excuses she shot full of holes. That in turn began to put a strain on our friendship. So, I started calling her less often." She motioned with her free hand. "Finding reasons I couldn't meet her for coffee or lunch. Then, finally, we both stopped picking up the phone. We haven't spoken in nearly three years."

"Obviously that troubles you. Why don't you call her now?" he asked.

"I'm embarrassed, I guess." Emily's laughter was rueful. "Donna was absolutely right about Reed, and that was before he proved what an absolute jerk he was by running around with my sister behind my back."

"So, to avoid embarrassment you will deprive yourself of her friendship now?"

Emily wrinkled her nose. The gesture wasn't intended to be sexy. He found it to be so anyway. "When you put it like that it makes me sound foolish."

"I'm sorry. That wasn't my intent."

"No, don't apologize. You're right, Madani. One hundred percent correct. And I am being foolish. I've missed her so much," she said with feeling. "I have other friends, of course, but Donna and I go back a long way."

"If that is so, it won't matter the length of time that has passed. She will welcome hearing from you."

"Yeah." Emily nodded, slowly at first and then with vehemence. "She will. I'm going to call her. First thing tomorrow. Or maybe even when I get home tonight. Thank you."

"You're most welcome, though really I have done nothing."

"You're a good listener."

"I try to be." It was a trait his father reminded him often enough would serve him well as ruler.

Emily angled her head to one side. "Have you and Azeem ever not spoken?"

"No." Madani chuckled. "He is far too fond of talking to remain silent for any length of time."

"How long have you known him?"

"Since boyhood," he told her, and couldn't repress the smile the old memories teased out. "If I tell you that he can be a bad influence on me, will you think it the truth?"

"Perhaps," she replied diplomatically, but then her lips curved. "Although it seems highly unlikely."

Madani laughed outright. "My mother said the very thing when we were boys. Azeem's mother as well. Even when the mischief we got into was entirely of his making, he managed to escape all blame."

"*Entirely* of his making?"

"Mostly." At her raised eyebrows, he amended, "Well, at least in small part."

Her laughter rang out, surprisingly robust. He liked hearing it. He liked seeing her looking so relaxed, especially after the afternoon she'd had. "It sounds as if they had you pegged."

"Pegged?" He turned the word over in his mind for a moment before understanding dawned. "Yes. I suppose they did."

"Besides, you don't strike me as the sort of person who would be easily led—even as a child and regardless of the temptation."

"No." He had not been easily led as child, nor as a man. Although he fought the urge, his gaze lowered to Emily's mouth, recalling the way it had felt against his. He swallowed hard. Temptation stood before him now in the form of a beautiful, sexy and exciting young woman. He wanted to know more of her, to know everything about her. He had neither the time nor the right. He glanced away, but because he could not completely curb his curiosity, he asked, "What sort of person do you think I am, Emily?"

"You're just fishing for compliments now," she accused on a laugh.

It was another unfamiliar phrase, but given the context of their conversation Madani figured it out easily enough. Chuckling, he said, "I suppose that I am. Will you be kind enough to indulge me?"

Emily's shoulders lifted in a shrug. "Why not?" But it was a moment before she went on, giving him the impression she was putting real thought into the exercise. "You come across as authoritative and very determined. It's clear that you know what you like and what you want."

"Yes." Indeed, he knew exactly what he liked, what he wanted. Not that he was free to do anything about it.

"I mean, white truffles, for heaven's sake." She blew out a breath and smiled. She was talking about food, which was just as well.

They reached a corner and, as they waited for the light to change, Emily continued. "I don't need to tell you that you're attractive. That night at the Hendersons', my assistant was sure you were a male underwear model."

He coughed. "That is a compliment, yes?"

"Oh, most definitely." She glanced around. "I'll point his ad out to you if I see one."

"I'll look forward to it," he said dryly.

She chuckled and, clearly enjoying his discomfort, went on. "You know, our waitress back at Fuwang's would have given me a serious case of food poisoning if she thought doing so would give her the chance to have you all to herself."

"You exaggerate."

She snorted. "She barely spared me a glance, even when I was ordering." Emily batted her long lashes at him. "She only had eyes for you, Madani."

"It is because I command attention." He said it tongue-in-cheek, even though from the cradle on his parents had taught him to be forceful, assertive.

"Right. You're also so humble," Emily deadpanned, drawing out his laughter. More seriously, she added, "You're obviously industrious and capable. You've created a very clever business opportunity for yourself. I think you're also generous, because your business opportunity in turn has offered the talented men and women of your homeland a way to market their wares overseas and make more money. In your own way, you're putting Kashaqra on the map."

Madani liked knowing Emily saw it that way. It was what he'd intended, giving his people a better way to earn a living, encouraging a positive image abroad for his homeland.

"What else?"

"You're insatiable."

"Insatiable?" It was an interesting word choice, he thought, aware of its other meaning. And apropos, because when Madani was with Emily that was exactly how he felt: hungry for more and not just sexually.

In their relatively brief acquaintance he'd figured out a few things about her, such as while she came across as fiercely independent and driven, she was also vulnerable and surprisingly unsure of herself when it came to being a woman. Madani blamed her ex-boyfriend for that, though her family appeared to have had a hand in it as well. They'd given her either-or choices.

She could be smart or beautiful like her coddled younger sister. She could follow her dreams or she could have a husband. They'd made her choose when no choice was necessary and, in fact, making a choice had robbed her of a full and truly satisfying life.

Emily deserved better than that. She deserved…so much more.

A blush bloomed becomingly on her cheeks, the product, he assumed, of her unplanned double entendre. "I'm referring to your ego. It needs constant feeding. But then I've yet to meet a man whose ego doesn't."

He didn't care for the comparison, but Madani worked up a comically wounded expression as he placed his right hand over his heart. "Despite all of your flattery then, are you saying you find me mundane?"

"Oh, absolutely. That's the word that springs to mind. There's nothing new or original about you." Her lips curved with an unintentional invitation. It took all of Madani's willpower to resist.

"But you are original, Emily Merit, which is why I will remember our time together in Manhattan for the rest of my life."

He took her fingers in his. He meant only to give them a friendly squeeze. He and Emily were no longer in Chinatown. For that matter, Madani hadn't the slightest idea of where they were. But as he lifted the back of Emily's hand to his lips for a kiss, that wasn't why he was feeling so utterly lost.

"Oh my God!"

His gaze flew to hers, but she wasn't looking at him. She was staring over his shoulder, a combination of excitement and disbelief evident in her expression. The ego she'd just accused him of having deflated like a punctured balloon. Not that she noticed. She'd already pulled her hand from his and was hurrying toward the window of a nearby building.

"This is it!" she announced, turning to grin at him. "This is exactly the location I want and—oh, my God!—it's available right now."

He read the real estate sign tucked in the window, noted the ample square footage. "It seems large for a catering business." Not to mention pricey, he thought, especially when her remodeled kitchen could accommodate her needs.

"It's not for catering. It's for The Merit." She said it with a lofty inflection, pride and excitement beaming in her expression when she announced, "My restaurant."

* * *

Emily watched the words sink in and part of her braced, ready for a negative reaction, which was how Reed and even her family had greeted her plans to open her own eatery. Madani, however, nodded in approval and smiled.

"What kind of restaurant will it be? Tell me about it," he invited.

"That's the wrong thing to say." At his frown, she explained, "I can go on and on about the plans I have."

He merely shrugged. "I have the time."

A moment ago, when he'd kissed her hand, she'd nearly melted into a puddle of hormones. She'd considered staging a repeat of the scene in her mother's living room, might have followed through, too, had she not spied the For Lease sign in the window. Thankfully sanity had returned. It was threatening to flee again as he stood in front of her, by all appearances genuinely interested in hearing her expound on her dream.

"Are you sure?"

Madani glanced across the street to where a martini-glass-shaped neon sign blinked over the entrance of Dean's Place. A smattering of tables was set up on the sidewalk outside. He pointed to the lone empty one and said, "It's a nice evening to sit outside. Let me buy you a drink, and you can tell me all about your restaurant."

It was just after eleven when Emily and Madani left the bar. Although Madani objected, she paid their tab. It was the least she could do after everything the man had done for her this day.

The Mercedes was at the curb. By the time they reached the car, Azeem was holding open the rear door.

"I trust you had a good evening?" he inquired politely, although a bit of the devil gleamed in his gaze when he glanced Madani's way.

"We did."

"I hope we didn't ruin yours," Emily added.

"Ah, Miss Merit, you are too beautiful to ruin anything."

"If you're going to be so outrageous with your flattery, you must call me Emily."

"Emily." He nodded. "Where shall I take you now?"

"Home, please."

Madani rattled off the address and a moment later they were on their way.

Seated next to Madani, she wondered how it was possible to feel exhausted and energized at the same time. She already had a million ideas for her restaurant, ideas she'd typed into her computer and referenced on a regular basis, adding to them, weeding out those that wouldn't work, using them as a pick-me-up on those days when her outlook needed bolstering.

Tonight, she'd come up with even more ideas. Despite the late hour, they were popping around in her head like pinballs. Some of them had come courtesy of Madani. The man was an excellent listener and sounding board. She appreciated his advice and the respectful way in which he offered it. Whenever Reed had given Emily suggestions, he'd made her feel like a dim-witted child for not having thought of them first.

As the car pulled to the curb, she held up the cocktail napkin on which she had jotted down some notes.

"Thank you." She waved the napkin. "For this and for everything else. I'm in your debt."

He shook his head. "Never."

"I enjoyed myself tonight. It's been a long time since I've gone out and let someone else do the cooking." Her laughter was rueful.

"You should do it more often."

"It's hard to find the time."

"You should make the time."

"All work and no play…" She'd said the same thing at her parent's house. At his frown, she added, "It's a saying. All work and no play makes Jack a dull boy. Or, in my case, Emily. And, well, it makes me a dull girl." She was babbling. It was the way he was looking at her.

"You're much too interesting to ever be considered dull, Emily."

She tried to laugh, but the sound that escaped was more of a sigh.

"Well, I'd better go." Before she could reach for the door, however, Azeem hopped out from the driver's seat and opened it for her.

Madani followed her. "I'll walk you up," he said.

"Oh, that's not necessary."

"Indulge me."

Azeem said something to Madani then in their native language. Even in the low light cast by the streetlamps,

Emily could see Madani flush. If his terse-sounding reply was any indication, in addition to being embarrassed, he was irritated.

Azeem, however, was unperturbed. Indeed, he laughed robustly. "Of course, my friend. But you are a fool."

Since Azeem had switched back to English, Madani did as well. "I will return in no more than five minutes." The words were said slowly and enunciated with care.

"No more than five minutes? A man should never admit to that."

Madani slipped back into his language for his reply and his inflection made it clear he'd just said something that could not be repeated in polite company.

"Is everything all right?" she asked when they stepped into her building's elevator a moment later. "Between you and Azeem, I mean."

"Fine."

Though it wasn't like her to pry, Emily said, "It didn't sound fine. And I can't help feeling I'm somehow responsible for the exchange."

"No. You did not cause our words."

"Maybe I didn't cause them, but you were talking about me. Weren't you, Madani?"

"Yes." He glanced away, sighed. "I apologize for both of us."

She pulled a face, seeking to lighten the moment. "Gee, was what you said about me *that* rude?"

He found no humor in her question. "No. Rest assured that Azeem has nothing but respect for you, as do I."

"But," she prompted.

"As I already mentioned, my friend can be quite outspoken in expressing his opinions. I have certain obligations, duties," he said softly. "I take them very seriously. I must. Azeem…we differ on how I should approach those obligations."

"If that was intended as an explanation, I'm afraid I'm still in the dark." She laughed awkwardly. Obligations. Duties. For the first time it struck her how little she knew about the man.

A bell dinged as the elevator reached her floor. She stepped into the empty hallway when the doors parted. Madani remained in the car. His gaze was intense. The way he dragged a hand through his hair hinted at frustration.

"Emily, I want you to know that…"

"Yes?"

"I wish…"

The doors started to close. They both reached out to stop them. "What do you wish?"

He blinked, smiled charmingly and let his hands drop. The turmoil she'd glimpsed just a moment before was gone from his expression.

"I wish you a good night."

CHAPTER EIGHT

"Who is he?"

Emily's sister demanded this even before offering a proper greeting as she waltzed into Emily's apartment late the following morning.

Despite a poor night's sleep, Emily had been in a terrific mood. First thing upon waking, she'd followed through on her promise to reconnect with her friend. She'd gotten Donna's voice mail, left a message. An hour ago, Donna had returned Emily's call and agreed to meet with her for drinks the following week. The conversation had been brief and on the awkward side. Emily had expected no less given the passage of time and the old hurts. But it was a start. Her good mood leached away with Elle's unexpected appearance.

"Hello to you, too," she muttered and closed the door with enough force to leave the locks rattling. "Just in the neighborhood?" If so, she would have to see about moving.

Whereas Emily was pretty sure she looked like the last

one standing after a cafeteria food fight—her apron was splattered with the ingredients of the half dozen recipes she'd worked on since dawn—Elle was fresh and radiant in a pale pink linen suit whose three-quarter-length sleeves offered an unrestricted view of the diamond bracelet Reed had given her to mark their engagement.

"Actually I sort of was. I'm meeting Reed at Herman's for lunch in an hour." Elle set her luggage-size Gucci bag on one of the stools lined up in front of the granite-topped island and sighed dramatically. "We're going over song selections for our first dance."

"Gee, that could take hours," Emily replied.

The sarcasm sailed over her sister's bleached-blond head. "I know, but he only can spare one. He's a busy and important man."

Which was why Reed wanted—*required*—a woman who had an open schedule so she could drop everything when he had a free moment to spend with her. With her restaurant dreams to pursue and a catering business to run, Emily had been a square peg to his round hole. Not so Elle. She and Reed complemented one another perfectly.

"Are you here to ask me for suggestions?" If so, Emily had some, though none was a song title.

"No. I thought we could…chat. We hardly had a moment to spend together yesterday at my shower." Elle shook her heavy cascade of blonde curls. The color was manufactured, but the texture was natural. Though Emily hated herself for it, she found herself fingering the ends of her stick-straight brown hair.

"So, who is he?" Elle asked a second time.

"Who is who?"

Her sister folded her arms over her chest, creating more impressive cleavage in the linen jacket. "Don't play dumb, Em. We both know I'm referring to the man you practically mauled in Mom's living room. It was all any of the aunts could talk about for the rest of the afternoon."

Indignation paired with embarrassment had Emily shooting back, "I didn't maul him. It was a kiss."

"It was more than a kiss and we both know it." Elle held up her diamond-heavy left hand to forestall Emily's retort. "Hey, I'm not finding fault. He's a yummy specimen. If my wedding to Reed wasn't just a couple of months away, I would be tempted to sample him, too."

Emily's mouth gaped open for a moment. Was it sheer nerve that caused her backstabbing baby sister to make that comment or could Elle really be that oblivious to its poor taste?

"Well?" Elle demanded when Emily remained silent. "Are you going to give me details or not?"

As if she was entitled to them? Em gritted her teeth. She needed something to do with her hands…before she used them to strangle her way to only-child status. She put the kitchen island between them, picked up the citrus zester and grabbed a lemon from the bowl on the countertop. With a bit more force than necessary, she shaved tiny bits of yellow peel into what was to become a marinade for a chicken recipe.

Cooking. It was her savior.

"Madani is a client, but we also enjoy one another's company." What she said was the truth, though for some reason she wanted to sigh with regret.

"I thought his name was Dan?"

"Dan. Yes. Short for Madani."

"Madani?" Elle repeated. "What's his last name?"

"Tarim."

"Madani Tarim." Elle's perfectly arched brows drew together. "Why does that sound familiar?"

"I can't imagine. Maybe one of the characters on your soap opera shares it."

Elle puckered her lips thoughtfully, but shook her head a moment later. "No. That's not it. But I've heard it somewhere and recently I think."

"I'll take your word for it." Emily dipped the tip of her index finger in the marinade for a taste and added another pinch of salt.

"Mom said you gave her the impression nothing was going on between the two of you." She snorted then. "Aunt Sally said if that was nothing, then every single woman in New York should be so lucky."

Emily resisted the urge to fan herself. Instead, she shrugged. "You know how Mom is. It's never a good idea to give her too much information."

"Is he…an escort?"

"What?" The word came out more shout than question.

"I'd understand completely if you—you know—had to hire a man to fill certain voids in your life. We all need… companionship."

Companionship. It was code for sex and they both knew it. Apparently Elle had counted up the months she'd been with Reed and deduced that Emily hadn't enjoyed a good, sweaty bout between the sheets since then. It stunk that her sister was half right. Emily had lived like a novitiate since then. Though truth be told she'd never found sex with Reed—who'd been her first and only lover—to be all that mind-blowing. She thought it was her. Maybe she just wasn't all that sexual. She knew better now that she'd met Madani. With a mere kiss on the back of her hand he'd caused a more intense physical reaction than Reed could muster with half an hour of inventive foreplay.

Still, Emily was outraged that her sister thought her to be so desperate and unappealing that she needed to pay for sexual fulfillment.

"Madani Tarim is not on my payroll in any way, shape or form," she snapped.

"Jeez, Em." Elle held up both hands. "There's no need to get so worked up."

"I'm not worked up. I'm insulted, Elle. Even you should be able to figure out why."

"Fine." Her sister rolled her baby blues skyward. "I'm sorry."

Yeah, she sounded sorry. Emily decided to let it go. "Forget it."

"So, is it serious?"

Emily chose her words carefully, well aware that every single one of them, in some fashion or another, would be relayed to her entire extended family. "I don't know that I'd call it serious. We're good friends."

"Good friends, hmm?" Elle's smile turned sly. "Is that another way of saying friends with benefits?"

The innuendo had heat flaring in Emily's cheeks. The topic just kept coming back to sex and, for a woman who had lain awake half the night thinking about it, she didn't need this now.

"Aren't you just full of questions this morning?" she evaded frostily.

"We're sisters."

"A fact that you tend to recall only when it's convenient for you."

Elle glanced away. "Come on, Em. I'm worried about you, okay? It's been months since you last came to a family dinner at Mom and Pop's."

"Three guesses why."

Elle ignored the jab and went on. "Given your crazy work schedule you can't have much time to go out with friends on weekends."

"I like my job."

"And I'd bet my favorite pair of Jimmy Choos that you haven't gone on a date since…"

"Since Reed?"

Elle moistened her lips. "Yes."

Emily set the zester aside and stared at her sister over the span of the island. "Are you feeling a little guilty?"

Emily wanted her sister to be. More than that, she wanted the apology that was long overdue. Perhaps then she would be able truly to put the sordid mess behind her and move on. She, Reed and Elle would never be one big happily dysfunctional family, sitting down to Sunday dinner at her folks' house, but an apology would help.

Elle didn't apologize, though. She crossed her arms and pouted. And it stunk that her sister could look so damned good doing something so childish.

"God, Em! You're so mean. Do you have to dredge that up again? Can't we move on already? It's been a year." Tears worked their way to the edges of Elle's baby blues, but her face remained splotchless and amazingly her eye makeup remained perfectly in place.

I've got to learn how to cry like that, Em thought.

"Gee, sorry. I don't know what I was thinking." Except, how like her sister to flip the situation around, turn herself into the victim and wangle an apology out of Emily.

Emily picked up the zester and went to work on the lemon again.

"I just want you to find someone who makes you feel as special as I do whenever I'm with Reed."

I thought I had. It took an effort for Emily to bite her tongue and she was glad she had, because she realized now, it wasn't true. Reed hadn't made her feel special. He'd made her feel…inadequate and even intractable for wanting to pursue her own dreams rather than help him pursue his.

"What we have together, it's such a fairy tale," Elle was saying. "You know like Romeo and Julia."

"Juliet," Em corrected.

"Right." She waved a hand dismissively. "Her."

The dreamy sigh that ensued had the same effect on Emily's nerves as fingernails being scratched down a chalkboard. Maybe she should point out that in Shakespeare's play the young, star-crossed lovers had both wound up dead.

She didn't. What was the point? Instead, she asked in exasperation, "How is it possible that we're sisters?"

Elle stared blankly.

"We have the same parents," Emily said. "In many cases we had the same opportunities."

Elle continued to stare blankly

"How is it possible for us to be such polar opposites? And I don't just mean in looks. I'm willing to work for what I want. You…you expect everyone else to do the heavy lifting for you. And do you know what stinks about that? They do. Mom and Dad have always given you a free pass."

Elle's expression went from blank to wounded. "I'm sorry that you've always been so jealous of me, Em. It's not my fault that my life has worked out so well while yours is so empty."

"Empty." She thought of her catering business, the satisfaction she'd felt watching it grow. And her plans for the restaurant, which continued to inch closer to reality. "Is that what you think?"

"Reed says—"

"Don't!" Emily held the zester out like a weapon. "I don't want to hear Reed's opinion of my life. I heard it too often when we were dating. Besides, we're talking about you. You're smart, Elle. You could do anything, *be* anything, if you just started applying yourself. Don't you have any ambitions?"

"Of course I do." She gave her hair an indignant toss. "I want to become Mrs. Reed Benedict in a wedding that will be the talk of the town for years to come."

Emily closed her eyes and sighed. They were back at square one.

"At least I'm not going to wind up old and alone." Elle raised her hand. "I don't want to fight. That's not why I came here today."

"No, you wanted to find out if I'd hired a male escort."

"I was hoping you'd found someone special to bring to my wedding," Elle said coolly. "I still haven't received your RSVP."

"That's because I haven't decided if I'm coming— alone or otherwise."

"But you have to come," Elle all but wailed. "You have to be a bridesmaid." Her genuine disappointment might have caused Emily to waver had she not added, "If you don't agree to stand up I'll be forced to have our cousin Constance in the wedding party, and she's put on so much weight since she got married."

Emily gaped. "Constance just had a baby, Elle."

"Hello. Three months ago. And at the slow rate she's losing the weight, she's still going to be at least a size eight in August."

"Tragedy," Emily muttered.

Elle ignored her. "Besides, the peach organdy I picked out does nothing for her complexion."

Emily had seen the dress. Nothing about its color or cut did anything for any of the bridesmaids' complexions and figures. But then, that was why Elle had chosen it.

"Say you'll think about it," she implored.

Because agreeing with her sister was easier than listening to her whine, Emily nodded.

"Great!" Elle clapped her hands together in childish delight before her expression turned calculating. "So, will you bring your new man to the wedding? Mom and the aunts are dying to corner him and pry out every last detail of his life. You should have heard the way they went on and on about him yesterday after you left."

Emily didn't need to have heard them. She could imagine the conversations perfectly. So, her relationship with the sexy and mysterious Dan was the subject of family speculation and gossip. That was just what she'd hoped for when she'd planted that kiss on him. Objective achieved.

So why didn't she like it?

Her grip tightened on the zester. "I don't think I'll be bringing him. I wouldn't want to put him through that."

Besides, long before Reed and Elle celebrated their first dance as husband and wife, Madani would be back in his homeland. Emily's heart gave a funny thump at the thought. She passed it off as regret. After all, the kiss apparently had left the impression with the Poor Emily crowd that she was having a good old time post-Reed. Once they learned the affair had gone nowhere—and given the efficiency of the Merit family grapevine, they would hear it before Madani's plane lifted off the runway—her first name once again would be preceded by a pity-garnering qualifier.

Elle frowned. "Oh. So you'll be coming solo."

"I haven't said I will be coming at all."

"Em," her sister wailed. "You've got to."

"Because I'll look better in the dress than Constance?" Emily nearly laughed.

"Of course not." Elle nibbled her lip. "But you will. Besides, I've paired you with Grant Barrymore. You know him."

Yes, she knew him. She also detested him. Reed and Grant were longtime friends. They had pledged the same fraternity in college, making them "brothers." But that hadn't stopped Grant from making a pass at Emily one night when he'd had too much to drink.

Wasn't anyone capable of loyalty or restraint anymore? Was Emily the only one who valued honesty and believed trust to be the foundation of a relationship?

Madani. The name and thoughts of the man blasted free from her subconscious.

He would, Emily decided. Any man who would let a woman kiss him the way Emily had and later the same evening leave her at the doorstep would understand restraint.

If Emily were in the market for a man, Madani would be exactly the sort she would fall for fast and hard. Good thing she wasn't in the market.

"Is that going to be edible?"

Elle's question brought her back to the present. She blinked at her sister. "Wh-what?"

"Whatever it is you're making. It doesn't look very appetizing." Elle's nose wrinkled.

Emily glanced down at the pulpy remains of the lemon clutched in her hand. She'd grated off every last bit of the peel and most of the bitter white pith. The marinade was ruined. She would have to start over.

Emily was on Madani's mind, starting with a sleepless Sunday night through the rest of the week. The more time he spent with her the more he wanted to spend with her. Add in that kiss and his mind was straying to forbidden places.

Friendship. It was what he'd offered her as they'd dined in Fuwang's. It was what he'd shown her later, when he listened intently to her plans for a restaurant.

Friendship. He'd never been friends with a woman before. Friendly, but not actual friends. He wanted so much more from Emily. But it was all he had to offer.

Sleep with her.

That was Azeem's unhelpful suggestion. He thought Madani should engage in a brief but mutually satisfying affair, maybe buy her a lovely trinket at the end of it. That way he would get Emily Merit and all women out of his system while he was still entitled to do so. He'd said so again Sunday evening—though thankfully in Arabic—when they'd arrived outside Emily's apartment.

Even after Madani had returned to the car—a full two minutes shy of the five minutes he'd predicted—his friend had continued goading him.

"I don't understand you. Why are you here with me when a young and beautiful woman is alone in her rooms and undressing as we speak?"

"Shut up and drive."

"Your mood would improve dramatically if you allowed yourself to relieve some frustration. I can turn the car around at the next light and take you back. I doubt she would mind the intrusion."

"No."

But his friend had continued as if Madani hadn't spoken. "In fact, from the way she looked at you tonight, I think she would welcome the intrusion."

"I said no."

"I could return for you in the morning, though not too early." He'd turned and winked. "You will have good reason to sleep late."

"Enough!" Madani had shouted as erotic images reeled through his mind.

Given the fierceness of both his tone and expression, he'd figured his friend would back down at the command, maybe even apologize for having gone too far.

He should have known better. Azeem snickered and not at all discreetly.

"At dinner tonight Emily asked me if it was difficult to be both your employer and your friend. I warn you, Azeem. If you keep it up I will be neither."

"Your threats would hold more weight, *sadiqi*, if I thought you actually meant them." He smiled, unperturbed. "We have known one another far too long."

"I was just thinking the same thing." Madani shoved a hand through his hair and exhaled loudly.

"You are not angry with me. You are angry with yourself."

"It is done, Azeem. How many times must I say it?"

"No. The engagement has not been officially announced. Your father will listen to you. He is a reasonable man, hardly provincial in his views. He has ushered much change into Kashaqra, brought our people into a new century."

"He honors the old ways."

"You are being a fool."

"Don't go there. Not again. Or at least not tonight." He'd rubbed his eyes, suddenly exhausted. "I am too tired for more verbal sparring."

"Because you know I am right," Azeem had said. In a more thoughtful tone, he'd asked, "Or perhaps someone else has started to change your mind?"

Now, four days later, Madani mulled his friend's words as he sat on the terrace of his apartment at The

Mark drinking a cup of the sweetened black coffee favored in his homeland. More than a dozen stories below, the midday traffic buzzed along on Madison Avenue, the blaring horns muted by distance and his own distraction.

If he thought a brief but satisfying affair with Emily Merit would get her out of his system he might have allowed Azeem to turn the car around that evening. There was no denying he was physically attracted to her and had been since their introduction in the Hendersons' kitchen. At each meeting during the two weeks since then his desire for her had only increased. As had his interest beyond the physical. That was the real problem.

He liked Emily, truly enjoyed her company. He admired her determination, the dreams she'd so carefully nurtured and refused to give up even in the face of adversity and heartache. She was amusing, thoughtful and incredibly bright. Not just a beautifully wrapped package like her younger sister, but one filled with riches and substance. Madani wanted to spend the next several weeks, even months, getting to know her better. He didn't have that luxury. Precious little time remained of either his visit to New York or of his bachelorhood.

One week after his dinner party Madani would return home. A month after that all of Kashaqra would mark the start of The Feast of Seven Days, which celebrated the country's overthrow of an oppressive ruler. As the celebration wound down his engagement would be announced.

His future was set.

He drained the last of his coffee. As sweet as it was, it turned bitter in his mouth. For as long as Madani could remember, whatever he'd wanted he'd gotten. Thanks to his wealth and rank, nothing ever had been beyond his reach.

Until now.

CHAPTER NINE

WITH two events on Merit Catering's schedule for the following day, Emily's kitchen was a beehive of activity Friday evening, and it had been since midafternoon.

At the island, Arlene was mixing up the crab meat filling that would be piped into pastry puffs and baked on location at the birthday party in Connecticut. All five layers of the cake had been baked and were cooling on the counter. The raspberry mousse filling was mixed and chilling in the refrigerator.

Emily had just returned from her favorite gourmet market for the last of the ingredients for Madani's dinner, including the fresh herbs and pricey white truffles. She'd planned to shop with Madani, but scheduling conflicts forced her to go solo.

Setting her shopping bag on the counter, she dipped her index finger into the bowl for a taste. "I think it needs a little more Worcestershire."

"I like it with less," Arlene said.

"I like it with more."

"And you're the boss."

It was an old argument, so Emily laughed.

Arlene grabbed the bottle of Worcestershire. As she added a few more dashes to the mix, she grumbled. "A bunch of bratty five-year-olds aren't going to care."

"No, but their parents might be more discerning when it comes to crab tarts. And if they like them the way Merit Catering makes them, they might hire us to do an adult event in the future."

"Pay attention, Sarita," Arlene said to the young culinary arts student who'd been helping out for the afternoon.

Emily regularly employed students from her alma mater, making up in on-the-job experience what she couldn't afford to give them in actual pay. She was grateful for the added help this day, even if the young woman had an endless supply of questions that kept breaking the rhythm Emily and Arlene had down to a science.

A knock sounded at the door as Emily carefully unpacked the truffles.

"Can you get that, Sarita? It's probably a delivery. I'm expecting some wine."

Even though Madani said he had everything he needed for his party, she'd picked up a couple of bottles of a special vintage for him. They were a thank-you of sorts not only for rescuing her from her sister's bridal shower but for listening so thoughtfully as she'd expounded on her restaurant plans.

"Um, Miss Merit," Sarita called a moment later. "It's for you."

She glanced over and her gaze locked with Madani's. His smile was slightly embarrassed, and all the sexier for it.

"I am catching you at a bad time," he said.

"No." Her palms felt damp. She wiped them on her apron. "I mean, yes. But come in."

Arlene cleared her throat noisily and mumbled, "An introduction would be nice."

"Oh. Right. Madani Tarim, this is my assistant, Arlene." Emily pointed to the other young woman. "And that's Sarita."

"Ladies."

He smiled. They sighed. Emily wanted to groan.

"So, what brings you by?" she asked.

"I brought some wine for you to try."

"That's funny," she said, thinking of the wine she'd ordered for him.

"Funny?"

Emily waved a hand. "Never mind."

"I planned to serve this tomorrow evening, but I wanted your opinion first. I wouldn't want it to clash with the menu you've so carefully planned." He held out the bottle for her inspection.

Emily read the label. She recognized the name of the French winery. The bottle hadn't come cheaply. In fact, it cost double what hers had. But that didn't surprise her.

Madani wasn't the sort of man to go halfway. "This was an excellent year for pinot noir, I believe. It should pair well with the fish."

"Care for a glass?" he asked. His gaze included the others.

"Now?" Emily glanced back at the kitchen where so much remained to be done. Even so, she shrugged. "I suppose a taste wouldn't hurt."

"I'll get the glasses." Arlene grinned.

Sarita was still staring at Madani with unabashed adoration. It was embarrassing, but understandable. Emily liked looking at him herself. She cleared her throat. "Arlene, grab four glasses from the cupboard. I think we've all earned a few minutes of downtime."

Two hours later the wine was gone. Sarita was, too, having left after half a glass to meet friends who'd called from a pub on Bleecker. Arlene was preparing to leave as well since she would be back early the next morning to wrap things up and load the catering van. She had finished the appetizers for the birthday party and done what prep work could be done for the entrées.

Madani was the only one who showed no interest in leaving. Not that Emily minded. It was no hardship to spend time with him. He'd watched the food preparation with interest, asking lots of questions that made it clear he'd never boiled water much less decorated a birthday cake, which Emily started on after Arlene left.

"This isn't exactly my forte," she admitted as she began spreading the raspberry mousse between layers of white cake. "I explained that to my client. In fact, I gave her the name of a bakery I do a lot of business with. But, she insisted."

"She must have faith in you."

"I think she just wanted to write one check and be done with it. She's a *very busy woman*," Emily intoned. "She must have told me that every time we spoke. It kind of made me wonder why she wanted to have a child." She added another layer of cake. "I'm busy, too. Probably busier than she is since Babs knows her and said she doesn't have a paying job. But I know my limits and I've determined my priorities."

"Are you saying you will never marry and have children?" Madani asked quietly.

The blunt question, which came just as Emily was leveling the second layer, caught her off-guard. She stopped midcut and glanced over at him. He was watching her closely.

"I won't say never, but it's looking doubtful. And since I see parenting as a two-person job, I probably won't be having kids."

Emily had made peace with the fact that her career plans were incompatible with a long-term relationship and parental responsibilities. Or she thought she had. But saying so now to Madani caused a dull throbbing to begin in her chest. She'd thought it a fair trade, but now she felt cheated.

"Is your decision based on what happened with Benedict?" he asked.

"Yes and no." She finished trimming the layer and set the blade aside. "The reality is, I work a lot of nights and most weekends. Reed didn't want me to succeed at my career for a variety of reasons, my schedule included."

Madani spat out something in his native tongue. Given the sharpness of his tone, she didn't need to ask for a translation. Her lips tipped up. "Yeah, I know. Reed's a first-class jerk."

"The phrase I came up with was a little more descriptive," Madani replied dryly. "He's intimidated by your success. It makes him feel like less of a man."

She smiled fully. "I realize that now. It takes some of the sting out of the fact that he cheated on me and with my sister."

"He didn't deserve you, Emily."

Her smile faded. He said it with such sincerity, with such utter authority, that she wanted to cry. She exhaled slowly instead and admitted the truth. "He was right about one thing, though. I'm pretty much married to my work and I will be for the foreseeable future."

"Even when you open The Merit?" he asked.

When, he'd said. Not *if*. The ache in her chest went from dull to piercing. Madani believed in her. He understood that her restaurant was no more a whim than catering was a hobby.

"Especially then. At least at first. Control freak, remember?" She laughed tightly. "What about you?

Your job involves a lot of travel. That has to be hard on relationships."

It occurred to Emily that even though she felt she knew Madani so well, she was clueless when it came to his personal life. He could be involved with someone. Involved, hell. For all she knew, he could have a wife and kids back in Kashaqra. No, she told herself. He would have mentioned them before now, especially after that kiss. Even so, she held her breath as she waited for his reply.

"I wouldn't know."

She had no right to the relief she felt. Nor did she have a right to ask, "Do you think you'll marry one day and start a family?"

"Yes. I will marry." His tone was resolute and oddly grim. His expression bordered on bleak.

"No need to sound so happy about it," she teased, hoping to lighten his mood.

But he sounded every bit as ominous when he replied, "I will do what must be done." That was all he offered on the topic before changing subjects. "Have you called on the building for your restaurant?"

She'd been so excited about it the other night she'd wanted to telephone the real estate company right away. Only the fact it had been a Sunday evening had stopped her. By Monday morning, reality had tempered her excitement. She was in no position to buy or lease the space, which meant she had no business wasting a real estate agent's time.

"No. It will be a good year before I've saved up

enough money to approach the bank and expect someone in the loan department to take me seriously."

He frowned. "What about investors?"

She scooped up the filling and began spreading it atop the cake layer. "I've considered that route. The Hendersons even said they would stake me, but I'd rather the risk be all mine. Well, mine and the bank's." She shrugged.

He frowned. "But the building, you said it was the perfect location and the square footage ideal."

Yes, she'd said that and still felt that way, which only made it more difficult to resist calling for details and requesting to see the inside.

"It is the perfect location for The Merit and I loved the building's architecture. But the timing is off." She laid the spatula aside and sighed. "I almost wish I hadn't found it. Knowing it's there, available and I can't have it makes it harder, you know?"

"I do. Exactly." His gaze was intense, tortured. "I, too, have found something special. Something I want very badly and cannot have." He reached over to tuck the hair that had escaped her ponytail behind her ear. Almost to himself he murmured, "Yet I cannot stay away."

Emily's mouth went dry at the same time her knees turned to liquid. No, he couldn't mean...

"You'll be leaving soon," she said softly. "Maybe being back in Kashaqra will help you forget whatever it is."

But he shook his head. "It will not matter where I am. Here or half a world away." His throat worked a moment before he confessed, "I will still want to be with you."

"Madani—"

"I want you, Emily. It is as simple as that and as complicated."

He closed the scant distance between them. When his hands framed her face, she closed her eyes. *Tell him to go,* she thought. *Tell him to stop.* She said nothing at all, instead luxuriated in his touch and waited for the moment their mouths would meet. When they did, she moaned. Her reasons for steering clear of men were sound, but they didn't negate basic need. That's what this was, she assured herself. Sexual need. It was building inside her now, like the cake she had been carefully erecting layer upon layer under Madani's watchful eye.

Thanks to hard work and sacrifice, she had a thriving catering business. One day, she would open her restaurant. But right now what Emily wanted, what she craved above all else, was this man.

In her mother's living room, their passionate kiss had been for show. Because of their audience, when it had ended, all of their clothing had been intact and their hands in politically correct places.

Well, no one was watching them now.

The kiss deepened. In the privacy of her apartment, Emily gave in to temptation. Her hands strayed from the safety of his shoulders and trailed across the firm expanse of his chest. Beneath one palm, she could feel his heart beating, the cadence fast and strong. Heat radiated from him and spiraled through her. All the while, the kiss went on. It was thrilling, maddening. By far the best kiss she'd ever experienced. Even so, Emily was determined to have more.

She clutched the soft fabric of his shirt in her hands, wrinkling it even as she contemplated ripping it. No doubt it was designer label, and as such obscenely expensive. The thought had her refraining. Her fingers found the placket of buttons instead and she began weaving one after the other through the hole.

By the time the task was complete Madani had started one of his own. As his mouth cruised across her cheek and then down her neck, he untied her apron and tossed it aside. Free of that layer, he tugged the hem of her shirt from her skirt. The shirt was a conservative pullover, beneath which she was wearing an equally conservative bra. It seemed an eternity before she was divested of the former. She helped him out of his as well, pushing the fabric down his arms and took a moment to admire his form. Madani was beautiful. Physical perfection. And the way he was looking at her made Emily feel the same. A forgotten part of her reveled in the sensation. She'd always been confident as a chef. As a woman, she'd questioned herself. Madani's frank appreciation, though, had her stopping the unhealthy practice. For that alone she would remember this man, this moment, for the rest of her life.

Then she was in his arms, hot skin pressed to hot skin, and coherent thought once again fled.

"Emily." Madani moaned and then mumbled something unintelligible.

She understood perfectly.

Even though they were in the kitchen, her bedroom was mere steps away. But the countertop just behind her was much closer. As if he'd read her mind, he lifted her onto it, changing the dynamics considerably. Emily was half a head taller than he was now, and she liked where his gaze was drawn.

When it came to her figure, she wasn't voluptuous, but she filled out a bra well enough. Too bad the one she had on was plain white cotton and came from a department store. Had she anticipated their encounter, she would have made sure to be wearing one of the silk and lace numbers she'd bought a few years back at a pricey boutique.

She decided lingerie was overrated when he leaned closer and deftly undid the fastener. She felt the heat of his breath and then the heat his breath inspired. Either eventually would have stoked the mercury into triple digits on a thermometer. Together they accomplished the task handily. She was going to combust soon. She simply didn't care. In fact, she was eager to give herself over to the flames.

With the hope of improving his access, she levered backward. She intended to lay her palms flat on the counter for support. Unfortunately one of them wound up in the bowl of raspberry mousse, the other in the side of the not-quite-finished cake. Just that quickly reality inserted itself. Emily issued an oath and straightened. She had no business kissing him, let alone working her way to complete satisfaction. Madani was sexy, smart, fascinating and kind, but he was a client. Besides, she knew all to well that certain ingredients didn't mix well with her career.

"I'm sorry." She whispered it.

"Perhaps I am the one who should apologize. Your dessert is ruined," he said softly.

He retrieved a damp dishcloth from the sink and handed it to her, averting his gaze as Emily wiped up her hands and then fumbled for her bra. The moment was as ruined as the dessert, and they both knew it.

He grabbed his crumpled shirt off the floor along with Emily's. She waited until they were both fully dressed before saying, "I have to get back to work."

"Yes." He nodded toward the smashed cake. "And now you have more of it."

"I don't mind." It was a lousy thing to say given the circumstances. Oddly, he nodded and looked almost relieved himself.

They walked in silence to the door. It was a dozen steps of pure torture during which Emily nearly asked him to stay. Forget work. Forget the cake. She could buy one in the morning. But that was only putting off the inevitable. They had no future. She'd known that before things got out of hand.

"I'm sorry, Madani. I've acted very unprofessionally," she began.

He laid a finger across her lips. "No. I am the one

who should apologize. I took advantage of the situation. I had no right." He glanced away, his tone more fierce when he repeated, "I had no right."

Ashamed of his behavior and aching for something that went far beyond sex, Madani slammed out of Emily's apartment. He took the stairs rather than waiting for the elevator. As he stalked across the lobby to the exit he marveled that he hadn't broken his neck given the reckless speed at which he had descended. But he'd had to get away from her before he gave in to desire, capitulated to primal instinct and committed the unforgivable.

Azeem wasn't waiting at the curb. Madani realized too late that he hadn't given his friend a time to return. Nor had he called for him. He would have to do that, but not just yet. He needed to think. And so he began walking, aimlessly at first and then with a destination in mind. An hour and a couple of phone calls later, he was standing outside the building Emily loved when the Mercedes pulled up. Azeem's amused smile melted away the instant Madani climbed into the front passenger seat.

"What has happened?" he asked.

"Nothing."

"You are talking to me, *sadiqi*. What has happened?"

"Not nearly enough." Madani laughed harshly, though that wasn't why his throat ached afterward. "I shouldn't have gone to see her tonight. I don't know what I was thinking." Through the car's window, he studied the building, recalling what Emily had said earlier that evening about finding what she wanted at the wrong time. "In some ways I wish I'd never met her."

He half expected his friend to start in again with an argument about bucking the marriage arrangement his parents had brokered on his behalf so long ago. But Azeem replied enigmatically, "I know exactly how you feel."

The remainder of their drive to The Mark was accomplished in silence.

CHAPTER TEN

FOR THE FIRST TIME in her professional life Emily considered standing up a client.

How could she face Madani after last night? She'd kissed him in abandon, stripped him of his shirt and then allowed him to return the favor. If she hadn't leaned back and put her hands in raspberry mousse and white cake, they would have made love. She wanted to be grateful that sanity had returned before the deed was done, but gratitude hadn't managed to navigate past her still tangled-up hormones. It would have been really, really good sex. And she hadn't had sex of any sort in a very long time.

The irony of the situation wasn't lost on Emily, either. Her job had, in a very literal sense, again proved incompatible with romance. Business needed to be her priority, her focus. Not a man and a relationship that had no chance of succeeding.

After he'd gone, she'd baked more cakes and mixed up more filling. She barely managed a few hours of restless sleep before her alarm went off the following morning. Thus, it was no surprise she was in a foul mood and not operating up to speed. Her hastily reconstructed layer cake was leaning like the famed tower in Pisa, Italy.

Arlene came in as Emily finished the last sickly looking rosebud.

"That's..." Noting Emily's dark expression, her assistant angled her head to one side and proclaimed, "Nice. Very nice."

Emily tossed the bag of frosting onto the counter. "Go ahead and say it. It's off. I'm off. Nothing is going according to plan."

She wasn't only talking about the cake. Madani's face flashed in her mind. She could pretend she was disappointed and out of sorts because they hadn't had sex, but the truth was, it went deeper than that. As foolish as it was, she kept trying to figure out a way they could work around her crazy hours and his visitor status.

She wanted to cry then and it must have showed. Arlene reached over and gave her shoulders a quick squeeze. "Don't sweat it, Em. I'll call Tiffany at Cakes for Every Occasion. She's bound to have something that will work for a kid's birthday party."

Yes, Tiffany would save the day, but Emily was starting to fear there would be no saving her heart.

At twenty minutes to five, she sucked up her pride and packed Arlene's car with everything she would need for Madani's meal. Emily had given her assistant use of the van since the party in Connecticut was much larger.

"Ready or not," she murmured upon reaching her destination.

She'd never catered a party at The Mark and she couldn't help but be impressed when she was ushered up to Madani's gorgeously appointed Tower Suite. Azeem held the door for her, taking over the loaded cart she was pushing. With a smile, he invited her inside. As illogical as it was, she was disappointed. She didn't want to see Madani, but she did, if only to discern how he was doing.

"The kitchen is right this way," Azeem said.

On the way from the foyer they passed the dining room. The table had already been set with lovely gold-edged china and crystal water goblets. The wine and cocktail glasses were arranged on a tray on the sideboard.

"If there is something you need, you have only to ask," Azeem assured her when they entered the kitchen.

She glanced around. "Everything looks to be in order."

More than in order. The room was as large as her kitchen and nearly as well equipped, she thought, noting the brand name on the appliances. For a man who only visited Manhattan on business a handful of times each year, and who didn't know how to boil water, Madani enjoyed excellent accommodations. Indeed, his were better than the vast majority of native New Yorkers. His export business must be truly thriving.

She began unloading the cart and got down to business. An hour later, as she checked on the sea bass,

Madani's guests began arriving. Emily could hear snippets of their conversations coming from the other room along with Babs Henderson's unmistakable laughter. She wished Madani would come by and put an end to her nervousness. Until she saw him, spoke to him, she was going to worry how their first encounter after almost having sex was going to make her feel.

Her luck, he picked the worst time to walk into the kitchen. She was in the middle of dishing up the hummus dip. She looked up, saw his handsome face and her hands faltered. The next thing she knew a large spoonful of it wound up in the freshly baked pita chips instead of the serving bowl.

"Sorry about that."

"No. I should apologize for startling you."

"It's not your fault."

"I must insist that it is," he replied.

How ridiculous. They were arguing over who was to blame. Some of her awkwardness ebbed away. "Fine. It's all on you, Madani. For shame."

He smiled briefly before sobering. "I was worried you would not come today."

Though Emily had very seriously considered leaving him in the lurch or perhaps swapping places with Arlene, she asked casually, "Why wouldn't I come?"

"We didn't part on the best of terms last night."

"Actually I think we did. It was for the best that things ended before… before they could continue." Heat flared in her face.

She didn't care for the fact that he nodded instead of arguing. "Still, I was worried that I had—how would you say?—crossed the line."

She recalled the way she'd divested him of his shirt and held up her arms so he could pull hers over her head. Fairness demanded she say, "I think we crossed it together."

Madani smiled, albeit sadly. His tone, his words held an uncomfortable amount of finiteness when he told her, "It's a memory I shall cherish. Emily, I have something I need to—"

Before he could finish, the kitchen door swung open and a middle-aged woman entered. She was dressed in a dove-gray uniform and a pair of thick-soled white shoes.

"Good evening, sir," she said to Madani.

"Oh, Emily, this is Mrs. Patterson, my housekeeper. She will be serving dinner this evening and helping you with anything you require in the kitchen."

"Mrs. Patterson." Emily nodded.

"Well, I should go. You have work to do and my guests are arriving."

"I'll have Mrs. Patterson bring out the hummus dish and pita wedges. That will give your guests something to snack on before they have to take a seat in the dining room. The penne pasta first course is ready as soon as you are."

He nodded and left and, even as her heart took a tumble, Emily got down to business.

Twenty minutes later, Mrs. Patterson returned to the kitchen after serving drinks and appetizers. She cleared her throat. "Excuse me, Emily. Your presence is requested in the dining room."

Although it wasn't unheard of to be summoned from the kitchen during a dinner party, being summoned during this one had her heart hammering. She tucked any hair that had escaped the net back beneath it, smoothed down her chef's coat and, after taking a deep breath, walked out.

"Good evening." She glanced around the table. The Hendersons were there. Another couple looked familiar, too, although she couldn't recall their names. "I trust everything is all right?"

"Fine. Exceptional, as a matter of fact. But..."

Her heart skipped a beat. "But?"

"We would like for you to join us."

"For dinner?" She blinked in surprise. She hadn't seen this coming.

"Please," Babs said. "You know how I am about odd numbers. Our host has agreed to humor me."

"What about your social secretary?"

"If Stella were free this evening I'd call her and make her come. But she has a prior engagement. Besides, you are such an interesting conversationalist, Emily."

She glanced at Madani. His neutral expression gave no clue as to his feelings about the invitation.

"Azeem?" she said hopefully. At least the driver was wearing a suit.

He shook his head. "Apparently the car needs to be washed and waxed."

At this time of night? Sure it did.

"Come on, Emily. The housekeeper can bring another place setting. I'll even move down and give you the chair next to our host."

Babs and her damned quirks. Emily could have killed the socialite. She settled for pointing out the obvious without going into too much detail.

"I'm working tonight, Babs." Not to mention that she still felt awkward around Madani. And then there was the not so small matter of her appearance. Her hair was pulled back and tucked under a requisite net and she was outfitted in a uniform while the other guests wore designer-label evening apparel.

"You can pop in and out as need be while the remaining courses are served," Babs said generously. "We'll all understand."

Emily divided a glance between Madani and the socialite. "It's very kind of you to want to include me, but I'm sure Mr. Tarim is only being polite. I'm his *caterer.*"

His brows rose at the emphasis, as if to remind her that being in his employ had not kept her from nearly winding up horizontal with him the night before.

"It was not mere politeness on my part. I wish for you to join us, Emily," he said.

Put that way, how could she refuse?

She took her time plating the sea bass, hoping to get control of her emotions. She could do this without making a fool of herself.

While Mrs. Patterson served the entrée, Emily dashed

to the powder room just off the kitchen. There was no help for her attire, but she removed the net and unpinned her hair. Despite a vigorous finger-combing, it remained crimped in some places and flat in others. Well, it would have to do.

When she returned to the dining room, Babs had moved to make room for her. Emily took the seat next to Madani, laying a cloth napkin across the lap of cotton work pants. *Fool,* she thought. And that was before Babs unintentionally tossed out a verbal grenade.

"The sea bass is delightful, Emily." She glanced around the table. "Denby and I are so proud of her and all she has accomplished. We practically discovered her and here she is five years later, making a meal for a sheikh."

Emily's polite smile dimmed in confusion. "A sheikh?"

"Sheikh Madani Abdul Tarim." Babs frowned. "He didn't allow me to formally introduce him that day in my kitchen, but I assumed you knew."

Emily's ears had begun to buzz. She turned to Madani, feeling oddly betrayed. "You're a sheikh. You told me you were the owner of an export business."

"I am. Among other things."

"You might have mentioned those other things included being the ruler of a country."

"I am not the ruler." He cleared his throat and a dull flush stained his cheeks before he added, "Yet."

"Uh-oh," Babs said sotto voce. "It looks like I may have opened up a can of worms."

Emily reached for her water glass. "No can of worms.

I was mistaken about what he did for a living. That's all. But it doesn't matter. I'm only the caterer. It's not like the sheikh owed me the truth."

"Oh. Well, it's a good thing you feel that way," Babs said. Lowering her voice, as if that made any difference when other diners could still hear her, she said, "For a moment, it almost sounded like maybe the two of you were... involved."

"We're not involved," Emily said.

"No," Madani agreed.

"Of course you're not," Babs said with a vigorous nod. "How could you be when Madani is engaged to be married?"

Engaged!

To think a moment ago Emily had been flummoxed to discover he was a sheikh. Her throat worked spasmodically now. It was a good thing she'd already swallowed the sip of water she'd taken. She camouflaged her reaction by dabbing her mouth with her napkin. Too bad the square of fabric wasn't bigger so she could hide behind it and give in to the tears that were stinging her eyes.

"Emily—" Madani began. Beneath the table, his fingers brushed her thigh.

But she turned to Babs. "Yes, he's engaged. And me, well, you know me, Babs. My career is my life."

How she got through the rest of the meal she didn't know. But she did and with a surprising amount of dignity. She even contributed to the conversation, offering her two-cents on global trade. All the while she politely ignored Madani and the hand he periodically rested on her thigh. Dessert was served to rave reviews. Afterward, she excused herself. Her work here was done.

She was packing up her supplies when he entered the kitchen.

"Emily, I owe you…"

She rattled off a dollar amount. At his frown, she clarified, "What you owe me. The truffles cost more than I anticipated."

"I don't care about the money." He was every inch the wealthy ruler when he waved a hand in dismissal of the sum. "I want to apologize."

"For lying to me?" she asked. "Or for cheating on your fiancée?"

"I didn't lie. Nor did I cheat."

"You're engaged!"

"No." Emily's heart lifted, only to plunge again when he added, "Not yet."

"Please don't tell me you think that makes me feel any better," she whispered. "I was…and you…we nearly…"

"I know." He heaved a sigh. "I can only imagine what you must think of me, but I did not mean for any of this to happen."

Okay, did he think *that* was going to make her feel better?

She crossed her arms. "Coming by my apartment last night, staying even after my assistants left, that wasn't an accident, Madani. Or Sheikh Tarim." Her hands fell to her sides. "What do I call you now?"

"I am the same man, Emily. Sheikh is only a title."

"No. I don't know you." She exhaled wearily. "I don't know myself. But at least I'm not in a serious relationship with someone else and trying to pick up a little on the side." Her eyes began to sting. "When were you going to mention her? Or were you going to at all? And here I thought you were so different from Reed."

Madani's heart already felt pulverized, but Emily's mention of her philandering ex-boyfriend delivered a punishing blow. It didn't matter that he hadn't set out to hurt or deceive her, he was guilty of both.

"After what happened yesterday…I was going to tell you everything tonight."

"Well, Babs saved you the trouble."

"I mean before the dinner party." He'd paced his bedroom, knowing Emily was in the kitchen and that he owed her the truth. He'd tried to come up with the right words to explain not only his situation, but what she had come to mean to him. But English eluded him despite his longtime fluency. He'd actually had to write out his apology, first in Arabic and then translate it. Finally he'd gone to see her. "But Mrs. Patterson interrupted me and my guests were arriving."

"Your guests." Her face bleached of color. "Go out and see to them. You're the host."

"You are more important to me," he insisted.

"No." Her eyes turned bright. "Please, if you care about me at all, for the sake of my personal and professional reputations, go out there before they begin to talk. As it is, they have reason enough to speculate on the exact nature of our relationship."

He nodded. He would do as she asked. He'd caused her enough distress. "Promise me you will not leave before we can talk."

"What is there left to say?"

"Promise me." His thoughts turned to the real estate deal he'd struck on Emily's behalf that morning. It had cost him a bundle, but it did little to repay the debt he owed her. "I have something for you."

It was almost an hour before his guests left and Madani could return to the kitchen. Emily was sitting at the table drinking a glass of water.

"Thank you for waiting."

She shrugged. "I said I would."

"I have something for you." He pulled some papers from the inside pocket of his suit coat. "It's my way of saying I'm sorry."

She unfolded the document, a legal agreement for the purchase of the building whose location she'd said was perfect for her restaurant. As he watched, her confusion gave way to comprehension. He waited for a smile, expected some joy. What he got was white-hot fury.

"What is this?" she demanded.

"It's a purchase agreement." He frowned. "I bought the entire building."

"And, what, you're just *giving* it to me?"

"Yes. I want you to have it. You deserve it."

It became apparent immediately that was the wrong

thing to say. "Because we nearly slept together? Gee, would I get a small country if we'd actually had sex? Is this your idea of payment for services rendered?"

Madani's eyes widened. He hadn't considered that Emily might view his gift in such an ominous light. "No. Don't think of it like that. My intention was only to make you happy, and to atone for my behavior last night."

She crumpled the papers, tossed them aside. "You lied to me, Madani. You have a fiancée!" Before he could argue, she said, "Excuse me, I forgot. You're not actually engaged yet. But that's semantics in my book. If you love her enough to consider proposing, you should love her enough to be faithful."

"I do not love her! I love…I love…" He released an oath in his native tongue. "You make this so difficult."

She said nothing, though her eyes had grown wide. Under her watchful gaze, he paced the length of his kitchen. The truth. He needed to reveal the last damning bit, that part that he'd hidden even from himself. Maybe then some of this pain would go away. He stilled, faced her.

"I love *you*, Emily.

"You love… No!" She shook her head and his heart ached anew.

"As preposterous as it may seem, I think I started falling for you the moment Babs introduced us." Had that really been a couple of weeks ago?

"What about your fiancée or girlfriend or whatever? Did you just fall out of love with her?"

"I never fell in. In truth, I barely know her." He walked to the table and smoothed out the documents. "It is an arrangement, not much different than the purchase of this building. It was brokered by our parents when I was but a boy."

"An arranged marriage?" She appeared skeptical. He needed to believe she also was relieved to hear that he didn't love Nawar.

"Yes. They still have those in my country. They are falling out of fashion and favor, especially among the younger generation, but…" Madani lifted his shoulders.

"Are they…legally binding?"

"Not according to the laws of Kashaqra, but morally…" He thought of his father, again saw Adil slump to the floor. In this case, Madani's future was etched in stone. "I am obligated."

"So you will go through with it."

Jaw clenched, he nodded.

"I see."

No, she didn't. He needed to make her understand. Madani took the seat next to hers and reached for her hand. "You say that I lied to you, Emily. Yes, I did. I lied to myself, too. I thought I could be satisfied to merely spend time with you, to be your friend. But the longer I knew you… You fascinate me on every level. I have never met your equal."

He watched her swallow before she said, "You claim to love me, yet in the same breath you spell out what the future holds for us, or rather, for you." Her voice grew hoarse. Her eyes were bright with tears. "What do you expect me to say to that?"

"I do not know." He'd never felt so powerless, so hopeless and lost. "Perhaps there is nothing for you to say."

Yet he waited, masochist that he was, hoping she would return the sentiment.

Emily pulled her hand from his and stood. "An apology is all I'm due. I accept yours. But I can't accept this." She nodded toward the papers. "It's…too much."

To his mind, it was not nearly enough. Given the chance, he'd give her the world.

"Please," he urged, rising to his feet. "I want you to have it. Opening The Merit is your dream. Let me help you make it come true."

"No."

Her dream?

Emily pondered that as she drove home. Was owning a restaurant *all* she wanted in life? She'd thought so. She'd been quite certain, in fact. Until Madani told her he loved her.

Part of her had thrilled at his declaration. God knew, it had taken restraint she hadn't been aware she possessed to keep her true feelings from spilling out. A glance at the big picture had made it easier to hold them in. He wasn't free. Sheikh or no sheikh, his destiny had been decided long before they'd met, and Emily wasn't part of it.

He'd offered her the building for her restaurant as a consolation prize—one heck of a consolation prize, but a consolation prize nonetheless. Here was her dream on a silver platter. The problem? It wasn't her only dream any longer.

CHAPTER ELEVEN

WHEN Madani answered the phone early the next morning after a sleepless night, it was his mother, and her tone warned him that she was not happy.

"I have called four times in half as many days. Unless you have been stricken too ill to dial a telephone, I will expect both an explanation and an apology."

"I have no excuse, Mother, so I can only apologize. I'm sorry if I worried you."

"As your mother, I expect to worry. It comes with the territory."

"Well, then, I hope your mind is now at ease."

"It would be, but you sound unhappy." Leave it to Fadilah to decipher his emotions from the opposite side of the planet.

"I am not unhappy," he lied, and poured more coffee from a brass *cezve*. "Preoccupied would be a better word choice."

"*Hmm*. Nawar is preoccupied as well," Fadilah

replied, misconstruing his meaning. "Or so her mother tells me. Have you spoken with her?"

He chose to act obtuse. "With Nawar's mother?"

"Not with Bahira," she chided. "Nawar."

Madani could count the number of times he and his betrothed had spoken over the years, either in person or on the telephone. None of their communications had been spontaneous or terribly personal. And none had occurred in recent weeks.

"No. But I trust she is well."

"Yes. I met with her and Bahira for lunch the other day to discuss the menu for the feast. We want it to be extra special given its significance this year. That is the reason for my call."

He sipped his coffee, barely listening. The mention of menus had him thinking of Emily. "I'm sure whatever the three of you decide will be fine."

"Normally I would feel the same way, but Nawar has made an interesting suggestion."

The comment snagged his attention. "Regarding?"

"She said as a way to pay homage to Kashaqra's growing recognition abroad—thanks in part to your efforts to promote our artisans and craftsmen—the menu of the final feast should be international with a sampling of foods from around the globe."

Food…now Emily was definitely on his mind and, though he knew it was pure folly, an idea began to germinate.

"How does Bahira feel about Nawar's suggestion?" he asked diplomatically.

"Bah!" Fadilah spat. "Bahira is too narrow-minded. If it were up to her Kashaqra's borders would be lined with barbed wire fences to prevent outside visitors, and television and the Internet would be banned because of their corrupt influences. She does not welcome simple change much less that which breaks from tradition."

"And you, Mother?"

"I believe in honoring the traditions that have been handed down through the centuries. In doing so, we honor our ancestors. But I like Nawar's idea for the final feast. Besides, the calendar year contains three hundred and sixty-four other days during which our people can dine on what is familiar." He pictured his mother's mouth turning down as she shrugged.

"So, am I to cast the deciding vote?" he asked.

"You give yourself too much credit," Fadilah chided. "I've already had my head together with the palace chef about the menu."

Madani swallowed. His mother adored the portly Riyad's preparation of regional dishes, but having eaten at some of the finest restaurants abroad, Madani was well aware of the chef's failings when it came to other types of cuisine.

"It's nice to be needed," he inserted dryly. "So why was it necessary to reach me?"

"Nawar thought you might have some favorite dishes that we could include."

He thought of the sea bass and the caramel trifle he'd dined on just the night before. "I do, but Riyad is not experienced enough to do them justice."

"He can learn."

"Or perhaps he can be taught." Foolish or not, the idea grew. He gave it voice. "There is a chef here with whom I've become acquainted that I may be able to persuade to help with the feast. This chef is very skilled with a variety of cuisines."

"Riyad won't like it…" his mother began. Then, "Oh, very well. If we are to serve your favorite dishes it makes sense to have them cooked to your liking. Hire whomever you wish."

After the call ended, Madani scrubbed a hand over his face. What he was thinking was absurd, insane. Assuming Emily agreed with his plan, and that was far from a given, he would be putting himself in the excruciating position of being with her without *being* with her.

Perhaps it was just as well that she hadn't said she loved him, too. That would make it all the more difficult to subjugate his feelings and mask his emotions around his family. But his pain would be worth it if Emily agreed to earn from him what she'd refused to accept as a gift.

Emily was meeting Donna for drinks, hoping to repair their damaged friendship. She locked the door's dead bolt and tucked her keys in her purse. When she turned to leave, she nearly ran into Madani's chest.

"Hello, Emily."

God, he looked good. She wanted to wrap her arms around him, confess her true feelings and beg him to find a way out of his arranged marriage. For that matter, she wanted to slug him a good one for being so seemingly perfect that she fell for him.

Instead, after silently cursing fate, she steadied her rioting emotions, rallied her pride and said with forced indifference, "I'm just on my way out."

He nodded. "I should have called."

They both knew why he hadn't. She wouldn't have agreed to see him.

"Well, I need to be going. Whatever you came to say will have to wait for another time." Such as the next millennium.

Emily started toward the elevator. When he fell into step beside her, she opted to take the stairs instead. No way was she going to tempt her pathetically weak resolve by spending even a short ride to the lobby in a confined space with him.

"It can't wait, Emily. I must leave soon."

"Oh, that's right. Back to Kashaqra and your almost bride-to-be." The accusation echoed in the stairwell.

"Yes," he agreed flatly.

Emily gritted her teeth. So *now* he was all for being open and honest. "I fail to see what that has to do with me."

"I assume you have not changed your mind about accepting the building."

"No."

"Then I have a business proposition to make."

That stopped her. She turned and stared at him. "I don't understand?"

"Each summer in my country, we celebrate the Feast of Seven Days to mark the long-ago ouster of a repressive ruler who all but starved to death many of the Kashaqran people. In the capital city, the feast is very elaborate and everyone is given time off from work to join in."

It sounded exciting and exotic, two things Emily's life wasn't…or hadn't been, until she'd met Madani.

He was saying, "As is the tradition, members of my family oversee all of the capital city's preparations, including the menu."

Despite her better judgment, her curiosity was piqued. "Menu?"

"This year will include delicacies from all over the globe." Just as her epicurean juices began to flow, he added, "At the final feast, my betrothal to Nawar will be announced."

Her interest soured. "So, it's going to be an engagement party and the whole country's invited to help you celebrate."

She started down the stairs.

"Unfortunately the palace chef is not what I would call competent when it comes to cooking other kinds of cuisine," he said, again in step beside her.

"I see your dilemma." Emily picked up her pace.

"I would like to hire you to assemble the menu and then assist the chef and kitchen staff in the preparations."

She couldn't have heard him correctly, which was why she stopped a second time and gaped at him.

"I am asking a lot. I know."

A lot? Try too much. Last night he'd said he loved her. Today, all he apparently loved was her cooking. And she'd thought her heart was done breaking.

She lifted her chin. "I'm sorry, Sheikh. It sounds like a wonderful opportunity, but I'm going to have to pass. I don't do big events. Too assembly-line for my taste, remember?"

"I remember. Believe me, Emily. Nothing that occurred during our time together will ever escape my memory."

Why did he have to say something like that? Why did the same have to be true for her?

"If you say yes, you will be generously compensated," Madani said after a moment. He pulled a sheaf of papers from his pocket.

Figuring she knew what they were, Emily gritted her teeth in indignation and let anger take the lead. "I thought I made it clear that I cannot and will not accept that."

"As a gift." He nodded. "But what about as payment for your time and talent?"

"I'm no expert on Manhattan real estate, but that building has to be worth millions of dollars."

"Yes, my original offer was too much. I realize that, which is why I have decided to retain ownership of the building. In return for your catering services, I will allow you to use the square footage at street level for the next three years rent-free."

"No."

"Two years, but no less. You would be—what do they say?—selling yourself short."

Emily shook her head, but Madani didn't relent.

"At least take a few days to think about it before giving me your final answer."

"It's not going to change."

"A few days," he repeated. "Please."

"Why?" she demanded. "Why are you doing this to me, to yourself?" She hated that the words wobbled.

"I want you to have your dream, Emily." He'd said the same thing the evening before.

How ironic that the man she'd been in a long-term relationship with hadn't been supportive at all on this matter, while the man with whom she could have no future, stood fully behind her.

"Dreams change," she murmured. At Madani's frown, she said briskly, "I can make The Merit a reality without you. The only difference is the timeline."

"You don't need me." She heard pride in his tone even as his gaze turned sad. "Your independence and determination are just two of the qualities I've come to admire. You are also an astute businesswoman. What I am asking you to consider is a business arrangement."

They reached the lobby and he held the door for her. As she passed by, he brushed his knuckles lightly over her cheek. In a voice ripe with anguish he said, "You will never know how deeply I wish I had more to offer you."

* * *

"So a sheikh says he wishes he could offer you more." Donna sipped her apple martini and sighed. "You've really come up in the world since Reed Benedict."

After some initial restraint and awkwardness, the two friends had apologized, hugged, cried and then fallen back into the easy camaraderie that had long marked their relationship. Two martinis later, Emily had opened up about Madani. She'd told her old friend everything, including the heated interlude in her kitchen, Madani's declaration of love last evening and what had transpired just an hour before on her apartment's stairwell.

"Just a wealthier version of the same."

"You think so?"

"You don't?"

Donna shook her head. "First of all, he urged you to reconcile with me. That makes him a saint in my book. Reed must have been pleased as punch when the two of us stopped speaking."

"He didn't like you," Emily agreed diplomatically.

"He hated my guts and it was mutual." Donna lifted her shoulders dismissively before going on. "Unlike Reed, your sheikh believes in your talent, so much so that he bought you a damned building for your restaurant."

"He's not my sheikh."

Donna ignored her and sighed again. "Why can't I meet a man like that?"

"He's also the closest thing there is to engaged, yet he never mentioned it. Remember?" Emily reached for her drink.

"That was wrong of him, I'll admit. He should have been up-front. But in his defense, it *is* an arranged marriage. It's you he loves."

Warmth trickled through Emily. She blamed it on the gin in her martini. "He's going to wed someone else."

Donna's expression turned sympathetic. "I'm sorry, Em. But look on the bright side. At least he's not marrying your sister."

"There is that." Emily set her drink aside and lowered her head into her hands. "Oh, Donna. What was I thinking? I shouldn't have gotten involved with him in any way except professionally. My schedule is too hectic."

"So? You can't let what Reed did dictate your views on men and relationships. Reed was the wrong guy for you. When the right one comes along, everything will work out because both of you will be willing to make any necessary sacrifices to see that it does." Donna took a deep breath before going on. "At the risk of jeopardizing our friendship again with my big mouth, I think you should call your sheikh and accept his business offer."

"He's not *my* sheikh." Emily raised her head. "He's *nothing* to me. He can't be."

"Then you should have no problem working for him again," Donna replied lightly. More seriously she added, "Look, Em, a million other caterers would kill for an opportunity to put something like this on their résumés. Imagine the cache it will give you not only as a caterer, but when you open your restaurant. Emily Merit, chef to the sheikh."

"Have you forgotten I would basically be catering his engagement party?"

"I didn't say it would be easy. But you know how in the old Westerns when a cowboy gets bit by a rattler he cuts the spot open to suck the venom from the wound?"

"You think it would help me get over him."

"Couldn't hurt." Donna shrugged. "Besides, you've dreamed of opening your own restaurant forever. He's putting the opportunity within reach right now. Separate the professional from the personal, Em. This is the chance of a lifetime."

"I don't know." But God help her, she was wavering.

Donna grinned. "And then there's the real bonus. It will take you out of the country on the day your sister gets married."

Emily told herself that was the capper: professional fulfillment *and* an airtight excuse for skipping Elle's nuptials. It had nothing to do with the fact that she was eager to see Madani's homeland and experience firsthand his culture, even if only so she could let him go.

After reaching her decision, she waited two days to tell him. She caught him the morning he was to leave for Kashaqra.

"I've decided to accept your offer," she said as soon as he came on the line. "I'll come to your country, help with the menu preparations for your...your feast."

"Emily, I—"

She talked over him. "This is an excellent business

opportunity. A friend of mine helped me to see that. As she said, in addition to the other compensation you have offered, helping with the feast will give my professional reputation a substantial boost. As such, it's an offer too good to refuse."

Her words were greeted with protracted silence. Finally, he replied, "I am glad you are able to see it that way."

"I do have one request, though."

"Yes?"

"I wish to leave before the big announcement."

There was only so much venom she was willing to suck.

During the month between the time Madani returned to Kashaqra and she was to arrive for the feast preparations, Emily compiled dish selections, which she e-mailed to him. Each time she received the same reply: *Many thanks. I look forward to your arrival.—M*

Did he? Or was he just being polite?

She didn't take time to ponder it. She was too busy. Exhaustingly so. In addition to her hectic catering schedule—which had picked up as word of her cooking for a sheikh spread, courtesy of Babs—Emily spent her mornings with a contractor at the building that was to house The Merit. She'd loved it from the outside, had known immediately that the location was prime. The inside, however, needed work and a lot of it to make it conform to her vision.

Already a couple of walls had been moved to accommodate more seating in what was to become the dining room, and the site of the new kitchen was set to be renovated. The work would wipe out her savings, but Emily felt confident that with no lease to pay for two years, her bank would approve a loan to cover kitchen appliances and start-up costs.

She was excited about the restaurant. How could she not be? Still, she'd expected to feel a greater sense of fulfillment and satisfaction. Instead, what she felt at times was empty. It didn't help that Madani was always on her mind.

Her cell phone trilled as she paced through sawdust at The Merit. She grimaced upon answering since it was her sister.

"Emily, I'm at the bridal salon and I need to know this very minute if you are going to stand up in my wedding. Final alterations have to be made no later than next week and the dress is going to have to be let out if Constance is to wear it," Elle complained.

Emily rubbed her eyes wearily. "I've told you time and again I'm not standing up in your wedding. I won't be there, period. I'll be out of the country on a job."

Her mother wasn't happy about it. Her father had even stopped by the apartment to lecture Emily on her obligations to the family. She'd held firm despite the guilt and pressure. Elle, as self-serving as ever, made it easier.

"Oh, that's right. You'd rather go to Kenya and play chef for that sheikh guy."

"Kashaqra. It's one continent over."

Elle snorted. "Whatever. Geometry was never my strong suit." Emily decided to let that one slide.

"God, you are such a hypocrite!" Elle shouted.

"Excuse me."

"You're still upset about Reed seeing me behind your back, yet the guy you were all over at my shower cheats with you and you're all forgive and forget."

Emily's stomach knotted. "What do you mean?"

"I told you his name sounded familiar. That's because he was featured in *Chatter* a couple of months ago. I found the magazine in my nightstand this morning and reread it. Imagine my surprise upon discovering your boyfriend topped the list of the World's Hunkiest Billionaires. I was happy for you until I got to the part about him being taken. Apparently you have no problem being the other woman."

"I didn't know about his…status," she said slowly.

"You would have if you read something other than recipe books."

"Well, I don't."

"You do now," Elle said pointedly.

"I'm going to Kashaqra on business."

But she knew she was lying. She was going to Kashaqra to say goodbye.

CHAPTER TWELVE

"WHAT are you thinking?" Azeem shouted the question as he marched into the office.

Madani glanced up in surprise. "Excuse me?"

"The person you've asked me to collect from the airport is Emily Merit. She is the American chef hired to help with the feast preparations."

Azeem's face turned a deeper shade of red and he let out a string of expletives.

Madani rose to his feet, confused by his friend's rage. "What is your objection? Emily is very good at what she does."

"She must be, for she has you thinking with something other than your head," Azeem shot back.

Madani was grateful for the expanse of desk that separated them, because the insulting comment made him angry enough to want to take a swing.

"Take care with your words," he warned. "You go too far."

"No. It is *you* who goes too far." Azeem's thick hands

fisted at his sides, proof of his own restraint. "You are bringing your mistress here, flaunting her in Nawar's face just days before the betrothal announcement. I know you do not love Nawar, that your marriage to her is but the result of a bargain struck to bolster family alliances. But this…this is an outrage! I will not stand for it."

Some of Madani's fury ebbed into confusion over Azeem's vehement defense of Nawar's honor. He decided to stir things up in the hope of eventually making them clearer. "I believe you were the one who suggested I have a fling while in Manhattan. You even chided me for leaving Emily's apartment that one evening and offered to take me back."

"Yes, but that was when—" Azeem's mouth snapped closed and he glanced away.

"When what?"

"Nothing."

"Don't hold back now, *sadiqi*," Madani drawled.

"When I thought there was still a chance you might not go through with the wedding. You seemed drawn to Emily. We hoped…"

"We?"

Azeem closed his eyes and said nothing. His defeated posture spoke volumes. Understanding dawned. Madani wondered why he hadn't realized it before. "You love Nawar."

His friend didn't deny it. When his gaze returned to Madani, it was filled with devastation, but nonetheless direct. "If you are going to marry her, you will honor her. You will treat her with respect. I will not stand by and watch her humiliated either in private or before the entire country."

"Emily is not my mistress. I give you my word that is not why I made arrangements to bring her to Kashaqra."

"Then why?"

"I wished only to give her an opportunity, one she richly deserves but would not accept outright." Madani explained briefly about her restaurant plans and the real estate deal. He sighed then. "Foolishly, perhaps selfishly, I am eager to see her one last time and know that she was once in Kashaqra."

Azeem studied him a moment. "You are in love with her."

"I am." He expected his friend to start in again on finding a way out of the marital arrangement. Instead, Azeem dropped heavily into the chair on the opposite side of the desk.

"How is it possible, *sadiqi*, that we have both fallen in love with women we cannot have?"

Later that afternoon, when Azeem went to the airport to meet Emily's plane, Madani didn't go with him. He wanted to welcome her to his homeland, perhaps take her on a tour of the capital city, but the encounter with Azeem made it clear he couldn't risk the spread of rumors. Neither Emily nor Nawar deserved to be put in such an unflattering light and forced to fend off the resulting gossip and character attacks.

That didn't keep him from pacing his rooms in the palace waiting for word from Azeem that she had arrived safely.

Emily felt as if she'd been whisked into a fairy tale. She'd felt that way since the plane touched down at Kashaqra's largest airport. She'd expected, foolishly hoped, that Madani would be there to greet her. But it was his driver who stood at the gate perusing the faces of deplaning passengers.

"Hello, Emily. I trust your flight was uneventful," Azeem inquired politely when she reached him.

"Yes." She'd experienced a lot of turbulence, all of it internal.

She forgot about it as the car, a Mercedes similar to the one he'd driven in Manhattan, left the airport and headed to the palace. She'd scoured the Internet for information and images of Kashaqra. None of it prepared her for the reality. The countryside was surprisingly homey and while not lush due to the arid conditions, nothing about it was barren. It was sprinkled with humble homes and farms.

In the distance, mountains rose up, stretching majestically on the horizon. Long before the car reached them, Emily would arrive in the capital city. Already she could make out a modern skyline. The closer the buildings drew, the more intrigued she became about the place Madani called home. Seeing it answered some of her questions, and created others. He was to rule one day.

Was it what he wanted? Or, like his marriage, was it another aspect of his destiny that others had determined?

When they reached the city limits, the rooflines along the well-tended streets grew taller and more elaborate. She'd grown up in New York, taking feats of engineering for granted. She let her head fall back now and gazed through the sunroof at buildings that, while not quite as tall as what could be found back home, were every bit as amazing.

"This city has some incredible architecture," she murmured.

"It does."

She lowered her gaze, noting the sidewalks where vendors were hawking their goods and people sat outside at cafés eating and sipping beverages. "It's not so different from Manhattan."

She caught Azeem's reflection in the rearview mirror and smiled.

"I believe our city has two million fewer residents than yours does, but yes, it's similar. I think that is why Madani feels so at home in both places."

A dozen questions bubbled to mind—not about the country, but about the man. She bit them back and listened instead as Azeem noted some sites of interest. The last one he pointed out, however, left them both frowning.

"Down that street is the large park where much of the festivities will be held, including the food tents." More quietly, he added, "It also is where Madani's parents will announce his betrothal on the final night."

This time, Emily wasn't able to suppress the question that most weighed on her mind. "Is he happy, Azeem?"

"Are you happy?"

Emily blinked, as surprised by his question as the knowing look in his eyes.

"What reason would I have to be otherwise?"

"The same reason as Madani perhaps?"

When they arrived at the palace a few minutes later, Emily's nerves were jangling. The time was at hand. But when she entered a grand hall with mosaic tiled floors and arched ceilings, Madani wasn't there to greet her. Emily chided herself for thinking he would be. A sheikh, one whose engagement was soon to be announced, surely had better things to do with his time than meet the hired help.

"If you will come this way." Azeem led her down a corridor to a cozier room set up with comfortable chairs and sofas that were upholstered in rich hues. Three women were inside. Was it Emily's imagination, or did the young one smile sadly at Azeem?

One of the older women stretched out her hand in the standard Western greeting and confirmed Emily's worst nightmare when she said in perfect English, "I am Fadilah Tarim, Madani's mother. Welcome to Kashaqra, Miss Merit."

"Thank you." Should she bow, curtsy, genuflect? Even as Emily contemplated proper protocol, Madani's mother was introducing the others.

"This is Nawar, my son's bride-to-be. And Nawar's mother, Bahira."

All of them were lovely and fashionably attired. Emily felt frumpy in her wrinkled rose blouse and camel trousers. For one terrifying moment, Emily wondered if she was going to be ill, but she managed to hold down the contents of her stomach and offered a weak smile. "It's a pleasure to meet all of you and may I offer my congratulations?"

She thanked her lucky stars they also spoke English since her grasp of Arabic was severely limited.

"Thank you." Nawar nodded. Her smile was sweet, but again seemed sad. "Of course, it is not official yet."

"It will be soon enough." This from Bahira.

Nawar's complexion paled. Apparently Emily wasn't the only one suffering from nausea.

"Our chef has prepared several of the recipes you sent in advance of your arrival. My son is critical of his results. He says you are a much better cook."

"That's too kind."

"We are pleased you could come and lend your expertise to this year's feast," Fadilah said.

"Yes, especially given its added significance." Bahira eyed Emily with unabashed speculation, before saying something rather heated in Arabic.

Madani's mother flushed, whether out of embarrassment or anger, Emily wasn't sure. She smiled tightly. "You must excuse my friend. In her excitement she has forgotten to use English."

Bahira was undeterred. "I said I am surprised to find that the chef Madani insisted on is so young and attractive."

It was Emily's face that heated this time. "I am highly regarded in New York. If references would put you at ease about my qualifications, I will gladly supply them."

"That will not be necessary," Fadilah inserted with finality. To the other matron she said, "Young women, attractive or otherwise, pursue professions and often rise to the top, Bahira. It is unfair to discount Miss Merit's abilities based solely on her appearance."

"You are right, Fadilah." Nawar's mother tipped her head to one side as if in concession, but her gaze remained cold.

"We won't keep you, Miss Merit," Fadilah said. "You must be tired after your long flight. I will ring for a maid to take you to your room. If there is anything you need, simply ask."

The only thing Emily needed was a stiff drink. She'd made a mistake by coming here, a huge one. She'd thought she could be professional, concentrate on the contract between her and Madani and forget about the contract between his family and Nawar's. But as she'd looked into the lovely face of his bride-to-be, all she could think was, Madani loves me.

This was ten times more painful than staying in Manhattan, outfitting herself in peach organdy and watching Reed marry Elle.

Forget her career. Forget closure and sucking out venom. She couldn't do this.

* * *

Madani paced his rooms with the desperation of a caged animal. Emily was under the same roof as he was and as far away as ever. He could not go to her, not even on the pretext of welcoming her to his homeland. A knock interrupted his thoughts. He answered the door to find his mother standing on the other side. One look at her expression and he knew whatever she had to say was not going to be pleasant.

"The American chef you hired is a woman!" she shouted, sweeping into the room with her arms crossed and her eyes flashing. "A young and beautiful woman."

"That makes her no less capable."

Her head jerked in a nod. "The very thing I told Bahira when she commented on it. But I doubt my assurances stopped her concern. Nor will they stop the rumors that are bound to swirl. What possessed you to do this, Madani?"

"She is an excellent chef. Brilliant. You will see when you sample her work. She will put Riyad's cooking to shame. She is beyond compare."

"There is something you are not telling me," Fadilah accused. Then her tone turned pleading. "Madani, your engagement is to be announced soon. Now is not the time for…for…indiscretions." She waved one delicate hand.

He reached for it, squeezed it. "I am not being indiscreet. That I can promise you."

Fadilah freed her hand from his to lay it against his cheek as she had often done when he was a child. It could not soothe the ache he felt now.

"But you have feelings for this woman that go beyond professional."

"I will marry Nawar as is expected. I will not do anything to upset Father."

She frowned at that. "Your father is fine. His health is far from fragile these days."

"And it will stay that way."

Fadilah turned to leave. She stopped at the door. "This Emily Merit, who is she to you, Madani?"

"She is…" *The woman I want to wake up to after a long night of lovemaking. The woman whose mind I want a chance to change about marriage and children. The woman whom in a very short amount of time I have come to love beyond all reason.* But he shook his head, denying his desire, denying his heart. "It doesn't matter. She can be no one to me."

CHAPTER THIRTEEN

EMILY found her way to the palace kitchen the following morning. She would leave as soon as it could be arranged. Before then, she would do her best to see that the feast preparations were under way.

She was showing the palace chef her technique for making an apple almond tart's thick crust when Madani's mother entered.

"Riyad." Fadilah smiled at the heavy-set man. "I need to speak to Miss Merit in private. Will you leave us for a moment?"

When he was gone, Emily dusted flour from her hands and waited. It was a moment before Fadilah said, "I have a problem, Miss Merit. It involves my son."

That made two of them. Striving for nonchalance, Emily said, "He is well, I hope?"

"Physically, yes. Emotionally, Madani is…confused." Fadilah fussed with the elaborately embroidered sleeve of her dress, giving her words time to sink in. "All of Kashaqra will soon learn of his betrothal to Nawar.

Though the announcement will be made officially, it has been common knowledge among many of our people for years. He may have mentioned to you that the agreement between our families was made when he was a young boy and Nawar a baby."

"He mentioned it."

Fadilah nodded. "He has, most inconveniently, I might add, met someone. I think he believes himself to be in love with this woman. I think perhaps she may even have tender feelings for him."

"I do," she replied honestly. "But you needn't worry. I am not here to try to stop anything."

"Then why did you come?" The question seemed more like a challenge.

Emily didn't want to discuss the feelings that had brought her here, so she only said, "Business. I was hired to help prepare the feast. It's the opportunity of a lifetime."

"Madani mentioned that you run a successful catering company in Manhattan." Fadilah motioned toward the tart crust on which Emily and Riyad had been working. "Having sampled some of your work this past week, I see that my son did not overstate your skill."

"Thank you. I am opening a restaurant, too."

"I would imagine doing so takes a lot of money, especially in Manhattan."

"It does." Emily notched up her chin and said, "That's another reason I'm here."

"But those aren't the only reasons, are they?" Fadilah's gaze was shrewd.

"No. I wanted to see Kashaqra."

Fadilah's brow puckered. "Why?"

"It's…it's Madani's home, part of who he is."

"You wanted to see my son again."

"One last time, yes," Emily admitted around the lump in her throat.

Fadilah studied her for a maddening moment, before saying, "In many ways, Miss Merit, I am a business-woman, too. My family is my business. And so I have an offer to make you."

"An offer?"

"I will pay you triple the amount you've been promised if you leave Kashaqra in the morning."

Though she'd already planned to leave, Emily's stomach knotted. "I signed a contract with your son."

"Contracts can be broken. Think about it and give me your answer later today."

As she stared at the door through which Fadilah had left, Emily knew contracts weren't the only things that could be broken.

It was madness, but when Madani spied Emily in the courtyard garden later that day, his resolve to stay away from her fled. As she admired the lush blooms on one of his mother's rosebushes, she looked incredibly beau-tiful and deeply troubled.

"Hello, Emily."

She started at the sound of his voice. "Madani. I wasn't expecting… It's lovely out here."

"My mother's doing. She tends the rosebushes herself."

"Yes, she's very hands-on," Emily murmured.

He wasn't sure what she meant by the comment. In any event, he had no desire to discuss his mother. Work seemed a safe topic, so he asked, "How is the restaurant? Any new developments there?"

"It's funny you should mention that."

When she would have dipped her head, he put his fingers beneath her chin and raised it. "You are happy, yes?"

She had to be happy. Knowing he was helping her dream materialize was the only thing that mitigated the torture he was experiencing having her so close.

"I thought I would be. I should be. The restaurant is what I've wanted, dreamed of. But…"

"But what?"

"It doesn't matter."

"Everything about you matters to me."

She shook her head and pushed to her feet. "No. That's just the sort of thing you can't say. And it's exactly why I must leave."

"Leave?"

"I shouldn't have come to Kashaqra. I thought I could do this."

"Do what?"

"Put on a professional exterior, pretend my heart is not breaking. I can't, because it is. It has been ever since Babs told me you're going to marry someone else."

"Oh, Emily." How was it possible to be miserable and

elated at the same time? Madani gave in to the need to touch her and reached for her hand. "I've missed you."

"Don't say that." The demand lacked heat, but she pulled her hand free.

"I only speak the truth."

"Lie to me!" she pleaded. "Don't you get it, Madani? I don't want the truth from you. That only makes it worse. Lie to me. Tell me you don't think about me. Tell me you haven't missed me. Lie," she pleaded a second time.

"Why?"

She shook her head, backed up a step. The answer was there in her eyes, but he needed to hear the words.

He took both of her hands in his this time. "Say it. Just once. Tell me you've fallen in love with me. Say the words. Please." They would have to sustain him for a lifetime.

"I love you," she whispered brokenly. He swore her declaration echoed off the stone walls.

"Emily." He tugged her into his arms and whispered her name a second time just before their mouths met. Need. Madani ached from it. But before he could lose himself in the kiss, she was pulling away.

"I can't do this. I…can't," she cried miserably.

When she turned to leave, he let her.

Emily waited until her emotions were under control before requesting a meeting with Fadilah. Unfortunately only so much could be done with her red-rimmed eyes.

"You've accepted my offer," the older woman deduced.

Was it Emily's imagination or did Fadilah look disappointed?

"Not exactly, but I do wish to return to Manhattan. Today. Or as soon as possible."

"As soon as possible?" The other woman's brows rose. "That can be arranged, of course, but I am curious. When I first broached the subject, you mentioned that you'd signed a contract with Madani. Does he know that you've changed your mind?"

"I...I think so." Had she told him? Emily wasn't sure. "Will you see to it that he knows?"

Fadilah's disapproval was palpable. "Of course. What reason should I give for your hasty departure? I assume you will not want him to know of our earlier conversation."

"My sister is getting married this weekend. I wasn't planning to attend the ceremony." To think, Emily had once thought attending would be too painful. "We had a falling out."

"But now you have decided to make amends."

"Yes. It will make my parents happy."

Oddly, Fadilah frowned at that.

"I'm packed and I've left Riyad with step-by-step instructions on how to prepare the dishes that were selected for the feast. Everything will work out for the best."

Fadilah's frown deepened. "Perhaps. I will inform Azeem of your plans and have him bring a car around within the hour. Before you leave, I will give you the agreed upon funds."

Emily rose. "Thank you, but that isn't necessary."

* * *

"Emily is gone?"

Madani stood in the doorway of his parents' private sitting room. His parents had requested to see him. Of all the topics he'd thought they might want to discuss, Emily was not one.

"She left this evening for the airport. Her flight to Manhattan is probably boarding as we speak," his mother said.

"But the feast starts in a matter of days."

"Riyad will see to it," Adil replied with a shrug.

Fadilah chuckled as she reached for a slice of pear. "He is more than happy to do so since he considered it an insult that you brought in an outsider in the first place."

"But we had a contract," he argued weakly.

"A lucrative one." His mother smiled. "But I offered her more money to leave."

"What!"

"Calm yourself. She didn't take it." Fadilah waved a hand. "Now, stop hovering in the doorway. Come sit down. We have much to discuss."

Madani hadn't even taken a seat yet when his father announced, "I'm disappointed in you."

He landed heavily on the chair's cushion. "I didn't mean for this to happen."

"But it did and you said not a word. Indeed, you allowed the preparations for your engagement feast to continue, you even invited this young woman here to help with them."

"I wanted to see her and I wanted her to see Kashaqra," he explained, hoping to keep his father's blood pressure low.

"Because you love her," Adil said.

It was Madani's heart that felt ready to give out now. "Yes."

"Yet even now you would marry Nawar." His father's gaze narrowed.

"I…no. I cannot." He split his gaze between his parents, waiting for the fallout, praying his father would remain calm.

Adil remained more than calm. He grinned. "Finally, my son, you are acting like a ruler."

"I don't understand."

"Madani, I held firm on the marriage contract because I believed you would eventually come to love Nawar. She is, after all, a fine young woman and your arguments against the arrangement didn't have anything to do with your heart. They do now."

"Yes."

"You love Emily." Fadilah smiled. "And she loves you, too. Which is why she fled. Will you go after her?"

"But what about the feast? Nawar?"

"I think we can handle them, both. So?" Fadilah's brows rose.

Madani's response was to jump from his seat and bolt for the door.

* * *

Emily made it through the wedding ceremony, smiling as instructed during the hour-long photo shoot in the church afterward. Nothing could make her feel worse than she already did and that included wearing the hideous peach organdy dress whose puffy shoulders made her look as if she should be playing offense for the New York Jets.

At the reception, she raised her glass of champagne in toast to the new Mr. and Mrs. Reed Benedict and choked down the overcooked food, all while ignoring the pitying looks her aunts and cousins tossed her way.

The only thing that kept her from going insane was Donna's presence. Her friend had insisted on coming with her. They were seated at separate tables for the meal due to Emily's wedding party duties, but once the plates were cleared and the music started, she brought Emily a gin and tonic and hustled her to a secluded corner of the banquet hall. Music pulsed from the huge stereo speakers. But that wasn't why Emily had a headache.

"Hang in there," Donna said. "The bridal dance will be over soon and we can leave."

"Can't wait."

"We can burn your dress in my fireplace. I bet it will go up in a matter of seconds, no lighter fluid necessary."

"Sure." But she was barely listening. What was Madani doing right now? she wondered. What was he feeling? His engagement would become a matter of public record in less than twenty-four hours.

"Hey, Em." Donna elbowed her side. "There's a guy looking at you. A really good-looking guy."

"Don't mention men to me, good-looking or otherwise. I've sworn off of them. And this time I mean it." She took a liberal swig of her drink and coughed after swallowing. "God, this tastes like straight booze. Did you have them put any tonic in it?"

"He's coming this way. Maybe he wants to ask you to dance."

Emily stirred her drink without looking up. "Not interested."

Donna whistled. "God, I think he could be that underwear model whose picture is plastered all over the city."

Her head snapped up and she scanned the crowd. No. It couldn't be, but then she spied Madani and the breath squeezed from her lungs. She rose on shaky legs, met him halfway across the room. That put them in the center of the dance floor during a fast song. Half a dozen gyrating couples were forced to move around them. She didn't care.

"I can't believe you're here. *Why* are you here?" She had to shout the words to be heard over the music.

"I came for you."

"But your engagement—"

"Has been called off to the relief of nearly everyone involved."

"I don't understand."

The song ended. The dance floor cleared. Murmurs began among the guests. The DJ came on the microphone. "Someone has requested a slow song for the couple now on the dance floor."

Emily glanced up to see Donna standing next to one of the speakers. Her friend raised her glass of gin and tonic and grinned. Madani took Emily's hand. Without the thumping bass, the music didn't seem as loud. Or maybe it was just easier to hear Madani since she was in his arms, her temple pressed to his cheek.

"I think you should know that your mother offered me money to leave the country."

"Yes. It was her way of being sure that you truly love me. It was a lucrative sum, I understand."

His chest rumbled with a laugh, but Emily wanted to be clear on this point, "I didn't take her money."

"Nor would you take anything from me."

"It's only right."

He leaned back, his expression as intense as his tone. "No. It's not right. Your restaurant, Emily—"

"I'll open it someday. Or I won't. Oddly enough, it's no longer the most important thing in my life, though I still plan to do it eventually."

"Maybe you can open a second one in Kashaqra."

She liked the sound of that. "Maybe." She frowned then. "Speaking of contracts, you made it seem as if the arrangement with Nawar's family was set in stone."

"I thought it was. Or, perhaps for the sake of my father's health, I resigned myself to believing that. But after seeing you in the garden, I couldn't lose you. I was determined to find a way around it." The arm around her waist tightened as if he never planned to let her go. "Then I didn't have to. It turns out, my father wants me to marry the woman I love."

"Love." She smiled, felt her heart lift. "It's an impossible emotion to deny."

"It is indeed."

Emily's eyes filled with tears. "You're here. I can't believe you're here."

He stopped dancing and dried her damp cheeks. "Where else would I be, where else *could* I be, when I love you so much?" He turned to the crowd of guests, many of whom were openly gawking. "I love her," he said loudly.

The commotion his announcement caused all but drowned out the music. Elle wasn't going to be happy to be upstaged, especially on her wedding day. None of that mattered right now.

"I love you, too," Emily told him, returning to his arms for a kiss.

When it ended a few minutes later, the sleeves of her peach gown were crumpled a mess, and the spray of flowers that had been in her hair had fallen to the dance floor.

Madani tugged at the collar of his shirt. "Please tell me you don't need to stay."

"I don't." Emily smiled. "What I need—all I need— is you."

HER ARDENT
SHEIKH
KRISTI GOLD

To the real "jewels" in this series:
Jennifer Greene, Sara Orwig, Cindy Gerard and
Sheri WhiteFeather.
Thanks for taking me under your wings, and then
letting me fly.
I couldn't have done it without you.

Kristi Gold began her romance-writing career at the tender age of twelve, when she and her sister spun romantic yarns involving a childhood friend and a popular talk-show host. Since that time, she's given up celebrity heroes for her favorite types of men, doctors and cowboys, as her husband is both. An avid sports fan, she attends football and baseball games in her spare time. She resides on a small ranch in central Texas with her three children and retired neurosurgeon husband, along with various livestock ranging from Texas longhorn cattle to spoiled yet talented equines. At one time she competed in regional and national Appaloosa horse shows as a nonpro, but she gave up riding for writing and turned the "reins" over to her youngest daughter. She attributes much of her success to her sister, Kim, who encouraged her in her writing, even during the tough times. When she's not in her office writing her current book, she's dreaming about it. Readers may contact Kristi at P.O. Box 11292, Robinson, TX 76116, USA.

One

He had never seen anyone quite so beautiful, nor heard anything quite so intolerable.

Sheikh Ben Rassad pretended to peruse the antiques displayed behind the shop window as he watched the young woman walk away from the adjacent local dry cleaners.

She clutched a substantial garment covered in clear plastic—and sang in a pitch that could very well wake those who had long since returned to Allah. Ben would not be surprised if every hound residing in Royal, Texas—pedigreed or of questionable breeding—joined her in a canine chorus.

She sang with a vengeance, optimism apparent in her voice. She sang of the sun coming out tomorrow, although at the moment bright rays of light burnished her long blond hair blowing in the mild April breeze, turning it to gold. She sang as if tomorrow might not arrive unless she willed it so.

Ben smiled to himself. Her enthusiasm was almost contagious, had she been able to carry a decent tune.

As she strolled the downtown sidewalk, Ben followed a comfortable distance behind his charge while she searched various windows. Although she was small in stature, her faded jeans enhanced her curves, proving that she was, indeed, more woman than girl.

Ben had noticed many pleasing aspects about Jamie Morris in the weeks since he had been assigned to protect her covertly. His fellow Texas Cattleman's Club members had originally requested that he guard her against two persistent men from the small European country of Asterland. The men had been sent to investigate after a plane en route to Asterland had crash-landed just outside Royal—a plane Jamie Morris had been on. She'd been bound for her arranged wedding to Asterland cabinet member Albert Payune, a man with questionable intentions and connections. Jamie had walked away from the crash without serious injury or further obligation to marry. Although the suspected anarchists had returned to their country, she was still not safe. The marriage had come with a price. Quite possibly Jamie's life.

Because of Jamie's ties to Payune, Ben had secretly memorized her habits in order to keep her safe, guarding her with the same tenacity he utilized in business. Though she was a magnificent creature to behold, duty came first, something he had learned from his upbringing in a country that starkly contrasted with America and its customs.

Now he must protect Jamie from Robert Klimt, a man believed to be Payune's accomplice in planning a revolution in Asterland—a man Ben suspected to be a murderer and thief. Klimt had escaped not hours before from his hospital bed after languishing for weeks from injuries sustained in the crash. Obviously the club members had underestimated the man's dangerous determination, and Ben despised the fact they had not been better prepared.

At the moment, he needed to question Jamie Morris about the crash. Make her aware that he would be her shadow for however long it took to apprehend Klimt. Ensure her safety at all costs. In order to accomplish his goal, she would have to come home with him.

Carefully he planned his approach so as not to frighten her. Yet, considering all that she had been through the past few weeks, he doubted she was easily intimidated. And he suspected she would not like what he was about to propose.

But the members of the club depended on him. Little did Jamie Morris know, so did she.

Jamie took two more steps, stopping at the Royal Confection Shoppe not far from her original location. The song she sang with such passion died on her lips. For that Ben was grateful.

She stared for a long moment at the display of candies with a wistful look of longing. Ben studied her delicate profile, her upturned nose, her full lips, but he had never quite discerned the color of her eyes. He suspected they were crystalline, like precious stones, reminding him of his family's palace in Amythra, a place far removed from his thoughts more often than not in recent days. Reminding him of Royal's missing legendary red diamond and trusted friend Riley Monroe's murder. Reminding Ben of his mission: to find the missing red diamond and return it to its hiding place with two other precious stones. The jewels' existence had been known only in legend, but they were very real. The Texas Cattleman's Club members served as guardians over the heirlooms, as set out by the club's founder, Tex Langley. No member took the duty lightly, including Ben. And he was as determined to protect Jamie Morris in the process of recovering the jewel.

Jamie turned away, but not before Ben caught another glimpse of her plaintive expression. Then she began to whistle as she moved to the curb toward her aged blue sedan parked across the downtown street. He must make his move now.

The squeal of tires heightened Ben's awareness, the bitter taste of danger on his tongue. He glanced toward the grating noise to find that a car was headed in the direction of the sidewalk, aimed at an unsuspecting Jamie Morris.

His heart rate accelerated. Sheer instinct and military training thrust him forward, in slow motion it seemed. *Protect her!* screamed out from his brain.

As he reached Jamie, the vehicle's right front wheel swerved onto the sidewalk. Ben shoved her aside, out of danger, sending her backward onto the concrete in a heap. Her head hit the pavement with a sickening thud. The car sped away.

Ben knelt at her side, his belly knotted with fear—fear that he may have caused her more harm in his efforts to save her. "Miss Morris? Are you all right?"

When Jamie attempted to stand, Ben took her arm and helped her to her feet, relieved that she seemed to be without injury.

She grabbed up the bag from where it had landed next to a weathered light pole, brushing one small hand lovingly over the plastic. "I'm okay."

Concerned over her condition, he grasped her elbow to steady her when she swayed. "Perhaps we should have you examined by a doctor."

She stared at him with a slightly unfocused gaze and as he had suspected, her eyes were light in color, verdant, clear as an oasis pool. A smile tipped the corner of her full lips as she touched the kaffiyeh covering his head. "White

Sale in progress at Murphy's today?'' With that, her eyes drifted shut, and she collapsed into Ben's arms.

He lifted her up, noting how small she felt against him. Fragile. Helpless. Had he failed to protect her after all? If so, he would never forgive himself.

Lowering his ear to her mouth, he felt her warm breath fan his face. He laid his cheek against her left breast and felt the steady beat of her heart. A wave of welcome relief washed over him, and so did an intense need to shelter her.

A small crowd of Saturday-morning shoppers began to gather. Sounds of concern echoed in Ben's ears. "Is that little Jamie Morris?" someone inquired. "Is she dead?" another questioned. An older gentleman asked if he should dial 911.

"No," Ben stated firmly. "I shall find her proper medical attention."

Her injuries must be worse than they appeared, but at the moment he needed to get her away from the open street. Away from imminent danger. Although he had not seen the culprit, he knew who had been behind the wheel—Klimt— yet he did not know where he had gone.

Tightening his hold on Jamie, Ben crossed the street and headed for his car. She still clutched the bag, but her body lay limp against his chest.

Thankful that she was small, he laid her across the bench seat of his sedan and tossed the bag into the back. He quickly rounded the car and slid into the driver's side, grabbing for the cellular phone and hitting the speed dial to access Justin Webb's private number as he pulled away from the curb.

"Yeah," Webb answered, the noted physician sounding suspiciously as if he had recently crawled from bed. Ben suspected that either his new child or his new wife, had kept him up all night. He believed it to be the latter.

"We have a serious problem, *Sadíiq*. Someone has tried to run down Miss Morris in a car, then escaped."

"Is she okay?"

Ben studied Jamie's face resting near his thigh. Her eyes fluttered open, and she mumbled something he did not understand. "I pushed her away before he could do serious damage. She stood on her own before fainting, but she has struck her head on the pavement. At the moment, she is in and out of consciousness."

"Is she bleeding?"

Ben searched for signs of blood with one quick glance over Jamie's curled form. Blessedly, he saw none. "Not that I see."

"Can you rouse her?"

Ben shook her shoulder. "Miss Morris?"

She curled her knees farther into her body and her hands against her breasts. She smiled up at him for a moment before drifting off again.

"Yes. But she falls back to sleep. I will take her to the hospital."

"Don't," Justin said firmly. "If Klimt did this, then he could be waiting for you there. Take her to your place. Talk to her. Try to get her to stay awake. I'm on my way."

Ben clicked off the cell phone and tossed it onto the floor. He shook Jamie's frail shoulder again. "Miss Morris?"

"Hmmm…?" Her eyes fluttered open.

"Where are you injured?"

"I'm fine, just fine," she muttered, then inched closer to him and rested her head on his thigh, facing the dashboard, one hand cupping his knee beneath his djellaba.

She stroked delicate fingers up and down his silk trouser leg and mumbled, "Nice."

Ben's flesh quaked beneath her random touch. His thigh

muscles contracted, not in protest but in pleasure. He did not find her proximity nice at all. He found it intoxicating, as was the scent of roses filtering through his nostrils. And his thoughts at the moment were anything but nice.

"Mother."

Ben briefly took his gaze from the road and looked down on her innocent face and half-closed eyes. "What about your mother?"

She tried to raise her head then let it drop back into his lap. "Dress. Mother's dress."

Obviously she referred to the garment she had retrieved earlier. It must hold great sentimental value, the reason why she had made haste in reclaiming it from the sidewalk.

Ben laid a hand on her silky hair and stroked it gently. "Do not worry. It is here, safe from harm."

Looking somewhat satisfied, she turned her face and nuzzled her nose against him.

Precisely against the crease of his thigh, a place no female of good conscience would ever rest her face on a red-blooded Amythrarian male who had not been with a woman in a while. To Ben's misfortune, Jamie Morris was not thinking of his celibacy at the moment. She simply was not thinking at all.

He inched to his left. Jamie followed. He could go no farther without exiting the car. It seemed this predicament had forced him between a rock and a hard door.

Staring straight ahead, Ben commanded his desires to remain at bay. He attempted to concentrate on driving. Concentrate on getting her to safety. Concentrate on anything but Jamie Morris's face in his lap.

On the outskirts of town, where city dwellings and pristine lawns gave way to flat desert-like terrain, every curve of the rural road brought Jamie's face closer to dangerous territory—and Ben's tenuous control closer to snapping. He silently scolded himself several times. Scolded his weakness for this woman when he should be thinking of her well-being, not his stubborn male urges.

The white pipe-fence gates to the Flying Longhorn Ranch, his Texas home, could not have welcomed him any sooner. Fortunately, Justin Webb's sports car was parked in the drive, its owner standing on the porch leaning back against the Austin-stone facade, awaiting their arrival.

Gently moving Jamie's head aside, Ben slipped out and rounded the car to lift her into his arms. He strode quickly to where Webb was standing.

Once he was on the porch, Justin told him, "Take her inside."

Ben complied, carrying her into his guest room with Justin close on his heels. Inside the room, he carefully laid Jamie on the silk brocade spread covering the bed.

Justin pushed past Ben and perched on the edge of the mattress. Raising Jamie's blouse, he unsnapped her jeans and touched her abdomen in several places. "Her belly's still soft."

Ben imagined it was. Soft as the feather mattress beneath her. "Is that favorable?"

"Yeah. She's not flinching. No apparent tenderness."

Jamie tried to brush Webb's hands away and mumbled, "Leave me alone. I'm tired."

"I've got to do this, Jamie. Just hang on." Justin continued kneading her belly, examining her ribcage. He regarded Ben over one shoulder. "Help me get these jeans off. I want to check her limbs for possible broken bones."

Not normally reluctant to undress a woman, Ben found his own hesitation surprising, to say the least. "She stood after the accident. I believe that would indicate nothing is broken."

"That was adrenaline working," Justin said. "She might

have some swelling that could say otherwise. If so, we'll need to take her to the hospital.''

Ben felt as though invisible hands prevented him from moving forward. "I shall summon my housekeeper to assist you."

Justin looked back with a frown. "Come on, Ben. I know you've seen half-naked women before. And I know you were guilty of getting them that way."

Ben was without a response. His friend did not realize that, under different circumstances, undressing Jamie Morris would give him much pleasure. But he must resist the tempting thoughts. Now and in the future. If he desired to keep her safe, he could not allow the distraction.

While Justin slipped the denim down her narrow hips, Ben forced himself forward to remove her running shoes and tugged the jeans away from her slim legs. Immediately he averted his gaze from the thin scrap of white lace covering her womanly secrets. He cursed the carnal urges trying to surface. Cursed his sudden weakness where this woman was concerned.

Stepping away from the bed, Ben busied himself with folding the jeans in order not to stare at Jamie's lush body. After what she had unknowingly done to him in the car, the last thing he needed was to view Jamie Morris naked as a babe.

"No broken bones, as far as I can tell," Justin said. "She doesn't appear to be in any pain when I touch her. She does have an ugly bruise starting to surface above her hip."

"My fault, I imagine," Ben said, keeping his eyes focused on a painting across the room as he laid the jeans on a nearby chair. "I pushed her harder than I'd intended."

"You saved her life, Ben. Don't be so hard on yourself."

Ben finally turned his attention back to the bed, grateful

the physician had covered Jamie's lower body with the spread.

Justin rummaged through the black bag he had brought with him and removed a stethoscope. He slipped it beneath the woman's blouse to listen to her heart. He then returned to the bag and drew out a small light, opening one of Jamie's eyelids, then the other, and shone the thin ray into each eye.

"Hey, are you in there, kiddo?" he asked.

Jamie opened her eyes, recognition dawning in their green depths. "Dr. Webb?"

"Yeah. The one and only. Can you tell me where you hurt?"

"My head hurts like a son of a gun," she muttered.

Justin raised her head up and examined her skull. "A nasty knot you got there."

"I'm just so sleepy." Jamie yawned and closed her eyes again.

Justin rose from the bed and faced Ben. "Her pupils are reactive, so she probably just has a slight concussion. You can let her sleep, but be sure to wake her periodically. Call me if she has any other symptoms, more pain, severe vomiting, or if you can't get her to wake up. I'm going to see what I can find out about Klimt."

Ben fought down the sudden panic. "You wish me to remain with her? Alone?"

Justin gave him a good-natured slap on the back. "Yeah. You can do it. I'm only a call away. If you even suspect her condition has worsened, then dial 911. The paramedics will be here in no time. But I'd bet she'll just sleep it off."

Ben respected his fellow Texas Cattleman's Club member and would prefer not to insult him. However, he still had questions. "Do you know this for certain? Forgive me, but you are a doctor who fixes imperfections."

"Believe me, Ben, before I took up plastic surgery and went into private practice, I saw my share of all kinds of trauma overseas. You have to learn to assess injuries on a moment's notice. Jamie will be fine. She's a tough kid. She's been through a lot lately. Probably exhausted on top of everything else.''

Ben felt somewhat reassured. "Yes, I believe you are right. She stays up very late into the night, I have noticed."

Justin sent him a lecherous grin. "You've been taking this protection stuff pretty seriously, haven't you?"

Stiffening, Ben raised his chin, hoping to hide his guilt. "I was charged with protecting Miss Morris. I have been watching her, as you and the club members agreed I should." He would not admit that it had been his pleasure.

"Well, just keep doing what you're doing. I'll check back now and then throughout the evening."

As soon as Ben and Justin said their goodbyes, Ben quickly made his way into the kitchen to summon Alima. The housekeeper stood at the stove wearing stereo headphones, a habit she had recently adopted during most of her domestic activities. He doubted she even realized they had a guest.

Ben allowed her this concession, knowing it was futile to argue that she might miss the doorbell or phone if she could not hear due to the country-and-western music blaring through the portable CD player. At times he cursed buying her the gift for her sixtieth birthday. But he would do anything for her. She had been with him since his birth, and she was his only connection in America to his culture. He could not function without her care. Not unless he chose to have dinner at Claire's Bistro every day, or live in squalor.

Perhaps that was why he hadn't concerned himself with finding a wife. Alima provided for all his needs—except one. His thoughts turned to Jamie Morris and how she had reminded him that those needs had been neglected in recent months.

Wanting to get back to Jamie, Ben tapped his house-keeper's plump shoulder. "Alima."

She slipped the headphones away from her ears and released an impatient sigh. "Yes, Hasim. Lunch will be ready soon."

"That is not what I need at the moment. I need you to come to the guest room with me."

She favored him with a bright smile. "Is someone coming to visit?"

Alima enjoyed visitors, and lately there had been none, something she had mentioned often to Ben. He considered that as long as Jamie Morris was in his care, she could provide company for the older woman. "Someone is already here. Come." He gestured her forward and followed her to the room.

Alima's mouth dropped open once she saw the young woman lying in the bed in a tangle of sheets. The feminine attributes Ben had tried to avoid viewing were again exposed.

Ire turned Alima's eyes darker than moonless midnight. "Hasim! What have you been doing with this *bint*?"

"She is not a girl. She is a grown woman." Even to his own ears, Ben sounded defensive, as if he had engaged in disreputable acts with Jamie Morris. Admittedly, he had imagined a few in the car.

With a sigh, he turned his attention to Alima. "It is not what you think. She's been injured. Dr. Webb has examined her, and I am to make sure she is all right until she wakes. I believe she will be more comfortable if you undress her."

"It appears, Hasim, that you have already done that."

Ben clenched his jaw and spoke through his teeth, his patience now a slender thread on the verge of severing. "I did not undress her. Dr. Webb saw to that for the examination. Find something for her to wear, then put it on her." He pointed to the door. "*ruuHi!* Now."

Alima left the room, muttering a litany of Arabic curses followed by a prayer for Hasim bin Abbas kadir Jamal Rassad's wicked soul.

Jamie flailed about, twisting, turning, trying to escape the terrifying images.

The plane crash. The fire. Debris. Lady Helena's cries.

No. Not the plane.

A car coming at her. Flying through the air. Falling. Falling.

A stranger's arms around her.

She tried to sit up but couldn't. Someone held her down.

Fighting for her life, she balled her fist and struck out at the unknown assailant. An iron grip caught her wrist.

"Shhh, little one. You are safe now."

The voice wasn't threatening. More like soothing. A lover's voice.

Jamie blinked several times to focus and stared into a face that would make Adonis hang his head in shame. A white cloth of some sort, secured by a thin gold band circling his forehead, covered his hair but framed a strong jaw shadowed by whiskers. Mysterious eyes regarded her, the color somewhere between rich earth and molten steel. She saw concern and compassion there, and something familiar. But she'd never met him before. She'd definitely remember that, even though at the moment her memories were nothing more than fragments.

"Where am I?" she asked, her voice weak.

He loosened the grip on her wrist but didn't completely let her go. "You are safe."

Jamie tore her gaze away and did a frantic visual search of her surroundings. The room was a kaleidoscope of color and texture, from the rich aqua bedspread covering her to the ornate vases on the nearby black-lacquer end table. Tapestries hung from the bright yellow walls and pillows of every conceivable color rested on a white chair to her right. Sheer mosquito netting flowed beside her from the top of the bed. Practical, she thought, considering the size of the pests in Texas. Was she still in Texas?

No way. This was an exotic place. Beautiful. Foreign.

"Miss Morris, there is no need to be afraid."

He knew her name.

She stared at the stranger once again. Was this Payune? Had he had a change of heart and decided to marry her after all?

Not likely, and she certainly hoped not.

Payune was reportedly nearing fifty. This man was in his mid thirties at best. And his clothes would indicate that he wasn't from a small European country. They didn't wear robes and cover their heads in Asterland, did they? Of course not.

This dark, handsome stranger was Aladdin in his prime. Valentino reincarnate. A desert knight.

Oh, Lordy. She'd been sold into slavery.

A ridiculous concept, Jamie realized. But not as ridiculous as being sold like prime livestock into a marriage to a man she'd never met, arranged by her father for the sake of his failing farm. Had she been kidnapped by this stranger? Did he expect her to do his bidding, too?

Why not? He was practically lying on top of her, all hard, muscled male. Every inch of him, from his solid chest pressing into her breasts to his muscular thigh braced between her legs. Not to mention all points in between, some that were way too obvious not to notice.

Whoever he was, she intended to let him know up front that she didn't like being manhandled by strangers who had designs on her body.

Still pinned beneath his substantial frame, his face only inches from hers, Jamie struggled to squirm out from under him. The more she squirmed, the tighter his grasp on her wrists, the more aware she became of his strength…and his undeniable maleness.

"Be still, Miss Morris," he said, his warm breath drifting across her face, his low voice strained. "You will hurt yourself."

At the moment, she wanted to hurt him. Sort of.

Clenching her jaw tight, she spoke through her teeth. "I don't know what you're thinking, buddy, but if you expect me to be your love slave, then think again."

He looked altogether confused. "I am here to protect you. I need your promise you will not attempt to run away. Only then will I let you go and explain."

Whether or not she tried to run away would depend on his explanation. Still, she thought it best to agree. Considering how her luck had gone lately, she was prepared for anything. "Okay. You can get up now. I'll stay put like a good girl."

With a guarded expression, he unclasped her wrists and sat up but remained seated on the edge of the bed, leaving little distance between them. "I am Sheikh Hasim bin Abbas kadir Jamal Rassad, Prince of Amythra, currently residing in the city of Royal, in the state of Texas. You may call me Ben."

Thank heavens. No way could she remember all those names in her current state of mind. But now she remembered him. Or at least remembered hearing about him. The gossip mill claimed he was filthy rich. A mystery man relatively new to Royal, who kept to himself. A member of the exclusive Texas Cattleman's Club. But no one had bothered to mention his good looks. If you went for the tall, dark, exotic type.

"So tell me, Prince Ben, where am I?" she asked.

"You are in my house."

"And how, pray tell, did I get here?"

He rubbed his chin. "You do not remember the car?"

She searched her brain, an effort in pain thanks to her throbbing head. "I remember I'd just picked up the dress." *Her mother's dress.* She tried not to panic. "Where is the dress now? I have to know."

He laid a comforting hand on her shoulder. "It's hanging in the closet over there." He indicated two double doors across the room. "It is safe."

She felt somewhat better. At least the dress had survived. And so had she, for now. "I remember someone pushing me. Then falling."

"I'm afraid I was the one who pushed you to the ground. That is how you struck your head."

That explained her mother of all headaches. "Why?"

"To avoid the car coming at you." His face turned suddenly serious. "You are in grave danger, Miss Morris."

As if she couldn't figure that one out herself. "And what, exactly, does this have to do with you?"

"It was decided by the Cattleman's Club members that I should protect you. Your connection with Albert Payune has put you in a precarious position."

How much more bizarre could her life get? "Connection? We didn't have a connection! I've never even met the man."

"Once you are feeling better, I will explain further."

"I feel fine!" Jamie sat up in a rush only to encounter

a pounding pain in her skull and a wave of dizziness. She lowered her head back onto the pillow. "Okay, maybe not that fine."

Concern was reflected in his dark eyes. "Dr. Webb has examined you. He believes you suffer from a slight concussion. He ordered me to make sure you rest."

So she hadn't dreamed Dr. Webb's appearance after all. "He was here?"

"Yes. He checked you thoroughly and said you need to 'sleep it off.'"

Her eyes felt as heavy as two-by-fours. The same two-by-fours pounding her temples. "That's a good idea. Think I'll take another little nap."

The sheikh stood in one graceful move and hovered above Jamie, straight and strong and gorgeous beyond the legal limit. "I will be nearby. If you need anything, please do not hesitate to call for me."

Jamie felt a little woozy, but she didn't know if it was from the bump on her head, or the man standing above her. "Sure."

He studied her for another moment, sucking her in with those dark eyes, as if he were a human vacuum and she a tiny speck of dust. "I will make sure you are safe. As long as you are with me, no harm will come to you."

With that, he left the room.

Jamie stared at the door long after it closed, wondering how the heck she'd gotten into this predicament. Her father, of course. If he hadn't agreed to the blasted marriage arrangement, complete with a hefty reward, she would have lived the rest of her life never knowing anything about Albert Payune or Asterland. Or Sheikh Ben Rassad.

Okay, so maybe meeting the prince was a high point in all this mess. She had to admit he was definitely easy on the eye. A little too macho, maybe. But he had seemed genuinely concerned for her safety. Regardless, he still had lots of questions to answer, and soon.

Jamie yawned again. Too tired to think about anything but sleep at the moment, she closed her eyes and snuggled down into the soft bed, Prince Ben's words echoing in her ears.

As long as you are with me, no harm will come to you.

Amazingly, she did feel safe. Secure. Protected.

After sleep again overtook her, Jamie dreamed pleasant dreams, not nightmarish images of doom. She had visions of desert sand, starlit nights…and her role as the love slave of a sexy sheikh named Ben.

Two

The soft moans thrust Ben to his feet. He had dozed on and off while keeping vigil at Jamie's bedside but now found himself wide-awake, worried over her distressed state.

Lowering himself to the edge of the bed, he stroked her silky hair. "You are safe," he said softly. "I am here. No one will do you harm."

She continued to thrash and muttered, "Please."

A fierce surge of protectiveness streaked through Ben. Without thought, he slipped into the bed beside her and cradled her in his arms. She curled into him, her back to his front, fitting perfectly against his body. Although the room was dim, washed only in moonlight, he could see that the sheer muslin gown Alima had dressed her in rode high up her thighs. With one hand he drew it down, contacting smooth warm flesh. He quickly covered her with the satin sheet.

Torture, Ben thought. Or perhaps a test of his strength. Yet he was only a man, not superhuman, and his body reacted as any man's would. But he would not let her go until she had calmed. He'd simply think of other things aside from her petite body, her round breasts, her bottom only inches from treacherous territory.

He tried to recall his impending appointments. His investments. His upcoming summer trip to Amythra to visit his mother.

His mother.

She would most surely be shamed by his reaction to the helpless woman in his arms. She would expect him to be strong. Maintain a steel reserve. She was stronger than any woman he had known, except, perhaps, Jamie Morris.

Yet at the moment, Jamie seemed vulnerable. Quite different from the hellion who had tried to deliver a blow to his face earlier. The woman who had serenaded the population of downtown Royal without caring who might hear.

She was most definitely strong. Determined. And she would never fit into his culture for that reason. He had witnessed his European mother's struggles with his native customs on many occasions. But she had loved her husband dearly, and had adjusted as best she could. Now she was left alone in a place that still remained foreign to her, even after forty years. For that reason, Ben must visit her soon. After he was assured that Jamie Morris was safe.

Jamie stirred again, interrupting Ben's thoughts and driving him to the brink of insanity. Her firm buttocks wiggled against his very overheated manhood. As soon as she settled, he would leave her and return to the cold, empty chair, although that thought held no appeal.

Holding Jamie Morris did, and he cursed the fact that he had not been with a woman in quite some time. Surely this was the reason for his reaction. Weeks had passed since he had returned home. In his country, there were women readily available to care for his needs. Experienced women who considered taking him to their bed an honor because of his station. The couplings were without emotion and left him with a sated body and an emptiness deep in his soul. An emptiness he did not care to acknowledge.

Jamie Morris was different from those women. She aroused feelings in him that he had rarely experienced in his thirty-six years. Aroused his need to protect. To keep her safe. That desire lived so strong within him that he knew he would die before he let any harm come to her, if he could prevent it.

He had covertly watched her for several weeks, had memorized her habits. He knew she woke every morning at 6:00 a.m. and took her coffee and the newspaper onto her apartment's small verandah. She returned to the same spot every evening and stayed with a book late into the night. She was still very young, and he was very jaded. She was an innocent; he was world-weary. Yet at times he had glimpsed loneliness in her expression, as if she craved companionship. He could relate.

But he could not consider his loneliness tonight. He must remember his duty. He was here to protect her, not to sample her luscious body.

Ben sent up a silent prayer of gratitude when Jamie stopped moving, her breathing now deep and steady. At least she slept.

Ben, however, would not for quite some time.

The dream was so nice, Jamie didn't want it to end. The visions were so very real she could still feel her imaginary lover's arms wrapped around her.

Unwelcome light penetrated her closed lids and the fragrant smell of coffee teased her senses. Resisting the distractions, she snuggled further into the heavenly bed.

Her mind still caught in a pleasant haze, she reached for a blanket to cover her head. She contacted something that didn't feel the least bit like her grandmother's handmade quilt.

Her eyes snapped open. What the heck was that? She didn't own any pets. Her gaze traveled downward to discover exactly what she was clutching.

A hairy arm. A large hairy arm that certainly didn't belong to her—unless she'd grown a spare during the night. Definitely male, she decided, after surveying the golden skin laced with prominent veins, the large square fingers attached to the end of a hand. A nice hand. Very nice.

Nope, she knew where her arms were. Connected to her shoulders, not to her hip.

Coming fully awake, she sat up with a jolt and yanked the sheets to her chin. It was all coming back now, one frame at a time, like a slide show. She wasn't in her own bed, and she wasn't alone.

Who had relieved her of her senses? How could someone have crawled into her bed without her knowledge?

"What is going on?" she hissed, then cried "Ouch!" when she pushed farther back and her sore skull bumped the headboard behind her.

Only then did she realize that the arm was an extension of a real live half-naked man whom she didn't recognize, until she met his dark gray eyes now staring up at her through a fringe of sinfully long lashes. The man who had occupied her dreams.

Prince Ben, savior sheikh.

He slowly ran a hand through his thick mussed hair—hair as dark as the Texas crude that had made Royal so prosperous. "Did you sleep well?"

Now suffering from sexy sheikh shock, Jamie couldn't force herself to utter one word.

When she continued to stare at him, his mouth curled up in a smile that revealed deep grooves framing his mouth and enhanced fine lines around his eyes. A smile that would melt an iron washtub. Dark whiskers scattered above his well-defined lips and granite jaw made him look a bit on the sinister side. Sensually sinister. She figured he probably had to shave twice a day. A beard like that would definitely promote whisker burn during long kisses. She'd just bet he could kiss the bloomers off Betty Mays, Royal's spinster county clerk.

And he was in bed with *her*. Jamie Morris, who didn't even kiss on the first date.

"Well?" he asked, his voice deep and raspy.

"Well what?"

"Did you sleep well?"

"Yes, thank you." She had found her voice, but where was her brain? This was no time for pleasantries. "No! I mean…why are you in bed with me?"

He rolled onto his back and stacked his hands behind his head, giving her an intimate view of the tuft of hair under his arm. Jamie looked away and contacted his bare chest. Her gaze followed the path of dark hair that began as a silken mat between his pecs then thinned to a stream over his abdomen before disappearing into the waistband of a pair of striped pajamas. And just below that…

Oh, my.

Like someone viewing a horror film, Jamie didn't exactly want to look, but she couldn't tear her eyes away from the hypnotic sight, even if her life depended on it.

Suddenly realizing he was speaking, she pulled her gaze back to his face. His grin deepened, causing her cheeks to fire up like Manny's grill at the Royal Diner.

"You were having bad dreams. I worried you might hurt yourself if you thrashed about too much."

She didn't remember a single bad dream. A very good dream, yes. "Oh."

"So I took the liberty of holding you until you calmed. I apologize if my presence in your bed has alarmed you."

"I wasn't alarmed exactly. Just a bit unnerved." Jamie was still unnerved, but she wasn't suffering from fear, as he'd assumed. She was more afraid that her dreams had been real, and he wasn't telling the absolute truth.

She chewed her lip for a moment, trying to decide how to broach the subject. Asking point-blank seemed like the sensible solution. "Did we..." How could she ask him *that?*

He impaled her with his night-sky eyes. "Did we what?"

Do the wild thing. Make whoopee. Shuffle the sheets.

She couldn't force herself to say any of those things.

He had the nerve to smile again. "I am waiting."

Jamie got the distinct feeling he enjoyed watching her squirm like a night crawler on the end of a hook. "You know...you and me...together. In the bed."

His smile disappeared, replaced by a dark, sensual expression even more disarming. "Did we make love?"

"Yeah. Did we do that?"

"Why would you assume this?"

She didn't mind mentioning the dream, but she refused to reveal that he was the prime subject. "Well, because I was out of my head. And you are in bed with me. And then I had these images of hands...and things." Lots of things.

"Someone hurting you?"

"No. Just the opposite."

He rolled to his side and faced her again with his elbow bent, one palm bracing his cheek, his eyes darkened by something Jamie couldn't quite name. "Do you mean hands touching you? Perhaps a mouth on you, kissing every inch of your body until you writhed with pleasure? Someone making love to you until you could not breathe, yet you wanted more, until you found yourself begging for the very thing you feared, giving everything over to sensation until you were lost, body and soul?"

He spoke in a low steady tone that made Jamie shiver and sweat, all at the same time.

She somehow managed to speak, with effort. "Yes, something like that."

His smile crept in once again, slowly, and only halfway. "No, Miss Morris. That did not happen between us. If it had, you would know. And you would not so easily forget."

Without further comment, he pushed himself up and left the bed with graceful movements, like a panther progressively stalking its prey. And Jamie sat with her mouth gaping like a sprung screen door, feeling as boneless as putty, her body immersed in heat and her head reeling from his words.

As he walked to the chair across the room, Jamie couldn't help but notice the way his pajamas tightened with each stride, revealing a bottom that would best be described as a true work of art. He picked up a heavy blue robe and slipped it on, covering his artful bottom, much to Jamie's disappointment.

He faced her again, this time his expression all-business, unreadable. "You must be hungry. I will have my housekeeper bring you a tray so that you may regain your strength."

She would need all the strength she could get to fight his control over her. Her desire to know him. All of him.

Shaking off the covers and the stupid thoughts, Jamie

scooted to the end of the bed and touched her toes to the luxuriously carpeted floor. She needed to get out of here. Away from him. The danger she might face outside was nothing compared to the danger this man posed to her sanity and her sudden urges. "Yes, I'm starved. But I can eat after you take me back to my apartment."

"I am afraid that is not possible."

"Why not?"

"You must remain with me until we find the man who is attempting to do you harm."

Jamie stiffened her frame and tried to stand. She felt weak as a newborn, every inch of her crying out in protest. One giant total body ache. Bracing her hand on the bedpost, she steadied herself to keep from falling in front of the man. She refused to let him believe that she couldn't take care of herself.

"Look, Prince Ben, I'll be fine. If anything happens, I'll call the police." Her spongy knees didn't want to support her.

He stepped toward the bed and caught her elbow when she leaned a bit. "You cannot do that. We cannot involve the police at this time."

This guy had too many rules, none of which she understood. He also radiated a sensuality that wasn't easy to ignore.

She stared up at him, only then realizing he was tall. Very tall. Intimidating-to-the-max tall. "Care to explain why I can't call the cops?"

"Trust me, Miss Morris, this is for your sake. The less you know, the better that will be."

Jamie decided he was sorely mistaken, and his determination to keep her in the dark grated on her already raw nerves.

Oh, well. She'd play along for now. She was too tired

to argue. "Since I can't go home just yet, mind if I use your facilities?"

His dark brows drew down with confusion. "Facilities?"

"Bathroom? I'd like to freshen up."

"Of course. I thought you might want to bathe, so I had my housekeeper set out some things for you. This way."

He held on to her arm as he guided her to the room across the hall. Once they reached the door, she expected him to leave. He didn't.

With her hand on the knob, she gave him her best sugar-sweet smile. "Am I allowed to have some privacy?"

"I thought you might wish me to draw your bath."

"So you can watch?" Jamie cringed. She sounded like she wanted him to watch.

He smiled and Jamie felt it down to her size-five feet. "However tempting that might be, I will allow you your privacy after I help you prepare."

"I'll manage. I'm feeling much stronger." *Liar, liar, pants on fire.*

"As you wish. If you find you do need help, there is an intercom near the tub—"

"I can handle this. I promise."

She backed into the room and slammed the door in his face. Slammed the door on those mysterious eyes and all that out-there sexuality. Turning, she leaned back against the wooden surface for support. But it wasn't the lump on her head making her feel like an overcooked noodle. *He* made her weak knees weaker and her shaky body shakier.

Determined to drive him out of her mind, Jamie concentrated on the huge room. A room big enough to house Sadie, her trusty blue sedan. An opulent bath straight out of her fantasies of what a bath should be.

Several black marble steps led to a mammoth whirlpool tub, a huge arched window its backdrop. The matching marble vanity top was graced with gold fixtures and two basins complimented by jeweled soap dispensers and tooth-brush holders. And laid out near one sink—for her benefit, she presumed—was a brand new toothbrush and toothpaste and two velvety black towels with a matching washcloth. On a freestanding gold rack near the toilet hung a lush red velvet robe and underwear. Her underwear.

Her underwear?

She reached back and planted both hands on her butt. No lines. No underwear. She wore nothing more than a too-large sheer ecru gown. The armholes, big enough to drive a truck through, hung all the way down to her waist. No wonder she was shivering.

Who had relieved her of her white lace drawers? And why had she just now noticed?

She'd been barely coherent, that's why. And obviously, the cad had undressed her. Bared her bod and taken liber-ties.

No way. He hadn't done anything lewd to her person. No doubt about it. Like he'd said, she would know.

Recalling his suggestive words, the thought of him un-dressing her again caused shock to course through her al-ready shocked body. And it annoyingly excited her.

Regardless, she planned to have a serious talk with the sheikh. Planned to inform him that, at the very least, un-dressing her without her permission was ungentlemanly. She valued her privacy, and although she wasn't all that modest, she did have high standards and certain expecta-tions. If someone was going to get her naked for the first time, then she darn sure better be conscious during the pro-cess.

A wave of nausea hit her like a raging bull. She slumped onto the step and considered the intercom.

No. She could do this.

With stilted motions, she managed to draw a bath and slip into the tub without passing out. The warm water soothed her sore limbs and made her feel a bit more human.

After luxuriating for a while, then attending to all her toiletries, Jamie felt halfway decent again. Now all she needed was some food, and to convince the sheikh that she needed to go home. But how could she do that in just a robe and underwear? Where had he hidden her jeans and shirt? Okay, so maybe he hadn't hidden them, but she wouldn't be a bit surprised if he had. No clothes, no escape. Obviously he was determined to keep her here against her will.

Well, Prince Ben was wrong if he really believed he could do that.

She slipped on her underwear and the robe, then opened the door and tried to gauge where she should begin in order to find him. Starting down the hall, she peered into several rooms, all bedrooms decorated in more bright colors, but she didn't come upon the man with many names, and probably many talents.

At the end of the corridor, wonderful smells drew her forward. The kitchen must be close, and maybe she would find him there. But before she reached her destination, she came to a den. It gave new meaning to the term *great room.*

The place was a combination of luxury and comfort. Old West meets Middle East. A set of horns hung near the vaulted ceiling over the massive white-rock fireplace, and, draped below, a purple tapestry with rainbow colors woven throughout traveled down the stone wall to the top of the hearth.

Jamie moved farther into the room and noted another opening and a hallway that seemed to go on for miles. In the immediate area, several chairs and rugs were set out in various locations across the gleaming hardwood floors, all in elegant dark colors. The whole place was velvet and marble, a sprawling ranch house most would only dream of, and something she'd not been exposed to in her twenty-two years. She had always appreciated simple. She liked simple. Not that she couldn't get used to luxurious.

Scanning the area, she honed in on a huge suede caramel-colored sofa set to one side of the fireplace. And in the middle of that sofa sat a man, reclining against thick cushions, reading a newspaper, his long legs stretched out before him, booted heels propped on the heavy oak coffee table. He wore jeans and a T-shirt. Threadbare jeans. Tight T-shirt.

Considering his lazy posture, his common ranch-hand clothes, he could be just any sexy-as-sin cowboy. But when he looked up, nailing Jamie with those iron-gray eyes, there was no mistaking his identity.

Prince Ben as Bad-Boy Cowboy.

Ben stared up at Jamie now looming over him dressed in an oversized robe, her eyes flashing anger, her delicate jaw set tight. He suspected she would soon demand more answers from him. Answers he was not at liberty to give her.

Tossing the paper aside, he dropped his feet from the table and straightened. "You are looking much better. Refreshed." With her damp hair falling just below her slender shoulders, her face freshly scrubbed, she was all softness and innocence. A celestial being.

"How dare you!"

She no longer looked angelic. She looked as angry as Alima when a tennis championship interrupted her American soap operas.

What had he done now? "I do not understand."

She clenched her fists and Ben braced for another swing,

but fortunately it did not come. "How dare you undress me and put me in that see-through gown. I have never in my life—"

"Miss Morris—"

"—met a man who thought—"

"Miss Morris—"

"—he could get away with taking off my clothes without me knowing it and—" She put a hand to head and looked as though she might faint.

He vaulted off the couch and circled his arms around her to prevent her from falling. "Miss Morris, you must calm down. You are still not well."

She looked up at him but did not push him away, or try to punch him. Instead, she leaned into him. "I'm fine, thank you very much!"

She did not seem fine. Her skin was pale, almost translucent, and she looked as though she might buckle. "I think not." He tightened his hold on her.

"I want to go home," she said willfully, belying her fragile state.

"I told you that is not possible."

She locked into his gaze, her chin raised up in determination. "You can't keep me here."

"I am hoping you will see that it is necessary in order to ensure your safety."

"I'll tell you what's necessary. I need to find a job." She grasped the front of his shirt. "I'm running out of money. My rent's due right now. Then the car payment." She sounded desperate, her voice pleading.

He rubbed her back to comfort her, all too aware of her breasts pressed against him. The way she smelled, fresh and clean. Womanly. He held her closer to anchor himself. "I will provide for you until the time you can return to your apartment. I will arrange to pay your debts and see to it that you are comfortable in my home for now.''

She stiffened in his arms. "I don't need your charity. I can take care of myself.''

Her attitude was the very reason he had never been involved with an American woman. Although he admired her independence, he did not always understand it, just as he did not understand his mother at times. Pride would not keep her safe, but he could. He would. "We will consider it a gift.''

"A loan,'' she corrected, seeming to give in.

A strong sense of satisfaction settled over Ben at the prospect she would agree to stay with him, at least for now. "We shall discuss your financial situation later.''

She relaxed somewhat. "Can I at least go home and get some clothes?''

"I will find you appropriate clothing.''

"I have to feed…uh…my fish.''

He took her arm and led her to the sofa, then brought her down next to him. It seemed best to put some distance between them. Simply holding her again resurrected more unwanted feelings within Ben. Feelings he did not welcome but could not seem to stop. Yet he must halt them. Remember his duty to her.

He sighed. "I will take you to your apartment where you can feed your pets and gather some clothes. But you must agree to come back with me.''

Her smile traveled all the way to her jewel-like eyes, causing Ben's pulse to race out of control. "Okay. Then it's a deal?''

"Yes, but first you must eat.''

She shrugged. "I'm not sure I'm all that hungry.''

He was, but not necessarily for food. He stood before he

lost his head, his control. "You can eat something. I shall summon Alima."

She slumped back onto the sofa. "Alima?"

"My housekeeper." And oftentimes thorn in his side.

Jamie shrugged again. "Okay. Does she do hot dogs? I'm really craving a hot dog."

Ben smiled in response. "I will see what I can do."

He then departed for the nearby kitchen to seek out Alima, glancing toward the sofa in the event Miss Morris should change her mind and try to escape. He hated holding her captive, and had he been less honorable, he might have led her to believe he *was* her captor, and she his slave. But honor was something his parents had instilled in him from birth, therefore he had no choice but to tell her the truth. As much of the truth as he could allow.

Alima was opening the oven door, removing fresh-baked bread. She turned around and tossed the pan onto the stove, then slipped the headphones away from her ears. "Is our guest awake now?"

"Yes. And she needs nourishment."

She lifted the lid from a heavy black pot on the stove. "I have prepared *simich* in a very hearty stew."

The wonderful bouquet made Ben's mouth water. "She does not want fish stew. She has requested a hot dog."

Alima narrowed her dark eyes. "I do not prepare hot dogs."

"You will prepare something like it. She is our guest."

She slapped the lid back on the boiling pot. "I will prepare something American, but I do no hot dogs."

There was no sense in arguing with her. With Alima, he chose his battles carefully. He would need her assistance with Jamie in the future. No matter how stubborn Alima could be at times, she was a kind woman. She had a way with people, able to soothe them during dire moments. Jamie would need Alima's kindness, for if she caused more trouble, put herself in more danger, then he would not be able to be kind.

"Bring the food into the living room on a tray," he said. "We will dine there."

"Do you wish the stew, Prince Hasim, or do you prefer the Texas food?" Her tone implied once again that she didn't approve of his burgeoning American tastes even though she was guilty of the same.

"I will have what Miss Morris is having."

Alima strolled to the refrigerator, muttering in Arabic under her breath as she yanked open the door and peered inside.

Ben returned to the living room to find Jamie curled up on the sofa, her eyes closed. But when he approached her, she quickly came awake and sat up. "I'm sorry. I just can't shake this sleepiness."

He still worried over her condition even though he had spoken with Justin several times by phone since the day before. The doctor had assured him that Jamie would be weak for a few days, but not to worry. Ben did worry, although perhaps he should be thankful she wasn't quite recovered. The potential for her to fight him would increase with her strength.

He joined her on the sofa. "Alima will bring you something satisfactory. I am afraid we have no hot dogs."

Jamie yawned. "That's okay. Right now I think I could eat just about anything if it stood still long enough."

"Then your appetite is returning. This is good."

She smiled. A pretty smile that withered Ben's insides like blades of grass in the sweltering Texas heat. "Yep. I'm feeling better," she said. "And right after lunch, you can take me to my place."

He should expect her persistence in this matter. She was not one to give up easily. "All right."

She smiled. "You promise?"

At the moment, he would promise her anything. "You have my word."

With her head lowered, Alima scurried into the room carrying a tray full of meats, cheeses and breads. She slipped it onto the table before them but did not raise her eyes to Jamie until Ben said, "Alima, this is Miss Morris."

Jamie held out her small hand to Alima. "You can call me Jamie."

Alima did not take the hand Jamie offered, as that would be disrespectful, but she did afford Jamie a smile. "I am pleased to have you in Prince Hasim's home, Miss Morris. If you wish anything, please let me know." She turned to address Ben. "Would Miss Morris be more comfortable dining at the table instead of here in the *mayaalis,* with the dead animals?" She gestured toward the cowhide rug draped on the floor in front of the hearth.

Ben repressed a chuckle. Jamie did not.

"I believe Miss Morris and I are quite comfortable here." He regarded Jamie. "I am afraid Alima has never approved of informality. She believes that my mother spoiled me by letting me run the palace, doing as I pleased."

Alima departed, muttering in her native tongue all the way to the kitchen.

"What did she just say?" Jamie asked.

"The monkey is a gazelle in the eyes of his mother. An Arabic proverb."

Jamie laughed, a rich vibrant sound that made Ben want to laugh with her. "I have to remember that. Maybe while we're stuck here together, you can teach me some Arabic."

There were many things he would like to teach her, the

least of which involved his native tongue. Or perhaps it *would* involve his tongue. And his hands, his body...

Thrusting the thoughts away, he said, "Arabic is best learned in an atmosphere where it is readily spoken. I only speak it with Alima on occasion and when I return home."

She took some meat from the tray and shredded it, then nibbled a few bits. "Where is home?"

"Amythra. A small country near Oman."

She took another bite and spoke around it. "Well, I'm not good at geography, so I'll take your word for it."

Ben placed some of the fare on his plate and opted to use a fork, unlike Jamie who used her fingers, licking them on occasion, causing a rising heat to stir low in Ben's belly.

He ate in silence while watching Jamie put her all into the meal. She ate as if ravenous. As if it were her last bite.

He suspected she approached most everything with heart and soul and unyielding determination. He imagined she would approach lovemaking the same way.

Again his body stirred, and he cursed the fact he had not dressed in his djellaba. American jeans could not hide his sins should he lose control over baser urges.

Crossing one leg over the other, he pushed his plate aside and leaned back against the sofa. Jamie did the same.

"That was wonderful," she said, rubbing her belly.

Ben visually followed the movement of her hand, imagining his own hand there.

He looked away, questioning his wisdom. How could he not touch her if she lived under his roof? How could he continue to ignore his desires if she was with him every waking moment?

He must. He would call on all his strength and avoid situations that might threaten his control. At one time he had not been in control, and his own father had paid the price. He had vowed then that never would he let anyone harm a defenseless human being, especially one he cared about. And he was beginning to see Jamie in that category, no matter how inadvisable that might be.

Needing to get away, he rose from the sofa. "Are you finished, Miss Morris?"

She stood. "Yes. And if you'll point me in the direction of my clothes, I'll change and we can head to my apartment."

"You will find your clothes in the top drawer of the bureau in your room. Alima has laundered them for you."

Again she smiled. "How nice. Remind me to thank her."

"Yes, and I will change, too."

When she stood, the robe gaped open, revealing the valley between her breasts. "Change into what?" she asked.

Into a madman if she did not close the robe. "My traditional dress." He reached for the robe and she stepped back. "I am trying to cover you."

She looked down. "Oh. This thing is too big."

He suddenly realized that not only would she be more comfortable in her own clothes, *he* would be more comfortable if she was wearing them. At least somewhat.

She crossed her arms over her breasts, much to Ben's relief—and disappointment. "Don't get me wrong, Ben, but wouldn't you be a little less obvious if you stayed in what you're wearing now? I mean, you're trying to protect me. When in Rome and all that jazz."

He bristled at the jab, although he believed she meant nothing by it. "It is expected of me," he explained. "Both in the business world and in my country. I have promised my mother that I will keep this connection to my birthright."

She looked away. "I'm sorry. I didn't mean to offend you."

"No offense taken. There are many things about my culture that most Americans do not comprehend."

She locked into his gaze and he saw true sincerity in the green depths of her eyes. "I'd like to understand."

In that moment, he had no doubt she would.

All their differences seemed to melt away, and Ben wondered if she would be the kind of woman who would understand him. Understand his ways. Understand the man beneath the prince.

Impossible dreams.

Three

Jamie relished the feel of the warm April sun filtering through the car's tinted window, the lush leather seat beneath her. The black sedan was the ultimate in luxury. Masculine, sleek, like its owner.

She regarded Ben with a sideways glance. "I like your wheels. But wouldn't a truck be more practical on a ranch?"

"I own two trucks. I travel in this because it's safer."

"Safer?"

"Bulletproof."

Bulletproof? Did he have a price on his head, too?

Jamie took in a deep breath and pulled a leg underneath her. She turned toward him as much as the seat belt allowed. "Why on earth do you need a bulletproof car?"

"Because of my family's influence, there are people who exist for the sole purpose of doing us harm. But since I've been in America, I have encountered no trouble. I have sent most of my bodyguards back to Amythra for that reason.''

Bodyguards and bulletproof cars. Obviously Prince Ben was important. A somebody. Royal, Texas, was full of somebodys. As a fourth-generation Royal native, Jamie's father had once been a respected farmer. But Caleb Morris had squandered that respect with frequent gambling and drinking binges since his wife's death. Jamie missed her mother, too, but her father still hadn't come to terms with his loss.

He was probably in Vegas now, blowing the money he'd earned for selling his daughter into marriage instead of taking that money and trying to salvage the farm. At least Payune had been gracious enough to let them keep the marriage funds for her "inconvenience and mental anguish," after he'd decided to void the contract.

She didn't consider an emergency plane landing a mere inconvenience or simple mental anguish. It had been terrifying. Although she was grateful that the wedding had never happened, she didn't have a dime to show for all her trouble. Her daddy had taken every last cent.

Burying the anger as she had for the past few months, Jamie glanced at Ben again, his eyes hidden by dark sunglasses. His features were angular, his nose sharp but not overly big. And oh, that kiss-me-quick mouth.

A classically handsome man. A man many women would want, not only for his good looks, but also for his wealth. She wondered why a good-looking prince with lots of money had never married. Then it occurred to her. Maybe he *was* married. To some woman back in his country. Maybe to several women. Did they still do that? Someday she'd find out more from Alima. But if the housekeeper was anything like her employer, Jamie realized that might never happen. So she might as well jump at the chance to find out for herself while the opportunity existed.

"Are you married, Ben?"

"No."

"Have you ever been married?"

"No."

A man of few words when it came to his personal life, she decided. "You don't have a woman waiting for you back home in your country?"

"No, I have no one waiting for me there."

"A girlfriend here?"

This time he smiled. "No, not here, either."

For some reason, that fact relieved Jamie. And her relief annoyed her. She wasn't about to play the role of his girl-friend while he insisted on handing out demands and trying to control her life. Like he'd really want her, plain old Jamie Morris from the country. "Don't you need some kind of heir? I mean, don't people who have royal blood need that?"

"My older brother, Kalib, has taken over the rule of Amythra since my father's death. He has five sons. Enough to supply Amythra with all the heirs my country will ever need."

"So while you were at home and your brother was having kids, what did you do?"

He fiddled with the radio and tuned it in to a station playing light jazz. "Before I came here to complete my education, I served as a commander in my country's military."

"Oh. So that's why you're so into this protection thing."

"I have been taught to protect those who cannot help themselves. Helpless women and children."

That made Jamie sit up straight and grit her teeth. "So you think all women are helpless?"

"Not all," he said, looking straight ahead.

"Good, because we aren't all frail little creatures waiting to be rescued."

"I would not assume that about you, Miss Morris. I believe there are times when you can take care of yourself." He glanced at her for a brief moment. "And times you cannot."

"And you can?"

"Yes. Many things are done out of necessity. Defending what you believe in to the death. Resorting to whatever means necessary to protect those in your care."

He said the words with such conviction, Jamie was determined to find out more about this overwhelming need he had to save everyone. "What do you mean by 'whatever means necessary?' Hurt someone? Maybe even kill someone?"

He shot another look in her direction then brought his eyes back to the road. "Yes. If necessary."

The admission hung over the car like a shroud. The images bouncing around Jamie's head were anything but pleasant. She deplored violence of any kind. But she found it hard to believe, considering his kindness to her that Ben could hurt anyone. "Have you had to do that? Hurt someone?"

His hands tightened on the steering wheel as if he had them around an imaginary neck. "Whatever I have or have not done in the past does not matter now. What matters is that I keep you safe."

The hard set of Ben's jaw told Jamie not to press, but she wondered if, in fact, he *had* hurt someone. Maybe even killed someone. Someday she'd ask again, but not now. Considering the way he continued to white-knuckle the steering wheel, obviously she'd already said too much.

Riding in silence, they passed through town on the way

to Jamie's apartment. A few tourists, mostly antique enthusiasts, occupied the afternoon streets. Retired folks who'd blazed the unbeaten path that took them to the small community of Royal, a place rich in oil, folklore and legend, and rich in rich people. Home to up-and-coming businessmen and women. Jamie's hometown that had changed and grown to suit the times. But she hadn't changed all that much. Not as much as she'd wanted. And now the prospect of returning to college to get her nursing degree seemed as far away as Ben's homeland.

When they passed the cleaners, Jamie suddenly remembered Sadie. "Where's my car?" She stared out the window and saw only an empty space where she had last parked. "Oh, heavens, they probably towed it. I can't afford to get my car out of the city lot—"

"Your car is safe."

Jamie leveled her gaze on Ben. "How do you know?"

"I have it stored in a garage at my ranch. One of my workers retrieved it at my request."

The man had considered everything. Taken care of everything. "Thanks." It was all she could think to say.

Once they pulled into the drive at the Royal Court Complex, Jamie quickly slid out of the car. But before she could make her way up the stairs, Ben grabbed her arm and stopped her progress.

"Wait," he said. "I must go first. Stay behind me."

Jamie opened her mouth to protest, but snapped it shut. She might as well let him have his way. His mother-hen attitude was something she'd have to learn to live with for the time being. She didn't have to like it, though.

Jamie let him pass and followed him up the stairs and into the hall, surprised that he went straight to 3C, her apartment. He withdrew her keys from his trouser pocket and held them up for her to indicate the correct one. She probably should be surprised he knew where she lived, that he even had her keys, but she wasn't. Nothing he did from this point on would shock her. In fact, she figured after everything that had happened—the stupid marriage agreement, the plane crash, the almost-hit-and-run, nothing would ever shock her again.

She was wrong. So wrong. When Ben pushed open the apartment door and she saw her upturned couch, her shattered floor lamp, her kitchen drawers tossed aside like yesterday's garbage, shock wasn't even close to what she felt.

"Don't move," Ben hissed, causing her knees to lock in place like the Tin Man without his oilcan.

He put up a hand, a silent command for her to wait on the threshold while he investigated. Blinding fear caused her temples to throb and her body to tremble. Not fear for herself. Fear for Ben. What if someone waited for him? What if several intruders ambushed him?

Jamie tried to convince herself that he would be fine. He had military training. But as far as she knew, he was unarmed.

A shaky breath of relief seeped out when Ben returned to the living room, all in one piece, and gestured her inside. "He is gone."

Moving forward on rubber legs, she took in the sight of her ransacked apartment. Nothing had been left in its place. Not one magazine, not one knickknack. Almost everything had been either destroyed or tossed aside, including much of Jamie's heart when she noticed her grandmother's porcelain angels in pieces scattered about their curio-cabinet home. Keepsakes passed on to Jamie's mother, then Jamie, and intended eventually to be passed down to Jamie's child. A symbolic death of a dream. Jamie's dream.

"Oh…no…not…." She bent to survey the horrible debris. How could anyone be so heartless? Why would anyone want to do this to her? What had she done to them to deserve such cruelty?

She fought back angry tears. Fought back sadness and frustration and a total feeling of helplessness.

"Jamie."

At first she didn't realize it was Ben standing over her, Ben calling her name. Then gentle fingertips circled her arms and lifted her up. Up into his strong embrace, his protective arms. He soothed her with words, some spoken in his native tongue, a language she didn't understand, but they made her feel safe.

Jamie clung to him, letting the tears come, unheeded, unwanted. She pressed her face into the fine silk of his robes, allowing his comfort. But only for a moment.

Pushing out of his arms, she let anger take the place of tears. "Damn whoever did this. Damn him to hell and back!"

Ben's dark serious expression stopped her ranting cold. "Did anyone give you anything when you were on the plane?"

Her mind was a muddled mess. As trashed as her apartment. So why was he asking about the plane? "What do you mean?"

"Were you given anything? An envelope? A package? Anything at all?"

"No."

"What about your luggage?"

"Destroyed in the fire. Every last shred of it."

He dropped his arms from around her and paced the room. "Did you have a bag with you that you carried off?"

"No. I had nothing with me but my mother's wedding dress."

Ben's gaze snapped back to her. "Did you have it with you at all times?"

"Yes. I was holding it when the plane made the emergency landing."

He walked back to her. "Was it out of your possession at any time?"

Why was he so interested in all these things? "I don't understand why you're asking me this."

Ben shook his head and paced some more, as if his thoughts only came if he kept moving. "There is something missing. Something we believe the man who did this is looking for. He thinks you have it."

Jamie stomped her foot, frustration replacing her grief over the break-in. "What is this something? Maybe if I knew, then I'd know if I have it."

"I cannot tell you. And if you had it, you would know."

Jamie rolled her eyes to the ceiling. "Oh, wow. I didn't know you spoke in riddles, too." She hugged her arms to herself, hating all the secrecy. Her father was a master at secrecy.

Ben stopped his pacing and faced her again. "I am sorry I cannot tell you more."

"Sorry?" She clamped her mouth shut against the oath threatening to spill out. "This is crazy. I'm just a good ol' Texas girl who made the stupid mistake of letting her father manipulate her into a marriage. All of a sudden, I'm thrust into some crazy scheme about some missing *something* and now I've got a target on my back."

"I will make certain he does not harm you."

The whole concept was so ludicrous, Jamie wanted to laugh. "You and who else?"

He seemed unaffected by her near hysteria, or her sarcasm. "If you would like to retrieve some clothes to take with you, I will escort you to your bedroom, then we must leave here. You may also bring your fish if you would like."

She would like to add foolish to frustrated since she'd been both. Not to mention frightened. Might as well tell Prince Ben the truth, even if he wasn't willing to do the same. "I don't have any fish. I made that up so you'd bring me back here. Seemed like a good idea at the time."

Ben smiled. A knock-your-feet-out-from-under-you grin. "Well, Miss Morris, you are very creative."

Darn him! Jamie couldn't help but smile back, although what she really wanted was to sit down on the floor, throw a tantrum and have a good cry. If there was such a thing as a good cry. Instead, she chose to look on the bright side. If Ben hadn't come to her rescue the other day, then this could have happened while she was in the apartment, alone. She might have been hurt again, or worse. And now he was offering to keep her safe and give her a place to live until... Until what? Would she ever really be safe again?

She couldn't worry about that now. She'd consider that later. Right now she wanted to grab some clothes and get out of here before the robber came back to finish the job, meaning finish her.

"Okay, let's go find some clothes." She stopped at her bedroom door, but didn't turn around. "And I really like it better when you call me Jamie."

"All right then...Jamie."

Pleasant chills coursed up Jamie's spine when he said her name. She sensed his closeness, felt his heat even though he remained a step behind her. And she wondered if being with Sheikh Ben Rassad was such a terrible thing after all.

In the back conference room of the well-appointed Texas Cattleman's Club, Ben affected attentiveness while listening to his fellow members discuss the recent events. In reality, impatience rushed through him as his thoughts turned to Jamie. He needed to get back to her immediately. Although he had put his workers on alert and posted a guard at the door, he would not feel at ease until he was with her again, seeing to her safety himself.

"Is that right, Ben?"

Ben's gaze snapped to Justin Webb when he realized the doctor was addressing him. "I am sorry. What were you asking?"

"The color of the car. Was it white?"

With a sigh, Ben leaned back in the chair. They had been through this before. "Yes. It was white."

"Winona did some checking for me," Justin said, referring to his wife who was also a police officer. "According to her, a white car was stolen from the hospital lot, the day Jamie was almost run down, so it's a safe bet Klimt was driving. They found the car abandoned right outside town, but we're pretty sure he wasn't strong enough to get too far on foot because of his injuries. He's still around here, somewhere."

Ben straightened again, thankful Justin's wife continued to keep them informed. "Yes, there has been no doubt in my mind from the beginning that Klimt drove the car and that he is still a threat to Miss Morris."

Aaron Black sat forward. Ben noted the diplomat's concerned expression and knew more questions about Jamie were forthcoming. "Have you asked her about the diamond?"

"Not specifically, since I believe the fewer who know about the diamond, the better. I have asked if she was given anything before boarding the plane. She says no."

Dakota Lewis frowned. "And she is absolutely sure, beyond a doubt?"

Normally the comment would not have bothered Ben. Lewis was retired from the United States Air Force, trained in the art of interrogation. Yet the need to defend Jamie burst forth and Ben could no longer control it. "Of course, I believe her. She has been through much. I do not care to upset her further by asking again and again."

Justin raised both hands, palms forward. "Whoa, Ben. We're not saying you should harass the woman. We just want to be sure she's not forgotten anything."

"She has not forgotten."

Matt Walker, Ben's neighbor and closest friend in America, finally spoke. "Okay. The diamond's still missing, and for some reason Klimt thinks Jamie has it. We just don't know why."

"And it's good he thinks she has it, even if she doesn't," Dakota added. "If he's connected to the revolution as we now suspect, selling the diamond is his only chance to raise money since we've recovered the emerald and opal. He'll eventually try to get to Jamie again and that's the way we'll catch him."

Ben narrowed his eyes. "Like a helpless lamb waiting for the slaughter?"

"We'll make sure that doesn't happen, Ben," Justin said. "But we have to find the diamond, and with any luck, return it to its rightful place, here with the others." He pointed toward the plaque in the grand salon that covered the hole in the wall containing two of Royal's legendary jewels. The third was still missing.

Peace, Justice, Leadership; the club's mantra etched across the plaque reminded Ben why he must endure the questions. Why he must see this through, not only for Jamie's sake but also for the town's prosperity.

"We need to put Klimt away for good," Matt said, "and we can't do that unless we find the man. I agree that he'll try to get to Jamie again. Unless he found what he was looking for in the apartment.'' He rubbed his jaw. ''Maybe he hid it there.''

''I don't think so,'' Aaron said. ''He's been hospitalized since the crash. When would he have had the opportunity?''

''The night he killed Riley,'' Justin interjected.

''*If* he killed Riley,'' Dakota said. ''We don't know for sure it was him.''

''It was him,'' Ben said adamantly. ''But I do not think he would have hidden the jewel in Jamie's apartment since she was home the night before the wedding. The luggage would have been a more likely hiding place. After all, the other jewels were found on the plane. I believe that the diamond was somewhere in her luggage and was perhaps lost in the fire.''

''We've looked in what was left of her luggage,'' Aaron added. ''We didn't find it. And we went over every inch of that plane.''

Justin leaned back in his chair and clasped his hands behind his head. ''Looks like we have no choice but to wait it out. See if he comes after Jamie again. If he doesn't, then he's found it and could be on his way back to Asterland. If not, he's still looking and that means Jamie's still in danger. If so, he'll try to find her, you mark my words.''

The thought of Klimt harming one golden hair on Jamie's head made Ben stifle an oath. He shoved back his chair and stood. ''If he touches her, I will kill him.''

The vow echoed in the room, all its occupants' eyes now trained on Ben.

Ben moved away from the table. ''I must return to her now. I will stay in touch.'' With a quick bow of his head, he took his leave, but not before he heard Matt's familiar Texas drawl.

''Yep, he's got it bad for her, all right. Let's just hope

his feelings don't interfere with him keeping her safe, and helping us get that diamond back.''

The words followed Ben all the way through the ornate grand salon and out the door. The overcast skies suited his black mood. He welcomed the impending thunderstorm that would truly complement his emotional turbulence.

The members were wrong. He would not allow Jamie Morris to keep him from his duty. He would prove to them he could resist all temptation, and that he did not have it ''bad'' for his charge. He was simply honor-bound to protect her. That was all it was or would ever be.

And that was what he told himself over and over, all the way home.

One minute he was vowing to protect her, the next minute he was gone.

Jamie walked aimlessly around the living room, not knowing what do about her situation. She'd tried to read some magazines to entertain herself, wishing she could turn back time. Wishing it was still December and she still had her old job back. Wishing she was living in her simple apartment and her only worry was trying to keep her dad from sinking farther into debt and depression. Wishing it was before the blasted notice had been posted all over town announcing Bride Wanted for Albert Payune of Asterland.

Never had she felt so alone, so out of place. Where was Ben now? Off planning her future? Deciding her fate?

He'd left an hour ago, barking demands about her staying inside. Staying away from the windows and doors.

Well, there wasn't any reason why she couldn't just take a peek outside. See what was going on. Surely there would be no harm in that.

Quietly she approached the front window and pulled back the heavy beige curtains. A man sat on the front porch, kicked back in the wooden glider with a shotgun resting across his meaty thighs. A Santa belly hung to his lap, probably the result of too much chicken-fried steak and beer. His ratty straw cowboy hat dipped low on his forehead, covering his eyes. Eyes that were closed, Jamie suspected. The piece of hay drooping from his mouth suddenly did a nosedive when his lower lip went slack.

If this man was Ben's idea of protection, Jamie would be better off with her own gun. Maybe she couldn't shoot straight to save her hide, but at least she wasn't napping.

Dropping the curtain, she stretched and braced her hands on the small of her back. She wasn't as tired as she had been, but she still felt the effects of getting up close and personal with the downtown sidewalk. The bruise on her hip was just plain ugly now, but the knot on her head had all but disappeared.

She felt bored, restless, in dire need of some kind of physical activity. She doubted Ben owned a treadmill, although he must do something to keep in such superior physical shape. Probably just came naturally for him, though. She couldn't imagine him dressed in gym shorts, working out at the local Y. Now another kind of workout she definitely could imagine.

My, my, Jamie Morris, you are turning into a bad girl.

The little voice in her head sounded remarkably like her grandmother. But her Nana had been gone for some time now, as had Jamie's own mother. Still, she thought about them often. Many times she had craved the company of a woman. Craved some honest-to-goodness motherly advice. Like now.

She suddenly considered Alima.

Would Alima talk to her? All she could do was try. It beat the heck out of talking to herself.

Jamie strolled toward the kitchen. Considering the spicy

smells coming from that direction, she figured she'd find the housekeeper there. She stepped into the room to find Alima busy at the island counter, chopping vegetables with a vengeance, her ears covered by bright yellow headphones.

Walking to the counter, Jamie stood in front of Alima in hopes of getting the woman's attention without scaring the wits out of her. After several minutes had passed, she tapped her on the arm.

Alima's gaze darted up from her task, and she stripped her ears of the headphones. She lowered her eyes. "I am sorry, Miss. I did not know you were standing there."

From the sound of the music coming through the headphones dangling about the housekeeper's neck, Jamie could understand why. She smiled at the woman. "Is there anything I can do to help you?"

Alima looked almost alarmed. "Oh, no, Miss. It is my duty to serve you. You must rest."

Jamie frowned. "I'm not even tired. Actually, I'm tired of resting. I'm about to go nuts just sitting around doing nothing. Surely you can think of something."

Alima surveyed the kitchen then pulled a barstool back from the island. "You may keep me company."

Conversation wasn't exactly a physical activity, but Jamie supposed it would have to do. Besides, she could find out more about the sheikh. She took her perch on the barstool and considered how she could do that. She guessed just coming out and asking would be the best place to start. "So, Alima, how long have you known the prince?"

Alima sent Jamie a kind smile. A mother's smile. "Since he was an infant. I cared for him then, as I care for him now."

"What about his mother?"

Alima's knife stopped in mid chop. "Her Highness cared

for him as well, but she had many duties to attend to and was in need of my assistance.''

''And you followed him here?''

''Not in the beginning. When he was still at the university I remained in Amythra. When he bought this house,'' she made a sweeping gesture around the room, her voice full of disdain as if it were below princely standards, ''he sent for me to attend to him here in America.''

''Where did he go to school?''

''The University of Texas in the city of Austin.''

Jamie smiled. From now on, she would think of Ben as Lawrence of Longhorn instead of Arabia. ''That's interesting. Do you have children of your own?''

A sadness passed over the woman's expression. ''No, Miss. Prince Hasim is the closest I have to a child. Allah did not see fit for me to bear children, but he was gracious in allowing me to care for the sheikh.''

A lump formed in Jamie's throat when she thought about her own mother, how much she had cared for her, coddled her and loved her. Jamie had been so very, very lucky. And seeing Alima's face, the maternal pride when she spoke of Ben, made her realize how much she would value having a child. Later. Much, much later.

The sound of a slamming door caused Alima to look up from her chopping and Jamie to slide off the barstool, ready to go for the nearby butcher knife in case the unknown apartment destroyer might come strolling in.

Instead, Ben entered, his face all hard lines and angles. His expression relaxed somewhat when his gaze contacted Jamie's. ''I see that you are safe, no thanks to J.D., my slumbering guard.''

Jamie laughed. She couldn't help it. ''Yeah, I noticed J.D. was snoozing.''

Ben's face hardened once again. "Did you go outside after I told you not to? Do you have a death wish?"

"I went to the window—"

"Did I not tell you to stay away from the windows?"

"I just took a peek—"

"That peek could have cost you your life!"

"But it didn't."

Ben turned away in a swirl of white and black robes as he left the room. Furious, Jamie followed. Of all the stubborn, hardheaded sheikhs she'd ever known...

Lord, she didn't know any other sheikhs except this one. But she had known stubborn men, namely her father. And the best way to deal with them was to let them know point-blank that they didn't have the upper hand.

"I'm going crazy!" she shouted at Ben's back.

He spun around to face her, fire in his steely eyes. "Better crazy than dead."

Jamie braced both hands on her hips, expecting steam to pour out of her ears at any moment. "Well, I might as well be six feet under the way you've made me a prisoner here."

In a rush, Ben grasped her arms. "Do not say that. Do not ever say that!"

Jamie tried to move away, but his grip tightened. "You're hurting me."

He finally dropped his hands. "I am sorry, but this is for your own good. This man will stop at nothing to get to you." At least he looked somewhat contrite.

"Who is this man?" she asked, hoping now he would give her just a clue.

"The man who wishes to hurt you."

Jamie rolled her eyes. "So we're back to that again."

"You need know nothing except that you are still in danger. And until this is no longer the case, you must stay on guard at all times. You must stay with me."

And in doing so, she'd turn into a blithering idiot. Not unless she could convince this obstinate prince that she needed some space. Needed to do something besides hang out in his house worrying about what would happen next.

Jamie remembered her mother saying that honey drew more flies than vinegar. Jamie turned on the honey, nice and thick. "Ben, I'm really, really going stir-crazy here. Can't we go somewhere? Anywhere? In the backyard? For a drive?"

"No."

She snapped her fingers. "I've got it. I know you have horses. I saw them out the window. We could go for a ride on your land. You do have riding horses, don't you?"

"Yes, but that is an insane idea. You would be a sitting target."

"How many acres do you own?"

"Fifteen thousand."

Jamie swallowed hard. And she'd thought her father's five-hundred-acre farm was more than enough to manage. "Okay, that's a lot of wide-open spaces. Couldn't we find one spot where we're hidden? I mean, with all that land, what are the chances he'll find us?"

"Too great for us to take."

She drew in a deep breath and called up all her reserves. "Look, Prince Ben, if you don't take me out of this house and on a horseback ride, I'll run away. I swear it."

"Then you would be a fool."

"I mean it. These walls are closing in on me. If you don't let me out of here, then the minute you turn your back, I'll be gone, and then where will you be?"

"The question is, where will *you* be? A victim?"

She hated his logic. Hated his unshakeable will. But she couldn't hate him, not when he was simply considering her safety. "Look, you'll either let me get out of here for a while, or you'll have to…have to…tie me up!"

The man had the nerve to smile. "Perhaps tying you up might be a pleasant option."

Turning, she headed for the door. She wasn't going to stick around for his mind games. "I'm going for a ride. If you want to come with me, fine. If you don't, that's fine, too. It's broad daylight. The man would be an idiot to come here when anyone could see him."

When she reached the door, Ben's hand came around her and slapped the solid wood surface. His warm breath ruffled her hair, glanced across her ear. "If you insist on doing this, I will accompany you on a horseback ride. And I will be by your side, trying to keep you safe. You'd best pray that I am able to do that."

Without thinking, she turned and circled her arms around his waist and gave him a solid squeeze. "Thank you. I really appreciate it."

He stepped away from her as if she'd slapped him instead of hugged him. "I will go change clothes."

"No!" She hadn't meant to sound so forceful, but she liked the thought of him riding with the wind whipping through his robes. Her fantasy come to life. She grabbed for a quick excuse. "It'll be dark soon. There's not time. Can't you manage with what you're wearing?"

He looked down, then back up at her. "Yes, I will manage with my clothing, but I must take something with me." He walked to the corner of the room, slipped open a bureau drawer and withdrew a metal object that glinted in the harsh overhead light. Jamie didn't have to see it to know it was a gun even though he quickly tucked it in the back of his slacks, underneath his robes.

Well, she would just have to put up with it in order to get her way and get out of here for a while. She hoped he didn't have any reason to use the gun.

Four

Ben silently cursed and called himself a fool while they rode through the near-barren terrain. He kept his eyes trained ahead as they passed through the oil fields, knowing each derrick could serve as a hiding place for Klimt. Even though Ben had kept men posted at the gate and several work hands riding the fence lines bordering the property, he still did not feel assured. His land was vast, and vulnerable in places. He did not have enough men in his employ to watch every area, every inch of barbed-wire fence where someone could easily slip underneath.

Yet he had allowed Jamie to talk him into this imprudent journey. But when she had looked at him with those innocent green eyes, he knew he would walk through fire to please her. And that weakness for her troubled him almost as much as the risk he now took. Angered him as well. He could not let down his guard.

With his free hand, he reached behind him and touched

the gun, but it afforded him little comfort. He prayed that Klimt would not have the resources, or the strength, to garner a weapon. Unless he stole one. That was a possibility Ben did not care to consider at the moment.

He glanced at Jamie and noted the brilliant smile on her face. Obviously she enjoyed her freedom. At least she rode in silence so that he might keep his ears tuned to the sounds. Blessedly, all he heard was the rush of the breeze through the coastal grass beneath them, the steady thump of horse hooves, and the occasional cow bawling in the distance.

She met his gaze and her smile melted into a frown. "Lighten up, Prince Ben," she said. "This isn't all bad."

"We must head back soon."

"Not yet," she said. "You promised me an hour."

An hour would be enough time for Klimt to find them. Why had he made such a promise? He knew why, but he did not care to examine his reasons. "The sun is going down, and it looks as though it might rain."

Jamie turned her face up to the sky. "Yeah. Smells like it, too. But it won't come for a while yet." She patted the leopard-spotted gelding's withers with one hand. "I was expecting you to own Arabians, not Appaloosas."

He allowed a brief smile. "They are well-suited to this country. My neighbor, Matthew Walker, has helped me establish a breeding program."

She gave the gelding another pat. "And what's this guy's name? I bet it's something exotic."

"Buck."

Her grin deepened, causing Ben's pulse to quicken. "Just Buck? That's funny."

"He was already named when I bought him."

She pointed at Ben's mount. "Let me guess. Barney?"

The sorrel stallion danced for a moment as if disturbed

by the insult. "He is called Fire, a part of his registered name."

"I guess that suits him." Jamie twitched in the saddle. "Can we lope for a minute? I'm tired of walking."

He'd expected her to ask sooner and had hoped for never. "We may trot, if you wish. I do not want you getting away from me for even a moment."

"Sure. Trot. Whatever." With that, she kicked the gelding into a gallop.

This time Ben verbalized his curses as he cued the stallion into a run. He managed to catch up to her, and, although he shouted at her to slow down, she did not heed his command.

Only when they approached the tree line surrounding a pond did she pull up. Ben stopped beside her, resisting the urge to tug her from the saddle to give her a healthy shake. Or a long kiss.

"This is beautiful," she said, her eyes wide. "It doesn't look like it belongs here."

Ben understood her admiration. He'd discovered the place the first time he had ridden the fields. The pond was framed by a few ancient live oaks that had survived the unforgiving elements. Yellow and lilac-colored wildflowers lined the banks that dipped down to the water's edge. An oasis of sorts—as close as he would get to one in this place called Texas.

Jamie continued to stare, silent, as if drinking in the sight. Ben studied her delicate profile, her soft lips, the column of her throat. He visually followed the path downward to her high round breasts. Heat coursed through him when he imagined kissing that same path, her flesh in his palms, naked and soft. His whole body seemed to lurch, reminding him that he did not dare give in to desire. Duty was of the utmost importance.

He cleared his throat to speak. "I come here often to think."

She turned her vibrant eyes to him. "I can see why. It's beautiful."

So was she, Ben thought. "Yes, it is."

With both hands on her hips, she leaned back in the saddle. "Boy, am I sore."

Without thought, Ben dismounted, led the stallion to a tree and tied him loosely to one branch. When he turned, he expected to see Jamie following suit, but she remained in the saddle. He walked to her and held out his arms to assist her. She braced her slender hands on his shoulder.

The act of helping her dismount should have been simple. But nothing about Jamie Morris was simple. Ben realized that fact when he slid her down the length of him. He had not meant to hold her so close. Perhaps he had, but not consciously. Regardless, she *was* close—so very close—that every place their bodies contacted, flames were left in the wake.

In his logical mind, he knew he should step back once her feet met solid ground. But he did not. Could not. She streaked her tongue across her bottom lip, fascinating him. Inviting him. He could not refuse such an invitation even though he knew to do so would be the most inadvisable thing he had done thus far.

Lowering his head, he captured her mouth, seizing the opportunity to sample what he had only imagined until now. Her lips parted, both surprising and delighting him. He slipped his tongue inside, softly, cautiously, not wanting to frighten her, or give her the excuse to pull away. Not until he had his fill of her, as if that were possible.

She readily accepted the play of his tongue and even engaged in some play of her own. Ben pulled her closer, but not close enough. His djellaba provided a barrier between them and for that he should be grateful. Had he been wearing his normal riding clothes, jeans and shirt, she would know how much this kiss was affecting him. How much he wanted her.

Jamie melted against Ben, relishing the feel of his strength, the spicy scent of his cologne. She pulled her hands from their resting place against his chest and slipped them beneath the robe so that she could span the width of his strong back. Feel the muscles she had admired on several occasions.

She heard a moan, but she wasn't sure who it had come from. Right now she felt like moaning all the way to Oklahoma and back. Never had anyone kissed her this way, with such a thorough gentleness, with only a flutter of his tongue in slow, fluid movements that made her feel like a bundle of hot, feminine yearning.

She was lost. Totally, completely disoriented, consumed by a raging need as unfamiliar to her as were the customs of this man now kissing her until she thought she wouldn't have a brain cell left in her head once he was done. She hoped he'd never be done.

Feeling incredibly brave, she slid her hands down his back, slowly, slowly, intending to rest them on his hips. Then she touched the cold hard steel of the gun.

Ben pulled away, looking as shaken as she felt. "We must go." He walked to the stallion busy gnawing on a leaf from a low-hanging branch.

Shocked, Jamie couldn't move. Not an inch. It was as if the kiss had melted her feet, cementing them to the ground.

With the reins in one hand, Ben turned back to her and looked around. "Where is Buck?"

To heck with Buck, Jamie thought. Where was her brain?

Glancing behind her, she noticed Buck wasn't there. He wasn't anywhere in sight.

"Buck's gone," she said, thankful she had found her voice.

Ben scowled at her. "Did you not tie him?"

"Of course not. You didn't give me a chance after you dragged me out of the saddle."

"I did not drag you. You came willingly."

"And you willingly put me in a lip lock."

"I do not remember you protesting."

Jamie didn't remember much of anything except the way he'd made her feel. "How did you expect me to say anything when you had your...your..."

"My mouth occupying yours? I believe you asked for my attention by opening your lips to mine. Is that not so?"

Jamie wasn't sure why they were playing this blame game. They were both to blame. And quite frankly, had she to do it all over again, she wouldn't change a thing. Even now, as he stared at her with those gray eyes the color of the near-night horizon, it would take only one move toward her, and he could have her again. All of her. Right here in the grass surrounded by flowers and weeds with the threats of a storm and a murderous man hanging over their heads.

She had really gone nuts. But it was Prince Ben's fault. He was driving her insane.... Crazy. Crazy for him.

And somehow, some way, she would have him again. She wanted more kisses. More of what she had never experienced in her twenty-two years. If she was in danger, she might not live to see twenty-three. Heck, life was a gamble. She could get struck by lightning, right here on the spot, because of her wicked thoughts. She refused to leave this earth without knowing what making love was all about. Without experiencing the heaven that existed between a man and a woman. And who better to teach her than the perfect prince named Ben.

* * *

Ben lay awake in his lonely bed for hours, wondering what he should do with Jamie Morris. What he could do about his weakness for a woman too hard to resist, even for a man who had spent his life practicing iron control. He could not afford to compromise her safety by again losing his head.

Rain drummed the tin roof above, a deluge that had come moments before they had arrived back at the ranch after they had finally located Buck. After the kiss. And Jamie, her skin dampened by the sudden downpour, hair wet, face innocent, had almost made him kiss her again. Instead, he had quickly retreated to safety, away from all that temptation.

A clap of thunder shook the walls, and he cursed the fact the storm muffled any suspicious noises coming from outside. His security system was the best money could buy, yet he still could not assure that a man as clever as Klimt— a man who had eluded them all—might not find a way to gain entry.

Aside from that prospect, he worried more about his feelings for Jamie. About his growing desire. Another threat to her well-being.

Perhaps he should make arrangements for Jamie to take up residence with another club member. But who? Certainly not his neighbor, Matt. He was planning to wed Lady Helena in the near future and they needed their time alone. Not Justin Webb and his wife, Winona. They had the responsibility of a child recently adopted by the couple. Aaron Black and his new bride, Pamela, awaited the birth of their firstborn. Which left only one member, retired air force colonel, Dakota Lewis, who had lived alone, estranged from his wife, for the past three years. As long as Ben had known the man, he had never heard Dakota mention being with another woman, perhaps because he still longed for his wife's company.

Yes, Ben could trust Dakota Lewis to keep Jamie safe. But what if he had been deprived of lovemaking so long that Jamie tempted him as well? Although Dakota was an honorable man, he was still a man.

Ben tightened his hold on the pillow in his arms, a poor substitute for a woman. For Jamie. He could not stand the thought of anyone touching her. Except for him. But he could not have her. Neither would he allow someone else to have her as long as she was in his care.

He was the only logical choice. The only one to protect her. He had made a vow, and he would not break it. He'd promised to keep her safe, and he would, even if that meant keeping his distance from her. He refused to let his desires override his common sense.

Rolling over, Ben flattened his face against the pillow. Did he really believe ignoring Jamie would be so easy? Did he truly think he could rein in his libido when every word she uttered, every smile she favored him with, made his heart gallop in his chest and his body come to life?

He must be strong. If he had to hide behind cool indifference, even anger, then he would. After all, it was for her sake—and his sanity.

He had no choice.

"Ben?"

At the soft sound of her voice, Ben's head snapped up. He could make out Jamie's small figure in the doorway. She was dressed in a short nightshirt that barely covered her thighs, her arms crossed over her breasts. His body again reacted to her presence even though she stood several feet away.

Between the steady rain and the fact he had been so lost

in his thoughts, he had not realized she had come in. How well would his inattention to his surroundings serve her?

Rising to a sitting position, he draped his legs over the edge of the bed. "Is there something wrong, Jamie?"

She took a few steps toward him. "I'm just feeling a little uneasy with the storm making such a racket outside. And I know it's really childish of me, but do you mind if I sleep in here with you?"

Yes, he minded, but not because he did not want her in his bed. Because he *did* want her in his bed. In his arms. Very unwise. Yet his inherent need to protect her, make her feel safe, kept him from refusing her request.

Moving to the far side of the bed, he raised the sheet and patted the mattress. "Come."

Quietly she moved to the bed and slipped in beside him. Ben turned onto his back close to the opposite edge, fearing even a brush of her smooth skin would cause him to lose control.

He glanced at her and saw that she, too, had turned on her back, studying the ceiling fan that whirred above them.

"Can I ask you something?" she said.

"Yes."

"When you kissed me in the pasture, did that mean anything to you?"

He wasn't prepared to discuss this now, not while she was so close. So soft and warm beside him, although they were separated by several inches. But he still sensed her heat, smelled her fragrance, longed for her touch.

He rubbed a hand over his bare chest, imagining her slender fingers there. "Jamie, please know that I find you very beautiful. Yet I cannot let what has happened between us interfere with the job I must do."

"Protecting me?"

"Yes."

"If that wasn't the case, do you think there might be more between us?"

Turning his head, he studied the outline of her delicate features set against the shadows. "Perhaps, but my life is complicated. I come from a culture that has certain expectations. Women are very different in my country. I am not accustomed to American beliefs."

"You mean you're not accustomed to women with a backbone?"

"Women who do not understand the way I have been raised," he corrected. "I cannot change who I am, or what I believe."

"I don't know, Ben. I think everyone has the capacity for change." She laced her hands together and stretched her arms above her head, pulling the nightshirt taut over her round breasts. Ben tried to avert his gaze but could not, and his whole body paid the price for his weakness.

"So I would guess that you see me as some wild, frivolous twenty-two-year-old girl who doesn't have the sense to take care of herself," she said, sarcasm in her tone.

He saw her as a woman any man would want, as he wanted her now. Young, yes, but with insight beyond her years. How could he explain this to her? How could he tell her that she was a precious gift that some man, some day, would be fortunate to claim? But not him.

He no longer knew where he fit in the grand scheme of things, even where he fit into his culture these days. He had changed, and change was not necessarily good. He was bound to his birthright, to honor his father's memory. If he no longer knew who he was, or what he wanted from life, then how could he involve her in his indecision, his inability to fit into either his culture or the one he had recently chosen?

He could only attempt to explain and hope she would

understand. "I believe you are a strong woman, Jamie. That is a good thing here in America. In my country, it is frowned upon. We are much more progressive than most, but our customs are slow to change. I have never been involved with an American woman for that reason."

"Never? Not even in college?"

"No, but I have not lived a celibate life, as you might believe."

She turned her face toward him. "Then who keeps you from being celibate?"

"Certain women in my country."

"Prostitutes?"

"No. Not in the sense you think. No money is involved."

"Mistresses?"

"Yes." He wanted to move off the disconcerting topic. He sounded like a dishonorable man when in reality it was an accepted part of his culture.

He looked at her once again. "Go to sleep or we will both be exhausted in the morning."

"One more thing." She turned on her side facing him, slipped one arm beneath the pillow and curled a delicate hand against her chest. Lightning flashed through the curtained window, illuminating her eyes. "My marriage to Payune. It wasn't my idea. It was my father's. I was trying to help him out. He needed the money for his farm. I just wanted you to know that. I would never marry a man I didn't love otherwise. And never again would I even consider such an archaic thing."

Ben internally flinched over her comment. Arranged marriages were common in his country. Still, he had often wondered why a beautiful young American woman such as Jamie had agreed to a marriage arrangement. Now he knew—an attempt to save her father from himself. His respect for her increased tenfold. "Where is your father?"

Her quiet sigh echoed in the room. "I don't know. He left before I was supposed to leave for Asterland. He has a problem with gambling and drinking. He's been that way ever since my mom died over a year ago. I've tried to help him, but he won't let me."

The sadness in her voice made Ben want to hold her, shelter her. He remembered how much his mother grieved his father's death at the hands of a dissident. How much she still grieved. And Ben had been too young to save his father from that fate and his mother from that grief. That was the reason he had vowed never to let harm come to anyone he cared about. But because of his mother's fortitude, she continued on with life as best she knew how. A testament to her strength.

"I am sorry about your mother," he said. "And your father's problems. Perhaps he will come around with time."

"Thanks. I hope so." She smiled. "What about your parents?"

"My mother is well in Amythra. My father died many years ago, when I was only a boy."

Jamie touched his arm. "I'm sorry, too, Ben. What happened to him?"

He truly did not want to discuss something so painful, but when Jamie looked at him expectantly, he had the strongest urge to tell her, reveal something he had never told another soul in America. "He was murdered at the hands of a extremist member of my father's opposition. As I said, I was very young. I was by his side when he was attacked outside the palace, yet I could do nothing to stop it."

"That's why, isn't it?" she said, her voice only a notch above a whisper.

"I do not know what you are asking."

"This whole protection thing. Your honor. It all has to do with the fact you couldn't save your dad."

How well she could read him. How well she seemed to know and understand his deepest secrets. "Yes. From that day forward, I vowed to defend and protect innocent people from those who have no regard for life."

She took his hand into hers and gave it a gentle squeeze. "If I haven't said it before, thanks for protecting me. I really do appreciate all you've done for me."

If only she knew how much more he wanted to do for her, including making love to her in ways that would make her cry out with pleasure. "You are welcome." He closed his eyes against her scrutiny. Guarded himself against sexual urges he could not ignore. Guarded himself against rising emotions he dared not claim.

He felt the mattress bend and sensed her turning over. Again he opened his eyes. He rolled to his side, facing her back, yet resisted the temptation to reach for her. Pull her against him. Lose himself in her.

"Ben, just one more question."

Hadn't she said that a moment ago? He hoped this would be the last request so he could try to sleep, if that were possible with her in his bed. "Yes?"

"Are you ever afraid?"

He was afraid now. Afraid of his growing feelings for this woman who seemed so strong, yet so vulnerable at times. Afraid that some day he would no longer be able to battle those feelings and would then give in to a yearning so intense, it almost consumed him. But he must resist, for many reasons.

"We must learn to face our fears," he said. "Otherwise, they will destroy us."

He heard her yawn again and prayed she was ready to sleep. "I think that's great advice. I'll remember it."

Silence stretched between them, and just when Ben thought she had fallen asleep, her silky voice broke the quiet. "Ben?"

More questions, he surmised. "Yes."

"Would you just hold me? I'd feel much better knowing you're close."

Against good judgment, Ben pulled her to him, much in the same way he had that first night. It took all his resolve not to turn her over into his arms, kiss her with all the emotion welling inside him. Prepare her body for him. Make love to her as if the dawn would never come.

The steady drone of spring rain kept time with his pounding heart. Drawing on his inner strength, he remained still, and waited until her breathing grew deep and he knew she slept.

Only then did he relax. Only then did he pull her closer, stroke her hair, savor her fragile body curled into his.

Only then did he whisper, "Jamie Morris, what have you done to me?"

Five

Jamie was just about at wit's end.

Two whole days and he'd barely talked to her. For two whole days he'd made it a point to avoid her, like she was a virus. Some contagious disease that threatened his health if he came near her.

Between mysterious meetings and business dealings, most conducted in the privacy of his home office, Ben had all but said she was a nuisance. An unwelcome guest.

Last night at dinner, she'd asked him to pass the salt. When he had, their fingers had touched, and he'd pulled away as if he'd been burned. The shaker had tumbled from her hands, spilling the salt. Out of habit, she'd tossed some of it over her shoulder for luck. Obviously that old wives' tale hadn't worked. Ben had only muttered an apology then gone back to reading the financial page of the paper. No luck there.

She'd resorted to telling jokes just to see if he would

laugh. Every now and then she'd managed a smile from him. She'd even told him about her plans, her ambitions, things she'd rarely told other people.

But she hadn't returned to his bed after he had told her that she wasn't his type. Well, big deal. That didn't mean he had to be rude. Or that she couldn't change his mind.

She'd had enough of his avoidance. Had enough of reading every magazine on the premises, cover to cover. Had enough of watching soap operas with Alima, the daily bedroom scenes only providing fuel for her dreams and the fire in her body Ben had stoked with his kiss. And, most importantly, she was fed up to here with Ben's continued withdrawal, his annoying silence.

Today she was determined to end it, even if she had to tie him up and force him to talk to her.

Jamie smiled at the thought of Ben shackled so she could do with him what she wanted, and what she wanted had nothing to do with talking.

You are a very bad girl, Jamie Morris. This time her mother's voice filtered into her conscience.

Jamie tuned out the scolding as she walked in to the living room, surprised to find Ben seated on the sofa instead of in his office, dressed in his cowboy clothes—torn jeans, ragged T-shirt, worn boots. He held a cordless phone propped between his jaw and his shoulder.

She couldn't decide whether she liked him as cowboy or prince. Both, actually. She liked him any way she could get him, which lately had been neither way.

His Arabic words, interspersed with English, floated around the room like cottonwood through spring fields. A soft lyrical sound, as if he spoke to a loved one. Maybe even a lover.

The jealousy hit Jamie full-force. Okay, so maybe he'd

lied about having a girlfriend from his country. Maybe he'd lied about a lot of things. It didn't matter.

She was with him now. She wanted his company. She wanted to give, and to receive all that he had to offer as a man. In doing so, she'd just have to protect her heart.

But first she had to convince him that she had certain needs he wasn't meeting. It had all started with that kiss, and she'd always been one to finish what she'd started.

Tiptoeing to the back of the sofa, she began kneading Ben's shoulders and the rigid muscles beneath her fingertips. He reached up and grasped her right hand but continued his conversation. She still had one unoccupied hand and didn't miss a beat with her massage.

"I must go now, Mother," he said, then clicked off the phone and tossed it onto the nearby end table.

Mother? So he hadn't been talking to a girlfriend after all. Jamie was filled with relief, and a strong determination to get his attention.

She dropped her hand and joined him on the sofa, leaving a comfortable distance. She didn't want to get too close—yet.

"That was your mother?" she asked.

Ben stared straight ahead. "Yes. She wants me to return to my country soon for a visit."

Jamie tried to fight back the disappointment. "Will you be leaving then?"

"No. I told her I could not because of unfinished business. She is not happy about it."

"I guess that's why you're so tense. You really do need to relax, Ben."

Only then did he look at her. "I will not relax until I see to it that Klimt is captured, and you are safe."

The name sounded familiar, but she couldn't hang a face on it. "Klimt? So that's the man who's after me?"

She could tell by the look in Ben's eyes that he regretted the slip. "Yes. Do you know him?"

Jamie chewed her bottom lip and searched her brain. "I remember the name. Is he from Asterland?"

"He was on the plane. He sustained injuries that until recently, kept him hospitalized. He escaped the morning you were almost run down."

"He was driving the car?"

"So we assume. And you have something he wants. Or he thinks you have."

Here we go again. That mysterious *something*. "What could I possibly have that he wants? I don't have anything anyone would want."

Ben locked into her gaze with those damnable gray eyes. "You are wrong. You have much that a man would want, although Klimt is after an object that has nothing to do with your feminine attributes."

At the moment, Jamie didn't give a darn what this mysterious man named Klimt wanted. She only knew what *she* wanted. Ben's kisses. Ben's hands on her. Anywhere. Everywhere.

She inched closer and brushed back a dark curl from his forehead. "Where's Alima?"

"At the market with J.D."

Jamie wanted to shout with glee. "So we're alone?"

His well-defined chest rose with the deep breath he drew. "Yes, we are alone."

"Good." Jamie moved closer, flush against his side. Oh, how she wished she had more experience in seducing a man. Her one boyfriend, Billy Joe Adams, had been all hands. After spending two years fending off his weekend groping, she'd eventually broken off their relationship with her virginity still intact. The boy had bored her to tears. All he wanted was a make-out session in the back seat of his father's revamped '56 Chevy. Jamie had wanted sweet words and gentle touches, not a tongue jockey with more moves than a seasoned wide receiver.

She wanted romance. A slow and easy seduction. Sweet, sensual words. Then and now. She wanted a man, not a boy.

She wanted Ben.

Considering the set of Ben's strong jaw and rigid frame, she doubted he could offer her what she wanted most. Correction. She doubted he *would* offer her what she wanted, needed. She had absolutely no doubt that he could handle it quite well, if he had a mind to.

Well, she'd just have to give it her best try, and see where things went from there.

Leaning closer to Ben, she traced a path along the tear at the thigh of his worn jeans. The dark hair on his legs tickled her fingertips, and tripped her pulse into a frantic rhythm. "Looks like you should've sent Alima for a new pair of jeans. These are threadbare."

"Stop."

"Stop what?" She smiled and sent her fingers back in motion, circling the bare flesh on his taut thigh. "I'm just making an observation."

"It is not your observation that is troubling me."

"What *is* troubling you, Prince Ben?" Her voice came out in a throaty whisper, taking her by surprise.

"We cannot do this, Jamie. What happened the other day cannot be repeated."

She lowered her voice to a teasing tone. "Why not? Don't you like the way I kiss?"

"I liked it too much."

Jamie was overcome by such power. A power that made her feel as if she could conquer the world, and maybe even Ben's resistance. "Then I don't see a problem. You won't let me leave the house, so why not spend the time getting to know each other better?''

She was beginning to get the hang of this, and she really, really liked being in control. ''You're a man, I'm a woman, and we both have certain needs.''

His expression didn't change, his face as hard as granite. As beautiful as polished stone. ''What needs do you have that are not being met? I have opened my home to you. If you wish something special to eat, I will be more than happy to tell Alima. If you wish me to get you some rental movies, I'll send one of my men. Tell me what you desire, and I will see to it that you have it.''

''I desire you, Ben. Just you.''

Letting her eyes drift shut, she braced for the impact of his lips on hers. Nothing.

Opening her eyes, she found him studying her, looking completely composed, but at least he hadn't moved away.

''You do not know what you are asking,'' he said, his voice deep and husky.

''I know exactly what I'm asking. Just a simple kiss, Ben.''

''Kisses are not simple, Jamie. You have no idea what will happen beyond that kiss. I cannot promise you that I will stop. Many nights I have imagined what it would be like to hold you, to take you beyond the limits you have only dreamed of.''

Now she felt totally breathless—and optimistic. ''I've dreamed of you, too. Every night for the past week.''

''But my duty to you prevents me from doing what I would very much like to do with you. To you.''

Jamie sat back and released a frustrated sigh. Regardless of his sexy words, the man was as immovable as a boulder. ''What does duty have to do with this? Or is it that I'm not good enough for you? Maybe you'd prefer a princess to a peon?''

He cupped her cheek with strong yet gentle fingers. "You are probably too good for me." He stroked a thumb back and forth over her jaw. "Fine as the most expensive silk. Pure. Too pure. Too innocent."

"I'm not that innocent." Okay, so maybe Billy Joe had barely reached first base, but Jamie was primed for a home run in Ben's arms.

She covered Ben's hand with hers and slowly slid it downward—past her throat, beyond her collarbone, and laid it on her breast. "Touch me, Ben. I need you to touch me. Kiss me. Prove to me that I'm good enough for your attention."

Before Jamie could prepare, she found herself laid out on the sofa, underneath Ben's large lean body. And he was kissing her. Boy, was he kissing her! And with an urgency that sucked her breath from her lungs. He thrust his tongue between her lips in a slow, fluid rhythm, and she felt it everywhere.

Every muscle, nerve, private place ached for him. Ached for what she knew he could give her. He made her feel all woman, and he was definitely all man.

He broke the kiss and framed her face in his palms. "Damn your beauty, your persistence," he murmured. "I will give you what you need."

Then he kissed her again and sent his hand underneath her knit shirt, cupping her breast through lace. She wanted more. So much more. She wasn't even sure what exactly *more* meant, but she'd know it if he gave it to her.

Slowly he lifted her shirt and released the front closure of her bra, then pushed the barrier aside. For a few moments he simply stared at her, then stared at his finger as he traced a path round and round her nipple. He muttered something in Arabic before raising his eyes to her. "You are exquisite."

For the first time in her life, Jamie actually felt exquisite. Lowering his head, Ben sent brush-stroke kisses down the cleft of her breasts, homing in on her taut flesh with lips as soft as the featherbed she'd slept in since that first fateful morning.

Something deep within Jamie told her she should stop him. Not because she didn't want this. She simply didn't want to fall in love with him. She needed to be in control, and right now Ben was controlling every move with his wicked mouth and roving hands.

When he suckled her breast, she shuddered from the long-awaited sensations. He lifted his mouth and placed his lips to her ear. "Do you still want more, my Jamie? Have you needs that I have not yet met?"

"Yes." The word came out on a sigh.

"Then so be it."

Pulling her to face him, with agonizing slowness he traced a line down her sternum to her belly with a fingertip, pausing at the waistband of her shorts. He kept her locked into his gaze with hypnotic eyes. Then he kissed her again, all the while toying with the snap, but not opening it. Jamie thought she might actually scream at him, Just do it! Before she totally lost it, he undid the snap with one smooth move. She felt the track of the zipper as he lowered it and held her breath, waiting, wondering, hoping he wouldn't stop. She would die right on the spot if he didn't follow through.

He slipped his fingertips beneath the denim, drawing her shorts farther down her hips. But he didn't remove them completely. He didn't remove his hand, either. Instead, he worked his way beneath her panties, but went no farther.

A pleading sound bubbled up in her throat, brought about

by impatience, by desire, by a need so great she wasn't sure she had the strength to face it head-on.

Then he found her secrets with his strong fingers, steadily stroking her as if she were something fine. Something to be cherished. He whispered in her ear, more words she didn't understand. But she could imagine. She didn't have to imagine what he was doing to her; she could feel it.

She wound tighter and tighter as he centered on her tender flesh. Her body moved beneath his hand of its own accord. She couldn't seem to control it. She couldn't control anything at the moment. Not the moans from her mouth that Ben tried to silence with another kiss. Not the steady throb of desire and the building tension beneath his clever fingers. Not the climax that overtook her in strong breath-stealing swells, causing her body to pulse wildly out of control.

She whimpered like a child and clung to Ben in fear he would let her go. If he did, she would drift away to another dimension and might never come back again.

She drifted anyway. Shattered into shards of sheer feeling, as if she were made of crystal. Slowly she descended from heights she'd never dreamed she could achieve. Her respiration returned to her in slow degrees. Her eyes felt drugged, her body heavy, but it wasn't from Ben's weight. While she was recovering, he had gotten up from the couch and stood looking down at her.

She stared up at him, confused. He didn't seem at all pleased. In fact, he looked madder than a hen in a coop full of barking dogs. He might be furious at her, at himself, but he wasn't unaffected by what had happened between them. The proof was there for anyone to see, right below the waistband of his tattered jeans.

Jamie lowered her blouse and rose on bent elbows. "What's wrong?"

"You should not have to ask." He sounded irritated, his face hard as steel. A monument to an unbendable will.

"Ben, I'm—" She had no idea what to say. What could she say? *Ben, I'm really needing you. Ben, finish what you started. Ben, dammit, get back here right this instant.*

She reached out her arms to him. "Please, Ben. Don't leave me. Stay here with me." *Make love to me.*

He perched on the edge of the sofa and took her hand into his. "You do not understand, nor do I expect you to. I have broken a vow to myself not to let this happen between us. I do not wish to hurt you." He touched her cheek reverently. "But I fear I already have."

He rose slowly, looking pained and more than a little worried. Maybe even regretful.

Jamie grasped for the right words. "But—"

"There is nothing more to be said. I am sorry. I should not have done what I did."

Jamie's desire was replaced with frustration that he would just drive her over the edge then leave her so unsatisfied. Himself unsatisfied. "I'm glad you did do it, Ben. I have never felt that way before. Ever. And you're not going to make me feel guilty." She worked her shorts up her hips and sat up. "But if you're too stubborn to realize that I'm a big girl who knows her own mind *and* body, then you're hopeless."

A wry smile formed on his lips. "Then you do understand. I am hopeless, Jamie. Hopeless when I am around you. But it will not happen again. You can trust me on that."

He turned to leave without another word, and Jamie's heart sank to its lowest point in her life. But her determination grew to the length of a football field.

Prince Ben was in for a big surprise. He could try to fool her with his duty and honor, she wasn't falling for that. But was she falling for him?

Nope, she wasn't going to do that, either. She'd somehow convince him that the chemistry they shared was natural. And there would come a time when she would have him. All of him. Now she just had to come up with some plan to make him see it her way.

"Klimt's still around, Ben."

Ben strangled the phone's receiver, trying to digest Matthew Walker's words. "Are you certain?"

"Yeah. I rode out to Miller's place on Old Tackett Road. A man fitting Klimt's description stopped by there yesterday, according to Miller's foreman, Gus."

"What did he want?"

"To use the phone. Long-distance. He gave Gus some money after the call."

"Does he know who Klimt contacted?"

"Nope. Gus just said he spoke in some language he didn't understand. I suspect he probably called Payune."

"Then we should be able to prove it."

"I thought about that, but Justin says he doesn't want to get Winona in trouble, so we can't go asking for phone records yet. Not unless we want to involve the police. Right now we need to let Klimt make the next move and hope he'll lead us to the diamond, since he seems to be getting more desperate."

Which meant Jamie was in more danger, Ben thought. "I will tell my men to be exceedingly cautious."

"Yeah, you do that. And keep an eye on Jamie."

Ben had kept more than an eye on Jamie earlier, and the simple memory of how she had felt beneath his hands, looked in his arms, her cheeks tinged pink, her eyes soft with satisfaction, made him want to climb the walls now closing in on him. "I have been watching her closely and I will continue to do so. But I am not certain how long I will be able to convince her to stay here without telling her the whole truth."

"You've got to try. The less she knows, the better." Matt chuckled. "You'll just have to use every trick in the book to make her stay. I have faith in you."

Ben clenched his teeth to keep from cursing. If only Matt knew how little he deserved that faith. "I will do my best to convince her to stay, but she is not so easily swayed."

"Okay, if you say so."

"Anything more?"

"No. We're just keeping our ears to the ground, trying to find out more about the plot to overthrow Asterland's government. Looks like we might be forced to send Dakota Lewis over there after all."

Ben felt an overwhelming sense of relief that they had chosen Dakota for the mission. The last thing Ben needed was an assignment to Asterland when he had promised his mother a trip home in the near future. "He would be the natural choice."

"Yeah, but we're not ready to do it just yet. If we're lucky, Klimt will not only lead us to the diamond, he'll also lead us to Payune. With that proof, then maybe we won't have to do anything. We can just let the Asterland officials handle it themselves."

Ben prayed that would happen soon, and that Klimt would make a mistake and find himself caught before he again tried to get to Jamie. Then Jamie could return to her apartment, and Ben could go on with his life. His lonely life. "I must go now, Matt. Keep me informed on what you might learn of Klimt's whereabouts."

"You bet. And Ben, one more thing." Matt cleared his

throat. "No one here expects you to be a saint. Things happen. I found that out the hard way, but I don't regret meeting Helena. So if you and Jamie—"

"You have no worries there, *Sadíiq*. I do not intend anything to happen between us. I only intend to keep her safe." What a liar he had become.

Matt released a grating laugh. "Yeah. That's exactly what I said about Helena. And look at me now, just a few weeks away from getting hitched and damned glad about it."

Ben was happy for Matthew Walker, but he would not allow himself to fall into that same trap. Marriage was something he could not consider, especially with a woman like Jamie. An American woman full of life and optimism, a need for independence.

No, he would never be the man to make Jamie Morris happy. She was too innocent, no matter what she claimed. Too good for a man like him.

She'd just have to be his mistress.

That thought haunted Jamie all afternoon. Amazing that she could even think at all after what Ben had done to her, but since then, she'd been thinking as much about what he'd said several nights ago in his bed. About the women who served him. What did they have that Jamie obviously didn't? Maybe she should just come out and ask him? Like he'd really tell her.

As usual, he had retired to his office, and she to her lonely bedroom to mull over her situation. Refusing to read another magazine, she'd done a lot of mulling over the past few hours. Now she was determined to take action.

Tossing her book aside, Jamie went on a quest for information, in search of answers. And the one person other than Ben who might put to rest her curiosity was Alima.

She found the housekeeper two doors down in a guest room, wearing her usual plain gray cotton dress and white apron. The room was much the same as Jamie's, brightly colored and luxurious, but still empty by all rights, except for Alima who roosted on the edge of the bed, tuned in to her favorite soap opera on the small TV, a vacuum cleaner nearby. She was hiding out, Jamie suspected, since Ben was at home, squirreled away in his office. He hadn't been in the best mood lately.

Silently Jamie slipped onto the bed next to Alima. "So who's the good doctor pursuing today?"

Alima shot Jamie a sideways glance. "The *SaHafi.* Newspaper woman. The one who is, how do you say in English?"

"Loose?"

"Yes. She goes from one man to the next. Such terrible morals, that one has."

What a perfect lead-in. Maybe her luck was changing. "Speaking of loose women, tell about those in your country."

Alima turned her attention to Jamie, probably because of the commercial break. "I do not understand."

Jamie pulled her legs up and crossed them in front of her. "You know, *those* women. The mistresses. What do they do to please a man?"

Alima clucked her tongue. "A young girl such as you should not worry about these things."

Jamie raised her chin a notch. "I'll be twenty-three in two months, long past the need for a nursemaid. I'm sure as heck not worried. I'm just curious." For reasons she didn't dare reveal to Alima, Ben's surrogate mother. "Well, how do they please a man?"

Alima hid her face behind her hands for a moment before revealing a toothy smile. "There are many ways."

"How many?" Jamie cringed at how anxious she sounded.

"Countless. In my culture, these women learn to please by learning to be pleased, letting a man guide them."

Jamie's eyes widened. "How do the men learn?"

"At a very early age, the men are given a book that instructs them on how…" Alima looked away. "I should not be telling you these things."

Jamie touched her arm. "I won't tell anyone. What kind of book?"

"A book describing places on a woman's body, where to touch them to make them…" Alima averted her gaze, "…ready for the man."

Well that explained a lot about Ben. Just the thought of his touch made gooseflesh pop out all over Jamie's body. She had been more than ready. She still was. "So they have this book, they read it, and then they practice with these women?"

"Yes, that is the way."

"And do the women receive a book?"

"No. They must learn from the men."

That figured. Jamie wondered what happened to those poor women who had the misfortune of coming upon a rotten teacher. "So they learn by doing."

"Yes. They learn how to entice. How to undress to drive the man to—" Alima studied Jamie long and hard, wariness calling out from her near-black eyes. "I have said too much."

"No, really. Tell me more."

"Why do you ask me these questions?"

"I told you, I was just wondering."

"And you have no other reason?"

"Well, in case I might encounter a man from your cul—"
Jamie had done it now. She could tell by the suspicion

on Alima's face. "Not that I would anytime soon. I mean—not that there's any man around here that I would encounter in *that* way." Not that she wouldn't like to, and soon.

Alima sent her a knowing smile, taking Jamie by surprise. "Should you come upon this man, it is important you remember that he has been taught to remain in control. It is a strong woman who can break that control. Yet her strength lies in her willingness to quietly do his bidding."

"You mean to be passive." The word left a bitter taste in Jamie's mouth. She hated passive. She'd never viewed women as the weaker sex, at least not herself. But if being passive and restrained in her seduction would break Ben down, make him give her his all, then she'd do it. Once, and only once. Because if she didn't have him soon, she'd go nuts.

Standing, she put her best smile forward. "Thanks, Alima. You're the greatest."

"And you are a devious child." At least she said it with a grin, making Jamie feel a bit less guilty.

"Not devious, just interested." So maybe it was a teeny-weeny lie.

Alima went back to her TV program as Jamie headed to the door.

"Miss Morris."

Jamie turned to find Alima still staring at the tube. "It's Jamie. I prefer you call me that."

"As you wish, Jamie," she said, without turning around. "I have seen the book."

Jamie took a step forward. "You have?"

"I came upon it in the sheikh's library while dusting. It is placed next to the fourth book on the top shelf. Very pretty flowers on the cover. It is an English translation."

Jamie was now beyond shocked. She was flabbergasted. "Sounds like a very interesting read."

"I would not know. I do not read English well. There are many pictures, though."

Obviously Alima had sneaked a peek. "You certainly speak English very well."

"Prince Hasim is a good teacher of the American language. I believe he would be a fine teacher in many areas."

Jamie walked to the bed and gave Alima a hug. "Thank you."

Before Jamie released her, Alima patted her hand and said, "Be cautious, my child. A woman who strives to lose her innocence may lose her heart to one who cannot give his in return."

"Thanks. I'll remember that."

Jamie left the room with Alima's cautions echoing in her brain. If she followed through with her plan, would she be in danger of losing her heart to the sheikh, a man who obviously had no interest in love?

No, she would not allow that. If she could keep from it. She couldn't consider that now. At the moment she needed to find the book, then find a way to practice passive.

Six

Jamie really wanted to tear his clothes off.

Not an appropriate thing to do considering they were sitting at the dinner table with Alima nearby in the kitchen. But having spent the afternoon reading "the book," complete with colored illustrations, the images still danced around in her head—images of Ben and lovemaking. Although the book was tastefully written, the pictures and text left nothing to the imagination. Especially Jamie's imagination, which at the moment was working overtime.

Alima scurried into the dining room with a platter full of fragrant meat, vegetables and pastries.

"What is the occasion, Alima?" Ben asked, the first words he'd spoken since they'd sat down.

She set the platter in front of Jamie and began piling the fare onto Jamie's plate. "I do not understand."

"First you bring us the oyster stew, and now this." He gestured toward the platter. "You normally do not serve *máaza* unless it is a special event. And if you do not quit filling Miss Morris's plate, there will be none left for me.''

Alima nodded and began serving Ben his food. ''It is in honor of our guest.'' She raised her eyes to Jamie who saw a helping of amusement there as big as the mountain of food on her plate.

''I see.'' Ben raised his glass of wine and tipped it toward Jamie. ''To our guest.''

Jamie clinked her own glass against his in a toast. ''And to my very accommodating host.'' Who she hoped would be much more accommodating as the evening progressed.

Sipping the wine slowly, Ben regarded her with his steel-colored eyes, but she couldn't begin to read what he was thinking. ''Is there anything else you wish from Alima?''

''Not that I can think of. I have everything I need.'' *At least from Alima.*

Ben dismissed the housekeeper with a sweep of his hand and the woman quickly left. He took his gaze from Jamie and centered it on the wineglass. ''Did you have a pleasant day?''

Jamie wanted to laugh. He had no idea how pleasant her day had been. He should, considering the episode on the couch. ''It was okay. After you ran off, it was just the usual, watching a little TV, that sort of thing.'' *Thinking about what you did to me on the sofa. Reading an Arabian sex manual.*

''I have made arrangements with your landlord,'' he said without looking at her. ''He has agreed to keep your apartment available for you. I have hired several men to watch over it should Klimt happen to return.''

''Great.'' She didn't want to think about her apartment or the fact that a maniac was still on the loose. All she could consider was Ben sitting before her, dressed in his casual clothes, his jaw shaded with evening whiskers, looking much too sexy to ignore.

Time for plan A, Jamie decided. Getting Ben alone. "After dinner, do you mind if we talk a while before I go to bed?"

He raised his eyes from the glass to her. "Something important?"

"Yes, I guess you could say that." Important to her, anyway.

"Shall we discuss it now?"

"No. Later. After Alima goes to bed."

"As you wish. I have something important to discuss with you as well."

Did she dare hope that he'd changed his mind? Could he possibly want to show her that he did want her? How silly for her to consider that. Nothing had changed in a matter of hours, at least not with Ben and his almighty conviction. Obviously she had her work cut out for her tonight.

After they had dined in silence, Alima cleared the plates while Jamie joined Ben in the living room. This time he took the huge leather lounge chair, leaving Jamie alone on the nearby sofa.

He might as well have erected a brick wall, Jamie thought. This was going to be harder than she'd imagined.

A few minutes of awkward silence passed before she asked, "What did you want to discuss with me?"

Ben rubbed large fingertips up and down the arm of the chair, bringing to mind his touch, the way he had reduced her into a pool of need with his sturdy fingers. "Klimt has been seen in this vicinity."

Jamie's eyes snapped up from Ben's hands to meet his glance. "How close was he?"

"At the ranch adjacent to Matthew Walker's, which is next to mine."

Too close for Jamie's comfort. "Did someone call the police?"

"I told you that we cannot involve the police. If we do, Klimt will not lead us to what we're looking for."

"Oh. The *something*."

"Yes, and I have made sure my men are on guard."

An idea came to her, sharp and clear even if she hadn't planned it. "I know I'd feel much better with you in my room."

"Perhaps that would be a good idea."

This was too easy. "I'd appreciate it."

"I will move the chair by the window."

He wanted to sleep in the *chair?* A chair could prove to be a challenge. Did they mention chairs in the book? "Okay. If that's what you want. But we have slept together before and—"

Ben's frown stopped Jamie in mid sentence. She looked from Ben to find Alima standing only a few feet away.

"If you do not need me, I shall retire for the evening," Alima said.

Ben checked his watch. "It is only 8:00 p.m. Are you not feeling well?"

Alima kneaded her hands, looking a bit flustered. "No, Prince Hasim, I am simply tired. I shall go to my room immediately." She turned to Jamie. "Good evening, Miss Morris. Should you require anything through the night, please do not hesitate to summon me. But remember that I go to sleep with my music playing in my ears, so I do not hear a sound until I remove my ear phones much later."

With that, she turned and left the room. Left Jamie with her mouth gaping open and a smile that wanted to surface. Alima proved to Jamie once again that she was a wise woman. She knew exactly what Jamie intended for Ben, and she had all but given her permission.

Jamie almost laughed at Alima's obvious matchmaking attempts, but all humor died when she saw Ben's serious gaze. "Do you know what is wrong with her?" he asked.

"Wrong? No. She looks fine to me." Time for a subject change. "As I was saying, Ben, you don't have to sleep in the chair. You can stay on your side of the bed, and I'll stay on mine." Which didn't mean she couldn't accidentally roll his way, catching him off guard.

"That would not be advisable."

Darn his stubbornness. "You don't have to worry about me attacking you in your sleep." She would make sure he was still awake before she made her move.

"I am not worried about you." His dark eyes burned into her, causing Jamie to shiver. "It would be best if I keep my distance."

Jamie shrugged and pretended indifference. Time to institute plan B. "Suit yourself. But before we continue this conversation, I want to take a quick shower and get ready for bed. Then we can talk some more."

"All right. I shall do the same, and I will be waiting here for you when you return from your bath."

They stood at the same time and although they remained several feet apart, tension hung thick in the air. Before Jamie gave everything over to impulse, she turned and headed to the bathroom.

Once inside, she slipped off her clothes and released a ragged breath. Every inch of her body responded when she thought about what she planned to do next. Would she really have the courage to seduce him again? Would he stop her, or worse still, turn away? And if she were successful, would she be strong enough to resist the emotional entanglement already threatening her heart?

No doubt about it, with each day that passed came another reason to like him. His honor and honesty. His overt sensuality. Two days ago, she'd managed to unveil more of the man beneath the prince, and she admired what she had discovered—a born protector with a will as strong as reinforced steel and a vulnerability he tried to hide behind a tough facade. But she was beginning to see that vulnerability—that chink in his armor—more and more. She wanted to know everything about the man she had come to admire. The man she could easily love.

She shook her head, trying to shake the cobwebs from her common sense. *No, no, no!* She refused to fall in love with him. Ever.

Just short of entering the shower, she caught sight of the vanity counter and halted. Laid out next to the sink was a gown much like the one she'd worn the first day of her arrival. But this one was a pale peach color and twice as sheer. Next to it sat a bottle of pink-tinted liquid.

Making her way to the sink, Jamie picked up the bottle. She flipped open the lid and sniffed, then placed a few drops in her palm. Oil. Strawberry-scented oil. She held the bottle up and studied the unreadable label. Unreadable to someone who didn't know a scrap of Arabic.

Alima the Headphoned Housekeeper playing matchmaker.

The woman had made herself Jamie's partner in crime. Who else would leave instruments of seduction? Certainly not Ben. He wouldn't even agree to get in bed with her, much less provide her with a naughty nightie and a bottle of fruity oil.

This time Jamie did laugh, allowing her mirth to bubble over. She felt exhilarated, alive and prepared for whatever challenge Ben had in store for her.

Poor Ben. He had no idea what she intended, but he would, and soon. Very soon.

Ben had no idea what Jamie Morris was up to, but he had his suspicions. Every move she had made, every word she had spoken, made him recognize how very hard she would be to resist. A cold shower had done nothing to squelch his desire for her, not that he believed it would, even though many extolled the virtues of icy water in enabling a man to forget his lust. Rubbish, as his mother would say.

Settling back on the couch, Ben waited for Jamie, afraid to face her, excited by that prospect. He silently prayed she would dress appropriately and not descend upon him wearing the nightshirt that barely disguised her feminine charms.

A few moments later, Ben sighed with relief, thankful that Jamie had reentered the room wearing a heavy robe. Yet, even encased in red velvet, he could still imagine the woman beneath. Every curve, every crevice. The thoughts would surely be the death of him.

Averting his gaze from the gaping bodice of the robe, he said, "I presume you enjoyed your bath since you have been gone for almost an hour."

Smiling, she continued to stand, one hand hidden away in the robe's pocket. "Yes, it was nice. I enjoy a long bath. It clears the mind and relaxes the body, so to speak." She took a few steps forward until she was standing above him. "How was yours?"

Every blessed thought left his brain when soft feminine smells filtered into his nostrils. "How was my what?"

"Your shower. I assume you took one since your hair's wet. Although I wonder, since you still have on your jeans."

Jeans that grew tighter with each coy look she sent him.

"Yes, I showered. I felt it appropriate that I remain in most of my clothes." And he cursed the fact he had not put on his shirt. Perhaps his subconscious was setting him up to fail. Or testing his strength.

With a devilish smile, Jamie slipped the robe from her shoulders, revealing everything to him through the film of a sheer gown—her round luscious breasts, the shadow between her thighs, the curve of her hips. But before he had time to savor the sight, she was on her knees before him, staring up at him, her emerald eyes alight with desire. He had seen that look earlier, and there was no mistaking it now.

"Jamie," he said, caution in his tone. "I beg you to consider what you are about to do."

She ran a slender finger up his thigh. "Relax, will you? I just thought you looked a little worried during dinner. A little uptight. I'm here to help. Your wish is my command."

He wished she would leave him to his misery. How could he relax when she was so very close, only partially dressed, looking like temptation incarnate? "I am fine," he said, his jaw tight, his frame rigid, his belly clenched, belying his conviction.

"Yeah, right. And I'm Marilyn Monroe."

Inching forward on her knees, Jamie slid both palms up his thighs and parted his legs, then moved between them. Ben clawed his way back to reality. He must stop her now, before he could not.

"Jamie, I do not think—"

She slid her hands further up his thighs and brushed a fingertip over his groin. "For once, would you just stop thinking, Ben? Just try to feel. Enjoy the moment."

Rising farther up on her knees, she feathered kisses along his ear, his neck, then lower still across his bare chest. Ben grasped the sides of her head, intending to pull her away.

But as if he had lost his will to fight, he followed her movements as she laved her tongue across his nipple, much in the same way he had done to her earlier that afternoon.

Coherent thought ceased for a time until Ben's self-control took over. He lifted her face. "Jamie, we have been through this. We cannot do this."

She smiled. "There's no 'we' involved at the moment. I'm doing this. Just me, and all you have to do is sit back and take pleasure in it. That's all I'm asking of you."

Dipping her hand into the pocket of the robe, she withdrew a bottle of liquid and placed several small drops in her palm, then tossed the bottle aside. With long slender fingers, she worked the oil up over his shoulders, across his chest to his abdomen, drawn tight against the sensual assault. All the while Ben grasped the arms of the chair to keep from touching her. Keep from grabbing her up and kissing the life out of her. Keep from carrying her to his bed.

If she wanted to play this game, he would let her for the time being. As long as he remembered not to let things progress beyond the point of no return. Yet, at the moment, the feel of her delicate hands stroking his body robbed him of his resolve to stop her.

"Ben," she whispered against his belly, then washed her tongue in his navel.

Give me strength.

His plea went unheeded as Jamie released the snap on his jeans. His erection strained against the denim and he longed for the freedom that only Jamie could give him. But at what cost?

Before he could consider what she was doing, she had his fly completely open. He managed a smile when she looked up at him, shock in her expression. Perhaps her fear would stop her as nothing he could say would.

Her eyes widened. "You don't have anything on underneath these, do you?"

"I find that unnecessary under the circumstance, do you not agree?"

"Oh." She looked down again as if uncertain what to do next.

If she had never experienced the sight of a man aroused, perhaps that would convince her she was playing with fire. That consideration, and the fact Ben could no longer stand the torment, led him to slip the denim down his hips, revealing everything to her eyes. Blessed freedom at last.

Jamie continued to stare and repeated, "Oh."

"Does my body frighten you, Jamie?"

She shook her head and ran a fragile finger down the length of his shaft, sending tremors coursing throughout his entire being. She touched him again, this time with oil-slick palms, tentatively at first, then more boldly. She had regained her composure while Ben's slipped farther away with every touch.

Without removing her hands, she raised her eyes to him and said, "Does this please you, Sheikh Rassad?"

He could not remember the last time he had been so pleased, or so achingly hard from wanting a woman. "Yes. It pleases me very much."

"What else would please you?"

He clung to his last shred of will. "For you to stop this torture before it is too late."

"I don't want to stop. I want to return the favor for what you did for me earlier today."

Exactly what he feared. "That is not necessary."

"Oh, I think it is."

Jamie Morris was not an innocent, that much Ben decided before his thoughts began to slip away. Considering the way she touched him, caressed him with fine silken strokes, obviously someone had taught her well, and he hated that someone, although he had no idea who he might be. Hated him because he had been the first man to touch Jamie, and Ben had mistakenly assumed he would be her first.

At the moment, Ben could not consider her with another man, doing this to another man. He was on the brink of totally losing control, but he would not allow it to happen here. And when she lowered her head as if to take him into her mouth, resistance was no longer an option.

With an animal groan, he moved her aside and stood to step out of his jeans, unable to contain his overpowering desire for her. Damn the consequences. He needed to have her—be inside her—as much as he needed air to breathe.

She gave a little squeak of protest when he scooped her up in his arms. "Ben, I'm not done yet."

"Oh yes, you are most certainly done," he whispered as he passed through the living room toward the other side of the house. Toward his bed and the promise of pleasure. Toward the point of no return. "But I am only beginning."

Jamie now realized what it truly meant to be swept away by an Arabian knight. Engulfed in Ben's strong arms and heady male essence, she rested against his hair-covered chest where the thrum of his heart beat out an erratic rhythm against her cheek.

She was breathless, thrilled and a tiny bit afraid of what she had unleashed in Ben.

He entered the room and kicked the door closed behind them, then brought her down on the bed in his arms. Ben's arousal pressed against her belly, robbing her of her voice. Muted light filtered in from the adjoining bathroom, allowing her to make out the fire in his dark eyes.

"Do you know what you have done, Jamie?" he said.

She had her suspicions. "I've finally managed to see your bedroom again." A weak attempt at humor, Jamie decided, especially when she noticed Ben wasn't smiling.

He pushed the hair from her forehead and framed her face in his palms. "I believe you underestimate your power. Tell me now, while you still have the opportunity, if you wish to go forward. If you are uncertain, I will let you leave. But if you do not stop me, then I promise I will see this through."

Jamie didn't hesitate for a moment. "I want this, Ben. I have for a while now."

"Then it is done."

He kissed her thoroughly, hurling a spear of heat that settled in intimate places craving his touch. His tongue danced against hers, moving in and out between her parted lips. He teased and tempted her until she shifted restlessly beneath him.

Breaking the kiss, he pulled her up and worked the gown up and over her head. His expression was almost frightening in its intensity. She wasn't necessarily afraid of him, but she was more than a bit apprehensive over the intense desire sparking in his eyes—worried over whether or not she would please him. What did she know about the art of lovemaking? Not nearly enough.

His features softened when he touched her cheek, his gaze roaming over her face, seeking, searching. If he expected to find some hesitancy there, he wouldn't. She was determined not to let him see anything but longing.

"My Jamie," he whispered as he touched his lips to her temple, her cheek, her jaw. Then he sent his hands on a mission down her body, lingering at her breasts, fondling her until she shook with the force of her need.

"You tremble," he said. "Are you afraid?"

"No."

"Do you desire more?"

To say no would be one whopper of a lie, regardless of her concern. "Yes."

"Then lie back. Let me show you all the ways a man pleasures a woman."

Lying down sounded like a great idea to Jamie. She felt as weak as a starved woman. In some ways she was starving—for Ben's undivided attention. And she was getting it. Boy, was she getting it. His lips drifted down her neck then closed over her nipple. Her back arched as if it had a mind of its own, thrusting her chest upward, giving Ben better access. Slipping his hands underneath her back, Ben paid equal attention to both her breasts, and it was all she could do not to cry out from the pleasure.

Jamie couldn't seem to stop shaking. She wasn't the least bit cold, either. In fact, she was hot. So hot she could melt the mattress.

Ben sat up and straddled her thighs, then took a nearby pillow, placing it under her hips. He brought her hands up to his face and touched his lips to each of her palms. "I want to kiss you," he said.

Jamie reached up to cup his jaw in her hands and tried to draw him back to her eager mouth. He wouldn't budge.

"A more intimate kiss," he said. "I do not want you to be afraid."

She was more excited than fearful. Maybe a little of both. Did he really mean what she thought he meant? Only one way to find out. "Okay." Her voice sounded small compared to Ben's.

Then he lowered his head to nuzzle his face between her thighs, and she knew exactly what he had meant. The promise of a kiss like none she had ever known.

At the first intimate contact of his tongue on her vulnerable spot, Jamie's hips rose off the pillow.

"Be still," he said, his voice a gentle command.

Be still? How could she be still when her body wouldn't let her? Somehow she managed not to move too much, even when he delved deeper, using his tongue, his lips, to drive her to the threshold of the ultimate insanity.

She couldn't stifle the sounds leaving her mouth, sounds as unfamiliar to her as this act he performed with such tender persuasion. Lights flashed behind her closed lids. Sensations overtook her, not unlike those he'd created with his touch earlier that day, but more intense. He increased the pressure of his expert mouth until Jamie thought she might actually scream. Then the sensations overtook her as the pressure began to build and build, driving her toward release.

Jamie was totally captive to Ben's will as he continued with his kiss. Nothing could prepare her for the ensuing climax. Not a book. Not her imagination. Nothing.

The moan left her mouth regardless of her efforts to stop it. It was as if she left her body for a time, yet she'd never been so aware of every wonderful sensation. She didn't want it to end, but it did, leaving behind a slow dissolving heat and a sense of total euphoria.

Opening her eyes, she met Ben's gaze and his crooked smile. Male pride, plain and simple. Some things were inherent in every man, regardless of their background.

"Did that bring you pleasure, Jamie?" he asked in that slow-burn voice that made her want to moan some more.

"Isn't it obvious?"

"Good. But I am not yet finished."

The man had the nerve to touch her *there* again, and again she didn't have the strength to fight the onslaught of feelings, nor did she want to. But before she toppled over the edge, he came back to her. She groaned in protest.

"Patience." His smile came full-force. "It is not over yet."

With that he pulled her closer to him. She felt the nudge of his erection, and braced her hands on his shoulders. She closed her eyes tightly.

As he began to enter her, he met the resistance Jamie knew would come with her first time. He suddenly stopped trying, and she kept her eyes closed against his scrutiny although she could feel his gaze on her.

"Jamie, please do not tell me—"

"Okay, I won't."

"Look at me." His tone demanded she comply, forcing her eyes open. "Are you a virgin?"

"As a matter of fact...yes."

He turned his face upward and released a heavy sigh. "Why did you not tell me?"

"You didn't ask."

He started to pull away, but she wouldn't let him. "You finish this, Ben. I swear if you don't, I'll never forgive you."

He studied her for another long moment. "Perhaps I'll never forgive myself for abandoning good sense, but logic be damned. If this is what you wish, so be it. I cannot resist you." With one hard thrust, he filled her completely.

Jamie winced and held her breath. Ben stilled against her, allowing her body time to adjust to his intrusion.

"You tempt me to hurry," he whispered. "You feel so good surrounding me. Like velvet."

"Then hurry. Please."

It wasn't the pain that had her wanting him to get on with it. The sheer power of Ben's possession filled her with impatience. The pain had all but subsided, and in its place came a need so great she couldn't even begin to understand it.

He moved slowly, withdrawing a bit, then sinking deeper inside her. "Am I hurting you?" he asked.

"No. Not anymore."

His next move made her grit her teeth, not with pain but with intense pleasure.

"Did you feel that?" he asked.

Heavens, did she feel it! "What did you do?"

"I am searching for a special place."

He'd found it all right. Again. Then his hands seemed to be everywhere as he thrust inside her. He touched her in places she didn't know existed. With tenderness he took her higher, whispering words of praise. "My Jamie," he repeated over and over, and for a moment she truly believed she was his. He had branded her with his body, and now claimed her heart in spite of her caution.

Soon she couldn't think as she again embarked on another journey to sweet freedom. She didn't know exactly how he was managing to draw another climax from her, but he was, and she really didn't care how he'd done it. She only cared about how he felt in her arms, his power, his strength, his sensuality that called out to the deepest recesses of her soul.

This time, when she reached the summit, she cried out his name. And her name left Ben's lips, too, before he shuddered then stilled against her.

Pure joy had long been absent from Jamie's life, but now that joy had returned in Ben's arms. She wanted to sing. She wanted to cry. She simply held on to him, stroked his thick dark hair, kissed his solid shoulder, took to memory everything he had given her. Try as she might, she couldn't take back her heart. He possessed it now, just as he'd possessed her body.

Alima's warning came back to her.

A woman who strives to lose her innocence may lose her heart to one who cannot give his in return.

Jamie called herself ten kinds of fool. She had fallen in love with him—a man who couldn't love her in return.

Seven

Ben had never been so satisfied in his life. Jamie's fragile body fit perfectly to his, as if they were truly one. They had been one, at least for a few blessed moments.

Fearing he was crushing her with his weight, he moved to his side and regretfully slipped from her body. When he saw the glimmer of tears in her eyes, only then did he realize what he had done. She had told him she wanted this, but had she really known her own mind?

No. And he had acted on impulse, stolen her innocence. He had never bedded a virgin before, for many valid reasons, the most important being honor. He had learned during his upbringing that a man did not take something so precious without answering for his decision. His honor was now at stake, and only one option remained.

"We shall be married."

Jamie sat up in a rush and pushed back against the headboard. "Excuse me?"

Ben sat up too, resting his arms on bent knees. "We must marry now. I have taken your virginity, and it is only right."

Her eyes widened. "Now just a cotton-pickin' minute, Ben Rassad. In case you haven't noticed, this is a new century, and you're in America. That old virginity-marriage clause is no longer in effect."

Leaning over, he flipped on the bedside lamp. Seeing Jamie naked and flushed stirred his body to life again. He grasped the bed sheets and flung them across her body, covering all that temptation.

"I have told you I cannot change the way I believe," he said. "And I believe I am now obligated to marry you."

"Obligated?" Jamie clasped and unclasped a fistful of the sheet, a storm gathering in her green eyes. "I don't marry out of obligation."

"Are you certain? If I recall, you almost married Payune for that very reason."

"You jerk."

Ben wanted to take back his callous words. He wanted to tell her more, admit that he cared for her deeply. He did not know if what he felt was love, but he imagined it could be if given time. Yet he didn't dare admit that until he was certain. His honor also bound him to tell the truth.

Her eyes clouded with unshed tears, and he cursed the fact he had put them there. But what could he say to convince her that his intentions were honorable? He would simply have to try. "I would see to your every need. I would make you my princess. I would give you everything you desire—"

"Except love." She impaled him with her troubled green eyes. "But that's okay. I don't want your love. I don't need your love. I don't need anything, or anyone."

"Then you will not consider my proposal?"

"Not on your life. People don't have to marry this day and time because they have sex."

"Make love."

"In the absence of love, it's sex," she said adamantly. "I mean, women don't *have* to marry even if they get pregnant." Suddenly Jamie's eyes grew large. "Oh my gosh. *Pregnant.*"

The word echoed in Ben's ears. "Jamie, are you not protected against pregnancy?"

"How could I be? You've kept me cooped up in this house. And besides, it's your responsibility, too."

Ben had to admit he should have seen to that responsibility, but the thought had not entered his mind. This was not something he normally concerned himself with. "The women I have known in my country see to their protection."

Jamie narrowed her eyes and glared at him. "Well, great. We're not in your country, and I'm not one of *those* women. Haven't you heard of condoms?"

"Yes. Of course. I wrongly assumed you might be taking the birth control pill. You were very prepared in your seduction, so why would I not believe you would be prepared to protect yourself against pregnancy?"

"Because I'm an idiot." Jamie clutched the pillow to her chest. "This is just all I need."

All the energy seeping from him, Ben stretched out and rolled to face her. "Could you be with child?"

She worried her bottom lip. "I guess it's possible, but it was only once. Surely that counts for something. I mean, who gets pregnant their first time?"

He sought her gaze. "Many, I imagine, and all the more reason for us to wed. If you are carrying my child, you will be carrying another heir to my father's kingdom." And the son or daughter Ben had always secretly wished for, but never considered a possibility.

Jamie pushed off the bed, retrieved her gown from the floor, and slipped it back on. "I have no intention of marrying someone because I might be pregnant. And I sure as heck am not going to marry someone because I happened to lose my virginity to them during a fit of insanity." She spun around and headed toward the door.

He sat up quickly. "Jamie, where are you going?"

She paused with her hand on the knob, her back turned to him. "To my room."

He did not dare let her leave. Tonight he wanted her with him, for many reasons, the first being that he needed to ensure her safety. The second was much more selfish. He craved her nearness, wanted her curled up next to him until the dawn. Wanted to make love to her again and again, until they were both too exhausted to consider anything but each other.

Slipping from the bed, he caught the door before she could open it and leave. Both hands braced against the wooden surface on either side, he leaned into her and rested his face against the back of her head, drawing in the sweet smell of her damp hair. "Stay with me."

"Why?" she asked without turning around.

"I want you in my bed."

"You've already had me in your bed. Three times, last count."

"Yes, but tonight was different."

"You can say that again. And right now I wish I could take tonight back. I regret I've been so careless."

Ben had no regrets about making love to her. He only regretted that he could not give her what she needed, a promise of love. He had built armor around his emotions for so long, he did not know if he could rid himself of it. But perhaps he could try, if she would give him the chance.

He ran his fingertips over her hip, then grasped her waist to pull her to him. "I need to keep you nearby. Keep you in my arms. Keep you safe."

Jamie tried to ignore his low, whispery words, the feel of his arousal pressed against her bottom. She couldn't, but that didn't mean she had to do what he was asking. She longed to stay with him all night, but feared that by doing so, she'd give in to his demands and agree to his proposal. Agree to anything, for that matter. She refused to do that, give up her control. She wouldn't marry a man who didn't love her; she'd made that vow after Payune had called off their arranged marriage. She couldn't commit to a stranger.

Ben was no longer a stranger, but he didn't love her. Yes, he might desire her, but that wasn't enough to build a marriage on. She wanted love. She wanted *him* to love her. Stupid, senseless fantasies.

Jamie didn't dare turn around. Just one look in his dark eyes would have her melting like gooey fudge all over the carpeted floor. "I'm going to my room now. I need some space. Time to think."

"To think about what I have proposed?"

"No. I need to think about where I can go to get away from here. Away from you."

"You cannot leave until—"

"I know. Until you find this Klimt. I can find somewhere else to go. I know Lady Helena. She's right next door with your neighbor, Matt. I imagine she'll let me hang out there for the time being."

Ben pushed away from her, muttering in Arabic with a severity she'd never before witnessed. "That will not be necessary. You may remain here, and I will give you your peace. I shall not touch you again. And damn you for what you have done to me.''

She heard the slamming of the bathroom door behind her, and moved into the hallway on rubber legs. The tears came then, slow and steady, falling down her chin and onto the floor. She welcomed them as punishment for exposing her tender heart to Ben. It wasn't his fault; it was hers. She had shamelessly seduced him, not once thinking about the consequences. Not once realizing that something as intimate as making love could be so emotionally overwhelming. Ben was right, it wasn't simple, giving everything to someone.

Now he wanted to do the honorable thing and marry her. Make her his princess. No matter how much she cared for him, she couldn't do that. Not unless he said the words she needed to hear—*I love you.*

Ben braced his hands on the sink and lowered his head. Turning on the faucet, he splashed cold water on his face, yet it did nothing to relieve the inferno raging inside him, or the terrible ache in his heart.

Jamie had given him her body without hesitation, yet she refused to be totally his. He could not blame her. She deserved a man who could commit all his heart. A man who knew where he fit into this world. He was not that man. Still, deep inside he wondered if she could change him. Show him this elusive emotion known as love. Love between a man and a woman.

He loved and respected his mother and father as a son should, but he was uncertain he could ever let down his guard and bare his soul completely to a woman, although tonight he had come closer than he ever had before. Yet Jamie would not marry him, or so she said.

What if she now carried his child? He must make her

understand the importance of their union. But should she finally agree to the marriage, would he be doing her a disservice by thrusting her into a culture intolerant of strength in a woman? His mother had survived, with great effort. Jamie was much like her. He had seen what love had done to his mother, robbed her of spirit. Could he prevent that from happening to Jamie? The very thing that he admired most about her would be the one thing looked down upon by his people. Did it truly matter that much what his people thought?

Grabbing his pajamas from nearby, Ben slipped them on and walked back into the bedroom. He would go to Jamie. Talk to her again. Keep vigil at her bedside since she would probably not allow him in her bed. He still must remember his duty to her. He must guard her with his life. Tomorrow they would discuss the rest.

The bedside lamp and bathroom light shut off simultaneously. Instinctively, Ben's gaze snapped to the security system panel attached to the wall near his bedroom door. No red light glowed to indicate that the alarm was functioning.

Ben raced from the bedroom at a run, his heart keeping time with his gait, only one goal on his mind.

Reaching Jamie before it was too late.

The floorboard squeaked beneath Jamie's feet, startling her. The hallway was dark, very dark, and she felt eerily disturbed. Usually Alima left the bathroom light on for her. But not tonight.

Knowing Alima, she was probably trying to create an atmosphere for lovers. If the woman only knew how successful Jamie had been in her seduction—how hopelessly in love she was with Ben—would Alima tell her I told you so? Could be, and Jamie deserved her scorn and much more.

Feeling along the wall, Jamie found the doorknob to her room, turned it and pushed the door open.

A hand grabbed her arm and yanked her inside.

A moist palm clamped over her mouth, inhibiting her respiration.

Blind panic contracted her chest when she was pulled back against the unknown assailant. The stench of cigarettes and sweat seeped into her nostrils, causing her stomach to roil. But the feel of something cold and hard jabbed in her side made her want to collapse from fear.

"Miss Morris, so we finally meet again."

Jamie tried to scream but all she could manage was a moan. She tried to struggle, which only caused the man's grip to tighten on her mouth.

"Don't move, or I will be forced to harm you."

Jamie froze, her ears ringing, her heart pounding.

His evil chuckle made her quake. "I must say, Payune did not know what he was missing by ending your marriage agreement. He would be pleasantly surprised to know that one so young is such an expert lover." His demented voice was laced with a heavy European accent. A voice that seemed somewhat familiar to Jamie, but she couldn't remember where she'd heard it.

His whiskey-laden breath fanned the side of her face and she tightly closed her eyes. "I see that the sheikh has fallen for your charms. I am surprised he sent you to your room alone when he could so obviously have had you again. But I am grateful for that fact, since you have something I need."

Jamie bit back the nausea and wished with all her might she could bite him. Not possible with his hand held so tightly against her mouth.

"I want that wedding dress," he demanded, venom in his tone.

Why did he want her mother's dress? Did it have to do with that mysterious *something?* Obviously, but she had no clue what.

"I will uncover your mouth," he said, "but should you make the slightest sound other than telling me the where-abouts of the dress, I will kill you." He forced the gun farther into her ribcage, leaving Jamie no doubt he was serious.

Where was Ben? In his room, she decided, stewing over her refusal to marry him. She'd been such a fool, and her foolishness could very well cost her her life. Maybe even Ben's life. She prayed he stayed in his room, away from danger. Then she could die knowing he was safe.

What was she thinking? She wasn't going to die, at least not without a fight. She needed an opportunity, just a small window of time, and then she could act.

"Do you promise not to scream?" he asked. She nodded her agreement. "Good."

He slowly lowered his hand and turned her to face him. She coughed, gagged, then drew in several ragged breaths. Staring at his shadowy frame, she couldn't make out his features, but she could tell he wasn't very big. Maybe an inch or two taller than she. A point in her favor should she decide to make a move.

He fingered a lock of her hair and laughed, sending icy chills of apprehension up her spine like fingers on piano keys. "I am sorry we have no lights so I can see you better, but I'm afraid that is my fault. Although when I watched you and your lover in action, I did see quite well. I truly enjoyed your, what shall I call it? Display of affection?" He touched her face and she cringed. "Had I more time, I might partake of your talents. But I am in a hurry, so perhaps later then?''

"Over my dead body," Jamie hissed.

He jabbed the gun into her belly, causing her to wince. "That could be arranged, but first the dress. Where is it!''

"In the closet, over there." She pointed a shaky finger toward the double doors across the room. When the creep turned his head in that direction, Jamie took her chance. She thrust her knee up into his groin with all her might, hitting the bull's-eye.

Startled, he dropped the gun to grab his crotch. Jamie immediately turned and ran into the solid wall of a chest. This time she did scream.

"I am here, Jamie.''

Ben. Thank God.

Pushing her aside, Ben took the man to the ground in one heavy thud. Jamie's eyes had adjusted to the limited light, allowing her to look on in terror as Ben struggled with the assailant. Two dark figures rolling on the floor. Where was the gun?

A light flickered behind Jamie, casting frightening shadows on the wall. She turned toward the glow to find Alima standing in the doorway, holding a large candle.

"What is this?" Alima asked, horror in her voice.

"This is Robert Klimt," Ben growled. "Murderer. Thief.''

When Jamie realized Ben had the intruder pinned to the ground, she let out a breath of relief and moved toward the pair, Alima following close behind. After she grabbed a robe from the chair and slipped it on, she kicked something with her toe and looked down. The gun. Slowly she picked it up and held it trained on Klimt's leg, the only place not covered by Ben who now straddled him with his hands wrapped around Klimt's throat. The man's eyes bulged with panic. Jamie wanted to cheer.

"Bring the candle closer," Jamie told Alima.

Alima slowly moved forward and in the candle's glow, Jamie studied Klimt's small sharp features, the mole near his left brow, and remembered.

"He was on the plane," Jamie said.

"Yes. He was trying to escape to freedom." Ben jerked Klimt's head up. "Where did you hide the diamond?" The fear didn't lessen in Klimt's face, yet he didn't speak.

"Diamond?" Jamie asked. "What diamond?"

"The diamond this animal stole after he killed the club's bartender, Riley Monroe." Ben lowered his voice to a menacing tone. "Is that correct, Robert Klimt? You killed a defenseless man after you forced him to take you to the jewels?"

"I admit nothing."

Ben let Klimt's head hit the floor with a *thunk,* but kept his grip around the man's neck. "You will admit everything."

The man tried to wrench Ben's hands away but couldn't. He made a choking sound. "Again, I ask. Where is the diamond?" Ben commanded.

Jamie worried that Ben might kill Klimt before he had his answer if she didn't do something to stop him. "I think it has something to do with my mother's dress," she said quickly. "Or he thinks it does. He demanded I give it to him."

Ben loosened his hold on Klimt's neck. "Is that where we will find the diamond?"

Klimt looked a bit too cocky for someone with hands wrapped around his windpipe. "And what will happen to me if I tell you?"

Ben sneered. "It is what I will do to you if you do not tell me that should concern you."

"I will be no good to you dead."

"He's right, Ben," Jamie said, grasping for anything to help Ben regain some common sense.

Ben looked at her for a moment before again turning his attention to Klimt. "If I should decide to spare your life, you will be turned over to the Asterland authorities. They will deal with you as they see fit. Or perhaps I will release you to the Americans and let them handle this. First-degree murder in the state of Texas carries with it death by execution." Ben's ensuing smile was cynical. "Perhaps that would be best."

Klimt's eyes bulged with terror. "No. You cannot do that. I have diplomatic immunity. I am a respected man in my country. I am a—"

"—tays bawáal," Alima shouted, cutting off Klimt's protests. When Jamie stared at her, Alima added, "A pissing he-goat."

An adequate description, Jamie decided.

"Give me the bedsheet," Ben said.

Alima hurried to the bed, stripped off the sheet, and offered it to Ben. With one hand still clasped around Klimt's throat, he took the sheet then grasped Klimt's wrists and dragged him across the floor to the bed. He raised the man's hands and tied them to the bedpost, leaving him helplessly suspended with his arms over his head like a side of beef.

Ben turned to Jamie. "Give me the gun."

She'd forgotten she was still holding it. With shaking hands, she complied.

Stepping back, Ben pointed the pistol at Klimt's head. "Now, tell me everything."

"If I do cooperate, will you assure me that you will

speak to the Asterland authorities and tell them I have aided you in the investigation?''

"Is that in hope they will give you a lighter sentence?'' Ben's laugh was sharp, without humor. ''I would rather deal with you myself than risk that you will not be adequately punished for the crimes you have committed. For killing my friend.''

"I will not speak again unless I have your promise.''

Ben rubbed a hand over his shadowed jaw, indecision warring in his expression. ''I will see what I can do, but I make no promises where your country is concerned.''

Klimt lowered his head in defeat. ''I did kill your Riley Monroe because it was necessary. After he led me to the jewels, I could not risk him revealing my identity. I planned to sell the jewels to fund the revolution.''

"Is Payune connected to this scheme?''

"I act alone for the sake of the revolution.''

Jamie shivered to think her once-intended was somehow involved in all this mess, even though Klimt denied it.

"We recovered all the jewels but the red diamond,'' Ben said. ''Where is it now?''

"You will find the diamond sewn into the hem of the wedding dress.''

Ben's jaw tensed, and Jamie sensed he was barely hanging on to his restraint. ''You are lying. Miss Morris has told me the dress was not out of her possession.''

Klimt glared at her with hate-filled eyes. ''She is mistaken. The dress was taken to the cleaners two days before we were to depart for Asterland. I broke into the shop and put the diamond there myself before she retrieved it.''

Jamie's mouth gaped when she realized the man was telling the truth. How stupid of her not to remember. ''I'm sorry, Ben, I didn't even think about that. I was only thinking about after the plane crash.''

"It is all right, Jamie," Ben said in a gentle voice. "It no longer matters." He pulled her to his side, taking her by surprise. "Did this swine harm you, Jamie? If so, I will kill him now."

"No!" Jamie couldn't let Ben kill Klimt no matter what the vile man had done. Ben would then risk going to jail himself. "He didn't do anything except try to scare me to death."

"Then I will let him live. For now." He turned to Alima. "Go and find J.D. He should be on the porch, although I have my doubts since he allowed Klimt access to the house."

"Your man is on the porch, asleep," Klimt said.

"I'm right here, you sorry S.O.B."

Everyone looked toward the door where J.D. now stood holding a flashlight, a small trickle of blood streaming from his forehead. He pointed at Klimt. "This coward ambushed me, knocked me over the head with some kind of pipe. Then he stole my danged gun."

Ben walked to J.D. and handed him the weapon. "Stay here and make sure he does not move."

"You got it, boss." J.D. grabbed the gun and stood over Klimt, his lips curled up into a menacing snarl.

Ben took Jamie by the shoulders and turned her to face him, away from Klimt. "You are safe now."

Jamie could only nod when she saw the concern in his expression.

Ben walked to the closet and removed the wedding dress. He laid it across the bed carefully. Jamie and Alima gathered round as he examined the hem. With a fingertip, he tore away several threads and reached inside. "It is here."

Alima lowered the candle and centered it on Ben's large palm holding a round red jewel sparkling in the flickering light. Jamie had never seen anything quite like it, at least five carats, she assumed. Red in color, it resembled a ruby.

"Who does it belong to?" Jamie asked.

Ben closed his hand over it. "To the town of Royal, its rightful owners."

"I've heard the legend of the jewels," Jamie said, "but I never believed they really existed."

"Yes, they do. And you must promise you'll never tell anyone of their existence. To do so will again bring about more fortune hunters such as this one." He nodded toward Klimt.

Jamie vowed to carry the secret to her grave. "I promise."

"Go with Alima now," he told her. "I will return to you as soon as I make arrangements to have Klimt removed." He brushed a kiss across her forehead before turning to J.D. "If he should lift a finger, you have my permission to shoot him."

J.D. laughed. "That'll be my pleasure, boss."

Ben took the flashlight from J.D. then headed out the door.

Jamie glared at the man who'd almost killed her twice now, and had the strongest urge to kick him again. But he looked so small and pitiful. Harmless, actually. Still, she would like to vent her frustration somehow. Maybe she should just tickle him under the arms. Death by uncontrollable laughter.

Alima's hand on her arm prevented her from giving in to the impulse, which was just as well. J.D. might actually shoot him if she made the creep move, and she didn't want his death on her conscience no matter what he'd put her through.

"Come, child," Alima said. "We will go to the kitchen. I will prepare you a drink to help you sleep, and you can tell me why this man is hanging from your bed."

Eight

Ben stood at his front doorway watching until the taillights disappeared from sight. Justin Webb and Matthew Walker had just left with the red diamond—the last of the three stolen jewels—and Robert Klimt. They intended to lock both of them up—Klimt in the Cattleman's Club basement until they arranged for him to return to Asterland, and the jewel with the other two until they could find another hiding place. Now it was of the utmost importance that they make plans to thwart the impending revolution. But that would come later in the day. At the moment, Ben needed to see about Jamie.

After searching the kitchen and living room, he found her curled up on the small sofa in his bedroom, covered by a silk throw, her eyes closed. Dawn's light seeped through the curtained window, washing her beautiful face in an ethereal glow. She appeared angelic, at peace. For that Ben was glad.

Deciding not to disturb her, he turned away.

"Ben?"

Her magnetic voice pulled him around to face her again. "I did not mean to wake you."

"I wasn't asleep. I'm too afraid to sleep."

He moved to the sofa and pulled her into his arms. She trembled against him. "It is all right now, Jamie. He is gone. He cannot hurt you anymore. You are safe with me."

The warmth of her lips against his neck brought his exhausted body to life. Tipping her chin up, he kissed her face, tasted the salt of her tears. She had been so courageous, so strong, but now she wilted like yesterday's flowers. And he needed her desperately.

Slipping his arms beneath her, he picked her up and took her to his bed, following her down onto the satin sheets. She clung to him and sobbed. He held her, stroked her hair, brushed a kiss over her lips and whispered words of consolation. He knew not what else to do. He wanted to make love to her, but he was afraid. Afraid she would turn him away.

She didn't. Instead, she drew his head down and kissed him in earnest, clutching at the T-shirt he wore. Filled with impatient need, he sat up and tore the shirt over his head, then shed his jeans while she slipped her gown off and tossed it aside. He came back to her and ran greedy hands over her naked flushed body, taking each curve to memory. She arched against him when he drew her nipple into his mouth and suckled. She moaned when he slipped his fingertips through the cleft between her thighs. He found her wet and warm, ready for him. Yet he took his time, stroking her slowly to build the tension higher, until he knew she could hold out no longer.

When her breaths became sharp gasps, he joined with her, sinking into her tight sheath. She wrapped her legs about him, drawing him farther into her welcoming heat, and sending her farther into his soul. He wanted to temper his movements, savor the moment, but he could no longer ignore his own body's demand when she writhed beneath him.

Clinging to his last shred of control, he stopped moving and slipped from her body, determined not to succumb to his release until she had been fulfilled. Jamie gave a little moan of protest, urging a smile from Ben.

He sat up and grasped her waist. "This way will be better for you," he said.

It didn't take long for understanding to dawn in her expression when Ben lay back. She moved over him, straddling his body. Slowly, she lowered herself onto his shaft, her face melting into pure pleasure.

Ben steeled against the heady sensations and willed himself to hang on for a little longer. "You are in control, Jamie," he whispered. "Do with me what you will."

If he could give her no more, he could give her this.

Ben kept his gaze locked into hers. She was now in complete command of her body and his. He watched her expression change like a chameleon as she found independence in their lovers' dance. Her face went slack and her eyes drifted shut. Her bottom lip trembled and a long steady moan left her lips. Only then did Ben give in to his own release and let go as never before.

Jamie collapsed against him, her heart drumming at his chest to match the rhythm of his own heart. He held her tightly in fear she might slip away, as if she were a dream of his own making. But she was not a dream. She was real. So very real.

He had never experienced such satisfaction. Such a sense of total completeness. She had crept under his skin, stolen his heart and soul. And as sleep overtook him, he vowed he would never let her go.

"Where are you going?"

Jamie's hand paused on the open drawer before she picked up the last of her underclothes and stuffed them in the bag she'd brought with her. "I'm going home."

"No, you are not."

Her gaze snapped to his. Ben stood in the doorway dressed in his Arabian clothes, appearing commanding and in control, and oh so gorgeous. She looked away again, worried she'd give in to him if she didn't. "You can't stop me. Klimt's out of the picture, so that means I can return to my apartment, find a job. Get on with my life."

She sensed his presence behind her. "Then you will not consider my proposal?"

"I can't, Ben." She turned to face him, shocked by the hurt in his gray eyes. "I have to sort things out. Figure out what I'm going to do next. Be my own person."

"I will allow you to do these things."

"Allow me?" She grabbed the bag and carried it to the bed. "You see, Ben, that's the problem. I don't want any-one *allowing* me anything like I'm some teenager who doesn't know her own mind. I want to go back to school. I want to be an adult and take care of myself."

"Then you are saying you do not want me?"

Oh, she wanted him all right. She wanted him like noth-ing she'd ever wanted before. But she couldn't have him. Not when he saw her as nothing more than an obligation. "What we've shared has been great. You've taught me a lot of things, including the fact that I can make it on my own."

"Even after what we have experienced together, you would still leave me?" he asked, frustration in his voice.

"Would you give yourself so freely without anything in return?"

He had no idea what he'd given her, and she would never forget it. Forget him. "I have no choice."

"Yes, you do. Marry me."

"I can't."

His gaze slid away for a moment before returning to her, defeat in his eyes. "Is there nothing I can say to convince you?"

Yes, there was something he could say, but she knew in her heart he wouldn't. She swallowed around the boulder in her throat. "I'll never forget what we've shared. But I have to move on. So do you. You need to find a woman who can give you lots of babies and quietly tend to your needs. I'm not that woman."

"Yet you may be carrying my child."

"I'll deal with that if it has happened."

He came to her in a rush and grasped her arms. "If it is so, you must tell me. The child will be mine."

So now she understood all too well. Ben viewed everything as a possession. No way was she falling into that trap. "Like I said, I'll deal with it."

"I will not leave you alone."

"If you don't, I'll leave town."

"I will find you."

"Maybe, maybe not," she said, although she knew he had the money and means to find her, no matter where she might go. But she couldn't worry about that now. She hoped he would simply respect her wishes and stay out of her life. "Now would you please unhand me so I can go home?"

His dark eyes narrowed, and he pulled her to him. His lips met hers in a hard bruising kiss. A kiss full of frustration, of passion. Then he released her and stepped back.

"I will let you leave now, but remember, I do not easily give up. You may trust me on that."

Ben tried to concentrate on the conversation between his fellow Cattleman's Club members but again found it increasingly difficult, as it had been the last time they'd met. His thoughts kept turning to Jamie, the way she had driven away in her battered blue car that morning, out of his life, but never out of his mind.

"So he didn't say for sure whether or not Payune was connected?"

Ben looked up to find Aaron Black addressing him. "He claims he acted alone. But I do not believe him."

"Neither do we," Black said. "That's why we've decided Dakota will go to Asterland and try to straighten this mess out."

"Where is the diamond?" Ben asked.

Aaron Black hooked a thumb over his shoulder. "With the others behind the plaque."

"And Klimt?"

"On a plane back to his country," Justin said. "They promised to deal with him appropriately."

Ben released a harsh laugh. "I doubt they will do to him what he deserves after what he has done to Jamie."

The members exchanged knowing glances before Black spoke again. "I've been in touch with Kathy Lewis, and she's agreed to make the trip with Dakota."

Dakota Lewis's frame went rigid. "So she did agree."

"Yeah, and she's on her way here," Justin said.

Ben studied Dakota's expression, his anger evident in the way he gripped the arms of his chair. "I don't know why you all think that involving my ex-wife in this mess is going to help."

"She has connections to Asterland's queen," Matt said. "We need her."

Dakota tossed aside a pen and watched it roll to the floor. "Is there no other way?"

"Nope," Justin said. "It's the perfect cover. Husband and wife traveling to Asterland on the pretense it's a second honeymoon."

"It will never work," Lewis said, his tone laced with frustration. "I'm not that good an actor."

"Look, Dakota," Black said. "I know you and Kathy have a history, but you're just going to have to bite the bullet and think about what we'd be losing if the current Asterland government falls. We all have strong business connections there, and we owe it not only to the king, but to ourselves to try and prevent that from happening."

"It is the only way," Ben stated, knowing in fact that his investments would suffer if they did not succeed with this plan. And he would like nothing better than to have Payune punished for his involvement. After all, the man was responsible for putting Jamie in danger, whether Klimt admitted it or not.

"Then it's settled?" Justin asked.

Dakota looked away. "Yeah, it's settled."

Aaron Black stood. "Great. We'll be in touch. Right now I've got to get back to Pamela. She wants to go shopping for baby stuff."

Everyone laughed then, except Ben. He again considered that Jamie might be carrying his child. Would she tell him, or would she possibly leave town without him knowing for certain? He could not allow that. And if she did try to run, he would find her, as he had promised. He would use every option available to him. Perhaps she would come to him on her own. Perhaps he was insane for believing that might be possible.

Justin, Dakota and Aaron took their leave, but Matt remained seated across from Ben, surveying him suspiciously.

Matt leaned forward and folded his hands before him. "So, where's Jamie?"

"She has returned to her apartment."

"Oh, yeah? I thought maybe you two might have hit it off. I was thinking maybe you'd tell us we have another wedding to look forward to."

"She refused my proposal." Ben wanted to take back the admission the moment it left his idiotic mouth.

"Then there *was* more to it than Big Ben playing the bodyguard."

Ben shifted in his chair. "Yes, but I did not intend for it to happen."

"Neither did I, Ben, my boy. But it did. So what do you plan to do now?"

"I do not know."

"You're not going to just let her get away, are you?"

Ben drummed the table with his fingers, impatience closing in on him. "I fear she is already gone."

Matt laughed. "Ben, you beat all. I've never seen you give up on anything so easily. Unless what happened doesn't mean that much to you?"

Ben's gaze snapped to Matt's, anger seeping from every pore. "I do not view her in that light. I have come to understand her. To respect her. I have come to…" He let the words trail away, afraid to claim them. Afraid to voice them. To make them real.

"You're in love with her, aren't you?"

Ben tried to close off Matt's question, but to no avail. "I am not certain. I have never experienced love for a woman."

Matt grinned. "Do you feel like you've lost your best

friend at the same time you just came close to sealing a million-dollar deal and the contract fell through?''

"Yes.''

"Then face it, Ben. You're in love with her. Lock, stock and barrel. But any one of us could tell that the minute you walked through the door a few days ago.''

"It does not matter now. She will not see me.''

"Then you'll just have to try harder. Woo her.''

Ben frowned. "Woo her?''

"Yeah, you know. Do things for her. Make her realize she can't live without you.'' Matt slapped a palm on the table. "And I'll send Helena over to talk to her. We have the same situation in reverse. You and Helena are from royal blood, different worlds. Jamie and I are just plain folk. But Helena and I have worked out our differences. She could probably help.''

A small weight lifted from Ben's heart. "Do you think that would be possible?''

"It's a start. But you've got to participate, too.''

"I have no idea where to begin.''

Matt released a frustrated sigh. "Ben, use that head of yours for something other than your investments. Buy her nice things. Cook her dinner. Be creative.''

The purchasing of gifts was something Ben could manage without any trouble, but he had never even lifted a pot from the stove, much less prepared a meal. He supposed Alima could teach him something to make for Jamie. Perhaps hot dogs.

Ben rose, ready to put his plan in action. "I will consider your suggestions.''

Matt stood. "I'll send Helena to Jamie's soon. She'll be glad to get out of the house now that Klimt's been caught.''

Ben offered his hand for a shake. "Wish me luck, *Sadíiq*. I will need it.''

"I have no doubt you'll do fine," Matt said, grinning.

Unfortunately, Ben had grave doubts. But he vowed they would not stop him. He would not give up until he had Jamie Morris back in his bed, in his life, for good.

Jamie collapsed onto the sofa, relieved she had her old job at the hospital back. Her life back. Without Ben.

The man was truly amazing. She'd come home to her apartment expecting to dive into much-needed clean-up due to the break-in. Instead, she'd found everything back in its place, along with all new furniture, compliments of Sheikh Ben Rassad. Obviously he was trying to buy his way back into her life. Jamie refused to give in to those tactics.

But no matter how hard she tried to forget him, he'd preyed on her mind night and day for the past week. She didn't miss being cooped up in his house, but she did miss him. Terribly. She missed Alima, too. Although the housekeeper had never asked about Jamie's and Ben's relationship, Jamie suspected she knew what had transpired between them. Yet she'd never said I told you so. She had simply told Jamie to take care and not to give up on matters of the heart.

Jamie had all but given up. She had no desire to look for a replacement for Ben. No one would ever measure up.

The knock at the door startled Jamie. Glancing at the clock, she wondered who would be calling on her at 8:00 p.m.

Ben?

She was thrilled by that prospect, yet afraid to find him on her doorstep. What would she say to him?

When the bell rang, Jamie rose and moved to the door, steeling herself in case she should find a sheikh on the other side. She peered through the peephole, but it wasn't Ben at all. Lady Helena Reichard stood in the hallway, impeccably dressed, blond hair pulled into a neat chignon, her pastel-blue silk suit looking as though she, too, had been on a job interview.

Throwing open the door, Jamie grinned. "Helena? I can't believe you're here!"

Helena held up a large white box. "Yes, I'm here, and I brought some of Manny's apple pie. Can I come in?"

Jamie stepped aside. "Of course."

Helena moved past her, favoring her left leg, and set the box on the table before facing Jamie again. "Your apartment looks wonderful. You've been busy redecorating, I take it."

Jamie looked around as if seeing it for the first time. "Actually, I didn't do it. Ben…Sheikh Rassad is responsible for the changes." He was responsible for many changes, but Jamie wouldn't burden Helena with her problems, not considering everything the woman had been through since the whole Asterland mess had started. Helena had been burned in the crash, her ankle shattered, yet she had managed to come through like a trooper. Now she had a new fiancé in rancher Matt Walker, a wedding planned in the next few months, and a new life in America.

Jamie tried to tamp down the envy as she pulled back a chair at the sparkling new dinette. Helena deserved Jamie's admiration and respect, not jealousy over her good fortune. "Have a seat and tell me what brings you here."

Helena settled in and Jamie noticed the mesh glove hiding the burns on Helena's left hand. She felt an immediate pang of sympathy—and guilt over not going to see Helena the minute she'd left Ben's ranch.

"I thought we were due a visit," Helena said. "Now that things seem to be safer in Royal, thanks to your Ben, I decided we needed to talk."

"He's not *my* Ben," Jamie said adamantly, then regretted the harsh words. "I mean, he's just a friend. Was a friend. He was very good to me while I was staying at his place."

Helena raised a thinly arched brow. "Really? He's a very attractive man. Maybe you discovered a little romance?"

"Actually, I—" Jamie saw no sense in hiding it from Helena. Since the crash, the woman had been the closest thing to a good friend that Jamie had known. Except maybe Alima. And Ben. "Yeah, I guess you could say that. We became rather…close."

Helena sent her a kind, knowing smile. "So I've heard from Matt."

Jamie frowned. "Was Ben bragging about it? If he was, then I'm going to march right out there to the ranch and—"

Helena laid a hand on Jamie's arm. "No, he wasn't boasting. Matt told me that Ben's moping around most of the time—lovesick."

If only Jamie could believe that. "Take my word for it, he's not in love with me. In lust with me, maybe, but not in love."

"Are you certain?"

"Yes. He never told me he loved me. He did ask me to marry him after… Well, after we became close."

"After you made love?" Helena added without judgment.

Jamie needed to explain. She valued Helena's respect, and she didn't want the woman thinking badly of her. "I didn't exactly mean for anything to happen between us, it just did." She lowered her eyes, away from Helena's steady perusal. "Truth is, I seduced him, not the other way around. I couldn't help myself. I'd never been with a man before, and he was just so…so…"

"Irresistible?" Helena laughed. "I know exactly what you mean. I feel the same about Matthew. They're both enigmatic men, strong, passionate. Not easy attributes for a woman to resist.''

"You can say that again," Jamie said wistfully. "I've never met anyone quite like Ben.''

"Nor have I met anyone like Matt. And I love him with all my heart." Helena leaned forward, her blue eyes intent and serious. "Do you love Ben, Jamie?''

Jamie wanted to burst into tears, but she held back by sheer will. "I don't know, I guess." Why was she lying? "Yes, I love him. More than I ever imagined loving anyone. He's so stubborn and demanding at times. So different from me because of his culture. He's used to women being passive. I'm anything but that. I don't want to be that at all. I'm afraid if I accept Ben's marriage proposal, he won't be happy with the real me, and I can't change who I am.''

"Marriage proposal?" Helena placed a hand on her chest. "Matt didn't tell me Ben proposed to you.''

"Yes, he did, because he felt obligated to marry me since he 'took my virginity.' Have you ever heard of anything so backward in your life?''

"I find it honorable that he would care enough to ask you to marry him.''

"I don't want him to marry me because he feels obligated.''

"Maybe you should give Ben another chance to prove himself to you, considering how you feel about him.''

Jamie centered her gaze on Helena. "He's already proved his honor by protecting me. Now I want only one thing from him. I want him to say he loves me. Is that too much to ask?''

"From a man like Ben? Possibly. Words might not come easily for him. In fact, I'm not certain he realizes he is in love with you. But I gather he is rather pitiful right now and it's only a matter of time before he does make that realization. And look at it this way. He could have any woman he wants, but it seems he has chosen you."

Jamie stood and walked into the adjacent kitchen to make some tea. "I don't know if that's enough."

Helena joined her at the counter. "What I'm about to tell you is between you and me. I wanted to come see you, but I planned to do it two days from now when I came into town for my doctor's appointment. Matt convinced me to come earlier after he met with Ben. He told me the sheikh's a wreck, so he offered to have me come and speak with you."

Hurt niggled at Jamie's heart. "So this was a set-up orchestrated by Ben and Matt?"

"No, Jamie. I agreed to do it not because Ben or Matt wanted it, but because I want you to understand that no matter what differences two people might have from a cultural standpoint, love has an amazing way of spanning those boundaries."

Jamie tried not to hope. "Do you really think so?"

Helena put her arm around Jamie's shoulder and gave her a gentle squeeze. "All I'm saying is keep an open mind. Give it some time. Time really does heal all wounds." She held up her injured hand. "I'm counting on that. So have faith in your heart, and give Ben a second chance."

Should she really follow Helena's advice? Could she really open her heart that wide? "I'll think about it, but I haven't even heard from him. He's probably changed his mind."

"You never know," Helena said with a smile. "And if I were you, I'd be prepared for anything."

Jamie wasn't at all prepared the next morning when two floral delivery trucks pulled up at the curb while she was attempting to head to the hospital for work. The deliverymen opened their sliding van doors and carried in vases full of every flower imaginable, two at a time, while Jamie stood by speechless. By the time they were done, Jamie's entire apartment was covered in blooms, from roses to carnations to daisies and some beautiful orange blossoms that Jamie had never seen before.

They were all from Ben, or so the card on the largest vase full of pink roses declared. The message read, Marry me—Ben. Not Love, With love, I love you, or any endearment whatsoever. Jamie tried not to be too disappointed, but she couldn't help it. Ben was trying to buy his way back into her life.

Not a chance she would give in that quickly.

Once she reached the hospital, she picked up the phone and dialed his number. Fortunately, Alima answered.

"Is Ben in?" she asked the housekeeper.

"Jamie, child, is that you?"

"Yes, it's me. I need to talk with your boss."

"I am afraid he is not present. He has left today for Canada, and I do not expect him until tomorrow morning."

That was probably best, Jamie decided. If she heard his deep magnetic voice, no telling what she might say or do. "Just leave him a message, please. Tell him I loved the flowers, but I'm not a blooming idiot."

A long silence filled the line. "I do not write English well."

"Then tell him thanks, but no thanks."

"He will be most disappointed he could not speak with you. Should I have him call you?"

"No!" Jamie lowered her voice when she saw another transcriptionist peek from behind a nearby cubicle. "Just tell him what I said."

"As you wish, Jamie. I would like to say that I greatly miss your company. I have no one with whom to view my television programs."

"Maybe we can do that again some day." A promise Jamie shouldn't make. She had no intention of returning to the ranch. "You could come here to my place. I'm off on Thursdays. We could just hang around and watch the soaps all day. Veg out on the couch."

"I do not understand this 'veg out.' Do you mean cook the vegetables?"

"No, act like one." Jamie could picture Alima shaking her head. "Well, I need to go. And I miss you, too."

"I am glad," Alima said, a smile in her voice. "The sheikh misses you terribly. I believe he suffers from a broken heart."

Jamie's own heart dropped over the declaration. "I'm sure he'll recover quickly once he goes home again." Home to his mistresses with no commitment, no ties.

"He will not leave, although his mother has called several times since your departure. He claims he still has unfinished business."

"I hope he finishes it soon," Jamie said. "I'm sure his mother misses him, too." As much as Jamie missed him.

"I would assume that, but I believe his unfinished business involves you."

"There's nothing unfinished between us, Alima. It's over."

"Nothing is over until the large woman sings."

Jamie stifled a laugh. Alima had finally adopted some American sayings, even though they weren't quite accurate. "I suppose, but don't count on it."

"I only count on two things, dear Jamie. The sun rising in the east, and the power of love between a man and a woman. You would do well to remember that."

Alima said a brief goodbye and hung up, leaving Jamie to ponder her words. Yes, there was a lot of power in love, but Ben didn't really love her. He wanted to own her, and Jamie refused to be owned by any man. Even a man she loved.

Nine

"**D**oes Miss Morris know you're comin' here tonight?"

Ben smiled at the elderly landlord and prepared to lie.
"Yes, she knows. I am making her dinner." He nodded
toward the paper sacks in his arms.

The man eyed him with suspicion, angering Ben. He had
advanced the landlord six months' rent on Jamie's apartment after Klimt ravaged the place. He had spoken to him
several times by phone to ascertain that Jamie's apartment
was still safe. He had arranged for him to let the delivery-
man in to set up the new furniture. Surely by those gestures
alone the proprietor realized that Ben's intentions were
honorable where Jamie was concerned.

"Mr. Grable, I assure you that Miss Morris would not
mind you opening the door for me."

A long moment of silence passed before the landlord
spoke again. "Well, I s'pose it would be okay for me to

let you in seeing as how you did help her out with her rent and all.''

''Thank you for your consideration.''

With agonizing slowness, the man slipped a key in the lock and pushed open the door. He turned back to Ben, still looking reluctant. ''I sure hope she don't get mad at me. You be sure to tell her this was all your idea.''

''I will be certain to inform Miss Morris of your kindness.''

The man left Ben standing on the threshold of Jamie's apartment without further protest. Ben stepped inside, pleased to find that the flowers he'd sent were still intact, not torn to shreds. When he'd arrived home that morning, Alima had given him Jamie's message. That would not stop him from his mission. Tonight was only the beginning of his ''wooing.''

Making his way into the small kitchen, he set the bags on the small counter and surveyed his surroundings, feeling as foreign as he had when he'd first come to America.

How difficult could it be to prepare this simple meal? Economics had been his college major, and he'd mastered all the upper-level courses with ease. He had handled many of his own investments and had proven successful in all his financial endeavors. He could most certainly make hot dogs.

Ben rifled through the bag and withdrew the frankfurters, a can of Texas chili, a package of buns, and a small plastic bottle of mustard. The other bag held two bottles of champagne he'd had the Cattleman's Club's new bartender order. The best that money could buy, fitting for a grand celebration. Ben hoped that by the time this plan was complete, both he and Jamie would have something to celebrate.

Ben read the directions on the package of franks. They

were vague at best. With little time before Jamie returned home from her job, he opted to use the microwave, although he had never operated one before. Surely this would also be an elementary task. Opening a cabinet, he took out two gold-rimmed dishes. Fine china. He was pleasantly surprised that Jamie would own such nice things after claiming she had simple tastes.

Standing in front of the microwave, Ben stared at the buttons in hopes they would soon make sense. The directions on the hot dogs stated to heat each one for 30 seconds. Since he was warming three, Ben set the timer for five minutes to assure they were completely done. He had never cared for the fare, and he certainly did not enjoy the thought of eating cold wieners.

He wrestled with the electric can-opener for a time. The can of chili slipped from the magnet, landing on the counter with a thud. He poured the contents into a pan and set it on the stove with the temperature turned to High. Feeling proud that he had managed thus far, Ben smiled with satisfaction as he tore open the package of buns. Simple. Why had he believed this would be so difficult?

A loud pop startled Ben, and his gaze shot to the microwave that seemed to be shooting sparks. Opening the door, he found the plate shattered, and the inside of the tomb covered in pink fleshy remains. What had he done wrong?

No matter. He would simply follow the directions to boil the wieners. At least he had plenty left.

A foul smell, followed by a gurgling noise, drew his attention. The chili erupted from the pan like a volcano, splattering the white countertops and floor with brown-orange blobs. Ben immediately grabbed for the pan without thinking. The handle seared his hand and he dropped the offending pot back onto the stove, sending the chili down the front of his neatly starched white shirt.

Now he was a mess. The kitchen was a mess. And much to his dismay, Jamie was standing at the door, glaring at him.

"What are you doing?" Her voice was low and surprisingly controlled.

"I am preparing dinner." Ben grabbed for a nearby dish towel and began rubbing at the spots on his shirt, avoiding her steely glare.

"It looks like you've had a food fight."

Yes, he had definitely been fighting with the food, and he was losing the battle. But he vowed not to give up. "I will clean the mess."

Jamie walked to the stove, grabbed a spoon from a white vase holding several utensils and began stirring the chili. "It's just a tad burned, Ben. I don't think it's edible in this state."

"Do you wish your hot dogs without the chili? Or I can return to the market and buy another can."

Jamie shook her head. "No. I'm not hungry."

Ben was. Hungry for the taste of her, the feel of her. She was dressed in snug black slacks and a red silk blouse. The pants adhered to her small bottom, defining her curves.

She turned to him and leaned back against the counter as if she had sensed his gaze. "What's this all about?"

Ben streaked a hand through his hair. "I wanted to surprise you. Prove to you that I would make a good husband."

She searched the kitchen war zone before returning her gaze to him. "I don't think you have a calling for the culinary arts."

"True, but if we are married, Alima would do the cooking for us."

She pinned him with her crystal-green eyes. "I like to cook, actually. And I really like living alone." Her gaze faltered, leading Ben to believe that like him, she had not enjoyed being alone at all.

Cautiously he moved toward her and brushed a long lock of golden hair from her shoulders. "I have missed you in my bed. I have missed your singing and your smile. Have you missed me?"

"I'm doing...just fine." She looked anywhere but directly at him.

"I believe you are lying."

She met his gaze, the familiar anger in her eyes. "I believe you've got an ego the size of Texas."

"Believe what you will," he said, bracing his hands on either side of the counter, "but I know that what we shared still haunts your dreams, as it does mine. I do not believe you can forget how well our bodies fit together, how much enjoyment we have taken from one another. How much remains to be shared between us."

With that, he took a chance and brought his lips to hers, leaning into her so that she would know how much he desired her. At first she tried to resist, but soon she opened to him and allowed him entry to the sweet recesses of her mouth. His whole being was consumed in fire generated by the kiss. The play of her tongue against his, the feel of her delicate body molded to his, drove him to near insanity. He wanted to take her right there, shove their clothing down and drive into her with the force of his need.

"No!" She pushed him back and ducked under his arm. He turned to find her backed up to the opposing wall, arms crossed over her chest. "You're not going to do this again. I'm not going to let you."

His gaze lingered over her body then came back to her flushed face. "It seems you already have."

She paced the kitchen and stopped at the open microwave. "What have you done to my grandmother's china?"

She spun around to face him and pointed toward the door. "Get out."

"Why? Do you not wish to acknowledge what is between us? Would you continue to deny it?"

"What's between us is chemistry. I want more."

"I will give you everything."

"You can't."

He took a step forward. "Tell me what you need, and I will search to the ends of the earth to find it for you."

"If you are too dumb to realize what I need from you, then you might as well give up."

Ben truly did not know what she needed from him that he had not already offered. How could he make her understand that he would do anything for her? How could he convince her that his life meant nothing without her in it?

He struggled to find the words to express himself, but they caught in his throat.

She sighed. "Ben, I'm tired. Please leave now."

He saw no point in continuing to beg her. He had another plan to develop, one that most surely would impress her. "I will clean up, then I will go."

"No, I'll do it. Go home. Let Alima fix you something decent to eat."

He no longer had an appetite for anything but Jamie's presence. "You are certain you wish me to leave?"

"Yes, I'm sure."

The familiar ache again settled on his heart. He was failing miserably at being a worthy man in her eyes. Yet he could not stand the thought of leaving her for good.

"All right, I will go tonight. But I will return."

She stomped her foot. "Don't you get it? I don't want you here. I don't need you here. Would you stop being so damned stubborn?"

"I will not stop until I have convinced you that we belong together."

Her eyes grew hazy with unclaimed tears, turning them a deeper emerald. Right then the urge to hold her again lived strong in Ben. But he refrained from giving in. Perhaps he would leave her be for a few days. His absence might convince her that she did miss him.

He turned and headed toward the door. With one hand braced on the knob, he said, "Pleasant dreams, my Jamie. I will be having them about you."

Jamie spent the next few days in a mental fog. Ben didn't call. Neither did her father. Never had she felt so alone. So confused. At least she had her work at the hospital and a few new friends she'd made in recent days. She'd even stopped by the local pet store and bought two goldfish to keep her company. Not that they provided all that much companionship.

After working her shift, including a few hours' overtime, she came home exhausted one evening to find two boxes on her dinette table—one large, one small—and a note from her landlord stating he'd personally delivered them to make sure they arrived safely, as ordered by the "Arabian man."

Prince Ben strikes again. What was he up to now?

After making some hot chamomile tea, Jamie sat at the table and stared at the boxes for a while, the pocketknife her father had given her on her twelfth birthday clutched in one hand, the teacup in the other. After a few moments, her curiosity got the best of her. She set the cup aside and picked up the smaller package. Slitting it open with the knife, she found beneath the packing a gold box from the Royal Confection Shoppe. She loved that place and often stopped by the window to admire the display, but she couldn't afford to buy any of their expensive candies.

Opening the lid, she found an array of dark chocolates—her favorite—and in the middle, surrounded by the candies, a small blue velvet box.

Jamie held her breath as she opened the hinged lid. A ring, a brilliant oval diamond, surrounded by emeralds, twinkled in the glow of the overhead light fixture. She had never seen anything so beautiful in her life. It had to be at least two carats and no telling how expensive.

Slipping the ring on her finger, she found it to be a perfect fit. She wasn't the least bit surprised, knowing it had come from Ben. He would know her ring size. How, she couldn't say. But he would, as surely as he knew her weakness for rich chocolates, something she had never told him.

Jamie turned her attention back to the candy and found a slip of paper wedged between the edge of the box and the paper shells. She unfolded the note and read.

I chose the emeralds to match the color of your eyes, yet this ring does not compare to your beauty. I hope that you will accept it as a token of my feelings for you—Ben.

Feelings? What feelings? Okay, so maybe he did have feelings for her. Maybe he did care for her. So why couldn't he just say it?

She glanced at the other box and wondered how on earth he could top the ring. The side was stamped Fragile, leading Jamie to believe it was something that could break as easily as her heart had over the past few days.

Standing over the box, she again took the knife and carefully opened it. The inside was full of green squiggly foam packing. She dug through the curly worms in a rush, sending them flying like jumping beans all over the table and floor. Just beneath were several tissue-wrapped items. She tore into one and again couldn't believe her eyes.

A porcelain angel, and below that, more angels. All in varying shapes and sizes, many exact replicas of those belonging to her grandmother—the ones Klimt had destroyed with his careless disregard.

With each one she opened, another tear escaped down Jamie's cheek. How did Ben know how much these meant to her? How could he so easily bend her heart to his will?

Slumping into the chair, she clasped one delicate figurine in her hand and cried. Cried because she was so touched by the gesture. Cried because so many emotions crowded in on her.

She wanted to damn his persistence. She wanted to curse him for making her love him more. She wanted to call him and tell him to get his cute princely butt over here so she could show him her gratitude in wicked ways that would leave them both breathless. But she wouldn't. Not until she'd had more time to think.

With a sigh, she picked up the stack of envelopes that had come in the mail. Most were bills that needed to be paid. A lot of junk mail and credit-card solicitations. Some kind of notice from the bank. She opened that first, praying she wasn't overdrawn. Inside she found a letter, and her blood pressure rose with each word she read.

After she was finished, she slapped the letter on the table, yanked off the ring, and cursed the sheikh.

Ben Rassad had more nerve than a skydiver, and she was darn sure going to tell him he had gone too far this time.

Jamie stood on Ben's doorstep muttering a litany of curses that would have caused her mother to go for the lye soap. If only her mother were here now, telling her what to do next.

But she wasn't here, and Jamie had to handle this alone.

She punched the bell and waited, impatiently tapping her foot on the wooden porch, clutching the envelope in her hand. Earlier she had longed to see him again. Thank him. Hold him.

That was before she'd found the notice in the mail from the bank stating an anonymous benefactor had paid off the note to the farm in its entirety.

Anonymous. Ha! Jamie knew exactly who had that kind of money, and she was about to confront him. *If* he was home and not off rescuing some other damsel in distress.

The door opened to Alima, a bright smile on her face. "Jamie, you have returned! I am so happy to see you."

Jamie let go of her anger long enough to give the housekeeper a quick hug, then stepped back when she remembered why she was here. "Where's the sheikh?"

"In his study," Alima said warily. "Shall I summon him for you?"

"No. I think I'll just surprise him." Exactly like he'd surprised her.

Without waiting for Alima's response, Jamie strode through the great room and down the hall to Ben's office. She didn't even bother to knock.

After throwing the door open, she found him sitting at his desk, a stack of papers before him. She slapped the envelope in front of him. "How dare you."

He met her gaze with his serious gray eyes. "So you have come to see me after all."

"I've come to tell you that I don't appreciate what you've done. You had no right buying my father's farm."

He kicked back in the chair and propped his boots on the edge of the desk. Jamie tried not to notice his worn jeans, or the way his T-shirt strained across his broad chest when he braced his hands behind his head, the spattering of whiskers framing his sinfully sensual mouth. "I did not buy it. I simply paid off the note. Through my connections, I discovered the bank was in the process of foreclosing. Had I not put up the money, someone else would have purchased the farm and you would have lost everything."

She already felt as though she had lost everything. First her mother, then her father. More importantly, she'd lost her heart to this man sitting before her, looking confident and cocksure and way too sexy to ignore.

Jamie's pulse pounded in her ears. "I could've handled it myself had I known."

"Do you have that kind of money?"

"No…I…" Damn him! "I would have found it somewhere."

He slipped his feet from the desk and sat forward. "I have done this for you, Jamie. For your father. Can you not see that I care what happens to you both?"

She crossed her arms and shifted her weight from one foot to the other. "You don't even know my father."

"No, I do not. But I do know where he is. I have spoken with him."

Jamie dropped her arms to her sides and fisted her hands. "Where is he? How did you find him? I've asked everyone I know, and not one soul knows where he is."

"As I have told you, I have the means to find anyone."

Worry suddenly replaced Jamie's anger. No matter what her father had done in the past, she was still concerned for his well-being. "Is he okay?"

"He is safe. He has been residing at a private treatment facility. A place in the southern part of Texas that aids those with alcoholism. He has been getting help for his problem."

Jamie wanted desperately to cry, but she held back the

threatening tears, kept her hurt in check. "Why hasn't he been in touch with me?"

Ben stood and moved around the desk to face her. "He assumed you were married and living in Asterland. He used the money from the arrangement to pay for his treatment."

Jamie felt both relief and sadness. She had very much misjudged her father's motives. And she very much wanted to see him, to hug him, to tell him how proud she was of him that he was getting help. To scold him for not trying to contact her. "Will you take me to him?"

Ben rubbed a hand over his jaw. He wanted to do this for her, but he had promised her father to wait until he was ready. "He is not quite finished with his treatment, but he will be soon. I have made arrangements to return him here when he is released."

Her green eyes flashed anger, deep and penetrating. "I guess you've thought of everything, haven't you?"

How could he convince her that he had her best interest at heart? What could he say so that she would understand he still wanted her with every thread of his being?

Taking two steps forward, he touched her cheek. "I would very much like to report to him that he is invited to our wedding."

"No."

He took her into his arms, hoping he could weaken her resolve. "I am sorry. I do not mean to pressure you. All that I ask is for you to consider my proposal. I am willing to give you as much time as you need. I will see to it that the farm is put back in order for your father's return."

She wrested out of his arms and moved away. "He'll want to pay you back. And I insist you let him."

Ben's frustration increased. "I will not deny him that. But it will not be necessary if he is in my family. I protect my own."

A steady stream of tears flowed down her face. "Don't you get it? I don't want your protection. I don't need your money or your gifts. What I need is—" She shook her head. "Never mind."

"What do you need, Jamie, that I cannot give you?"

She swiped at her eyes. "I suppose you'll have to figure that one out yourself."

She slipped her hand in her jeans pocket and withdrew the ring he had so carefully chosen for her. Taking his hand, she placed it in his palm and closed his fingers around it. "Here. Maybe you'll find someone else who can wear this. Someone who's interested in your money and your station and your protection. That person's not me."

"I do not want it back."

"Neither do I." She turned away and headed for the door, but before she left, she faced him again. "The angels are beautiful, but I'll be returning those, too."

"I will not accept them. They are a gift to replace those you have lost." And he knew in that moment he had lost her.

"Fine. Thanks. As soon as my father returns, he'll be in touch about paying you back."

"And you will not see me again?"

"I can't, Ben. It's too hard."

He clung to the last of his pride, yet he must ask once more, but only once. "And you will not consider being my wife?"

Another rush of tears streamed down her face. "No."

He strode forward but kept his distance although the need to hold her, kiss away her tears, lived strong within him. But he would not let her leave until he had said all that he needed to say. "Should you decide that you need me, for any reason, I will be here for you."

"I appreciate it."

"You have my word, I will not bother you. If you change your mind, then you will have to come to me, for I will not ask anything of you again."

Then she disappeared out the door, out of his life.

He returned to his desk and sank into his chair. Tossing the ring aside, he rested his elbows on the solid surface and placed his head in his hands.

His chest constricted with the weight of his sadness, his remorse. He recalled his mother telling him that a shattered heart was the greatest pain anyone could endure, even a man. At the time, that concept seemed ludicrous. But that was before Jamie Morris.

Why could he not tell Jamie with words how he felt? He had been trained to be the best soldier. He had been groomed to be a proper prince. He had strived to be a learned businessman. Yet he had never been taught the ways of the heart, nor could he voice these strange emotions piercing his soul.

He had also learned when to accept those battles he could not win—and he could not win Jamie Morris.

That did nothing to ease the deep ache in his heart. No matter how long he searched, he would never find another woman who had touched him so.

But was he really so ready to give up this fight? His tenacity had seen him through difficult times. Would he simply walk away from something so precious?

He would have to consider that tomorrow. Tonight he had arrangements to make to return Jamie's father to her. At least then he would have some peace knowing that she would no longer be alone. Unlike him.

You have my word, I will not bother you. If you change your mind, then you will have to come to me, for I will not ask anything of you again.

Jamie had spent countless hours thinking about Ben's declaration, about him. Only moments ago she'd considered going to the ranch, telling him she'd been wrong. She wasn't sure what she would say. All she knew was that she needed to see him again as much as she needed air.

But he wouldn't want to see her unless she agreed to marry him. Could she do that not knowing how he really felt about her? She wanted desperately to believe he loved her. At times she truly thought he did. So why couldn't he tell her?

She shook her head. When it came right down to it, she hadn't told him, either. Maybe if she had, it might have made a difference.

The doorbell rang, and Jamie knew it was him. Prayed it was him. Now she would get her chance to tell him exactly how she felt. How much she loved him.

Slowly she opened the door, and discovered she'd been wrong. It wasn't Ben at all.

Sheer joy replaced the disappointment when she recognized the man standing on her porch. A man who had meant so much to her for so long.

His neatly combed silver hair, his careworn face were as familiar to her as the town she'd grown up in. He stood tall, his body still straight and strong despite the fact he had lived the life of a hardworking farmer and had suffered the loss of the woman he loved more than life itself.

"Daddy!" Jamie threw herself into her father's arms, hugging him tightly, crying some more even though she had mistakenly believed she was fresh out of tears.

"I missed you, baby girl." He set her back but kept his weathered hands braced on her shoulders. "My, my, you are a sight for these old eyes."

"So are you." She swiped her face with the back of her hand and tried to look stern despite the fact she wanted to shout with joy. "You've got a lot of explaining to do, Caleb Morris."

He dropped his hands from her shoulders, lowered his eyes and pushed up the sleeves of his faded chambray shirt. "Yeah, I know it. And I got a lot of apologizin' to do, too. So if you'll hear me out, I'd like to explain."

Jamie closed the door behind him and showed him to the couch, taking her place beside him.

"Are you feeling okay, Daddy?" she asked with concern once they'd settled in side by side.

He smiled. "Yeah. Better than I've felt in a mighty long while. Haven't had a drink in months."

"I'm so glad. But you're looking a little thin."

"I could say the same for you. You're as skinny as your mama when I married her." Sadness flashed across his expression and centered on Jamie's heart.

She hugged him again. "I know how much you still miss her, Daddy. I miss her, too. But she'd be so proud to know you've gotten help."

He clasped his hands in front of him and dangled them between parted knees, surveying the floor. "You know, Jamie girl, I ain't never held much stock in dreams, but your mama came to me in one right before I left. She told me to get on with my life in that voice she always used when I was late for supper."

Jamie smiled at the memory. "I can just imagine that."

"She mentioned you, too. Told me to take care of you. That's why I did it."

"You should have done it for yourself."

He slowly met her gaze, shame in his weary blue eyes. "Not the treatment center. I meant the wedding arrangement. I wanted you to have a better life than what I could give you. I figured if you got out of this town and moved to that Asterland place, then you could finally have the fine things you deserve."

Jamie spoke through another rush of tears. "Oh, Daddy, I was happy just being your daughter. I'd have found the money to go back to school eventually, at least after you got back on your feet again."

"I wasn't sure that was gonna happen at the time. I know now that selling you into marriage to a man you didn't love wasn't a good thing. But I also thought that maybe if you didn't love him, you wouldn't hurt so bad if you lost him."

Jamie let the tears roll down her cheeks, unheeded. "I know now how bad that hurts, and I'm surviving."

He studied her with questions in his eyes. "Are you talking about that young man, Ben?"

She had no idea how much Ben had told him about the relationship, but she assumed he must have mentioned something. "Yes, I guess I am."

Caleb straightened and took her hands into his. "Are you in love with him, Jamie girl?"

This time she looked away. "'Fraid so."

"Well, I'd like to say I'm sorry about that, but I'm not." He tipped her chin up and forced her to look at him. "No matter how bad it hurt to lose your mother, I wouldn't take back one minute I had in her presence. She was a gift from God, that woman. I have peace knowing she sleeps with the angels."

"I understand that, Daddy, but I'm afraid Ben might not have those kind of feelings for me."

He frowned, deepening the lines around his eyes. "Are you tellin' me that man doesn't love you?"

She shrugged. "He's asked me to marry him, but he hasn't said he loves me."

Caleb let go a sharp laugh. "I didn't tell your mama I loved her, either. Not for a long time. In fact, I believe I finally said so one day down at the creek right after…'' He cleared his throat and a blush tinged his ruddy cheeks. ''Never mind that. I just didn't know any pretty way to say it. Guess I was a coward.''

''Ben's no coward.'' Jamie was shocked at how defensive she sounded. She steadied her tone. ''I'm just not sure how he feels about me because he's never really said.''

Rubbing his chin, Caleb stared off into space for a moment before returning his gaze to Jamie. ''Well, now, I just spent the good part of two hours on one of them private jets with the man having a long conversation.''

Jamie's mouth gaped. ''Ben?''

''Yeah, and all he could do was talk about you, what a fine daughter I'd raised. I barely got a word in edgewise.''

''Are you sure we're talking about Ben Rassad? Sheikh Ben Rassad?''

''He said his name was Ben. He had one of those curtains on his head and some kind of robe. Never seen a man wearing a robe 'cept at bedtime.''

''That would be him.''

''Well, since we're talkin' about the same man, I pretty much think that he does love you. If not, he's got one hellacious case of the flu 'cause he looked mighty lovesick to me. Sounded that way, too.''

Was her father right? Hope welled in Jamie's heart. ''So he drove you over here?''

''Yep. After we got to Royal, he delivered me here himself.''

Jamie squeezed her father's hands. ''And he just dropped you off?''

''Nope. He's downstairs waiting with one of his men. Said he wouldn't come up unless you said it was okay.''

Jamie's heart leaped into her throat. ''I do want to see him. To thank him. But I don't want you to leave—''

Caleb stood. "Jamie, I'm plumb tuckered out from the trip. I need to get over to the farm and see what's what. Jeb and May Prentice have been seeing to the place for me, but I want to check it out myself."

"You could stay here. I mean, is that a good idea, going back to the place—"

"—where I lived with your mama all those years?" He nodded. "I'm to the point now where I can deal with those memories. She's still there watching over me."

Jamie rose from the sofa and drew him into another heartfelt hug. "You've come a long way. I'm so proud of you."

"I'm proud of you, too, Jamie girl. You're the one good thing I ever did in my life. 'Cept for marrying your mama. Now I'm going to head on back and give you your time with your fellow."

"Speaking of him, there's something you should know about finances and the farm before you go," she said hesitantly, afraid of his reaction to Ben's gesture. Her father had an abundance of pride.

"You mean the fact your Ben paid it off?" Caleb grinned. "He told me about it. Said I could pay him back when I took in the first crop. I still have some of that Asterland fellow's money left, too. Unless you think I ought to give it back seeing as how you didn't marry him?"

Jamie laughed through residual tears. "No, Daddy. It's yours to keep. Believe me, I earned it."

His brows drew down in confusion. "How's that?"

Jamie walked him to the door, anxious to see Ben now that her father was well on his way to recovery. "It's a long, long story. Too long to tell you tonight. But tomorrow I'll come by and fix you breakfast, then we can have a good long visit."

"Okay, then. That sounds mighty good. That rehab place

fed me slop I wouldn't even offer the hogs." Caleb leaned and kissed her cheek. "I'll send your young man on up. I'm thinkin' you both have lots to talk about."

"Yes, Daddy, that we do."

Jamie watched her father head away, his gait quick and determined, so unlike the man he had become after her mother's death. She had so much to be thankful for. They both did. And she owed so much to Ben. She planned to tell him tonight. If he decided to come up.

Ten

Jamie leaned against the door for support and waited for Ben's arrival. She was dying to see him, to hold him, to tell him that what he had done for her, for her father, was more than anyone had ever done for either of them. To show him how much he meant to her.

A few minutes later, a steady knock caused Jamie to push away from the door, her pulse pounding in her ears.

She opened it to find Ben standing on the threshold wearing his traditional clothes and a killer smile, holding a bag from Claire's.

She nodded toward the bag. "What have you got there?"

"Dinner for two. Your father said he would not be joining us. J.D. has driven him home. I decided that Claire's would be preferable to my attempts at preparing dinner, although I would be willing to try again if you are willing to take that chance."

"With you cooking dinner?"

He pinned her with his gray eyes. "That, and other things."

"What other things?"

He sighed. "I would like to start over, Jamie. Prove to you that I am not the ogre you claim I am. Since you left me, I cannot eat or sleep. I cannot concentrate on my work. I can only think of what we have shared, how you felt in my arms. I miss your laughter. I miss the way your eyes light up when I touch you. I even miss your singing. So if you will grant me another opportunity to—"

Jamie grabbed his arm and pulled him inside, silencing him with a kiss. The bag dropped to the floor. She didn't care about food at the moment. She didn't care about the fact she was dog-tired. She didn't care about anything but Ben, the way he was kissing her back with such power that she thought her legs might not hold her any longer.

He hadn't said he loved her, but he was coming mighty close. And tonight, no matter what, she wanted to be with him, make love with him, even if it was only one more time.

As if he'd read her mind, he hooked his arms underneath her knees and lifted her up, much as he'd done that first night they'd made love.

Again she was swept away, not only by his powerful arms, but also by her feelings for him. Her love for him.

Once in the bedroom, Ben slid Jamie down the length of him and murmured, "I did not expect this reaction from you. I believe that you have missed me, too."

"Okay, I admit it. I have missed you." She couldn't seem to draw enough air into her lungs. "But I didn't expect this reaction from me either. I say let's just go with the flow."

He rimmed the shell of her ear with his tongue. "You

will receive no argument from me, but I have been traveling all day. I am in need of a shower.''

Jamie smiled up at him. ''Me too.''

''Then perhaps that is where we should begin.''

''You don't have to tell me twice.''

Jamie slipped off her blouse and shimmied out of her slacks. Ben tossed his robes aside, raked the kaffiyeh from his head, then tore at the white shirt he wore underneath his robes, sending buttons pinging around the room like pea-sized gravel. After he snaked out of his slacks, they stood before each other totally naked.

The raw hunger Jamie saw in Ben's eyes made her shiver, made her want him right then, but she let him lead her into the small bathroom. He turned on the shower before bringing her against him for a long lingering kiss. A kiss full of promise and passion like none she had ever known before him.

Breaking the kiss, he took her hand and together they stepped beneath the lukewarm spray. They stood for another long moment and took in the sight of each other until Jamie began shampooing his thick dark hair, and he returned the favor. Covered in slippery suds, they laughed, they kissed, engaging in water play—a pleasant prelude to what would come next.

Jamie reached behind her for the shower gel, placed a few drops in her palm, then began to lather Ben's chest through the swirl of dark hair.

His sexy smile drove her to near insanity. ''You would have me smelling like Alima's fresh-cut flowers?''

She returned his smile, sending her hands down his belly and farther still. He was completely aroused, and she was completely in awe.

''Are you complaining?'' she asked, tracing a fingertip down the solid length of him.

He sucked in a deep breath. ''No. You will hear no complaint from me if you continue this.''

She watched his features grow taut as she continued to caress him, memorize every inch of him. His eyes drifted shut and she knew he was close to coming unwound. Very close. And she felt such power.

Suddenly his eyes snapped opened and he circled her wrist in a steel grip. ''Enough. You are driving me insane.''

''That's the idea, Ben,'' she said, sounding incredibly coy.

''Not yet. As I said, this is only the beginning.''

With that, he picked up the gel and spread some in his palms, then knelt down and washed her feet, one at a time. Jamie stared down on his dark head bent in concentration and realized that he was playing the role of slave. She had never expected that he would do something so subservient as bathing her feet. But then she had never expected to meet anyone like him.

He raised his gray eyes to her as he slid his large palms up her calves to the inside of her thighs, pausing just before he arrived at the point of her greatest need.

Standing once again, he took hold of her shoulders and backed her up against the cold tiles. He lowered his mouth to her breast and suckled one, then the other. Jamie moaned her pleasure, knowing it *was* only the beginning of his special brand of sensual torment. And she loved it.

He ran his hands down the curve of her waist, the flare of her hip, and cupped her intimately. ''I belong here, Jamie,'' he whispered. ''Inside you. One with you.''

His masterful fingers delved into her needy flesh, making her quiver, making her beg. ''Ben, please—''

''Shhh, Jamie. You need not speak. I know what you need. I can feel it.''

Oh, boy, she could feel it, too. The steady building of

pressure, of heat, when he found her center and settled there. He continued to stroke her straight into oblivion. She cried out when he brought her to a climax so great she thought she might never recover. But she did, enough to scold him. "No fair. Now I'm ahead of you."

"Not for long, my Jamie." He brushed a kiss over her cheek. "Not for long."

Without bothering to dry off or turn down the lights, they made their way to the bed and sank onto the patchwork quilt, tangled together like clinging vines. They faced each other and continued to touch and explore, fondle and caress, until Ben said, "I can wait no longer."

Neither could Jamie. She craved the feel of his body inside hers. But when she tried to guide him to her, he moved away and left the bed.

Confused, Jamie sat up and found him rummaging through his pants pocket. "Ben, what are you doing?"

"I have brought the condoms." He slipped onto the edge of the bed and held up the plastic packets, at least five, for her inspection.

She couldn't repress a smile. "It doesn't matter."

He frowned. "I believe it does. At least to you. I want you to know that I will do whatever you wish of me."

She snatched the packets from him and tossed them aside. "I *wish* for you to make love to me. Now."

"Are you certain?"

"I've never been so sure of anything in my life."

Without words, he moved over her and sank into her waiting body, joining them on a level that went far beyond the physical. He moved slowly, with care, setting a perfect rhythm. Setting Jamie on fire with his increasing thrusts, his fine caress above the place where they were joined.

Suddenly he stilled and bracketed her face in his palms. "You are everything to me," he whispered. "You invade my waking hours. You have captured my heart." He kissed her softly. "And I love you with all that I have to give, my Jamie."

Had she heard him right? She couldn't find the heart to ask, afraid she had dreamed it.

"I have never known such feelings before," he continued, "And I can no longer deny them."

Tears of joys spilled from the corners of her eyes. "You have no idea how much this means to me. For the longest time, I believed I was nothing more to you than a possession."

His smile was so beautiful, so sincere, it brought fresh tears to her eyes. "How could you be my possession when it is you who owns me?"

He kissed her deeply then. A kiss that held a promise for the future. Jamie knew right then that she belonged with him. They belonged to each other.

Again he moved inside her, touching her in places begging for his attention. Touching her heart and her soul. And when she could no longer hold back the tide of pleasure, she gave in to the release with abandon as Ben shuddered and called out her name.

In the aftermath, Ben turned to one side, taking Jamie with him. She brushed a wayward lock of damp hair from his forehead. "My answer is yes."

His smile was teasing and a little bit wicked. "What would the question be?"

Obviously he wasn't going to make this easy for her. She couldn't blame him, considering how many times he had asked, and how many times she had refused. "You know. The one you've been asking for a few weeks."

"The one involving marriage?"

"Yes, that's the one. And if the offer still stands, then

yes, I will marry you and drive you crazy and have your babies.''

He cupped her face in his large hands. ''More than all the gold in the world, I want you to be my wife. I will put no one before you. All I need is the promise of your love.''

She held him tightly. ''Ben, I do love you. I think I loved you the moment you woke up in my bed that first morning.''

He kissed her gently. ''Then you will promise to wake with me every morning, and come to my bed every night? That you will be with me always?''

Never had Jamie felt such freedom. Such honest love. ''Yes. Always.''

He rolled her beneath him once again. ''Good. That is all I will ever need.''

Her tummy rumbled. ''How about food?''

He laughed then, a deep rich sound that made Jamie want to laugh, too, from the pure joy of it. ''Are you saying you are hungry?''

''Starving.''

His eyes darkened with intense desire. ''So am I, and after I am done with you, we can have dinner and plan our wedding.''

She was late, but not for the wedding.

Jamie still had forty-five minutes to get ready for the ceremony and about one minute before she would know if she was, in fact, carrying Ben's child.

Perched on the edge of the vanity stool dressed in her old terry robe, she stared at the white plastic stick resting near the sink and waited for the sign that would tell her yes or no.

A watched pot never boils.

Jamie released a nervous laugh when she recalled her

mother's words. She'd have to remember to teach Alima this particular American saying.

The remaining seconds ticked off while Jamie impatiently tapped her foot. Then suddenly, a plus sign appeared, leaving no doubt in her mind she was pregnant.

Pregnant.

She'd somehow known for a while that she was carrying Ben's baby. A baby created by two people who had found each other against all odds. Created by two people in love. Jamie felt truly blessed.

But when should she tell Ben?

She consulted her watch. Time was wasting. She still had to dress. Her father would be at the apartment any moment now to escort her to Royal's city park, the place they'd chosen for the ceremony.

After the wedding, she would tell Ben. This news could wait for now, until the right time. Until tonight, when they were alone. She didn't want anything to detract from this glorious day when she would marry the man she loved more than life. Just as her parents had loved each other.

Quickly she applied her makeup and curled her hair. Once she was satisfied with her appearance, she retrieved her mother's dress and slipped it on. A perfect fit.

Lovingly she caressed the white lace overlay. Funny, she'd told Helena last month she had no intention of wearing it anytime soon. Now she was wearing it and she was going to have a baby. Ben's baby. Things had certainly changed in her life in record time. And she couldn't be happier.

The doorbell sounded and she answered the summons, finding her father waiting for her. He looked so very handsome in his Sunday suit, his bright smile flashing against his tanned rugged face.

He held out his hands for her to take and smiled a proud-papa smile. "You look as pretty as your mama did when she wore that dress all those years ago. She would be so proud of you." A single tear drifted down his cheek.

Jamie tried to thwart her own tears with a smile. "Stop that right now. If I cry, I'll ruin my makeup, then we'll never make it on time."

He hooked his arm and she slipped her own arm through it. "Then let's not keep your Ben waiting," he said.

"No, let's not." She had kept him waiting long enough.

Ben stood beneath the gazebo waiting for his bride. The April day was unseasonably warm, and the tuxedo he wore decidedly uncomfortable. He supposed his discomfort had as much to do with nervousness as the weather. He would not be at ease until he had Jamie by his side. Not that he thought she would not show for the wedding. He was simply ready to begin their life together.

Matt stood nearby, speaking with fellow Cattleman's Club members Justin Webb, Aaron Black, Greg Hunt and Hank Langley. Moments before, Forrest Cunningham had walked away from Dakota Lewis who now remained back from the others, looking disinterested and perhaps a bit sad. Ben assumed he was contemplating the mission he would soon undertake in Asterland with his estranged wife. If luck prevailed, it would serve to bring the couple back together once again—as was meant to be, according to Aaron who had known them quite some time. Although the man denied any feelings for his wife, Ben and all the other members knew better. And Ben could certainly relate to Dakota's pain over not having his love with him. The short time he had spent without Jamie had seemed like centuries.

The statue of Tex Langley, the Texas Cattleman's Club's founding father, stood off in the distance. A crowd of onlookers had gathered around the ropes that segregated several rows of white chairs lined up on the lawn for the invited guests. Ben assumed that a wedding between an Arabian sheikh and a local woman would garner much interest in the small town. At the moment, he wasn't concerned over the masses. At the moment, he wanted to see Jamie.

The sound of a woman crying drew his attention. Alima sat on the front row dabbing at her face, sobbing now and again, much louder than most would deem appropriate. She had told him that morning how honored she was to stand in for his mother who was tending her latest grandson, the sixth born to his brother. Alima's sobs grew louder when the string quartet he had hired began to play. He believed her tears were those of joy. Or perhaps the classical music was not to her liking. At least she had come without the blessed headphones.

Several guests turned to the direction of the street. A spattering of excited voices acknowledged the arrival of the white limousine pulling up to the curb.

Ben's heart vaulted in his chest and pounded in anticipation when he saw Jamie's father exit the car. And then his bride slipped out in a flowing white dress. His Jamie. His love. Soon to be his wife.

The guests who had been mingling began to make their way to their seats, many noted citizens of Royal, including several members—old and new—of the Texas Cattleman's Club.

The Justice of the Peace moved to the gazebo next to Ben, along with Matt Walker who would serve as the best man. Matt's fiancée, Lady Helena, who would also bear witness to their union, took her place on the opposite side. The couple exchanged a look, one of love beyond all limits. A few weeks ago, Ben might have scoffed at such a thing, but now he truly knew the power of love. A love he had never thought possible.

Ben turned toward the crowd and watched with pride as Jamie made her way toward the gazebo. She walked with grace and shone in the mid-morning sun like the fine jewel that had brought them together. The mild breeze, smelling of freshly mowed grass, ruffled her golden hair, ringed on top by a circle of white flowers. The locks curled over her breasts and glistened in the sunshine, bringing to mind that day when Ben had first viewed her leaving the cleaners with the dress she now wore, singing at the top of her voice. That day that had nearly ended in disaster but instead had brought them to this treasured point in time.

The dress flowed to the ground and fit her curves to perfection. Ben mentally scolded himself when the image of removing it slowly from her body filtered into his brain.

The quartet began to play the traditional "Wedding March" as Jamie started up the aisle. Her smile was luminous, giving Ben such a resounding joy. He had finally made her happy, and it had taken not objects nor gifts, but only a few simple words.

Once Jamie and her father had scaled the first of the two steps, Caleb Morris turned and kissed Jamie on the cheek, then offered her hand to Ben. "She's all yours," he said. "Treat her like the gift she is, cause if you don't, I've got a loaded .22 and a case full of shells." A grin melted his serious expression.

A spattering of laughter came from the audience, and Ben smiled in kind. Jamie looked mortified.

Ben bowed slightly. "You have my word, Mr. Morris."

Taking Jamie's fragile hand into his, Ben helped her up the remaining step. When she met his gaze, he noticed a fine sheen of tears in her eyes.

"Are you ready for this, Prince Ben?" she asked.

"I have been ready for weeks."

Jamie turned and handed her bouquet to Helena who smiled and said, "Amazing what love can do, isn't it?"

"Truly amazing." Jamie turned back to her soon-to-be husband and drew in a deep cleansing breath.

Debonair was the first word that had come to mind when she'd seen Ben waiting for her at the end of the aisle, dressed in a tailored tux, wearing his traditional kaffiyeh, looking strong and commanding. *Beautiful* was the second, and it much more aptly described him at the moment as she glimpsed the adoration in his gray eyes.

He brought her hand to his lips. "You are more exquisite than I could ever imagine."

"And you look much too good to be true."

The Justice of the Peace cleared his throat, signaling he was ready to begin the ceremony that would unite them forever. Not once did Ben look away, his voice clear and composed as he repeated the vows. Jamie wished she could say the same for herself. Her voice trembled, shaky with stubborn tears of joy that wouldn't go away. But she managed to get through it all the same.

Once they had exchanged rings, plain gold bands that Jamie had insisted on, the Justice of the Peace announced that Ben could kiss his bride. Ben cradled her face in his hands, and she slipped her arms about his waist.

"I love you, my Jamie."

"And I love you, Ben."

Then he melded his lips to hers in a long, lingering kiss that made Jamie forget where they were.

Fire rose to her face when everyone began to applaud and several hoots and hollers rose above the din.

Finally they parted and with hands clasped, walked back down the aisle to more applause. Once they were in the waiting limousine, Caleb and Alima joined them for the trip to the legendary Texas Cattleman's Club for the reception. When they settled in, Jamie and Ben on one seat, the housekeeper and the farmer on the other, Alima eyed Caleb from the top of his bolo tie to the tip of his shiny boots. But Jamie noticed Alima didn't look at all displeased by what she saw. Then Caleb shocked Jamie by smiling at Alima and introducing himself.

During the short drive, Jamie was content to cuddle with Ben in silence and listen to her father and Alima discuss Hank Williams and George Jones. Common ground shared by two very different people. Jamie could certainly relate to that.

They arrived at the club to much fanfare and hordes of people Jamie didn't recognize. She did, however, recognize the mayor, who greeted them inside the foyer of the Cattleman's Club. Jamie noted the plaque hanging above the entrance. Peace, Justice, Leadership. How well she understood that concept now that she had met Ben. He represented all those convictions, and much, much more.

Once inside the cavernous ballroom, Jamie could only stare at the flower-and-ribbon-bedecked walls, the fine crystal and china, the mammoth white cake graced by cascading pink roses centered in the middle of a long table surrounded by every kind of food imaginable. She'd never stepped foot in here before, and now she felt privileged to be among such honorable men. Privileged to be married to one of them.

Ben led Jamie to the table where Matt delivered a champagne toast and they performed the required cutting of the cake. Afterward, Ben introduced her to Aaron Black. She had already met his wife, Pamela, on the plane bound for Asterland, only now Pamela Black looked very different with her swollen belly and radiant smile, not a trace of the shy woman who had rarely spoken. Dr. Webb soon joined them with his wife, Winona, and a baby girl dressed in pink frills. Matt and Helena stood by, arm in arm, seemingly lost in their own world. Probably talking about their impending wedding, Jamie surmised.

Off in the corner, holding up the wall, was another man Jamie didn't recognize. He looked incredibly lost, and very, very distressed.

She tugged Ben's arm to garner his attention and discreetly pointed in the stranger's direction. ''Who's that?''

Ben bent and whispered, ''Dakota Lewis. Another member of the club.''

''What's wrong with him? He looks like he's lost his best friend.''

''That he has, I am afraid. I will explain later.''

Her heart went out to the man. Right now she wanted everyone to be as happy she was.

After more conversation, Jamie's feet began to ache. She needed to talk to Ben alone, let him know she was ready to leave. Her stomach felt a bit queasy, and she wondered if a woman could have morning sickness in the afternoon.

When Matt and Helena walked away, Jamie grabbed the opportunity and led Ben into an alcove near a long hallway.

He took her in his arms and grinned. ''Do you wish my attention, wife?''

''How perceptive of you, husband. Can we go soon?''

He nuzzled her neck, his warm breath playing against her already heated skin. ''Are you growing impatient to begin our honeymoon?''

''You hit the nail on the head.'' He was also stirring up trouble when he sent a string of kisses down the valley of her breasts, exposed by the dress's sweetheart neckline.

''I am more than ready to make love to you,'' he murmured, along with a few choice words that would make the flowers wilt, just like Jamie's legs. ''I believe there is a vacant conference room down the hall that should do quite nicely for what I intend.''

She grabbed his ears and tugged his head up, away from dangerous ground. "I believe you are a wicked man."

He pressed against her, signaling loud and clear he was having some very wicked thoughts. "I am definitely a man in need of his wife's attention."

"Then let's get out of here," she said in a breathless tone.

"I will say my goodbyes, then we can go. I have made a reservation at the Royalton Hotel. I am sorry we cannot have a proper honeymoon until all is settled with Asterland."

Jamie didn't dare ask what was left to settle. She'd let him keep his mysteries. Besides, as far as she was concerned, Asterland could fall off the face of the earth. "I'm really sorry your mother couldn't be here."

He had the nerve to cup her breast through the lace. "I fear she is very taken with my new nephew." He bent and rimmed her ear with his tongue. "And tonight perhaps we can make her another grandchild."

Jamie couldn't have wished for a more perfect opening. But if he didn't stop fondling her, she wouldn't be able to speak. "Too late for that, I'm afraid."

Ben's head snapped up and he met her gaze. His hand slowly dropped to his side. "What are you saying?"

"I'm saying I took a test this morning. One of those over-the-counter things, not the lab kind. But they're supposed to be pretty accurate."

"And?"

Jamie smiled. "It said that Sheikh Hasim bin Abbas kadir Jamal Rassad of Amythra is going to be a daddy."

His eyes drifted from her face to her belly where he reverently laid his palm. "I could not have hoped for a better way to end this perfect day." He met her gaze, pure joy in the dark depths of his eyes. "Except, perhaps, by making love to you all night."

"As long as your son cooperates."

He looked at her with love shining in his eyes. "I am hoping for a girl. One with hair of gold like her mother, and a strong heart to match."

Jamie felt as though that strong heart might burst with all the love she held for this prince of a man. "It doesn't matter to me. I will love it, whatever it turns out to be."

"As will I, as much as I love you."

She circled her arms around his waist and stared up at him. "So when are we planning to return to Amythra?"

"This summer if all goes as planned. My mother will not tolerate waiting much longer to meet her American daughter-in-law, and my brother will want to hold another ceremony in honor of our marriage, if you agree."

"Whatever makes you happy, Ben." She worried her bottom lip for a moment, thinking she had so much to learn about his culture. "We've never really discussed it before, but where do you plan for us to live?"

"Here, in Royal. You should be near your father. We can visit Amythra as often as possible. And as soon as our child arrives, we can determine when you will finish your schooling."

Jamie wanted to cry again. "You'd do that for me?"

"I would do anything for you. I thought you would realize this by now."

She realized that, and how very much she loved him. Never again would she believe a person couldn't change. "But won't you miss your family? Your home?"

He took her hands into his and placed them to his lips. "For many years I have not known where home is. Now that I have met you, I know." He bent and kissed her softly, then raised solemn eyes to her. "You are my family now, Jamie. *You* have brought me home."

* * * * *